With Trees on Either Hand

MURIEL HALVORSEN

Waubesa Press
P.O. Box 192
Oregon, WI 53575

© Copyright 1995 by Muriel Halvorsen Olson
Cover illustration by Muriel Halvorsen, electronically enhanced
Editing/proofreading by J. Allen Kirsch
Published by Waubesa Press of Oregon, WI
Color separations by Port to Print of Madison, WI
Printed by BookCrafters of Chelsea, MI

FIRST EDITION

ISBN 1-878569-24-4

To Lena S., Anne H. and Inga O.

INTRODUCTION

These days it has become my habit to drive the cows home from pasture each evening and when the cows are scattered that becomes a long hike. However, I've found the exercise brings a more restful night and, what's more, to be searching for the cows is not to be wandering aimlessly as I often see those of my age doing in town — the women peering with no pang of temptation at store-window displays contrived to entice a world gone young; the men shuffling along with lackluster eyes dimly marking the horizon, unsparked by curiosity as to what lies beyond.

In August, when the open pasture sears in the sun, I often find the cows in the draw that runs from east to west on the north forty; for there the grass remains green and succulent through even the hottest part of the season, protected on the south by a wooded ridge and canopied by elms that stretch their trunks long from the floor of the valley to reach the light.

On the north, the valley wall rises sharply to meet the church yard that borders the farm and, occasionally, I take the time to climb the bank and enter the cemetery; but I must pick my way carefully, as the caretaker throws the refuse over this bank and the discarded plants have taken root and grow mingled with wild flowers and fern so that the ground cover is profuse and tangled.

How far removed from the crags and fjords of Norway is this little patch of earth! Yet the names on the headstones read like a Norwegian baptismal roster: Kari, Thornbjorn, Marit, Rolf, Nicolena, Nils, Randilena — all these from just our own family plot.

As convention decrees, the husbands lie to the right with their wives buried to their left. But sometimes in the light of my knowledge of their lives, I rearrange the headlines in my mind's eye. Tante Marit would not have approved of this, my idle game of marker dominoes; she would not have had things any other way.

With Trees on Either Hand

PART I

CHAPTER I

There was no delay at Bergen. His arrival at that port meshed with the departure of the mail boat for the north, and he had but time to grab his bundle, sprint across the dock and board the vessel before it weighed anchor. But fingers of land beckoned the boat close for a touch again and again as they plied the sea-cleaved coastline, wearing his patience thin. Yet his face registered no emotion when he spotted against the northern horizon the familiar outline of the peak — that one that furnished the northern horizon the familiar outline of the peak that marked the entrance to the fjord of home — that one that furnished the mountain-cloistered fishing village of Lilledalen a channel to the outside world.

The boat probed the ragged shoreline, singled out the gap; the sails were trimmed for the passage that in the shadows of the overhanging cliffs was like going through a tunnel.

When abruptly the channel widened to reveal a calm body of water resembling a large inland lake, he strode to the rail with a purposeful squaring of his shoulders. Far down the length of the fjord he sighted the village piled into a cranny cluster of toy blocks tossed carelessly there by a child. It floated toward him... enlarging, bringing details into focus...

He noted that the fleet was in. With sails furled, the exposed masts, booms and gaffs made the waterfront an etching of vertical and diagonal lines against grayed rectangles of sheds at water's edge. Beyond the waterfront, sod-roofed cottages of fishermen nubbed the sides of the valley that ran up the mountain from the fjord and gave the village its name. Set apart high on a promontory overlooking the water stood the master's house, and, nearby, the church — its steeple puny against the background of peaks that towered behind it.

The mail boat was their only link of communication with the outside world, its arrival was always eagerly awaited by the villagers and the word quickly spread when someone spotted it coming through the gap. Thus, a group was gathered on the dock, and, close-in, he quickly recognized most of them despite the lapsed years, if not individually, then by family — the *Maas* height, the *Berg* nose, the *Dahl* chin. Family traits were catalogued in the mind through generations of forced proximity.

They, in turn, were scrutinizing him. Suddenly it became apparent that someone had identified him; the group surged forward in excitement. It was a rare thing for a native to return after having once made his way to the New World.

He stepped ashore and the line of watchers sagged to make room for him; then rejoined itself to encircle him — pressing in, touching, shouting to be heard.... Hadn't he found America to his liking? Had he already made his fortune? Was he home to stay?

He did not respond, but broke free and started to make his way to the village. The clamor died down. But they were not to be denied completely. Almost every family had a member who had emigrated, and now, as they walked with him, they queried him in the manner of a roll-call of former villagers. The vastness of the New World lay beyond the comprehension of these who had for centuries occupied the same small valley; they turned to each other in perplexity when he shook his head in the negative as each name was called. How could he have spent so many years in America and not have encountered *any* of the other villagers? When they reached the tavern, he turned in and the men followed, leaving the women to scatter and spread the news.

The cry "Rolf Monsrud is back" had an electric effect on the shored seamen. From every direction, as if drawn by a magnet, they converged on the tavern. There, encouraged by the credulity of his audience, Rolf held forth; his talk as strong and flowing as the *branvin* now that he had swung their interest from his intent to the opportunities of the new land, which was accomplished smoothly enough in their eagerness for him to verify their hearsay of a utopian America.

"—and you can plow *all* day and not hit rock?"

"All day.... Forever! A straight furrow to the Pacific and you'd never hit rock!"

"—and land enough for all who come?"

"Forties, eighties — even sections if you want it and can handle it."

These measurements meant nothing to them, he knew; but he ignored their baffled expressions: How could these sea people with their tiny plots scratched in between rocks possibly imagine one acre of flat, stoneless ground, let alone forty or eighty acres! "Now being able to handle it, that's the thing," he went on ; and started an explanation of the Homestead Act.

He paused in the middle of a sentence, his thought arrested by the glimpse of a figure passing by the window. He arose from his stool, walked to the open door. Some of the men followed. With his eyes riveted on the back of a young woman, he tried to sound casual when he asked, "Now who might that be?"

His brother-in-law, Nils Dahl, answered: "That daughter to Hans Maas — *Marit*. Every day she goes to the wharves to watch for a sail... the sail of your brother, Thorn. His boat is long overdue."

Nils interpreted the dark look that crossed Rolf as concern for the safety of his brother. But as Rolf's eyes followed the figure of the girl — swiftly receding with long-legged strides, Nils thought he heard Rolf mutter, "The devil with Thorn!"

❧

Unlike Rolf, the people of the village took Marit for granted; dismissing her six-foot height and the pride with which she carried that height with "that one is a Maas for sure." And Marit as well accepted it as her due as a Maas, not slouching in an effort to minimize as self-conscious young women are prone to do when they found themselves towering above their peers. She held her back straight, carried her head high. As if to crown her regal bearing, she wore her thick auburn hair pulled straight up into a high bun on the top of her head, a hair style that not only added to her height but emphasized facial features of a subtle feline quality — not beautiful, but striking: a bold forehead under which her slanted gray eyes were widely set, high cheek bones, and a short stubborn chin.

Yet, for all her height, Marit was not lanky, a fact Rolf took in with his back view and in spite of the ankle-length dress. And she would have fared his scrutiny as well had he gotten a front view — an aspect of soft contours.

All this was of fairly recent development, however. Hers had been a big-boned, raw-muscled, gangling childhood and adolescence, more boyish than feminine in behavior as well as appearance. It always had been her boast that she could whip any boy her age. It had not been an idle boast; she had proved it many times to her own satisfaction -- and to the despair of her mother, Randi Maas.

In the male-dominated society, the contempt allotted her for having been born female was, it seemed to her, manifestly uncalled for. Strong for her age, aggressive by nature and possessed of a flash temper, she had not been satisfied to merely strive for parity. *That* proved nothing! It had been her way to deliberately create situations that would give her an opportunity to show up her biological adversary, best him, her strategy being to draw out with taunts, then fix the point-of-no-return with challenge.

All this was not unapparent to Randi, and although it was her usual way to keep these skirmishes from her husband, once, out of patience and aware that Marit set up her targets, she had turned the girl over to her father for discipline. And although Hans had whipped Marit until her behind was welted, she had not broken. Never again, Randi decided with some admiration, and remorse when she coolly considered her daughter's redeeming virtues, which she was certain boded ultimate womanliness. For it was Randi's observation that Marit had a soft heart for any being — man or beast — that was weak or in trouble, a compassion that seemed to spring from an awareness of having been given more than her own share of strength. The combination was such that she could bloody the nose of the village bully, then hop-scotch all the way home so as not to destroy the hills of the ants on the pathway. She was a star pupil of church history and the catechism, and often in childhood play she had fancied herself a female St. Paul carrying the gospel to the "far-flung isles" — this often at the waterfront, standing in a rowboat directing a drafted oarsman. She was yet to learn that women were barred from positions of authority in the church. *If only she had been a boy....* But here, Randi checked herself. If it had been meant to be *so,* it would have been *so.*

On the day of Rolf Monsrud's return, Marit passed by the tavern without a glance and did not notice the larger-than-usual congregation of men there. She had come from the waterfront having first gone to the village church where every evening since the storm she had knelt at the altar rail to say prayers for Thorn's safe return, and then, to prove her faith, to the shore to watch for a sail.

In the three weeks that had passed since the gale, she had watched boats sail up the fjord several times, had stood *willing* them to be Thorn's. But each had proved to be one of the other boats of the scattered fleet — crippled, limping home for repairs; and the crew of each had spoken of the ferocity of the storm in tones of awe. Yet, in spite of the lapsed time, she did not doubt for a moment that Thorn would return.

She, as all seamen's women, stood apart from the sea, the *terra firma* of life, but Thorn was *of* the sea. It was to him mother, sweetheart and mistress all rolled into one — a passion compounded of respect, love and challenge. And she had not come between, had not bound him to herself too tightly; then, having loosed him, she trusted. The sea would not betray one of its own.

This was to have been his last voyage before their marriage. Had the storm not intervened, even at this moment they would be man and wife — the wedding was to have been a week ago today. She thought of this as she made her way home through the twilight, having lingered at the shore until the dark blue water of the fjord was meringued with night fog between the fluted rim of peaks.

All was in readiness, only awaiting his return. Her wedding costume — skirt, vest and cap — on which she had embroidered for months, lay across the chest in the room she shared with her sister. And the chest itself held the precious linens that had slowly accumulated through the years — a dowry milked in dribbles from the family's meager resources.

The greatest treasure was the lace tablecloth that had been handed down for generations to the eldest daughter when she married — a symbol of family continuity. A paradox considering its legendary origin: that it dated back to the days of Viking plunder and had been booty brought home by a sea-rover to present to a much-sought-after lady of questionable virtue as a persuader for favor. Fact or legend, the cloth existed but was never used, the gossamery vision much too fragile from age.

She was now on the path that led up the valley — a valley that was little more than a cleft in the rocks to the sides of which cottages clung precariously. Her home was next to the last on the path, the last belonging to the Dahls where Thorn had made his home when he was a child, and where he still stayed when not at sea.

They were almost of an age to the day, she and Thorn. And from the time the Dahls had come to live next door, she had shunned feminine companionship in favor of his; that is, until he was sent to sea at the age of twelve, a development to which she had contributed no small part. When Nicolena Monsrud, visibly pregnant, married Nils Dahl, a cottage was quickly raised at the end of the path. The child Marit observed all this with only passing curiosity, but her interest perked when, on the day the Dahls moved in with their scant furnishings, she caught sight of Thorn.

She eyed him for some time from behind the curtained window of her own home, measured him; then she sallied from the house. It ended in the usual way: She subdued him. Then, having settled the matter of supremacy, she attached herself to him, keeping a jealous eye on his every movement — the locations of their respective homes giving her the jump on him. His only respites were the short school sessions of spring and fall when he found refuge in numbers, and some weeks in summer when the few cattle of the village were herded together and driven up to the mountain plateaus for pasture, the village lads taking turns as herd boys. But for the most time throughout his childhood, Thorn had no alternative but to tolerate her company, even though it was not to his liking; at least, not then — not in the beginning.

⁘

Marit and Thorn were forbidden to set foot on the carefully-tended shallow garden plots that took up the little available space around the cottages, except to help with the weeding. The cliffs, wharves and fjord were their playgrounds.

It was one day when they were playing on the wharves that Thorn, to get at her, needled, "Some day I'll go to sea. You'll have to stay. Girls don't go to sea. That's one place you won't follow me, I'll bet."

He had her there; only men went to sea. She eyed him jealously. But that was years away, she thought; right now he was still at her mercy, and a shaft to the ego was in order. "Haw! You'd be green before you even reached open water"

Insinuating that he would get seasick! This was an insult of the lowest order to the Norwegian boy born of the sea. If only he had a boat, he'd show her!

A rigged skiff was anchored a little way off-shore. He eyed it covetously. It belonged to the master, as did the whole fleet; only the rowboats were at the disposal of the villagers. But even the *women* could handle *them;* they often used rowboats to gather kelp that they boiled and fed to the cattle.

Burning with the smart of her insult, he didn't hesitate long. "I'll show you! Someone'll be green. But it won't be me."

He jumped into a rowboat. She read his mind. "You wouldn't dare!"

He sat waiting for her to follow him.

He must be bluffing! She would call it. She got into the boat and he rowed out to the skiff. He boarded it; again she followed. How much further would he dare go?

He drew up the anchor, began to unfurl the sail. Now she became uneasy — maybe he wasn't bluffing after all. But he mustn't. "Stop it!" she commanded.

"Now look who's green."

Exalted at the fear in her eyes, he set the sail and the skiff started to move.

No boy could live near the sea and not have some knowledge of sailing, but he had never had a chance to try his hand at it. The boys were required to serve an apprenticeship with a seasoned seaman — often their fathers — before being entrusted with the tricky business of handling a wind-driven vessel. Now, in the thrill of trying his hand at the craft, any reservations he may have had vanished. Tacking, pointing, he aimed her prow for the open sea and tried to keep her on course.

He was too busy to think, but Marit was not. She had plenty of time to think. *What will the master do if he finds out?* The villagers revered the master almost as much as the minister. The minis-

ter fed the soul, the master the body. *To disobey the master is almost
like disobeying God himself!* And I'm just as guilty as Thorn is!

They skimmed over the water. Soon the village was left far behind. Thorn's dark hair was windblown, his face flushed. *What had
gotten into him?*

Now his eyes were on her. "What's the matter, don't you like
sailing?"

"Go back," she begged meekly.

Savoring having her at *his* mercy for a change, he laughed and
turned his back on her plea. Perhaps they would have sailed until
they reached the open sea had not Thorn spied another boat coming through the gap. He tacked about clumsily, and the other boat
chased them all the way back to the village, overtaking them at the
end of the race.

They were hauled from the boat. She was largely ignored, but
as she sprinted for home, she looked back once. One of the men
had Thorn by the scruff of the neck and was marching him firmly
up the trail to the master's house on the bluff.

Later, when she saw him coming home, she ran out to meet
him. She took it for granted he had been flogged.

"Did you holler when you got it?"

"Mind your own business." He swaggered away.

"Being flogged is nothing to be so big about," she called after
him. "I was flogged once — and I didn't yell like I bet you did ."

She was yet to learn the basis for his new-found bravado.

❧

The master had been fully informed before Thorn was brought
in. His words were sparse.

"Your name?"

"Thorn Monsrud, sir."

"Your age?"

"Twelve, sir."

"And you think you're man enough to go to sea?"

"No, sir. I mean yes, sir. I mean no and yes, sir."

Up until now he had stood shamefacedly, with eyes downcast.
But suddenly he straightened up, looked the master in the eye almost defiantly. "I mean, I know how to sail, sir."

"We shall see."

The master took an aloof interest in the lives of his beneficiaries; took pride in keeping himself posted on the vital statistics. Ignoring Thorn's presence and thinking aloud he tallied: "Orphan. Makes his home with his sister, Nicolena, wife of the net mender, Nils Dahl. Four little ones and another one on the way."

He stopped talking, stroked his beard thoughtfully for a few moments. Then he pronounced his verdict.

"Ten lashes, light," he said to the man who stood waiting aside in the room. Then, to Thorn, "Next time the fleet goes out, you will be assigned. I will look into the matter, place you where you can be of some use. But as half a seaman, mind you. At half pay."

Then he dismissed the matter by turning away, and the man again grabbed Thorn by the scruff of the neck, marched him out and carried out the master's chastisement.

When the door had closed, the master walked to the window, looked down at the water. The stern lines on his face softened... *Is this not Nicolai Monsrud's son? Now there was a man with salt water in his blood! If I had such a son... I'll keep an eye on this lad....*

꧁꧂

Marit kept her distance while Thorn was making preparations to go to sea. At least she would not give him the satisfaction of rubbing it in — of strutting his emancipation from her! To salve her ego, she told herself: I'll bet I could still lick him though.

Now they became strangers, elaborately ignoring each other whenever Thorn was home from sea. The truce came to an abrupt end, however, one summer evening when they were fourteen.

The encounter was not contrived. She had been sent on an errand to the Dahls by her mother. She knew Thorn was home, but she told herself it didn't matter. She would pretend he wasn't there and ignore him completely.

She ran across the yard, bounded up the steps. Just as she reached for the latch, the door opened suddenly, throwing her off-balance. Thorn — also in a youthful rush — plunged against her, reeling her back with the impact. She teetered for a moment on the edge of the step. Then, before his very eyes, she did a mortifying pratfall!

He shut the door behind him, stood on the topmost step looking down at her.

King of the Mountain! She sprang to her feet in rage. "You did that on purpose, you... you clumsy oaf.""

He came down the steps. "You take that back!"

"Who's going to make me?"

"I am."

"Just try."

And then they were at each other.

She was fully confident; he had not reached the growth spurt, and she was still bigger than he. But she had not reckoned with the rugged life he now led: the muscles toned by a boy's prideful struggle to do man's work and the nimbleness come of climbing masts. She was no match; it was a convulsive, but short bout. And it ended with his pinning her.

Then in the pale light, her body still struggling beneath his and her breath panting a heat in his face close above hers, an awareness came to him. "I'll let you up if you kiss me first."

She spat in his face. In natural reflex he brought his arm up to wipe the spit off on his sleeve. In a flash she wrenched free, threw him off and was up and away. When she regained the top of the steps, and with her hand on the latch for insurance, she paused. "I hate you! You're... you're nasty. That's what you are. Nasty!"

She opened the door and for a moment her figure was a framed hourglass in the light from the room; then she slammed the door.

The hourglass spun round and round. When it righted itself, the sands of his childhood had spun out. In one topsy-turvy moment Marit had become that compelling enigma: female.

When finally he stood to his feet, he faced the closed door. "You're for me, Marit, and I'm for you," he asserted aloud. "Only *you* don't know it yet. Or don't *want* to know it yet."

✼

For two years she did not speak to him, and he let her go her own way; at first, in the inhibited self-consciousness of adolescence, and later, with incipient masculinity, in amused tolerance of her transparent show of indifference.

But as young men would, a group was one day surveying the field of village belles. Inevitably, Marit's name came up.

"She'll make some man a good woman. But she'll take some taming," Ole Lie appraised.

"There are ways," one of the others picked up.

Thorn knew the turn the conversation would now take. "Never mind the ways," he blurted out.

They all turned to look at him. His face, now reddened, was read well by all. "So that's the way it is," Ole said, slapping him good-naturedly on the back. But the gleam in the eyes of some of the others did not escape him, Marit would have no truck with the likes of any of them! Maybe it was time he staked his claim.

It was spring, but the cows had not yet been driven to the mountain valleys. It was Marit's chore to milk the cow that was stabled in the small shed behind their cottage. Thorn waited at his window until he saw her go out with the bucket and enter the shed. Then he came out of the house and followed her.

The shed door was open to the mild spring air. Marit looked up to see him standing in the doorway. She said nothing, went on milking industriously. When her lack of sociability did not repel him she dawdled at the job, stretching it out, hoping he would tire of his little game — whatever it was — and leave. But he leaned against the door frame mooning. As if he had all the time in the world!

She could no longer stall. With a skillful tug, she managed to pull down one last full stream of milk. She took careful aim. It struck him full in the face.

In a moment he was again the boy Thorn, and she his torment. His eyes full of milk, he lunged at her blindly. "You hell-cat!"

She jumped up from the stool, slopping over the milk in the bucket to evade his first grab at her. But there was no way of escape; he kept himself between her and the door. Eventually, he cornered her, caught her.

She was braced for battle, But his hands, when they found her, were gentle, his voice even and his words logical. "Let's quit pretending, Marit. We aren't children anymore. You know how I feel about you. And you must feel the same way about me or you wouldn't try so hard not to show it."

The sudden pang of tenderness that shook her was alien. He saw it in her eyes — a look he had seen in the eyes of trapped animals, defiant, yet in their agony begging for the *coup de grâce*. He kissed her full on the mouth, and long. He felt her body supple in his arms like a willow in spring thaw.

The taming was accomplished. But not in the way his friends would have suggested. Thorn, knowing her pride, made her femininity, not a subordinate thing, but a complementary one — made her want to be a woman for *him.*

Once when he was holding her close he had whispered, "You and I will make great mates!" Her response to the implication of his words was shaking in its intensity.

❦

Marit, in her trek from the shore that evening, had now reached her own gate. Had Thorn been home, she would have looked toward the Dahls before she turned in. But her thoughts were still at sea; she did not see the stranger silhouetted in the window of their neighbor's house.

The family had eaten supper; the dishes had been cleared away. The younger children sat round the table, their heads buried in parochial books. Her father sat drawing on his pipe meditatively. Her mother sat mending, her hands always busy, even when she rested. She looked up with knowing eyes when her eldest child entered.

The sea cares nothing, Randi Maas opined to herself.

CHAPTER II

I t was not of nostalgia that Rolf Monsrud returned to Lilledalen in the spring of 1869. The death of his mother years before had released him from the hated pledge he had made to his father, and he had turned his back on the village within days of her demise; there had been no regretful backward glances.

His earliest memories were of another place; a place where big vessels docked with exotic cargoes and then set sail again, not to return for months or years — and sometimes not at all.

Had his father had a premonition on that last day before he embarked on the fatal voyage? He had often wondered; for it was on that final day of his home stay that he had called him aside and exacted the pledge: "If I don't return, promise me that you'll take care of her, that you'll never leave her!"

The urgency in his father's voice had frightened him. "But you'll be back... you always come back." Then, begging for reassurance: "Don't you..? No matter how long the voyage is?"

His father had looked away over his head, as if into a distance. The reassuring words had not been forthcoming. Instead, his father had mused, "I suppose I've spoiled her, given her too much. But I see so little of her."

He had looked up into his father's face. At that moment had found it unbelievable that he might never return, that he was mortal.

When his father spoke again, his voice was compelling: "Promise!"

He had not promised immediately; had tired to evade his father's eyes.

"Look at me! This is important. I'm talking to you as a man to another man."

As a man to another man.... He had then looked up into his father's eyes; had for a moment considered telling him the truth. But his father was blind — so blind to her that he'd never believe it!

❧

It happened shortly after his father left on one of his voyages. He was awakened in the night by voices, one of them male, and his first thought was that his father had returned — the voices came from his mother's room. Joyous, he jumped from his bed and raced down the hall to the door that was slightly ajar.

But in the room, lit by the street lamp outside the window, he saw his mother engaged in what, to his innocent eyes, appeared to be a scuffle with a stranger; a stranger he saw only in profile, with a wing of curled mustache protruding rakishly and a beret perched at jaunty angle over the temple. Years later when he was drawn into a free-for-all seaport brawl, he took singular pleasure in smashing the nose of a French seaman, spoiling his profile.

The naive Rolf took his mother's mock protests for the real thing and sprang to her defense, beating at the man with his fists, only to have his mother turn on him. She pulled him off the man, swatted him hard on the side of the head and showed him out the door. He heard the door slam loudly behind him as he fled back down the hall to his own room.

He had been nine then; but not many years passed before he realized the significance of Nicolena's brown eyes and more richly pigmented skin: The Monsruds were dark of hair, but had blue eyes and *fair* skin. And to add insult to deceit, his mother had named her daughter *Nicolena* — after *his* father and herself!

But he had given his pledge, and when his father was lost at sea, exercising his prerogative as head of the house, he was adamant in insisting the family return to his father's native village.

There were no strangers in Lilledalen, but the grubby life of a fisherman was not to his liking; on the day of his mother's burial he left the village "to look for bigger fish," as he put it.

He went first to Bergen, the place of his birth. He walked to within a few doors of the old home, then wheeled and retraced his steps to the waterfront and the aseptic smell of salt water. He made inquiries; found his way to the office of the shipping concern for whom his father had served.

The clerk who took his application looked up with interest when he stated his surname. "Monsrud... now, that sounds familiar. Would you be kin to Nicolai Monsrud?"

"He was my father."

Under the clerk's scrutiny, Rolf drew himself up taller, made an effort to measure up, although by now he had despaired of ever reaching his father's height. But after his silent appraisal, the clerk went back to his paperwork; only commenting, "I remember him well."

The noncommittal remark left Rolf feeling somehow put down. But this feeling vanished when, after some minutes of checking schedules, the clerk informed him that he was assigning him for a trial run to a vessel that was scheduled to ship out the very next day. The sooner the better, Rolf thought, eager to put this place with its memories behind him.

⚜

Rolf's years on the high seas coincided with the heyday of the clipper ships; vessels that, because speed was of the essence, sported

a cumulus cloud of sails. As cargo consignments went to the swift-
est, competition was keen and every voyage had the animation of a
race as the sea fliers strained to make port, set new time records.
Having proved himself a worthy seaman on his trial run, Rolf was
never without assignment. Seldom taking shore leave, he touched
at nearly every major port of the world — New York and Boston
among them — in his years at sea.

Each time he touched at Boston or New York, however, he felt
an elation, a buoyancy inexperienced in any of the other weary ports
of the world. It was as if the ports were open doors and he were on
the threshold, with others pushing past him to get in, almost carrying him along in their eagerness. Why not, he finally asked himself
one day; and yielded, left the sea.

But now, he found, his sensations were far different from those
of a foreign sailor on a few hours' shore leave. He was no longer
the rider of the wave, but a part of one, submerged in a tide that
bore ever westward.

For a time he worked in the coal mines of Pennsylvania. Drifting on, he worked the iron mines of Ohio, then in the lead mines
of Illinois. Finally deciding that the mole's life of a miner was not
for him, he moved on. Like many of his nationality, he had an af-
finity for the forests, and when he reached the pine heartland of Wisconsin he found that employment as a lumberjack was to his liking. In Wisconsin, he found the congenial companionship of fellow countrymen.

Wisconsin was poised on the brink of its great lumbering era
— an epoch that was to last for nearly fifty years. Only timber cruisers had penetrated far into the forbidding wilderness where a perpetual gloom was cast by the towering pine. The trees barricaded
by impassable underbrush and windfalls, the cruisers poled log ca-
noes in their function of appraising the uncut holdings. A resourceful
breed, they depended, except for the few staples they carried, on the
enveloping wilderness for their survival as they plied the streams.
But should they fail to gauge wisely the rifts and currents in the
unfamiliar streams, even those few staples could be swept away. They
also had to skirt friction with the natives, no small trick considering that in the pursuit of the interests of the lumber companies they
often infringed on the traditional hunting grounds of the various
tribes — although territorial rights were not delineated. A smatter-

ing of various Indian dialects was valuable and some cruisers became
linguistically proficient.

With streams as highways, company trading posts sprang up
along the banks, later to become nuclei for villages. But to the lumber concerns, this was secondary. The more crucial function the
streams performed was as the vehicle for floating the logs to market, and in the high tide of the spring, the companies appropriated
the state's waters, saturating them with a spectacular glut of cut timber, sometimes resulting in jams that might number in the millions
of logs. In the necessity to keep the logs moving, each year the ti-
tanic drive took its toll in the life and limb of the *river pigs,* those
men who rode the rafts and whose responsibility it was to untangle
the jams. Hazards notwithstanding, the harvest eventually reached
its various destinations and, fed by the pineries, remote cities downstream such as Dubuque and St. Louis became imposing lumber
distribution centers.

But these far downriver cities were of no interest to Norwegian
immigrants. Their mecca was Menomonie, headquarters of the
Knapp-Stout Lumber Company on the Red Cedar River of Wisconsin. If one could somehow make his way to this spot, he was
assured of a toe-hold in the New World, for Knapp-Stout was on
its way to becoming the largest lumber concern in the world and
no one who was willing to work was turned away.

The work day was from dawn to dusk six days a week. The food
consisted mainly of beans and meat, mostly venison, with individual
hunters boasting of having delivered more than a hundred deer in
one season to the camps. The pay started as low as twelve dollars a
month. Even so, with free board, many lumberjacks managed to save
enough money in one or two years to send for their families in
Norway.

With the arrival of families, however, permanency became a
necessity — a contradiction for a lumberjack, teams of whom would
move into an area, establish a camp and exist under the most primitive conditions. When the timber ran out, they would move on, a
denuded landscape the only testimonial to their passing. But in
passing, and with family life in mind, some took note of the fact
that the soil was rich and established homesteads.

Rolf picked his spot carefully. A main camp had been established at a river fork and in the area was a belt of high ground only

interspersed with pine and therefore of no interest to the company with so many tracts of solid pine available. The predominance of hardwood rather than pine was to him a peculiarity that attested to the fertility of the soil. He took three days off from work to hike the fifty-odd miles to Eau Claire to file his claim. Coming back, he walked all the last night to make it to camp again in time for roll call in the morning.

He was a landowner, a status he could never have attained in the homeland where land was kept in families and handed down from generation to generation! Well, not quite, he admitted to himself. He still had to fulfill the requirements of the Homestead Law in regard to tenancy and improvements and then it would be all his. He wasted no time in setting about this.

They had Sundays off. But work ended at dusk on Saturday night, not to resume again until daybreak Monday morning. So each Saturday night found him hiking from the camp to his holding, and the wee hours of Monday morning found him hiking his way back, the hours in between spent in improving the claim, often without sleep the whole time. But it was possible to go on working even at night in the light of the burning trees. Since there was no market for hardwood, burning was the only feasible way to rid the land of them.

He did not burn them all, however. The choicest he saved for a cabin, notching them as he went along. When the pile was sufficient, and on the promise of a keg of beer to make it worth their while, he raised the cabin one Sunday with the help of some fellow lumberjacks from camp.

Now he set his mind to the matter of furnishing the cabin. The bed he had provided for when he raised the walls, a corner of the cabin serving as part of the bedstead, was simply a matter of fastening a pole into one wall to form the outside rail of the bed and propping it up at the loose end with a stout post. Then, to hold the straw that would serve as a mattress, he laid poles crosswise between the rail and wall, toe-nailing them to a wall log. The table he fashioned from split logs, flat side up, also supported by stout wooden posts sunk into the dirt floor, using a similar structure for a bench. Boards braced and fastened to the wall became a cupboard. Lastly, he fashioned a stove from a barrel and rocks mortared with mud.

He was pleased that, save for nails and stovepipe, all this had taken no outlay of cash, leaving his savings nearly intact. In his opinion, there were better places to invest money than in housing — investments that would pay off in tangible value, monetary gain. He decided now that one such investment would be to buy a team of oxen. Not only would the oxen be a help in breaking ground, but they would increase his income; the logging companies doubled a man's salary if he furnished a team of oxen and, as a bonus, they furnished the fodder — no small consideration in an area where no land had been brought under cultivation and winter forage had to be hauled in from long distances on tote wagons.

⁓⁂⁓

Rolf was not by nature an innovator, but he was a shrewd observer and took every opportunity to drop in on homesteaders who were already established, taking pointers from their blunders and successes.

After a number of such visits, he made an observation. He lacked the most vital asset evident in successful homestead enterprises — a good woman! *Her* industry and capabilities made all the difference.

He had never before entertained the thought of marriage, but now, as a matter of business prudence, he decided to acquire a wife. But women were not easy to come by. Those who had married before they emigrated were lucky, he observed. They had good, obedient, unspoiled Norwegian wives — not like these Yankee women!

There were but two alternatives. The first was to wait for the tide of immigration to cast him a suitable mate — not likely any time soon and he wasn't getting any younger. That would be to leave it to chance, a critical thing to leave to chance, he calculated. The other alternative was to go back to the source, go back to Norway and pick one. That had the advantage of wide choice, he weighed; one could be exacting in his requirements. Strength was the main thing.

He decided to return to Norway. He left early in the spring, even before the drive. The sooner he left, the sooner he would be back to get down to the real business of his life, which had now become the homestead.

He used some of his funds to get to Boston, but saved passage fare by signing on as a crewman on a Norwegian vessel bound for the homeland. And now he had found exactly what he was looking for in Marit Maas.

Having taken up lodging in the home of his sister, occupying the loft bed that had been Thorn's, he was able to observe her at close range. There was no doubt about it. She was the pick of the lot!

❧

After their mother's death and Rolf's desertion, Nicolena and Thorn had been shunted from household to household as charity wards. Nicolena had earned their keep as a scullery maid and baby tender. The urchin Thorn was an unwelcome appendage to her like an extra digit, ignored except when he got in the way or made his superfluity glaringly apparent.

With the coming of Nicolena's adolescence there had been an unfolding of unusual dusky prettiness and a quick burst into voluptuous womanhood. This did not go unnoticed; men leered openly, and women began to cast a wary eye on her presence in their homes.

In turn, Nicolena was not long in becoming aware of her sultry magnetism. At first she played the game coyly; then, carried away by the unaccustomed attention and her sway, in wild abandonment. Finally, only the Dahls would have her. Nils, the oldest son, would have her completely.

Rolf was not in Nicolena's home long before he was made aware that she was a bitter woman. Nils was a poor provider; not being of sea calibre he took odd jobs — wood splitting, mending nets— and the lonesome coins he thus earned jingled more merrily in the tavern till than in his pocket. Consequently, conversing with Nicolena was as picking one's way through a prickly patch.

"Well, it's beginning to look like Thornbjorn is in more than a little trouble."

At the unfamiliar sound of the suffix, Nicolena looked up from the wooden washboard. The villagers had dropped the "bjorn" years before at Thorn's insistence. "I'm just Thorn," he had often said.

Her eyes were reflective. "He may yet return. They may have

made another port." With that she went back to her rubbing and grumbling. "I've got trouble enough of my own with four already and another one on the way, and that poor excuse for a man I've got."

Here was an opening; Rolf quickly probed it. "A big family is an advantage in the land of America. Each one means another pair of hands to help with the work. Not like here, where each means another mouth to feed. No one goes hungry there."

"No one... ever?"

"Not ever. " He thought of adding: That is, if you're willing to work; but thought better of it — that would leave *Nils* out.

"America must be heaven. All I've got in my belly half the time is just another one."

Her bitterness could be turned to advantage. He decided to risk disclosure. "I came back for a reason. I need a woman, young and strong. There is land to be cleared and broken, crops to be sown and harvested, sons to be sired.... I *want* a large family."

The rote rubbing ceased abruptly. She straightened up, looking at him alertly. "Do you have someone in mind?"

Should he risk it? He studied her face for a moment. "I have Marit Maas in mind."

Nicolena gasped. "But what of *Thorn?*"

"The devil take Thorn!"

He had not intended to be so blunt; he saw that she was taken aback. But a few minutes ago, she had said she had troubles enough of her own. "As I was saying, a big family is an advantage in America. Now, if you were *there....* "

She laughed mirthlessly. "And how would I ever get there?" Her eyes became pensive. "Unless.... You said you needed help. I could go back with you and leave Nils here."

Now it was coming his way. "It was something like that I had in mind. If you could swing Marit to me, I could send money to you later, for *you* to come. That is, when I get set up myself."

It was not hard to read her face. He saw the weighing, the dawning of hope; the hardening that told him he had won, had gained her as an ally against Thorn. *I hope Thorn never comes back,* he knew she was thinking.

"I've noticed the girl sets great store by you," he added pointedly.

Marit looked in on Nicolena every day. Her mother made a habit of sharing with her less fortunate neighbor, and there always seemed to be a little food *left over* each day for Marit to carry next door. Quite often, Nicolena needed a helping hand with the children and the work. Being almost family in her betrothal to Thorn, she did what she could to lighten Nicolena's load.

Marit had been aware that there was an older brother, but since they never heard form him, she had not taken him into consideration as a future brother-in-law. Now she felt she must.

Their first encounter was a disappointment. *He's not a bit like Thorn,* was her first impression. Then: *He's not interested in me — even if I am almost his sister-in-law.* For he never spoke to her, nor was she able to meet his eyes. For even though she was occasionally aware that he was looking at her, when she looked at him, his eyes moved away evasively. Soon she came to pay him little notice when she encountered him.

This, Nicolena observed. But it did not at all quell the seething volcano of hope that had now supplanted the hard-rock of despair inside her. First, she must undermine Marit's confidence in Thorn's return; she would have eyes for no other man until she came to believe Thorn was lost.

Her first attempts were dismal failures. "Our own father was a good seaman, but when it came his time to go...." She ended there, implying doom. But it had no perceptible effect on Marit, so she continued: "The sea takes its toll every year. Women who marry men who go to sea should always be *prepared.* And those who *plan* on marrying such men should think on this, too."

Marit made light of it. "Don't worry yourself for nothing, Nicolena. Thorn will be back. You'll see."

Nicolena decided to try a different tack. Now often when Marit came she found Nicolena's eyes red, as if from weeping — an effect Nicolena was able to quickly achieve whenever she had enough forewarning of Marit's coming to give her time to rub her eyes with an onion nub.

At first, Marit tried to comfort her. But finally out of patience, she lashed out one day. "You like to wallow in misery. That's *your* trouble, Nicolena."

⚜

Weeks went by and Rolf was becoming more impatient. Every day he watched Marit leave for her pilgrimage to the church. He was aware that she still went to the shore, that she still had thoughts only of Thorn and he fumed inwardly: Here I am, a man with bright prospects, a man who under other circumstances would be considered a good match by the father of a daughter of marriageable age....

For it really was something best left to the men, this matter of arranging suitable marriages. It was a matter of business, and women knew nothing of business. They were poor judges of what was best for themselves. Look at his sister Nicolena; she had the poor judgment to get herself caught with the most worthless of the pack!

Hans Maas had a good business head. Were it not for Thorn's spectre, he could go over the girl's head to her father, ask for her hand and be almost certain of being granted it on the basis of his bright future. But it wouldn't hurt to pay Hans Mans a visit; to feel him out.

"I see that your daughter still waits for a boat that will never come. It's best she forget about *that* one and start looking around."

"The boy knows the sea," Hans said simply, and Rolf sensed that Hans had a great deal of respect for the young man who was his future son-in-law, and also that he, as well as Marit, had not given up hope of Thorn's return.

The visit compounded Rolf's frustration. By now he should have been on his way back to the homestead, his future assured, with Marit in tow as the embodiment of his design for that future: A family dynasty in the New World — numerous, landed and prosperous. And now, no other would do. Marit had become a fixation in that design.

⚜

It was the custom of the day for each boat to have a figurehead. Carved by hand, some were grotesque; others were of great beauty.

Thorn, being skilled with the knife, had carved the figurehead for the boat on which he served, the figure being that of an eagle with outspread wings. In its mouth, he had carved a rope, strand by strand, running back so that it seemed to melt into the boat itself and making it appear that the eagle was pulling the boat into the wind on the strength of its wings. Marit had always admired it.

It was when she was watching on the wharf one day that a sail appeared far down the fjord. Her heart pounded hopefully, but again there was disappointment. It was Torger's boat. However, something in the stance of the crew — a certain urgency — caused her to linger on even after she had identified the boat.

The boat docked and Torger stepped off first. He was carrying something wrapped in sailcloth. When he reached her, he laid it at her feet ceremoniously; unwrapped it in ritualistic gravity.

There was no mistaking it. The eagle lay before her. Its mouth was torn — empty of rope, agape, as in horror. She turned without a word and started running blindly toward home.

Before she reached there, the church bell began to toll the news to the village — measured, with ominous lapses between the knells.

Others besides Marit had waiting and the finding of the floating figurehead was taken as the seal of doom by the relatives of the crew.

The mourners filed into the little church for the customary memorial service, their pace geared to a funeral dirge.

"Out of the depths have I cried unto Thee...."

Marit had attended many such services and the words the minister had spoken on those other occasions had seemed so comforting. Now the words rang hollow, reverberating meaninglessly in the echo chamber that was the emptiness inside her.

They filed out again.

Why doesn't our church have cloisters where one could go, she wondered numbly, where one could dedicate a life that was no longer of any use to oneself?

CHAPTER III

K nut stood facing the approaching storm. "I don't like the smell of it," he said, sniffing the wind.

Knut smelled everything: where the fish were running, submerged rocks, the enigmatic undercarriage of icebergs, good and bad weather, but they had come to respect his proboscidean hunches, for they were uncannily accurate. They had taken in the nets, checked ropes and sails and battened down. Now, as secure as they could make themselves, they stood steeled and waiting as the slate-gray storm bore down in an eerie twilight of lowered sky that obscured the boats of the fleet from each other; making the crew of each boat keenly aware that their fate was an individual thing.

The blast came as a pent-up blow from the mouth of a cyclopian monster enraged by a hot bowl of soup, hitting suddenly and lashing the sea into an instant fury. They took in sail, took up oar and bail to do battle — to vault the swells, to keep from being foundered in the yawning troughs.

Wall after wall of water came rushing, clawing, dragging; slipping, skidding, dropping. Time was only measured by the pendulum swings of the boat in the canyons of the sea. Hour after hour passed in a black, fluid hell. A creeping weariness was felt first in the muscles, then, way down to the marrow of the bone.

Thorn could never accurately state the time nor what it was they struck. But knowing that one of the treacheries of the sea is that a boat driven by the wind may at the same time find and iceberg bearing down windward with the current, multiplying the force of impact, he surmised from the devastation that it was an iceberg.

There was a violent, splintering jolt. Men were thrown against each other and into the sea. Some were pelleted against hard objects, the moans from their broken bodies mingling with the banshee-wail of the wind and the shrill plaint of wrenching timbers. No order to abandon ship was heard — a final fragmentation, leaving each man's survival in his own hands.

Thorn's leg was pinned. He tried to dislodge the heavy timber; but even as he tried to free himself he felt the boat breaking up under him. He clawed around in the darkness. His hand finally finding the familiar feel of rope, he pulled it to him and lashed himself to the timber, hoping it would float free.

It went under. Below, he tried to disengage himself. Just as his lungs were about to burst with the pressure of prolonged held-breath, there was a final great wrench and the timber floated free. But in the freeing he was struck a hard blow on the head by some segment of the debris.

When he regained consciousness, it was day; the sun was beating down on him. His first sensation was of thirst. He opened his eyes; the world spun in a vertigo of intense blues pierced by brilliant flashing lights. He shut his eyes again; tried to think, tried to orient himself. He raised his head, opened his eyes again and looked across a sea still rough and jittery from the chaos of the storm.... It all came back to him. He tried to raise himself to a sitting position, the better to take stock, but he was flattened by spasms of retching. When the biliousness had passed, he lapsed into a lethargy of exhaustion, uncaring that his face lay in the slime of his own vomit.

A keen sense of thirst again roused him. He struggled to a sitting position; noted that the timber, in breaking free, had taken with it some boards, that he was afloat on a raft of a rough sort. He scanned the waters; no other boat was in sight, not even a bit of flotsam that would give him hope of finding water kegs afloat.

He now realized the full seriousness of his situation. He could do without food for some time, but without water.... He looked up at the sun. It was in its zenith; he would have to wait for it to start to descend before he could of certainty fix the east, land would lie to the east. He lay back again, tried to save his strength, but gnawing thirst forbade resignation.

Off to his right there was a haze on the horizon. It might just be the shadow of a retreating storm or it might indicate a land mass — his blurry eyes refused to make the distinction. Yet he decided to try to work his way toward it, using his hands as paddles. After a time the sun told him he was headed in the right direction. It just might be land!

If he made progress, it was not discernible; what was more, he was soon exhausted. But evening brought with it coolness and a resurgence of strength.

The current alone would carry him to that shore — but that might be too late. *His lifeless body a feast for the seafowl....* That mental projection jolted him into action. He broke off two jagged loose boards to serve as paddles and flailed on through the darkness, the stars his compass. Some time before daybreak he lapsed into unconsciousness, his body still secured loosely by the rope around his middle.

Clad in skins and leathern-complexioned, the man who stood shielding his eyes from the sun seemed parcel of the bleak landscape behind him. The dancing waves played tricks on the eyes. He stood frozen for some time. But now he was certain; there was something! He turned and ran through the rocks to the group of hide-covered huts that was their summer camp.

It was the way of these people to watch for wreckage after storms, for in their meager existence even debris could be used to advantage. Hardwood timbers were especially coveted, so no time was lost. An alerted group ran to the shore, dragged their skin boats to the water's edge and set out like a flock of low-flying seafowl skimming over the water, paddle-pinioned.

When they reached their objective, they were so excited over the prize that they did not immediately concern themselves with the seemingly lifeless body lashed to it. Only after they had towed the timber to shore did they examine him, detect life. They carried him into one of the huts where they left him to the care of the women.

Children peeked shyly at him through the aperture and the women were only a little less shy. But finally one more bold than the rest came close, caught sight of the grotesquely swollen leg.

This discovery drew a group. There was a monosyllabic counsel, a decision made; one of the children was sent to summon the aged one. She hobbled in, muttered darkly at the sight of the damaged leg; briefly examined Thorn further. It seemed her wisdom was respected, for the others stood in silence until she was finished, as if waiting for a verdict. Evidently there was hope; upon her instructions they went scurrying away, returning shortly with a miscellany of unlikely materials.

They did their best by him, bringing to bear the ages-old remedies of their race. An evil-smelling poultice was applied to the leg and held in place by a skin casing; tallow was smeared on his sunburned face and cracked lips; potions were forced down his throat.

And he fought them all the way, so much so that they were forced to tie him down to minister to him. In his delirium he insisted that he must be up and away — and could not remember why. But there was a reason, a reason he should be someplace else. It was as a reprieve to the women when his fever rose and his condition worsened. Now there was tranquility. He lay very still — and silent.

⋘⋙

He opened his eyes. Recollection did not come at once, and for some moments he stared hypnotically at the patch of blue sky that shown like a shred of bright blue glass through the chink in the top of the hut. He tried to move and the leather bands that had been applied to restrain him cut into his raw wrists and ankle. It was suddenly as if he were a snared animal; he struggled to get free, although to do so mutilated his flesh, the restraints cutting in.

He became aware of someone moving about in the shadows that surrounded him. "Turn me loose," he begged feebly.

The Lapp woman started at the sound of his voice. She came closer. But, yes! The fever had broken! She ran from the hut and returned with one of the men who understood and could speak Norwegian.

"Untie me!"

The man complied, but it was of no great difference; his weakness bound him to the pallet as surely as if he were still bound. *And one of his legs....* It was as if it were lead!

The effort so far expended had exhausted him. He only mustered enough more strength to ask, "Where am I?"

"Lopphavet."

It was too much to think about now. He fell into a natural sleep.

Next morning he awoke clear-headed. His first thought was: I must let Marit know — let her at least know I'm alive.

These people led a primitive life, he knew; they neither wrote nor read. So paper and pen were unavailable. Yet, there must be some way.... He set his mind to it.

The next day he summoned the man again; instructed him to cut a piece off the bottom of his trouser leg. The man did so, using his bone knife. Thorn then instructed him to have the women boil it, bring the remnant back to him in the water in which it was boiled.

If the man was perplexed, his face gave no indication. He followed Thorn's instructions, returning later with the strange brew.

As Thorn had hoped, the dye had boiled out; it made a passable ink. He then asked for a feather and a piece of hide. Borrowing the man's knife, he whittled the quill to a point. He dipped it in the dark residue, and with an unsteady hand scrawled on the hide. *I'm safe, Thorn.*

After it had dried, he rolled it up tightly and addressed it to Marit. He fashioned thongs from more hide and bound it securely, then gave it to the man; instructing him to pass it on to the first Norwegian they might encounter on one of their hunting or fishing expeditions.

Now, he relaxed and lay back content to wait for strength to return. If it weren't for the leg.... The leg would take time. He wouldn't hobble home to Marit a cripple!

༺ঽৡঽ৶༻

From hand to hand and from boat to boat the leather scroll made its way; it was a miracle that it reached Lilledalen. It *did* reach Lilledalen. But Marit very seldom ventured to the waterfront these days, so it was handed to Nicolena to give to Marit, who was sitting with the babies so Nicolena could meet the mail boat that day.

On the pathway on the way home, Nicolena examined it out of curiosity — it was an odd thing. There was no return on it, but the moment her eyes fell on the address she stopped dead on the path. She had watched that hand form its first letters. She'd recognize that scrawl anywhere.

She turned off the path, unwound the thongs and threw them into some bushes. Then, sitting on a rock, she read the brief but weighty message.

Marit's faith had been rewarded — Thorn had survived! But what of her own hopes, her chance for a new life in America, her happiness? She tucked the scroll inside her blouse and went on home.

It had all gone so well — up until now! After Marit had given up on Thorn, she had been as dough in her hands, to maneuver as she wished. When she had drawn for her the picture of a land without women — uncomfortable, lonely, uncivilized — Marit had fairly jumped at the chance to go, to sacrifice herself. *Why hadn't she thought of this before, this weakness in Marit,* she chided herself.

The wedding day had been set. It was not to be an elaborate

affair, for Marit did not want it so. However, a fever of preparation prevailed. Although the wedding was to be simple, they would embark for America immediately after, and the list of provisions needed for the voyage — compiled from the letters of those who had crossed successfully — seemed endless.

It was the way of the time for the emigrants to provide all their own essentials for the crossing. So, to start with, there must be food enough to last for from six to twelve weeks — the variant factor being the wind. And because of the time element, perishability must be considered. Being baked were mountains of flat bread, a hardtack that kept well and packed compactly in chests. Grain was being ground for the preparation of grout, or mush, a staple of the diet. Salted and smoked meats and fish were being casked, also dried fruits and vegetables. Cheeses were being pressed, butter churned and crocked. Such staples as coffee, tea, sugar and flour were being measured out.

But food was a fraction of it. Rounding out the list were items of a medicinal nature: brandy, vinegar, wine, carbolic, sulphur powder, ointment, spirits of camphor and Hoffman's drops. And not to be overlooked were saltwater soap and fine-tooth combs. Last but not least, also to be packed were Marit's personal belongings and dowry.

Realizing that giving Marit the proper send-off to America was a tax to the resources of the Maas family, neighbors chipped in, no doubt with the thought that next time (hopefully) it might be one of theirs so fortunate. Even Nicolena, dipping into her meager larder, contributed with a generosity that was unusual for her.

Keeping busy, but in an aura of resolute silence, Marit moved through these days of preparation in the black of mourning. And she would not break mourning even for the ceremony. She had given the wedding costume she had so hopefully stitched to her sister Thora. It could be unseamed, the material salvaged for another day.

Also, it had seemed to her that it would be sacrilegious — a mockery — to exchange vows in the church with anyone other than Thorn. So they were married in her father's house, the ceremony reduced to a minimum: the simple exchange of vows of fidelity as required by the church.

Before they embarked, Nicolena had a moment alone with Rolf. Now, she felt, it was safe to tell him of the scroll.

"Burn it," he told her.

But she had already secreted it between the rafters in the attic where a board was loose and, busy as her life was, she never got around to carrying out his order. The scroll was forgotten until later — much later.

As the boat sailed out of the fjord and into the sea, Marit instinctively looked to the north for a sail, but the sun glinted off an expanse of emptiness. She turned and set her face to the south — and Bergen. There they would catch the vessel that would carry them to Liverpool and the ship of passage.

❧

Five days later Thorn returned home. When he walked in the door, Nicolena feigned shock, putting her hands up in horror as if at the sight of a ghost — but not before she had quickly scanned his face.

She had guessed correctly that he would get the news in the village before reaching home; his usually ruddy face was, in truth, almost as white as a ghost. "I don't believe it," he stated flatly.

In self-interest, she had not let herself think of Thorn, of what this would do to him. Now, in his presence, and at the sight of his stricken face, her voice was scarcely audible when she vouched, "It's true. Marit is on her way to America... with Rolf." Then, in a twinge of conscience, she made an attempt to rationalize for him. "They did find the figurehead...."

"Rolf!" He sat down hard, his one leg stiffly in front of him.

"Your brother does have a way with women."

That didn't add up! The memory of the mother he had lost as a little boy had always been shadowed by the figure of his older brother, the pall of fear he threw over her. And, somehow, he had always connected her death, his loss of her, with Rolf. Indelibly imprinted on his mind was the memory of her saying, "Your hate is killing me...." That, and Rolf's menacing face and his mother cringing from it.

"I remember too well his way with women! He'll destroy *her* just like...." His shoulders heaved suddenly, and he got up and went out.

He did not come back until the next afternoon. Nicolena did

not ask him where he had been — and if she had, he could not have told her. For he had climbed until night came, up and up, dragging the leg, savoring its protests of pain. And then on in the darkness, unmindful of crevasses and abysses, until he had finally stumbled. Spent, he lay where he fell and slept fitfully until morning.

His head cleared, he spent most of the forenoon making his way down again. Down, he spent some time on the shore looking out across the water, wild thoughts racing through his mind. He would pursue them, fight Rolf for her. But first, he must know more....

Again on the path to the cottage, he spied something to the side in the bushes. He took the few necessary steps to retrieve it, picking it up and turning it over in his hands. The jagged bone-cut edges of the thong were unmistakable.

It had to be true. Marit had *chosen* Rolf over him. She had gotten his message.

His face was no longer boyishly bland. "You've met your match now!" he said aloud.

CHAPTER IV

They could have booked passage on a Norwegian vessel at Bergen. But these ships, converted to cater to the emigrant trade, were of the slower sailing varieties, for people who have nothing waiting for them at the other end, Rolf reasoned when he made the decision to go to Liverpool, catch a clipper. But when they reached Liverpool, he learned that they had missed an outbound clipper by two days and that another was not due for several days. However, a packet was scheduled to sail the very next day, its destination Quebec. He made the necessary arrangements.

He was disappointed, but consoled himself with the knowledge that they might have done worse. The packets—sometimes known as Baltimore Clippers—could be outdistanced only by true clippers. Having been beaten out by the clippers for more lucrative cargo, they regularly plied the route between England and Canada, carrying passengers and manufactured goods on the outbound voyage and returning with cargoes of lumber. Usually rigged as brigs or schooners, they were full-bodied vessels with strong hulls and stout spars, sails and rigging. The decks were flush with a galley, and the long boat, lashed to the deck, often carried livestock and on this voyage carried goats to furnish the crew and first-class passengers with fresh milk. Also, for the first-class passengers, there were comfortable cabins, Below-deck was the steerage compartment.

❧

In the comparative brightness of the sunlit deck, the compartment appeared to be in complete darkness when Marit peered down the yawning hatchway. Yet people were entering — some had preceded her and others were waiting in line behind — so she made her way down the ladder, Having gained the floor, she saw that the only source of light was the hatchway through which she had descended and that one source was now being partially eclipsed by the persons entering.

Even before her eyes adjusted to the twilight so her sight could apprise her of the nature of the place, her nose warned her of its vileness. In the heat of the August day the air was stifling, intensifying the odors that wafted on it. It was repugnant. She had the instinctive urge to flee the place, but she forced herself to walk away from the light and scan about.

Her eyes took in a scene of confusion; it appeared that all the trunks, crates and boxes from every attic of Europe had somehow found their way to this place together with barrels and kegs of every size. Milling about in the jumble were women and children. The wail of one babe in arms seemed to rise from the mouths of them all.

Here, as it had in all manner of abode from cave to palace, the female nesting instinct came to the fore. Somewhere in the aggregate were their belongings; she decided to look for them. It became apparent that this was the reason for the milling about. Others were trying to locate their own things, and those few who had found them were extracting them from the common heap, assembling.

Marit picked her way from one motley pile to another. When she did finally come upon their own, her eyes had become so jaded from trying to spot the slight distinguishing differences of the containers that she almost passed them by.

She looked about for a likely spot in which to settle their own collection, but one location seemed to have little advantage over another; it was space itself that was at premium. She saw a small pool of emptiness by a bulkhead and lay claim to it by dragging a crate to the spot. She was able to shift all but the big box that held the huge iron scalding kettle packed with tools of wilderness scarcity that Rolf had acquired as a bonus of the homeland jaunt. That one would have to wait for the men, few of whom were in evidence. After having deposited their families aboard, most had gone back ashore to savor the last moments of unrestricted movement.

With all gathered, she sorted the containers out with a mind to their time of use. Those things that would not be needed until they reached the homestead she shoved to the back; to the fore she brought food, cooking utensils, clothing, the small box containing their toiletries, bedding. Again she looked about. She had been led to believe that rudimentary berths would be provided, but none were in evidence. Did that mean that they would have to sleep on the floor? She brought out their pallet, but did not spread it; there would be time enough for "making the bed" later, she decided, dubiously eyeing the filthy floor.

She had done all she could for the time being, and she now decided to compass the compartment, get her bearings. She had to pick her way, for aside from the array the emigrants had themselves brought on board, numerous obstructions blocked her way. Ropes and canvases were strewn about and sprinkled liberally throughout were numerous wooden buckets. *It would help some if we threw these overboard,* she thought, kicking disdainfully at one of the empty darkly-stained receptacles, and then stumbling over a crude wooden bench, one of several she had encountered.

The area was not partitioned, save for the one that shielded the privy that must serve them all; and that hardly more than a screen, a rough-boarded overture to privacy. She turned her back on it. *I'll hold back as long as I can,* she vowed.

She came upon the galley; its confines such that she estimated that only three — four at the most — could work there at one time. They would have to take turns. She looked about, tried to compute.

It was then she noticed a young mother struggling to set her own small world in order, her efforts hampered by the infant she carried on one arm and the distraction of trying to quiet its crying. The woman was startled when Marit reached out, took the baby from her.

"It think you can use some help," she explained, although she wasn't sure the woman was Norwegian, would understand. She had heard some of the mothers speaking to their children in a tongue that was foreign to her.

"Oh, I would be so grateful! If you could just hold him until I get things straightened out a little. I have a cradle somewhere...."

She located the cradle. "If I can just get the ropes undone."

Marit watched her struggle with the knots a few moments. "Here, let me try it," she said, handing the baby back to its mother. As she did, the blanket dropped from its face and she could see it was a very new one, just days old, she guessed.

When the infant had been deposited in the cradle and soothed by rocking, Marit said by way of making conversation, "The baby looks so young. You can't be long out of childbed."

"Only two weeks! But we felt nothing must stand in the way of our going to America. Even if I'd had to have it on the high seas we would have come. We'd been waiting so long for the fare, money Eyvin's cousin sent. As soon as it came we packed. But then I got sick. The baby came a little early. But we delayed only long enough for me to get back on my feet."

"Then you have relatives in America?"

"My husband has several cousins. We're going to them. And you? Do you have people to go to?"

"No. None of my people are there. Nor my husband's."

It was said matter-of-factly but the woman took it as need for reassurance. "Well, now you know me. So at least you'll know one person in America!" Then she thought to introduce herself. "My name is Anna — Anna Rolstad."

"And I'm Marit Maa— Monsrud. But America is such a big place. We'll probably never see each other again after we leave the boat."

"What's your destination?"

Marit hesitated. It really was no *place* — just wilderness. But she remembered Rolf's mention of a town. "My husband has a homestead in Wisconsin. I think it's near a place called Millwood."

Anna's mouth dropped open. "Why, that's where Eyvin's cousin lives — can you believe it? We'll be neighbors!"

It was as if they were old friends; a quick familiarity that would have been unlikely in the homeland where isolation bred distrust even of fellow countrymen from other districts, other valleys, over the mountains. But now, adrift from the homeland, reservation had dissolved in the need to cling to something; if not a common past, a mutual destiny.

"We'll stick together," Anna said, linking her arm in Marit's. They stood thus, observing the bustle about them.

"Something should be done," Marit commented.

"Something done..?"

"There's no privacy — no privacy at all! There could at least be curtains."

"Blankets?"

"We'll probably need them. But there's all these pieces of canvas and rope. It seems to me the pieces of rope could be strung up, canvas hung on them...."

"If only the men were here—"

"Why wait for the men? All I need is something to stand on."

Anna looked up dubiously. "You'd need a ladder."

"With all these boxes around?" Already she was piling one on top of another.

She had effected several curtained cubicles by the time the men began to return in tightly knit little groups, a noisy invasion with joviality that seemed a little too much — the back slapping and a show of bravado rather than genuine lightheartedness. Disbanding, they stood awkwardly about, at loose ends.

One very blond young man had taken his place by Anna's side and was observing Marit's efforts.

"Can you use some help?" he offered.

"The rope can be put to better use than that!"

It was Rolf's voice. They turned to him for an explanation.

"Have you ever been to sea, Eyvin?"

"No."

"I figured so. If you had, you'd know that all this...." he swung his arms wide, "must be tied down. Have you any idea what this place will be like if all these barrels start rolling around, the piles start tipping over? And mark my words, they will when we set sail!"

With that, he began gathering up rope himself. Eyvin did the same, as did some of the other men, seemingly relieved to have something useful to do. Each secured his own freight first; then that of others. But they ran out of rope before all was secure.

"Well, at least we're all right on this end," Rolf said with self-satisfaction, brushing his hands together. "Let the rest worry about themselves."

With the men putting an end to her project in their appropriation of the rope, Marit turned her attention to another matter. "I suppose it's time we start thinking about something to eat."

"I'm not hungry. My stomach's all tied up in knots."

"But you must eat! For the baby, you know."

However, they lunched on cold food, as did most of the other families. And many didn't eat at all, Marit noticed.

It began to darken even more in the compartment and one of the men took a lantern down from where it hung and attempted to light it, with no success.

"It's rationed," Rolf explained.

"Rationed hell! It's empty," the man said, holding the lantern to his ear and shaking it vigorously. "Are we expected to go to roost like chickens when the sun goes down?"

Just then, a seaman appeared at the hatchway; he came part way down the ladder and paused, so as to be able to look out over their heads. Then, in the light that came from above, he proceeded to read a paper that he carried in his hand.

Marit did not understand a word of it. Anna, who stood close beside her, whispered, "English, I would guess."

Marit could see from the faces around her that it was as much a puzzle to most of them as to her. Only Rolf's face showed comprehension, and when the sailor had finished reading, he said something that caused several men to spring forward, Rolf among them. He handed the paper to the first man who reached him.

The seaman went back up the ladder, and the man who now had the paper took his place on the ladder and started to read the paper once more, but again in a language that apparently many could not understand, Marit and Anna among them.

"Doesn't he think we can read for ourselves!" Rolf spouted.

"What's it all about?" Eyvin asked.

"The ship's rules. And that Kraut had the guts to set himself up as an interpreter! I'll bet there's more Norwegians than anything else on this ship!"

When the German had finished reading, he got nail and hammer and posted the paper. But this time, it had grown quite dark in the far recesses of the compartment and children were beginning to whimper.

Now the seaman reappeared carrying a can. He summoned the interpreter, who in turn explained — for those who could understand German — that it was the night's ration of oil and that when it was used up, there would be no more until the next night so they would do well to conserve it. Only when he had finished were the lanterns gathered up, the oil doled out.

When they were lit and hung on the widely-spaced hooks, everything that stood on the floor created a shadow trap that must be navigated with care lest one trip and fall over something. But navigating was unavoidable with the privy the busy port of call that it now was becoming.

The business of bedding down began, the pallets unrolled and shaken to fluff them, an exercise that filled the air with dust. Some were set to sneezing and objections were loudly voiced.

"What is this, a threshing?"

"Just spread them."

"Stop it!"

"Someone open a window." This last brought a few good-natured laughs.

The din subsided, followed by a self-conscious lull; with no privacy for undressing most adults retired fully clothed, save for their shoes and stockings, but mothers undressed their children so they could apply to their bodies the quicksilver salve that they hoped would guarantee a night undisturbed by the body lice of which they had been forewarned. In their weariness, they promised themselves that tomorrow they would begin the ritual of fine-tooth combing, another precautionary measure.

The rules said the lanterns must be extinguished by nine. The interpreter, who seemed to have become something of an officer in his own right, made the rounds and blew them out. They heard him stumbling back to his own pallet in the darkness. "Good enough for him," Rolf muttered.

It was some time before all voices hushed, particularly the voices of children asking for water; they would not receive their first day's ration of drinking water until morning. After a while, however, the slow, even breathing of slumber and occasional snoring told those who lay staring wide-eyed into the darkness that some had found sleep. From time to time, the shrill cry of an infant pierced the darkness, and although soon muffled, some of those who slept rolled over in an involuntary gesture of protest.

In contrast to the steerage compartment, all was fixed routine above and first light brought the order for the hands to man their stations. The anchor was catted — hoisted to the cat head. The mate gave the orders to loose the sails and men sprang aloft and cast off the gaskets. The mate then hailed the yards and "Aye, aye sir," echoed back in each case. Then the order, "Let's go," and the furled cocoons of sails burst into wings. The trimmed sails cupped the wind, the anchor was weighed and they were off.

The time-honored rite of getting underway had been executed in perfect British form without a hitch. Or so it seemed above. Below, pandemonium broke loose. In the steerage compartment, all sounds from above were amplified. The clank of the anchor on the deck awakened those who slept and when the sails caught wind, the lurch hailed unsecured baggage to the floor. Women screamed and snatched terrorized children from the floor where they were in danger of being trampled by the men who cursed as they stumbled blindly about in the shadows bumping into each other. Finally, one made his way to a lantern and lit it.

More lanterns were lit, and the canvas Marit had so laboriously strung up was yanked down to get at the ropes which were now needed for a "better use," as Rolf had warned. In time, order was restored, but not before some of the lanterns sputtered out, giving evidence of the close calculation of rations.

The rest of the lanterns were blown out and they settled down to wait for full light. But no rest was to be had. The children were now wide awake, many of them wailing, and the voices of mothers, themselves unnerved by the nearness of the sea breaking against the bulkhead, were heard trying to reassure them in their fright at the creaking and groaning of the vessel as it strained to follow the lead of the sails far above. Landlubbers that most of them were, even before daylight not a few succumbed to seasickness from the rocking. To this, not even the men were immune. The reason for the abundance of buckets now became apparent. Not all found them in time.

⚜

Morning brought a sorry mess to light, but also positive action as an antidote for the helpless mood of the night. Clean-up was the first order of the day, as ship's orders were that they must keep their own quarters clean. But it was of revulsion rather than compulsion that the women waited impatiently for the crew to appear with the water that they would use for the scrubbing.

After the clean-up, the scrub water, together with the other wastes, was handed up to be dumped overboard. Only then were the fresh water rations forthcoming: two quarts for each adult and one for each child. Some time was consumed as the women scrambled to get containers in which to collect their family's share. Then, thirsty as they all were, they dared not drink their fill, for the ration must also suffice for cooking. Parents pulled up-ended cups forcibly from their children's lips.

The afternoon was spent in the reorganization of floor space, the men the arbitrators in this matter. It was generally agreed that clear traffic lanes to the privy must be arranged. Also, the buckets were evenly distributed, and with everyone cautioned to take note of the precise location of the nearest one before lights-out. The baggage was restacked in such a way as to afford a little privacy for each bedding area, then tied down.

All this was accomplished with a great deal of gesturing and very little friction — at least, so it seemed. But there was an inordinate amount of switching about, With all the old rivalries and antagonisms coming into play, nationalistic boundaries were drawn, the compartment emerging a miniature Europe.

⚜

It soon became apparent that nationality and language were not the only barriers. One closely-knit little family stayed singularly aloof from the rest. They prominently displayed a statuette of the Virgin

Mary, and the woman had been observed fingering beads. When it was whispered to Marit that they were Catholic, she stared frankly; she had only *read* about Catholics — in church history. In her mind's eye, she had always visualized them in shadow, as if, somehow, their faces would give evidence of their "unenlightened' state. But they seemed to be blissfully unaware of the their lack, she observed.

But these she could excuse. Far less charitable was she to those of her own countrymen who were dissenters from the state religion and whose reason for going to America was for the freedom to wantonly practice their heresy in a place called the Territory of Utah, their fares to that place having been funded. *They* had the light and had turned their backs on it! These she would steer clear of!

Although meals continued irregular and little incidents spiced each day, life aboard ship assumed something of a daily pattern.

Time passed swiftly for the women, taken up as they were with the domestic problems of existence. Not so for the men. They found time heavy on their hands. The camaraderie of the first days had eroded under the stress of confinement. Every man soon knew every other's life history from beginning to end and listeners were apt to rudely turn away from an anecdote that had been repeated too many times. The only cohesiveness that was evidenced was in the eternal card games they played. But even in this diversion, raw nerves shorted out in quick flashes of temper. After one such flare-up, one man had withdrawn entirely and sat brooding by himself day after day.

Their irritability was intensified by the rule that forbade smoking — the comfort of a mellow pipe. Some still carried them in their mouths for the satisfaction they could gain from sucking on the empty bowls. Many resorted to chewing tobacco, a commodity that could be purchased from ship's stock, and women zealously donated pans to serve as spittoons. But as the men sat playing around the oversized crates that served as card tables, and in their preoccupation with the game and the difficulty of reading the spots in the dim light, they aimed only in the general direction of the pans and often missed their target. Marit sympathized with the women whose quarters were near those areas and, therefore, whose lot it was to clean them. She helped with the cleaning, mindful that Rolf had contributed his share to the mess.

A few passed the daylight hours in a cluster near the hatch, reading by the light it afforded. But one individualist spent his time and the light in whittling female figurines in a variety of poses. At first he offered these to his fellow passengers at a price but, finding no takers and having a seemingly endless supply of whittling wood, he started handing them out gratis. Women looked away in embarrassment when the men displayed the revealing forms — to the delight of the men, who teased by stroking them affectionately. Not a few found their way to the galley stove, cast to symbolic hell fire which the devout felt was their just due.

Most came to be so accustomed to the disruptions of the night that they slept through unmindful of wailing babies and those who groped their way to the privy. Some saved trips by misappropriating the slop buckets. This was particularly was this true in the cases of mothers with small children. If others heard, this too they ignored.

Marit was thankful that in the lack of privacy, Rolf kept to his own side of the pallet. But she was made blushingly aware that not all were so self-disciplined. Once when there was nearby heavy breathing and telltale rhythmic rustling, she pulled the corner of the pallet over her head to muffle the sounds, groveling as if the humiliation were her own.

❦

It was in the third week that they found the old woman dead in the morning. Traumatized by having been uprooted from her lifelong home, the voyage had been beyond her comprehension and day after day she sat and followed the movements of those about her with vacant eyes, only mechanically doing her son's bidding. But once she had cackled toothlessly when her daughter-in-law had tried to shame her by pointing a finger at her wet skirt and scolding when she did not make it to the privy on time.

"It's funny we've come this far without dropping some baggage," Rolf told Eyvin. "I've been on runs where the below-deckers dropped off like lemmings on march. We'll be lucky if we get by with losing only the old and useless — they're usually the first to go. Them and the little ones."

The callous remark caused Marit to glance apprehensively over to where Anna sat frozen by the side of her fretting baby's cradle. She had not heard. Just yesterday she had said, "I worry that I don't have enough milk. He never seems to be satisfied."

The interpreter informed someone above of the death, then came back to report that the body would not be removed until nightfall. "They don't want to upset the cabin passengers," he explained.

The son covered his mother's body with a blanket and throughout the day they tried to ignore it. But awareness threw a pall over the compartment.

Late that night, two crewmen came down the ladder with a lantern and a board slab. They shrouded the body with an old piece of canvas; then, informing that only the next of kin would attend the commitment, a small procession disappeared up the ladder.

Below they lay in silence, as if listening for something; a hymn perhaps, maybe even with a splash. But they heard nothing. Soon the son, his silently weeping wife and the two sniveling children returned, lighted to their quarters by a lantern held over the hatchway. The light disappeared and silence again prevailed for a time.

Then, into the darkness and to no one in particular, the son began to talk. "Not even a hymn.... It was all over so soon. The captain read something from a book — a prayer book, perhaps — a verse or two from the Bible. I think it was the Bible. One of the sailors held a lantern for him. Then they set the lantern down, lifted one end. She slid away, disappeared."

A little later, he asked into the darkness: "Do you think it makes a difference? I mean, not being buried on consecrated ground. Will she be resurrected with the rest?"

"That I can't say," said another voice. "But I've always understood that being laid away in consecrated ground has some bearing. At least, so it was in the homeland. Here.... well, I can't say. Maybe the rules don't apply at sea."

Remembering Thorn with a pang, Marit interjected vehemently, "Of course it's different at sea! Many good men have gone down. God would not be *so* unjust!"

With such firm conviction were the words spoken that further conjecture seemed pointless.

Most had imposed their own self-rationing, mindful that the length of the voyage would be determined by the wind. But by the end of the second week, the food began to taste stale. Two more weeks, and the butter had gone rancid with heat. That heat, coupled with humidity — the level of which was kept constantly high by the overhead drying of poorly washed diapers — had worked a ravage of blue mold on the dried foods. To add further to the shortage, the cereal foods were found to be infested with weevils. There were still the salted foods, but a saline diet increased thirst and the limited rations of the now-flat water did little to slake it, even though they added vinegar to counteract the flatness.

This deterioration of the food supply added to the burden of the women. It became a daily task to sort through their stores for something to eat that was not tainted. The bad they set aside, but the day came when they had no alternative but to eat the rejected. They could only hope that hunger would compensate for the off-flavors and that in the meager light it wouldn't be noticed that there were foreign particles in their bowls of grout.

There were those who were marking off time on their calendar sticks, and it was calculated that it was in the fifth week when dysentery struck. Aggravated by close quarters, it spread rapidly. Soon nearly half were down.

It had been the way to take up the bedding in the daytime to make more room, but now those who were still on their feet had to tread their way among pallets, not only to accomplish their now double share of daily chores, but to attend to those who were sick.

The Catholic woman was one of those who was down. She would allow no one but her husband to minister to her, and he was hard-put to see to their children's needs as well as hers. Most time-consuming was the feeding of the baby. Some of the women took turns at the task of chewing the food, spitting it out and spoon-feeding it, as was the mother's fashion. But even seeing this, the woman did not warm to the other women. Shortly, the baby too contracted the illness.

When Marit knew the baby was dead, she drew the father over to where the child lay. Seeing realization in his eyes, she left it for him to tell the mother in his own way.

She heard her cry out once, but then nothing more until the father returned from his lone pilgrimage to the rail with the body. Then, in the weakness of her illness, the mother's whimpers, like an animal in pain, filled the place.

At first they tolerated it in compassion, but when it went on and on it began to wear on them. "Can't he make her shut up!" someone grumbled.

Marit found her way over to where the woman lay. She tired to comfort her, but was pushed away.

The beads. She seemed to take great stock in the beads. Where were they? She felt through the surrounding debris with no success. Then, on a hunch, she reached under the pillow and pulled them out. She tried to put them into the woman's hands, but she would not grasp them. Her own hand she wiped on an apron after touching them.

Then Marit became aware that the husband was beside her. He took the beads from her hands, placed his wife's hands on them and led her fingers along them saying words in their own tongue. After a time, the wife's voice blended brokenly with his.

Marit returned to her own pallet. The rhythmic chanting seemed less offensive than the whimpering; some were lulled to sleep by it. After a while, Marit too went to sleep. But she was awakened once in the night by an outcry that was suddenly muffled, as if a hand had been clapped over her mouth. Then, again, the chanting.

Anna had not contracted the disease, but the salty diet and lack of sufficient fluid intake had reduced her breast flow to almost nothing. They had no success with spoon feeding because the baby was too young. He fought against it and when they did manage to force something into his mouth, he spit it out. His cries were becoming weaker and weaker.

Thinking of the baby who had died, Marit vowed; This will not happen to one of *ours!*

One morning she located a Norwegian who knew a little German and, with him, she went to the interpreter. "You'll have to go above and ask for milk for Anna's baby or it too will die," she conveyed to him.

Her urgency forbade his refusing and he mounted the ladder. But soon he returned, saying, "They said they have only enough milk for the needs of the cabin passengers."

"We'll see about that!" she said, brushing past him and his guttural *"Nein, nein! Verboten!"*

She gained the deck, accosted the first seaman she saw. "I want fresh milk for a sick baby!"

He indicated he did not understand her and pointed back toward the hatchway, at the same time advancing on her. When he reached her, he attempted to push her back, but she broke away from him.

The captain, I will see the captain himself, she determined. But where were his quarters?

Now a whole pack of seamen converged on her and tried to rush her. Two got hold of her arms. She wrenched loose and struck at them.

Drawn by the disturbance, a group of passengers who had been sunning on the deck gathered and stood gaping as if at a mad woman. She appealed to them, at the same time fending off the seamen.

Suddenly a distinguished-looking man broke away from the group and started elbowing his way to the hemmed-in Marit. The sailors gave way and soon he was fact-to-face with her. Marit pleaded her cause to him, and the man turned to the sailors for interpretation. Then Marit was enraged further, for it became apparent that at least one of them had only pretended not to understand her.

"She wants milk," he explained in English to the man.

"Tell him it's for a baby — a sick baby."

The sailor passed only the information.

"Give my daily measure to the sick child," the man said.

"But it's against the rules!"

"It's my measure. If I want to give it away, I will!"

Now one of the sailors left to consult a higher authority. He returned with the captain.

The captain consulted with the man, who was adamant. The captain issued some orders to the seaman and turned curtly on his heel.

Marit was informed that she would get the milk, but that "the captain wants it made clear that this is highly irregular, that it is only at the insistence of this gentleman that you are so favored, that it is only of his intervention that you were not tossed bodily down the hatchway to the hold where you belong; that there will be no more exceptions, that all you are entitled to is what the gentleman has proffered — has chosen to deny himself — and that another breach will not be tolerated."

Marit had stopped listening. She turned to the man, looked him levelly in the eye and said, "Surely, God will reward you!"

The sailor did not interpret but she knew the man understood. He shook her hand, saying "Godspeed!" He stood watch as the now calm Marit made her way decorously to the hatchway and descended.

The group of seamen broke up, and as they walked away one remarked to a companion, "These Americans and their democratic notions! No class, no class at all!"

The first measure of milk was delivered to the hatchway within the hour. Marit warmed it in a little pan, adding water to cut the richness and a little sugar to tempt the baby Peder's appetite. She carried the pan to where the infant lay. Now, how to get it into him?

A pessimistic Anna watched her prepare a pap from a torn piece of clean white cloth. Having twisted and tied the material, she dipped it into the milk, forced the little jaws open and inserted it. He drew on it hungrily. She held the pan close to his face and managed to transfer a noticeable amount before he tired in his weakness.

Now Anna, hope roused, took over the task. When he had slept, she reheated the milk, aped Marit's procedure. Soon he was taking the milk greedily and she was kept busy meeting his demands, which he made known lustily with increasing strength as days went by.

✧❦✧

It was fortunate that the voyage was drawing to a close. In the next several days three more succumbed and made their eerie shrouded departure through the hatchway by darkness. It was with almost unbearable longing that those who remained anticipated the day when they could again emerge into sunlight and fresh air, leaving behind this twilight limbo that now reeked of death.

The day did come: An exultant wave swept the compartment, lifting even the sick on its crest when a passing seaman shouted down the hatchway, "Land ho!"

There was again the clanking of the chain, the dropping of anchor. But now, they were informed, they must wait until the doctor from the island near which they were anchored made his inspection.

The waiting seemed interminable but finally the doctor appeared with bag in hand. He began making the rounds, certifying those who passed inspection. But they must all wait until he had completed the rounds, they were told. For only those certified well could enter Quebec, the port of debarkation. The sick must be removed, taken to the island and quarantined.

The doctor left, to be followed shortly by litter bearers. The sick were lifted on them, carried up and away, to the accompaniment of frenzied consultations among broken-up families.

It was yet another day before they left the boat. They heard those above leaving.... More waiting! When, ultimately, their turn did come to leave, there was a rush to the ladder. It was not a time for patience; not a few were rudely shoved back in the scramble.

This stepping into the light so bright made them rub their eyes from the blinding whiteness of it. It was as if waking from a nightmare. The deck gained, they at first stood looking dazedly around, then, landward.... America!

Rowboats swarmed about the vessel and from them hawkers temptingly help up their wares: fresh bread, buns, cakes, milk.... "Ignore them," Rolf advised. "You'll pay double for everything they offer." But many could not resist, dug into their pockets for coins and satiated themselves.

✦

Throughout the weeks in the compartment, Marit had envisioned a green shore, an Eden toward which they were steadily drawing. It was with a stab of disappointment that she viewed a landscape seared brown by the first frosts, and bare tree limbs. It was as if they had cast the singe of death before them. That greenness, which is life, had shrivelled at their approach.

And the city that spread itself before her hungry eyes did nothing to lift her spirits. It had a strange familiarity — as if she had seen it before. She puzzled over this. Then it came to her: in her childhood history book there had been a picture of a feudal town with serfs' huts squatting at the base of a castle. That was it, the town crouched at the foot of a great citadel. There was something of the Old World about it, not at all the sort of thing she had expected to see in America!

On shore, they paced with unsteady legs while they waited for their belongings to be unloaded, a long wait among a milling throng. Meantime, they appeased their hunger with buns and coffee that Eyvin purchased from a cafe on the waterfront.

The sun went down, taking warmth with it, and the air began to crisp. Some began making preparations to camp out for the night. But this was out of the question for Anna and the baby, so having secured their baggage for the night, they made their way to a lodging place.

As they walked, natives, intent on their own affairs, passed by. Their ears caught snatches of conversation in a still different tongue. Rolf knowledgeably informed them that the people in this city spoke French, not English.

"A lot it matters," Anna observed wryly. "They're both Finnish to me."

They chuckled at this quip at the expense of their sister country and her Ural-rooted language — an enigma to other Scandinavians.

The lodging place was an uncomfortable barracks-like building. Even so, it was with reluctance that they dragged themselves from bunk at sun-up next morning. But Quebec was but a pause in the trek of the immigrants, so again they boarded a boat, this time a river boat that drew much water under its load of human cargo together with the ever-present trunks and crates. They bore the sardine-packed jaunt in good form, however, for it was to be of short duration; at Montreal they would switch to train or steamer.

At Montreal, it was Rolf's decision to take a steamer and Eyvin deferred to his judgment. So again they found themselves on water, but steamers were a new experience to all but Rolf and time passed swiftly in their curiosity at this modern marvel that, instead of masts with ballooning sails, bore iron rods crowned by rising and falling pistons on its superstructure. Adding further to the spirit of adventure were the ingenious locks they ran on the voyage and, then later, open water — an inland sea so large that they could not see across, making it seem they had lost their way and were back on the Atlantic.

They steamed into Buffalo in the dusk of an evening, and in the twilight the busy port, lined with wooden warehouses, was so reminiscent of the homeland that Marit suffered a pang of nostalgia as they moved in for docking.

Again a boat was to be the conveyance for the next leg of their journey, but the large steamboat they boarded next morning was, in their eyes, a floating palace. Three-decked, spic and span with paint, and ornate with gilded decoration, the steamboat made them acutely aware of their own shabbiness when they crossed the gangplank. Of *immigrant* ilk, they were relegated to the lowest level and jammed together, but the appointments of even the lowest deck were such that they felt they had no cause for complaint.

It was not to be their last boat ride. At each city there was now the option of taking to the rails, but rails proliferated going east, diminished going west, and ran out entirely in the upper reaches of Wisconsin. By contrast, water routes to the west were well established, with regularly scheduled boats. Thus, in opting to travel by water, they would board three more vessels in traversing the Great Lakes.

❧

In was when they reached Chicago that Marit first discerned the raw edges of the new land — in the rutted dirt streets, the seemingly endless sprawl of wood frame buildings and on the outskirts, where many houses had a stable at the rear and animals rooting in yards. It was as if the city were swallowing up countryside in indigestible hunks. She also noted the manner of the people themselves — a quickened pace, a staccato way of conversing. "They sound like they think talking is a waste of time," Marit commented to Anna.

Her own spirit responded to the optimistic mood of the city, but the buoyancy was soon weighted. Within a few short hours, they stood beside a train with many boxcars. Some were labeled in big print: IMMIGRANT CAR.

After their possessions had been transferred to one of these and dumped in grand confusion in the middle of the floor with those of many others, they boarded. Inside they found backless wooded benches stacked along the sides. These they untangled and aligned against the walls. They sat down, attempted to compose themselves, for the overnight trip to Rock Island on the Mississippi.

The train huffed its way out of the city, then picked up speed. In upright positions and huddled together for warmth against the cold that crept into the unheated car, they rocked their way through the night....

Marit was dozing, swaying.... That cough... the rapid, labored breathing... her weariness, the jumped pile of effects... their help-lessness.... It was *then,* not now: *Johanes was having just another one of his croupy spells. But the next day they put him in a box and they held her up so she could see him and she wondered why he didn't open his eyes and look at her... Then they took the box with Johanes in it and put it in the ground and her mother cried and there had been no one to play with until Thorn moved next door. There had been Thorn....*

Some time before morning the car became quiet.

When they alighted to a world that was spectral-frosted, the father carried the dead child in his arms — a boy of five or six, hampered by the mother who persisted in tucking a tattered blanket about the child.

It would be three hours before they must board the vessel that would take them up the Mississippi. The father retrieved a spade from the heap of baggage and dug a shallow grave in the frozen ground of the railroad right-of-way while the mother held the body, refusing to relinquish it to men who offered their help.

A few gathered round, Marit and Anna among them, "to pay our respects." They sang from memory two verses of a hymn. Someone pulled a dog-eared Testament from his pocket and read a Scripture passage. The father rolled a boulder over the spot as a marker.

And still they went on: The man and his wife together with their two remaining children boarded the riverboat with the rest.

Now the passing panorama of shoreline held no interest for Marit; this last death had somehow depressed her more than any of the others. It seemed superfluous, like the last soldier to fall in battle before an armistice is called. If only he could have held out a little longer....

Will it never end, she wondered. Will there always be another river, another boat or, perhaps, a train?

Now there was a coming together of waters, a junction — Read's Landing. For those who would continue up the Mississippi, the twin cities of St. Paul and Minneapolis waited in awkward adolescence, stretching toward the grace and culture that are earmarks of mature cities. Non-identical from birth, sedate St. Paul looked with some disapproval on her brash sister across the river, and the seeds for a perpetual rivalry had already been sown.

The Twin Cities were not to be viewed by the Monsruds and the Rolstads; they would follow the Chippewa into Wisconsin. But Marit took the time at this crossroads of destinies to seek out the bereaved parents, for she had learned that they were bound for Minneapolis.

"Though we may never meet again, my prayers go with you. May God comfort you."

The mother looked back down the river. "We must go back. He must have a proper burial."

Her husband grasped her firmly by the elbow and steered her away.

❧

"So *this* is Wisconsin!" Anna said.

Marit's gaze followed Anna's dubious appraisal of the wilderness that hugged the shores; a monotony broken only by settlers' rough buildings and occasional villages which in their drabness matched the landscape. "It isn't pretty," she commented.

Rolf pointedly ignored their remarks and addressed Eyvin. "We're lucky we made it before the river iced. It's a long, rough ride by stage."

"How much farther is it?" Anna asked.

Again Rolf turned to Eywin. This way Rolf had of ignoring women was by now familiar to Marit. "Millwood is up a branch of the river. We haven't far to go."

Before long this was verified by a smoke haze that hung low in the sky over the trees. Upon rounding a bend, the town came into view — a parade of nondescript buildings strung along the water's edge. But high on the bluffs above the river, sophisticated white frame houses faced down their primitive surroundings in storied haughtiness.

She was to be favored with a closer look at one of these, for they were not to leave for the homestead until the next morning and when Eyvin's cousin came with a wagon to pick up Eyvin and Anna at the landing, the Monsruds were extended an invitation to spend the night at the Rolstad home.

After the men had loaded the wagon, they climbed aboard, the men perched behind, the women on the seat with the teamster. They passed through the town proper, left behind the shacks of log, tar and unpainted frame and followed a street that curved around the bluff to the top. On the height they turned in between the stone gateposts of an ample dwelling set back among trees in a large yard.

A woman rushed from the house to greet them warmly, but without embrace. Having welcomed many such, Inga Rolstad was wise to the possibility of more house guests than met the eye! "I will have baths ready shortly," she said candidly.

They drove around to the back and the baggage was unloaded into a shed. They were welcomed through a back door of the house into a room that was apparently the laundry. A large wood range crackled with fire and on its top, copper boilers filled with water were heating, droplets from their sides skittering across the hot surface of the stove top and burning themselves out like comets.

To this sizzling accompaniment they visited with Inga and were served coffee and pastries by a maid. When the water began to steam, the maid carried it by the bucketful to a large woodstove tub that stood in a corner behind a screen and added cold water to temper it.

"Who goes first — or shall we draw straws?" Anna jested.

"You go ahead," Marit told her.

Anna handed the baby to Marit, went behind the screen and threw her soiled clothing over it as she undressed. Inga promptly gathered up the clothing and popped it into one of the boilers on the stove. She replaced it with fresh clothing she brought out from somewhere back in the house.

From behind the screen, exclamations of delight came from Anna. "Can you imagine having enough water to sink yourself in from head to toe?" she luxuriated, half to herself.

When Marit's turn came, she told Inga, "Just lay my clothes aside. We'll be leaving in the morning."

Inga was a little embarrassed. "I don't know if I have any clothes to fit you anyway," she said, measuring Marit with her eyes.

"Oh, anything will do until tomorrow," Marit assured her.

The "anything" turned out to be an outrageous combination, but she donned the articles, revelling in their freshness.

As Marit bathed, Anna spent the time bathing the baby in a basin. Then they were welcomed to the house proper, leaving the laundry to the men.

Marit was surprised at the luxury of the home. There was a great deal of talk at the supper table and she gathered that the comfortable circumstances stemmed from lumber interests. In a moment alone with Anna before retiring, she whispered, "The future looks bright for you! Eyvin has good connections."

Then came the unbelievable softness of the bed, the sweetness in her nostrils of clean linens. Morning broke all too soon.

On this new day, Rolf was all business. He went to the bank, drew out some money and made arrangements for their transportation to the homestead.

She had been unaware that he had money put away. But then, he never had discussed his circumstances with her. The thought suddenly struck her that she did not know this man who was her husband.

He never ventured anything. In the first days of their marriage she had attempted to converse with him but had met with little success. When she asked him a direct question, he would sometimes answer curtly in as few words as possible but more often his only response was a grunt. She had given up trying, and he seemed to prefer it that way. But up until now, they had always been around other people, at least during the daylight hours.

In the alienation of the day, the intimacy of the night took on an aura of unreality. But she had inferred from unspoken but subtle nuances that the marriage act was just another one of those things endured by women, one of the many ordained duties of wifehood. As such, it seemed appropriate that she yield herself without complaint, even in the consummation, which had occurred aboard the vessel that carried them to Bergen. Afterward, she had lain awake remembering.... *When Thorn held me close.... Would it have been that way with him? Am I different from other women — that I wanted Thorn?* But she purged the thought from her mind. It hadn't been hard to do, taken up as her thoughts and energy soon became with the crossing.

Inevitably, the time came to take her farewell of Anna. They only stood looking deeply into each other's eyes, until the last moment. Then Anna came close, pledged in her ear: "If there is ever anything I can do for you, anything to repay you...."

"It was nothing. Nothing at all!" Marit lightly dismissed.

CHAPTER V

C onstructed with an awareness to the rigors of its function, the sturdiness of the tote wagon added to the seeming clumsiness of its movements and, loaded to capacity as it was now, it proceeded with a plodding motion as the cradles and knolls in the trail caught first one wheel and then another. And no soft earth cushioned the jolts, for the ground was hard from the freeze of the night.

Drawn by a two-span team of horses, the load was made up of a miscellaneous assortment of staple foods and hardware and, perched on top of it all, their own travel-worn possessions rode, tied down with ropes to keep them from being jostled off. Marit rode up front between the teamster and Rolf and from their crossfire conversation she gathered that the wagon was bound for a trading post with supplies.

In the first miles, the land was well-settled and mostly cleared of forest, the settlers clustering about established centers like broods of chicks around a mother hen, drawing some measure of security from proximity. A little further on there were homestead clearings and intermittent forest. Finally, only a few venturesome stragglers broke the continuity of the forest and, as the settled area was put behind them, the trail reflected disuse, became primitive.

Their progress was delayed for a time by a windfall. It seemed that this was a foreseen possibility; the teamster hopped nimbly down, took an ax from a holder on the side of the wagon and fell to hacking away. Rolf lent a hand. As the teamster limbed, he carried the debris to the side of the trail and deposited it in a neat pile. At last only the bare trunk of the fallen tree remained; using a cant hook, rock and crowbar, they managed to roll it far enough to the side so they could pass. "Now that's the advantage of two," the teamster commented. "If I'd been alone, I'd had to unhitch the horses to get that one."

Occasionally, the wagon rumbled across corduroy, great logs lad side by side like so many matchsticks to provide firmness for passage in swamps and treacherous bogs. A crude bridge spanned one stream, but twice Marit held her breath when the wagon rolled down an incline and the horses pawed to ford the stream on the precarious footing of the rock-strewn bottom.

They had left Millwood at mid-forenoon, but it wasn't until they had forded the second stream in mid-afternoon that the teamster halted the horses on the far side and announced: "Time to eat."

In a protected spot strewn with the ashes of former fires, he kindled a small bonfire. Taking a smoke-blackened pot from the wagon and filling it with water from the stream, he drew from his pocket a small packet, dumped the contents into the pot and set it on fire. He then unhitched the horses, watered them at the stream and fed them hay from the wagon.

In the meantime, Marit unpacked the basket that had been pressed on her by Inga Rolstad. When the teamster returned, he eyed the spread hungrily. By contrast, the flattened brown bag he drew from his pocket looked meager. "You're welcome," Marit invited.

"So are you," he said, motioning toward the steaming pot on the fire.

He ate with animal gusto, washing down the food with great gulps of hot coffee. Again and again Marit dipped her own cup into the hot brew; in spite of the bits of twig and leaf fragments that floated on top, she found it more to her liking than the milk that Inga had thoughtfully provided.

The meal was eaten in silence, so intent were they on sating their hunger. Marit was amazed at her own appetite; when she picked the basket up again, she found it much lighter.

The teamster doused the fire with water. "Can't be too careful," he explained. "If a fire ever got started in these trees, it wouldn't stop going 'til it got to Superior!"

He exaggerates, she thought, looking up at the trees, then realized the wisdom of caution as the towering spires seemed to close in and wash over her like a sudden sea swell.

There had been a run of conversation between the two men throughout most of the day, but now they fell silent, the teamster concentrating on forcing the horses forward. They seemed to be straining; they must be getting tired, she thought. But when they rounded a turn, she found they had been climbing. Through a gap in the trees, she had a glimpse of the horizon to her right, but it faded away in a blue haze. They were on the summit of a ridge.

Now the trail led downward, and whereas before the horses had been whipped forward, the teamster now stood to his feet and pulled on the reins with all his strength to hold them back from the bits, their shoes made half-moons in the partially thawed earth in their stiff-legged resistance to gravity.

Midday had been comparatively warm but now, on the north side of the ridge, the air developed a chill. She felt herself becoming cramped from the cold and the sitting.

As idea occurred to her. "Could I run alongside for a while?"

As usual, Rolf ignored her. She turned to the teamster.

"There isn't room to run alongside. The branches would whip you in the face," he said. Then, after a pause. "You could run along behind if you take care not to drop back. We haven't time to dawdle."

He halted the horses and she climbed down. "When you get out of breath, hitch on behind and ride," the teamster advised her.

She passed some miles alternately running and hanging on, and when the wagon was stopped again to rest the horses, she was glad again to take her place on the seat.

She had noticed an occasional trail branching off into the woods, and several times during the afternoon she had thought she smelled smoke in the air, yet there had been no visible settlers' cabins for a long stretch.

The men seemed to be in no mood to be bothered with questions, but she ventured to ask, "Do these trails lead to clearings?"

"Tote branches."

She made nothing of the reply. "I thought I smelled smoke."

"Indian camps."

Rolf said it in his usual sparse way; but, in her mind, the two words burst into kaleidoscopic images: Feathers, tomahawks, war paint — scalps! She eyed the tangle of pine and bare limbs, tingling at the thought that at the very moment one of the savages might be peering at her from concealment.

But it was not until twilight that she was treated to her first sight of the native American. They approached a clearing, and lining both sides of the trail ahead were mound dwellings. In her lethargy, it took some moments for their significance to penetrate her mind. But suddenly she knew and sat bolt upright, wide-eyed.

There were numerous campfires with figures moving about them, and when their wagon emerged from the shadows of the woods a shout went up and some of the figures converged on the trail.

Stare for stare. The faces of the Indians, stolid, gave no clue to their thoughts. But after her first swift deduction — that they were friendly — a look of bewilderment came over Marit's face. Their clothing was mostly of cloth, indicating that they had largely adopted the white man's mode of dress; one of the women even sported a print dress, albeit its former bright colors were dulled with grime. Here and there, tattered garments revealed sinewy limbs. It struck her that they looked just as white people would look under the circumstances: dirty, cold and even hungry.

The teamster suddenly reached over and snapped his whip at them. The motley group stumbled over each other as they scrambled to get beyond its reach. Rolf and the teamster laughed uproariously at this spectacle of awkwardness, but Marit felt a hot flush come to her face, not entirely in anger at the callousness of Rolf and the teamster. She was embarrassed for the Indians. Why did they give way so readily? The cowering retreat. Something didn't jibe.... *These* were not the fierce warriors of her childhood history. As the wagon drew away from the encampment, she muttered under her breath: "You could've at least let out a war whoop or two!"

A little beyond the encampment they stopped again, at a stream. She wondered if they would camp for the night, but it soon became apparent that this was to be but a pause to water the horses. They would not even take time to eat supper.

She had the foresight to take this opportunity to rummage through their baggage for a quilt. Her fingers were numb, she had trouble undoing the bindings and almost gave up. Later, she was thankful she had made the effort for as the night darkened, the cold intensified. Trusting in the quilt to keep her warm, she snuggled down, shut her eyes and fitfully slept, constantly bounced by the motion of the wagon.

Once she was startled wide awake by a piercing wail close to the side of the trail. "Devil!" the teamster muttered. She turned to him in the darkness, questioned him with a look, but he did not explain.

Time passed in a numb stupor and she was not aware that they had entered the settlement until the wagon stopped. She opened her eyes; dimly outlined in the darkness was a deeper rectangular darkness, a symmetry alien to forest. Her dulled mind defined it as a building.

The men let themselves to the ground in slow, stiff stages; she roused herself and did the same. Having gained the ground, she stood there dazedly trying to orient herself. She became aware of other figures — a lantern, someone unhitching the horses. A window sprang to a golden glow and she made her way toward the light. She found the door, felt for the latch — just as it was pulled open from within so she stumbled across the threshold. The teamster had preceded her; it was he who had opened the door.

Now fully awake, she looked about the room. It was small and appeared to be an office; there was a huge roll-top desk with swivel chair, a cot and a pot-bellied stove. From where she stood she felt the radiating warmth of the stove and did not wait for invitation; she went to stand by it and for a time was aware of nothing but the caress of heat on her chilled flesh.

"Pull up the chair," the teamster said, pointing to the swivel chair by the desk. As she turned to do so she suddenly missed Rolf. "Where's my husband?"

She did not wait for his reply but started for the door. "Perhaps he's waiting — I'd best go."

"Oh, sit down and relax," he said crossly. "Rolf has business to attend to."

"This time of night?"

Ignoring her question, he threw himself down on the couch, pulled a fur throw over himself and fell asleep almost at once in an explosion of hearty snores that attested to his relish of the long-awaited rest.

She pulled the chair to the stove and sat down. The combination of heat and exhaustion soon made her drowsy, unmindful of the peculiarity of her situation: nodding in a chair in the middle of the night in a strange place with a man who was not her husband snoring nearby — and Rolf off on "business."

❦

Rolf watched Marit enter the office and thought some of following her, informing her of the delay. But what he had to do seemed much more important to him than her possible perplexity so he wasted no time, setting off at once.

Impatient with the stiffness of his joints and muscles from the long ride, after he had turned a corner of the building, he jumped up and down briskly. Limberness restored, he set off at a fast pace.

He passed by the few buildings of the trading post, continued on for about a quarter mile out into the country, then turned in and knocked at the door of a cabin. After several insistent barrages of raps, he heard stirring and the sound of footsteps inside. A man opened the door a crack, peered into his face in an effort to identify him.

"It's me, Rolf Monsrud. I've come for my oxen and wagon. And the money."

The man hesitated a moment. Then, with a hospitality that seemed a little too much for the late hour, he opened the door wide. "Come in. Come in out of the cold!"

He lit a lamp, turned to face Rolf.

"Let's get on with it. I haven't all night."

The man cleared his throat. "I don't have the money."

"What do you mean you don't have the money? You've had all summer."

"There was an accident. I.... my back—"

"A deal is a deal! You can't expect to use my oxen and wagon all summer for nothing!"

"I intend to—"

"I'll have my money or—" Rolf paused, calculating, "or like value! I'll have a look around the barn."

With that he spun on his heel and walked out.

The man hastily lit a lantern, pulled on his clothes and followed him. When he reached the barn, Rolf was already leading the oxen to the wagon. The man held the lantern for him while he hitched them.

"I fully intend to pay you when I get back on my feet."

Rolf did not reply. He took the lantern from the man's hand, went back into the barn.

The place where the oxen had stood left a big gap. Now there remained only a cow, a heifer and a very young calf. Rolf scrutinized them.

From the door, the man pleaded, "I'd rather give you the money."

"You don't have the money," Rolf said in a tone of finality. He walked over to the cow, opened her mouth and examined her teeth. Then, by passing the calf, he moved to the heifer.

"She will do," he said, untying her. "I'll need hay, too."

"That comes to much more than our agreed price and you know it! You know how scarce cattle are in this country, and then *hay*, too."

Rolf went on as if he had not heard. He led the heifer out and tied her behind the wagon. Then he drove to the haystack and began to fork lay liberally.

"If I was in better shape, you'd never get away with this! You look out! Someday I'll come looking for you!" At that, he loudly turned and went back to the cabin. Rolf heard the door slam loudly.

Inside, the man spoke as much to himself as his agitated wife when he said, "Even Ole Bull himself couldn't strike a good note on that one. It's in the wood."

When Rolf passed on his way out, the cabin was dark again.

⚜

Marit was awakened by Rolf's hand on her shoulders. "I'm ready to leave," he said, shaking her roughly.

She followed him out; noted that it was still dark. Was there no end to this night? The wagon was parked next to the big tote wagon, and Rolf began tossing their things into the hay or the smaller wagon. She climbed in and settled them. Lastly, she retrieved the quilt from the front seat of the tote wagon where she left it. The smaller wagon was already in motion then she jumped on.

She wrapped the quilt around her and burrowed into the hay.

But the wagon rolled only a short distance before it came to a stop. Rolf called her to come and hold the oxen, then went to a darkened building and pounded on the door. A lamp was lighted and from the stacked shelves she saw through the wide window, she knew this was a store. Rolf was evidently buying groceries.

When he came out he was carrying a big bag of flour and a much smaller bag. Considering they were starting from scratch, the total looked inadequate.

"Are you sure you have everything?"

"What we don't have, we do without."

He used the word "we" as if it included a multitude, but as they moved away from the settlement, they were in solitude. Mimicking the inflection in her voice in her mind, she thought. *We* seem to be all alone.

She scanned the wilderness on both sides, lastly looking back. It was then she spotted the heifer plodding patiently at the end of a rope in the darkness behind.

CHAPTER VI

In the homeland, life had never been easy for the common folk, generation following generation in an unwritten caste system, with people even taking family names form the titles of the farms they tilled as cotters and, in the cases of seafaring families such as her own, sons following fathers to sea, but with little hope of a man ever owning a boat of his own. Consequently, their lots were contingent on the humor of their particular landlord or master.

But Norway had been a civilized nation for a thousand years, and certain niceties — refinements — were taken for granted. She had no preparation for the elemental existence she must now face.

As they approached it in the cold, gray light of that morning, the cabin looked cozy and inviting. But when she stepped in, it was to a room still in darkness, the light from the one small window absorbed by the dirt floor and unpainted log walls with taupe chinking of mud. When her eyes had adjusted enough to make distinctions, it was only to take in at a glance the rudimentary furnishings. She tried to hide her disappointment, but in spite of herself, a note of criticism crept into her voice when she said, "Only one window?"

"Windows let in cold."

He could have explained to her that the cabin was only temporary, that someday he intended to build a fine house, a house that would make her the envy of other women. He could also have pointed out to her that their own circumstances were enviable, that most were coming into the wilderness with no advance preparation, many with only the tools they carried on their backs, and their first shelter was a tent, wagon-box or even as crude as a windfall with pine boughs thrown over. And in his aversion to accounting to a woman, he did not even brag, as was his wont, that only he, of all the settlers in a wide radius, possessed the status symbol of the day: a yoke of oxen of his own. And at the moment, as he retrieved his gun from behind a rafter where he had secreted it for the summer, he could have assured her that they would not have to do without meat, that he was about to fill that need. But he shouldered the gun, went out the door without a word.

Well, such as it is, it's my house to keep, she chided herself after he had gone out, and immediately set about building a fire in the makeshift stove. It sprang almost instantly into a cheery flame, the wood having dried by the stove all summer. Then, to the accompaniment of its snapping, she methodically arranged the meager supplies on the wall cupboard, mentally listing all the things she would have to do without: sugar, eggs, milk, butter, potatoes, coffee....

Coffee.... How coffee-thirsty she was right now! The night's lack of sleep had enhanced her need of its stimulation and the prospect of doing without it day after day seemed unbearable.

But soon a more practical need took her mind off coffee. She was in the process of sorting out the things they had brought with them from Norway and the soil of weeks clung to everything she unpacked. How would she ever get them clean again without soap?

She knew the process; she had helped her mother make soap many times. She could save ashes, leach lye from them... but fat was the essential ingredient. How could she make soap without fat? She sat down on one of the uncomfortable benches, eyed the heap in disgust.

Such filth should be burned, she was thinking when Rolf walked in. He set the gun by the door. "I need help," he said, going out again. She threw on her wrap, followed him out the door.

He picked up a rope and headed into the woods. She dogged his steps. They led on and on, deep into the forest. Her eyes on the ground to keep from tripping on something, she almost bumped into him when he stopped. On the ground at his feet was a deer — a big buck. It took all their combined strength to drag it through the undergrowth back to the cabin.

She spent the rest of the day dressing out the animal, using her own uneducated judgment, for Rolf had again disappeared into the woods, this time with an ax and bucket.

Upon exploring the unfamiliar carcass, she came upon leaves of tallow. These she carved carefully away — though doubtful of the quality of soap wild game would yield. In contemplation she thought: *Mother would be disgraced!* Her soap was a thing her mother had always taken pride in.

She had finished the butchering and was in the process of preparing supper in dwindling light when Rolf returned. The bucket was heaped with honey in the comb.

That first night they went to bed at dusk. *Tomorrow, I will dip candles from the beeswax* was her last thought of that first day.

❧

Days flashed by in silhouettes of light and darkness, with light being extended into darkness from the play of the leaping flames of burning trees. Their presence was a hindrance to the tilling of the soil and snow reduced the fire hazard. The torch made short shrift of them.

Rolf's ambition knew no bounds and he would often work outdoors in the firelight until late into the night. She spent these long winter evenings knitting by the window-light of these same flames, saving on candles. In the long, lonely hours, she often engaged the heifer in a one-way conversation.

She had been puzzled when Rolf started partitioning off a corner of the already crowded cabin. It was when he began framing the manger that she realized the purpose. It was not to her liking at first, but her relationship with Rolf was so shrouded in silence, the heifer had become company for her and they had established a rapport of a sort. The heifer often responded to her voice with lowing. And she had come to include cleaning the heifer's quarters as part of her daily household routine, attending to its creature comforts as she would one of the family.

In addition to her household chores, during the days she helped Rolf clear land and in her busyness she would have lost track of time had she not counted it off on the calendar stick she had brought from home. It was her intention to observe Christmas.

She thought of how in the homeland preparations would have been in progress for weeks now, with the twelve days of Christmas a perpetual feast and the time-consuming task of assembling the spread completed by the twenty-third of December when they observed "Little Christmas Eve."

The meats alone were a production. The spiced meat-roll used flank as a starter. In it were placed more meat and seasonings, and it was then rolled up and sewn with strong thread, boiled until done, then pressed until cold. The head cheese called for a boiled hog's head from which the meat was cut off, spices added, then all put in a sack and pressed, and lastly, put to soak in salt brine. The *lutefisk* began with dried codfish which was cured by soaking in lye, then the lye leached out by soaking in many changes of water and, finally, before serving, heated just to boiling, with the resultant huge white flakes of fish served swimming in melted butter.

Tedious in the making were the huge potato flat cakes called *lefse.* Butter, cream and flour added to mashed potatoes to make a dough, they were rolled out paper thin, wound round a wooden stick and carefully unrolled again on the surface of the stove top and baked on both sides.

In addition to raised breads laced with fruits — called *Yulekake* — there must be a liberal supply of the traditional cookies — *Sandbakkelse,* rich, granular cookies baked individually in fluted tins; *rosettes,* made by dipping an iron in thin butter dough and then plunging it into hot fat to cook; *krumkake,* batter baked between the plates of a hot iron press and, while still warm, rolled into cone shapes on a wooden form; and *fattigman,* an egg-rich dough rolled out, cut into rectangles and deep-fried.

Rounding it all out there would be fruit-soup made from dried fruits and fruit juices, thickened with tapioca; and on Christmas Eve for supper, rich rice pudding with a hidden almond — a token of good luck for the coming year for the finder.

As a starving person dreams of mountains of food, even tastes it in his mouth, the remembrance of it all haunted her. She was so hungry for something different! Even a plain potato would be a treat! But Christmas came on and the essential ingredients did not; and no amount of ingenuity could compensate for their lack.

She did manage some cookies. She had found some nuts in the woods; these she shelled and crushed, added to a stiff dough she made of flour, honey and melted tallow. The end result left something to be desired. But the nuts did give them a flair.

⚜

On the twenty-fourth of December, Rolf hitched the oxen to the sleigh, then came into the cabin and changed to clean clothes. It was evident that he was planning an outing, the first since their arrival at the homestead.

He said nothing when he left. She trusted, however, that he would be back by evening; for in the old country, Christmas Eve was the apex of Christmas with the church bell ushering in the season, calling them to 5 p.m. service in observance, and the rest of the evening a family time. It was the days following that were spent in a lighter mood of celebration.

After he left, she took the ax and went out in the woods to look for a tree. The woods contained a scattering of white pine — a far cry from the Norway spruce. But she found a small pine perfect in size and form. It would do.

Having set it up and braced it securely, she cast about for decorations. At home the tree was hung with fruits, the gifts and small hand-braided baskets filled with goodies and specially dipped little colored candles. The most colorful thing she had was her dwindling supply of yarn. She strung the tree with it, taking care not to break or fray it so she could unstring it, wind it up again. She stood back. It just didn't look like a Christmas tree without candles!

It was then she remembered having seen some bright orange pods on a bush in the woods. She went and found the spot. Most had been blown away by the wind, buried in the snow. But she picked the remaining ones into her apron. Back at the cabin, she poked holes in them, pushed them on to the tips of the branches, distributing them over the tree. Now she stepped back and was quite pleased with the effect. By half closing her eyes she could almost make herself believe that the orange pods were flame.

She had been saving a choice venison roast and this she now put in her heavy iron pot. It was early in the day but long, slow cooking would make it more tender, she knew. Later she would add to the pot two partridge breasts. And she had concocted a meat roll from venison flank, though unspiced. At least there would be a variety of meats.

She found time toward evening to sit down and read the Christmas story from her Bible. In their familiarity the beloved words read like a cadence. She then did the evening chores. She went to the spring with the yoke on her shoulders and brought back two big buckets of water, one for them and one for the heifer, carried in a big supply of firewood, bedded and fed the heifer. She fed an extra large portion on this evening as was the custom in the homeland in acknowledgment of the animals' presence in the stable at Christ's birth.

It became dark, but there was no sign of Rolf. The meat was done. She took it off the heat and shoved it to the back of the stove to keep it warm. She did not light the candle, but sat in darkness. She was not lonely, for somehow she felt a bond with all humanity on this night and she sat basking in the glow of that feeling. "Peace on earth...." No spot on earth could be more peaceful this night, she reflected.

She must have slept, for she started with the feeling that a great deal of time had elapsed, but she had no way of knowing because Rolf carried his watch with him — their only timepiece. She put more wood on the fire; surely Rolf would come soon! In a relaxed mood, she lay down on the bed and fell into a sound sleep.

She was awakened by the sound of the sleigh runners squeaking over the snow as they passed by the window. She jumped out of bed, lit a candle and set about getting the belated supper on the table. She heard Rolf fumbling at the latch and went to open the door for him.

He stumbled in, almost falling against her. He had been drinking! But this is probably his way of celebrating Christmas, she rationalized. She had never known him to drink excessively before. He carried a bag; she took it from his hands and set it on the floor.

His hands freed, he fumbled clumsily in his pocket — drew a paper out and flung it at her. It fluttered to the floor. She picked it up and recognized at a glance her mother's handwriting. A letter from home! The first. What better Christmas present? And right on Christmas Eve!

Rolf had opened it. He must have been hungry for news from home, too, she concluded. But supper was ready and he must be famished; before she read it, they would eat.

"Go ahead and read it! Read about your Thorn — and his return...."

It didn't register. "Wh—what did you say?"

He laughed. She couldn't have heard right. She carried the letter over to the candle and quickly scanned through it, her face going white....

Rolf's hands were on her. "It's always him you think of, isn't it? Always him, even when we go to bed at night. You never think of me... that's why you're so cold...." His words were slurred; his finger dug into her flesh.

In shock, she confessed woodenly. "Yes... I did think of him... that way."

It happened so fast that she did not have time to throw her hands up in defense. He suddenly dropped his iron grip on her shoulders, spun around and hit her full strength across the mouth with the back of his hand. She staggered back, the taste of blood on her tongue.

She felt drained of feeling; no temper burst of adrenaline came to her aid. It was of sheer instinct that she side-stepped when he came at her. He missed her, crashed into the tree, taking it down with him.

The tree... he had knocked over the Christmas tree... the tree besmirched! Suddenly it seemed the lowest blow he could have dealt. Anger welled; her wits came into play.

By the time he got back to his feet and came at her again, she was fully alert. She artfully dodged his next lunge at her, which infuriated him even more. Now he came at her like an enraged bull, head down, charging, throwing his whole body against her. She managed to throw him off-balance, but in falling, he clutched at her, dragged her to the floor with him.

So it was to be a battle royal! Her strength was no match for his, she knew. It was a matter of avoiding the decisive pit of muscle against muscle — a matter of agility. Wriggling, arching, dodging, she wrestled him on the dirt floor. His soddenness was to her advantage, his movements delayed. Gradually she wore him down. Suddenly his body went limp. The combination of alcohol, effort and the heat of the room too much. He had passed out.

She dragged him to the bed and rolled him onto it, covering him. Then she sat down to reread the letter, this time slowly... word after incredulous word....

Thorn...Thorn had come back! And she hadn't been there! She was here, in this unreal place with unreal things happening. Wild thoughts, desperate thoughts.... She could go back.... leave tonight! She could write a letter, explain it all.... But could she? Could she justify her marriage to Rolf so soon *after?* After what....? Thorn wasn't *dead! She was married.* She was a married woman! She was no longer Marit Maas. And again and again the re-echoing thought: *What must Thorn think of me.... What does he think of me now....*

After a long time she felt the chill of the night creeping in, and like an automaton got up to replenish the fire. On her way to the wood box by the door she tripped over the bag on the floor, knocking it over. Potatoes spilled out.

Rolf awoke and rolled into a sitting position on the edge of the bed. He seemed in no mood to continue the fight. Instead, he was talkative. Talking to *her....*

At another time, the things he was saying would have embarrassed her. He spoke of women he had been with and the things he knew about women. He blamed her coldness for the fact that she had not conceived. It was important for him to have sons. She had failed him in this way....

For months she had tolerated his silence. But now he was talking. Talking as he had never talked before — on and on. But she didn't care, she didn't care at all. She wasn't even listening.

৽৽৽

They were in the dead of winter now. And not a small part of the chill was the cold realization inside her: She had made her bed, and now she must lie in it — *for every one of my remaining days on this earth....*

Even her knitting needles were stilled; she had used up the bountiful supply of yarn she had brought from home. But she had knit many pairs of socks and mittens, more than they would need for several winters.

A bold idea occurred to her. She knew that the lumberjacks needed warm mittens and socks, working outdoors all winter as they did; she would walk to the settlement and try to find a market for the excess of her supply. She did not tell Rolf of her plan. In the days since Christmas, she had developed a reticence of her own.

She waited until a day when he left early in the morning with the sleigh and oxen, giving her reason to believe he would be gone all day. Then, after doing her morning chores, she dressed warmly, gathered her knit articles into a bag, threw the bag over her shoulder and set out.

She knew the general direction of the trading post and it was a sunny day so she set her course by the sun. The trail Rolf had cut in leaving was the sole one for a way and she followed it, not certain it would lead her to the town until other single tracks cut into it. This assured her that she was on the main trail and that if she stayed on it, it would lead her where she wanted to go.

As she went along, the main trail became well-worn, making the walking progressively easier. Soon she found herself on the outskirts of the settlement.

It was bigger than she had expected. In the darkness of the night of their arrival, she had assessed it to be much smaller, but an outpost. But now she saw that, in addition to the numerous company buildings, the place had the aspect of a permanent village with a number of single dwellings, a dam and a short false-fronted main street.

A bit down the way on this street she saw a shingle on a building and made her way to it. It was a store, the same one where Rolf had purchased their first supplies. There was a flag in a holder over the door. When she got inside she discovered that the store also served as a post office. Mail protruded from a cubicled wall rack.

She approached the merchant, opened her bag and displayed her merchandise. "I'll take them all," he said.

She was relieved when he spoke Norwegian. "How did you know? That I'm Norwegian, I mean."

"I can spot a newcomer a half-mile away. And most of them hereabouts are Norwegian."

He took the bag, dumped the contents out on the counter —

counted out the pairs. "It's customary to take it out in trade," he informed her.

"I'll take money."

He did not argue; but also did not ask her price — simply drew some bills from the cash register and handed them to her. She examined the bills. The money was strange to her — she had no idea if the pay had been fair. Nor how much she could buy with the money.

She browsed about, tempted by all she saw; but most of all by the bin of coffee beans, the aroma of which hung in the air of the place. But she decided to replenish her stock of yarn first, see how she came out on that.

She gathered up skeins of yarn from the bin, took her selections to the counter. The merchant added up the tags, stated a price. She lay the bills down on the counter, attempted to decipher them. Impatiently the merchant scooped them all up and put them back in the cash register, handing her a few coins in change.

She made a pretense of browsing some more, but she had already decided. "I'll take coffee for the rest," she told him.

He weighed out the beans in a small bag, and she tucked it into her pocket. At the door she thought to ask, "Is there any mail for Rolf Monsrud? I'm Mrs. Monsrud."

"I know and, no, there was just one letter this winter for that party — the one at Christmas time." She quickly went out and shut the door behind her.

Out on the street again she asked herself: Was I bilked? She decided she had not been, for the yarn would knit into more than she had brought. And there was the coffee.... But I'll learn the money, she promised herself. Next time I'll ask him to explain the prices, let him know that even if I *am* a newcomer, I still have my wits! She didn't think to wonder how he knew she was Rolf's wife. And if she had asked, the merchant wouldn't have told her that the word was out in the small town that rolf Monsrud had gotten himself quite a woman in his shopping expedition to Norway.

It was nearly noon and the long walk had made her hungry. She saw no place resembling a cafe. Then she remembered that she had no money left anyway, only the coffee beans in her pocket. She turned off again at the corner and headed toward home.

She couldn't get the beans in her pocket off her mind. After months of abstinence, she was this close to a cup of coffee.

She had now come to the last building of the town — a shack. But there were curtains in the windows. No man would bother with pretty print curtains. And the merchant had said that most hereabouts were Norwegian. They could strike up an acquaintance over a cup of coffee!

Her knock was answered by a feminine voice and she took it as an invitation to enter. Walking in, she saw a young, fair-haired woman seated by the heater rocking a baby. "My name is Mrs. Rolf Monsrud — Marit. I was just passing by on my way home and I thought I'd stop in and make your acquaintance. I have no close neighbors."

The woman looked at her blankly. Then *she* spoke — she wasn't Norwegian after all! They both laughed at the awkwardness of their situation. But the woman let her know that she was welcome nevertheless by gesturing that she should seat herself on one of the chairs by the table.

From what little the woman had said, Marit had identified her nationality as German, a tongue that was no longer completely alien to her ears, nor even understanding; for in the fraternity of the voyage, she had come to know that many of the designations were similar to Norwegian. And she had even picked up some German words. But she did not have to make all the effort. The other woman, who said her name was Amelia, seemed avid for company and met her halfway. They hit it off well and, after a time, Amelia handed the baby to Marit, gesturing her to the rocking chair, while she set about preparing a lunch. It was only stew warmed over but to Marit it was a banquet: carrots, onions, cabbage. She hadn't had vegetables for months other than the potatoes Rolf had brought home for Christmas. Topping off the meal was prune sauce and a tart red jelly to put on the freshly baked bread.

A cup of coffee would be the crowning touch. But the pot stood on the cold side of the stove. Amelia hadn't thought to offer her coffee. Boldly she drew the bag from her pocket and handed it Amelia, who peeked into the bag, then apologetically let Marit know by gesture that the reason she hadn't offered was because she was out, but if Marit would permit.... She filled the pot with water, got out her grinder; soon they were visiting over coffee, with refills frequent.

Time slipped by so pleasantly that Marit didn't realize it was well into the afternoon when she got up to leave. As a parting generosity, Amelia packed a crock with sauerkraut, putting it in a cloth sling so Marit could carry it more easily. Marit, in turn, indicated that Amelia should keep the remaining coffee beans. But Amelia pushed the bag back and, in the end, Marit poured half of the remaining beans into an empty saucer that stood on the table. The last of it she returned to her pocket.

When she got outside she immediately noticed that the weather had changed. The day that had started out sunny had clouded. Dirty, gray clouds scudded low and from them an occasional snowflake drifted down. She would have to hurry! If it snowed much — covered the tracks — she would have trouble finding her way home.

She hadn't gone far before the scouting flakes had called down a barrage. But the deep furrows of sleigh tracks were still clearly visible. She started to run, one foot planted squarely in front of the other in the furrow. This awkward gait set the sauerkraut to swinging in the sling. She pulled it around to the front and clutched it to her as she ran, the other hand over her shoulder hanging onto the bag of yarn.

As it would in snowstorms, a premature twilight set in. To make matters worse, a wind came up, drifting the snow. At each juncture in the trail she became more confused; sometimes there was a trace of tracks, sometimes not. Eventually drifting snow obliterated tracks completely. Still, she sped on for some time before she would admit to herself that she was lost. And, by that time, it was almost dark.

She was not one to panic; but a way back a wolf cry had risen nearby and had been answered by another on the other side of the trail. Soon the howling seemed to come from every direction. Believing herself to be pursued by a pack, she ran blindly, attempting to put them behind.

It was just before total darkness set in that she had to stop to shift her loads and give her aching arms and cramped fingers a respite. It was only then that she spied the fresh footprints in the snow, so fresh that she could tell that they were pointed in the same direction in which she was going. Someone had passed this way just ahead of her! She must hurry, catch up before the tracks were erased to her by the wind.

She had gone but a short distance when the tracks turned in, led away from the trail. Now she must make the decision of whether to stay on the trail or follow the tracks, to be hopelessly lost in the forest should she lose them there....

She didn't hesitate long; she followed the tracks. This someone must *know* where he was going, she reasoned. And so intent was she on her swift, hunched-over tracing that it was only when the tracks were scrambled with those of others that she looked up to realize that she had broken into a clearing — a clearing of wigwams!

She had been seen; soon she was surrounded. She told them she was lost — forgetting in her confusion that they would not understand what she was saying. Several of them spoke English, she could tell. If only she knew the language!

Finally, she set down her burdens, knelt in the snow in the light of a campfire. She brushed the snow smooth and drew on it a rough map showing the approximate location of their cabin in relation to the settlement. She then drew in many side trails, gesturing to indicate that she was confused by all the trails.

They conferred among themselves. Then a young man came forward to where she stood, reached over and pulled the shawl back from her hair. She drew back — scalping came to mind. But though there were exclamations at the sight of her hair, no one made a hostile move. Instead it seemed that the young man had identified her by her auburn hair. He pointed at her hair, then in a direction of the wilderness.

The picture came to mind: The Indians were notoriously stealthy; she had been observed in the clearing of home from cover of the surrounding woods, her red-hued hair a distinguishing characteristic. It was an unnerving thought that she must take into consideration from now on.

Now the young man indicated she should follow him. Short hours ago she would have been leery had she even spotted one of the natives in the forest. Yet now she left the circle of light and went without hesitation into the wilderness alone with him.

He set out at a trot, an unslackening pace he kept up the whole distance. She was hard-put to keep up, tired as she already was from running and carrying the two bundles, burdens he did not offer to share. It was in a state of exhaustion that she saw that she had gained the clearing of home. She set down her bags, turned to the man. I

must give him something to show my gratitude, she decided, drawing off her warm mittens and handing them to him. He took them
in silence, turned and was immediately swallowed up in the swirling storm.

When she staggered in, Rolf was lying face down on the bed
fully-clothed. He jumped to his feet, seemed surprised to see her.

In a monotone, she explained, "I went to the settlement to sell
knitting.... I got lost on the way home.... an Indian led me...."

He seemed relieved. "That was all!"

He sat down by the table. "I'm hungry."

When they had finished eating, feeling somewhat relieved, she
began putting the yarn away . She could tell from his face that the
new supply of yarn pleased him.

Then, a surprising comment: "From now on you can take care
of the household needs with the money you make from knitting."

It was not sarcasm or reproof. He was turning the management
of the house over to her. Even though at her own expense, the prospect pleased her, tokening a less stringent future. She was glad she
had not brought out the coffee, evidence of money foolishly spent.
Tomorrow I will scatter the beans in the woods, she decided. But while
undressing for bed, in the pretense of fluffing the straw on her side
of the bed, she secreted the bag with the beans in it under the straw
on her side.

⚜

The next morning when she was at the spring she was suddenly
surrounded by a group of Indian women. One of them was wearing the mittens she had given to the Indian guide and, by pointing
at the mittens and the bare hands of some of the others, the woman
indicated that they, too, wanted mittens.

Marit was at a loss; she now had no extra mittens on hand. But
she motioned for them to follow her to the cabin, all the while rack-
ing her brain for a substitute that would please them.

Rolf was working in the clearing limbing logs and when he saw
the procession approaching, he dropped the ax and came to meet
them.

"They want mittens," Marit explained.

Rolf's face flushed in anger. Suddenly he put his hands to his

mouth and let out a bellowing "Ya-hoo!" It was his way of sum-
moning the oxen for feed.

His strange behavior startled the squaws and they backed away.
When the oxen — which had been foraging in the brush — burst
into the clearing, running pell-mell toward the group, the women
scattered and fled.

"We could have given them something," Marit reproved.

"They can grub for a living the same as the rest of us! If you
once start with them, they'll never stop coming."

Rolf, like most of the settlers, thought of the Indians as he
thought of the trees — a superfluity of the new land that stood in
the way of its development. There was talk of removing them to a
reservation at Lac Court Oreilles. To the Indians, on the other hand,
the business of laying claim to a piece of land as one's own — taking title — was a mystery, private ownership alien to their culture.
And, consequently, with their hunting grounds being steadily en-
croached on by the lumber concerns and the homesteaders, and with
all the fight taken out of them and too lately out of the wild to have
adapted to the ways of the white men, they had become afflicted
with a creeping inertia. Pilfering and begging were common.

But Marit was not familiar with any of this. *I'll find some other
way to help them,* she promised her nagging conscience as she went
back to her interrupted task of carrying water, a prolonged task on
this day because she was preparing to wash clothes. The task was
especially irksome in the snow of winter, for her long skirts became
sodden in the repeated trips to the spring.

It had once occurred to her that men's clothes were much more
practical for chores in the snow, that she could don trousers for her
trips to the spring. Then she had been immediately appalled that
such a thought should occur to her. The donning of male apparel
would surely indicate moral decay. It was explicitly forbidden in the
Scriptures! She felt that the very fact that such a thought should
occur to her was due to her lack of contact with the church and its
stabilizing influence. As a consequence, she had devised a way to
compensate.

Rolf worked on Sundays, but she could not bring herself to labor
on the Sabbath even to help him. So having some Sunday hours to
herself in the cabin, it had become her custom to hold her own
private service, even to the sermon, with one of her mental diver-

sions on weekdays being planning "next Sunday's sermon." These she would stand and give forth to the empty room. The heifer, over the partition, sometimes attested to her appreciation of this extended discourse with drawn-out mooing.

❦

Her trips to the settlement — now designated as Pine Fork from the name of the post office — were excursions she came to look forward to. She learned to memorize landmarks so that she would not become lost again.

The outings always included a stop at Amelia's. Not a small part of the pleasure of the visits was the contact with Amelia's baby, to whom she became very attached. It occurred to her that a baby was a lot of company.

She had blocked Christmas Eve from her mind, but now, thinking enviously of Amelia's baby, some of Rolf's words of that night came back to her....

Perhaps, after all, she had committed adultery with Thorn *in her mind* and maybe God was chastising her by "closing her womb" — a phenomenon not uncommon in the Old Testament. She vowed she would think of Thorn no more — in *any* way. Then perhaps He would grant her desire for a baby of her own.

But spring came on, and still she had not conceived.

CHAPTER VII

There is something about spring in Wisconsin that makes one hope in spite of herself. Even as early as February, the brightening days give a lift to the spirit. But the cold prevails, and February is allotted to winter. Not so with March; it is a disputed month with the seasons vying for the upper hand in a seesaw of tumultuous weather. But come April, winter loosens its hold. Then each ridge drains its slopes to the nearest valley and the valleys to the streams. The streams, in turn, tumble their way to the rivers, languid in their ice-bound banks, and the sudden influx tears the shroud loose and floats it downstream in massive chunks; the pressured river waters boil in their rage at the obstructions in their courses. After the run-off, the dun earth stands nakedly exposed — but not for long. Spring flowers soon delicately veil it. Even before the last patches of snow have dissolved, the hepatica pops out wearing a woolly green hood. At night and on cloudy days it draws the hood tight, but if the day be bright it throws the hood back and lifts its trusting little face to the sun's warmth. Later, stately trilliums nod knowingly to the violets at their feet, their heads ever hung in a deep purple mood, and spring beauty embroiders the woodlands with an orchid filigree. The trees also blossom: Oak and maple, the *grandes dames* of the forest, allow themselves only a subtle tracery of color for the occasion; birch and poplar, perpetual flirts, outrage good taste by hanging countless fuzzy gewgaws on themselves. Wild fruit trees — debutantes all — compete with each other for attention in coming-out gowns of frothy pastel. Finally, foliage breaks out in the ethereal green of spring, and the earth stands transformed by the miracle of regeneration.

And as if all that were not enough to lift Marit's spirits, spring brought with it two bonuses. First, the heifer dropped her calf, which meant there would be milk to drink, butter for the bread, cottage cheese and all that cookery magic dependent on the unglamorous creature called cow. Secondly, a homesteader, who had a wife and children, had filed claim on land adjoining theirs. The man had spent a night with them, sleeping on some straw on the floor. She had plied him with questions, learning the names and ages of each of the three children as well as the wife's name — Sana. *Sana Englien.* The name had a pretty ring to it, she thought. She could hardly wait to meet and welcome her.

But her first encounter with Sana Englien was not as she expected. She went to the spring one morning and was surprised to come upon another woman there drawing water, her back toward her. The woman did not hear Marit come up behind her and when Marit spoke, she started, dropping her bucket. She retrieved it and turned round, backing away at the same time.

"I'm Marit Monsrud. And I suppose you're Sana Englien?"

The woman nodded.

"I was surprised to see you. I didn't know you had moved in. How long have you been here?"

"Three days."

"*That* long? I thought... well, since we're going to be neighbors, I'd have welcomed you before this had I known. You see, you're our *first* neighbor."

"I know."

"Would you like to come up to our cabin with me for a little while? I can't offer you coffee, but there's fresh bread and milk."

"I have to go back. The children are alone."

"Alone....?"

"Odin left for the drive this morning." Then, after a pause, "We needed the money."

That meant he'd be gone for weeks. Marit did not know quite how to phrase the question. "But how are you living?"

"In a tent."

Marit thought of offering to take them in right on the spot, but she supposed Rolf should have something to say about it. She hesitated.

When Rolf came in to eat at noon, she took it up with him.

"Feed four more mouths! And where would we bed them?"

She acknowledged to herself that they would be hard-put to find room for four more people in their already cramped quarters, so she did not press the matter. Instead, she decided to pay Sana a visit to see if there was something she could do to help.

That same afternoon she made her way to the spot where the tent was pitched. A bright fire burned in front of the tent, but no one was about. The flap of the tent was partially raised, so she knelt down and peered in. Sana and the children were huddled inside.

"I've brought some milk."

At the word "milk," the three toddlers spilled out of the tent. Sana emerged with bowls and soon the children were seated round the fire, their faces moons of up-bottomed bowls. It was evident they were famished.

Sana stood apart, hugging herself with her arms.

"Are you cold? Come over to the fire."

She seemed to want no part of the scene. Her eyes darted about the tangle of woods surrounding them, as if looking for a way of escape. Then, after a few moments and without preliminaries, she stated flatly, "I didn't want to come into the wilderness. I didn't want him to go off and leave me here alone."

"You're really not alone. We're here."

"I was city-bred." It was her way of holding herself apart with words!

"Well, you're *here* now."

With that, Marit walked over to her, put her arm about her waist and firmly steered her over to the fire.

"This is a long way from the city, I'll grant you that. But it won't always be so wild. We already have a big clearing around our cabin, as you'll see if you accept my invitation to come for dinner tomorrow. And I'm sure that when the drive is done and Odin comes back, he'll clear land and build you a proper cabin."

Sana turned away from her reassurance, went back to the tent and started crawling back in. "Can I expect you tomorrow? Just follow the trail. After you round the turn, you'll see our cabin," she said to Sana's back.

She noted in leaving that Odin had left them with a good supply of wood — evidence of industry before he left. The days were fairly pleasant now, but the nights still were chilly.

They didn't show the next day. But having cooked enough for six, Marit carried the food to them. She found them huddled in the tent as the day before. "I was afraid we'd get lost," Sana said by way of explanation.

Every day thereafter, Marit found time to visit them, always carrying milk for the children. Once, Sana said, "I should pay you for the milk, but the last of the money went for the supplies he left us with."

"Pay me? I wouldn't think of such a thing!"

"It's charity."

"Nonsense. We're neighbors."

Although she knew it hurt Sana's pride, she couldn't bear to see the children do without milk, and continued to carry it to them each day. And once she brought a special treat for them — three hard-boiled eggs. Rolf had somewhere scrounged a hen and rooster; but she had foregone using any of the eggs, for the hen was in the process of laying a clutch and to steal eggs would be to lessen the hatch — the size of her future flock.

Some days when she went to the Engliens' tent, her efforts to make conversation with Sana were futile. Sana sat staring into the fire in some faraway world or her own. There came a time when she did not even acknowledge Marit's visits by coming out of the tent. She lay facing the tent wall, her back turned on a reality she would not, or could not, face.

The weeks thus went by and Odin returned; and with his return, Sana's despondency seemed to pass.

❧

The chores of the winter were child's play compared with the labor that the spring thaw brought.

Where giant trees had stood the fall before, receding snow exposed huge stumps rising as spectres of the departed as the snow melted. To remove them it was necessary to grub around each one until the roots were exposed like the spokes of a wheel, then sever them below ground level. At this point the strength of the oxen was coupled with theirs in pulling them loose, the oxen then dragging the trees to the edge of the clearing to be burned later.

They grubbed relentlessly; but for all their effort, they still had to seed around some still intact stumps. If the grain was to have time to mature before the cool or autumn, it must be sown early.

The intense shade of the trees had inhibited sod and the soil tilled readily to a seedbed under Marit's grub hoe. When turned over, the humus-rich bed gave rise to a heady earth odor under the sun's warmth. Once, seized by an abstruse urge, she scooped some soil up in her hands and buried her face in it. A shudder of gratification shook her body; she dropped her arms and the mass slid from her fingers. At her feet, the imprint of her face stared up from the earth.

❧

The seeding finally accomplished, there was a lull in the work. Marit, in her involvement with spring planting, had not been to Pine Fork for some time, and now, knowing that the cows were scarce — making, she guessed, a market for butter — she decided to churn an accumulation of skimmings and make a trip to the store.

She packed the churned butter in a bucket and chilled it in the spring before setting out. But the warm sun soon softened it. Although she stopped at a stream along the way and held the bucket in the stream to harden it again, it was in a liquid state when she reached the store. She haggled with the merchant, who refused to give her more than half-price for it, limiting her purchases accordingly. But her disappointment vanished when the merchant reached into the wall rack, pulled out a letter and handed it to her.

It was from Nicolena, but really not a letter, just a note, she discovered upon opening it. She took it in in a glance:

Don't forget our bargain. I still have the leather scroll. I didn't burn it like you said. I expect to be hearing from you soon.

It didn't make any sense, hardly worth the postage to send it so far. It was addressed to Rolf. Maybe he would know what it meant.

When she reached home, she immediately sought him out, handed it to him. His face reddened upon reading it, but he offered no explanation.

Instead, he said, "This letter was addressed to me. You have no business opening my mail!"

It must be some personal matter between Rolf and his sister, she concluded. There was no reason for her to concern herself with it, as long as it didn't involve her.

❦

Since returning to the homestead in the fall, Rolf had put all thought of Lilledalen behind him, including his bargain with Nicolena. Having put an ocean and a half a continent between himself and her, he had felt secure. But now her letter came as the opening of a door to a cold draft of a room that had been shut off.

He had prided himself that his decision to return to Norway to hand-pick a wife had been a shrewd one. Marit was all that he had sought in a woman — except, of course, for that business of her not yet giving any sign of presenting him with a son. But it really hadn't been that long. It was just that he wasn't getting any younger and it took a long time for children to get some size to them. He had been worried that he had revealed too much on Christmas Eve — he couldn't remember it all clearly — but evidently no harm had been done. In fact, some good had come of it from a shift in his tactics. He had learned that Marit was not a woman who could be beaten into submission, that the key to her subordination was her religious bent, her marriage vows being "holy" to her he was sure, as was everything else connected with the church. This religious quirk of hers was something to be encouraged, even though it meant he got no help from her on Sundays. She made up for it the other six days! Also, although the Christmas episode seemed not to have had any serious consequences, he decided it was a thing he would not risk repeating. He would never get that drunk again — Thorn or no Thorn!

That she still favored Thorn over him he was certain. But someday she would see that he had been the better choice. He but needed time to prove it to her. When he became a man of means, she would see!

This winter wasn't the way it was always going to be. He had to make the money last until the crop was in next fall or he would have to borrow — go behind. And getting behind would mean having to go to the pinery to work next winter. In which case he would not get more land cleared, which was the key to harvests that would bring in good income. If all went well, by next fall....

But he must do something about Nicolena. He couldn't be certain that she would not carry out her veiled threat — expose to Marit that she had been tricked into marrying him. She respected him as a husband and in all important matters deferred to him. It must stay that way.

He decided to hold off Nicolena by writing a letter promising that he would send fares as soon as he could afford it. At the same time he would make it doubly clear to Marit that she was not to open mail addressed to him.

It was only Nicolena's letters that worried him, but he did not make that distinction when he intimidated Marit by saying, "Opening other people's mail is the same as stealing."

He could see by the shocked expression on her face that the word "stealing" had the desired effect; the Ten Commandments were law to her. She didn't remember at that moment that it was he who had opened that fateful letter telling of Thorn's survival, the one she had received from her mother at Christmas, addressed to *her*. She had blocked all thought of Thorn from her mind.

On a bright June afternoon, a shadow from the open doorway fell across the cabin floor. Marit turned to see a stranger standing there, his hand raised to knock on the door. But this was no ordinary foot traveler such as had stopped at the door several times this summer to ask the way or for a meal or night's lodging. He was not dressed in the rough manner of the wilderness, but wore a black suit of shabby elegance. In his hand he carried a worn leather valise.

She invited him in and, after exchanging pleasantries about the weather, waited for him to give some clue to his purpose in coming to their door.

Noticing her questioning look, he said, "You are wondering what I am doing *here.*"

He spoke with an air of authority, and as if he expected her to *know* who he was. She did not want to make a blunder so she said safely, "Whatever your mission, you are welcome."

From her use of the word "mission" he took it that she had recognized him as a minister. "I consider it my mission to minister to the faithful in the far reaches of the wilderness. I trust you are one of the faithful?"

So he was a man of the cloth. But she did not want to commit herself until she was certain he was *their* kind. "I do my best," she side-stepped.

"This is my first trip through this area. I am endeavoring to establish a circuit. If it can be arranged, I shall be visiting at regular intervals hereafter. On such visits I shall attend to the essential rites — baptisms and marriages. But I also hope to hold services to sustain the faith of the believers."

She looked him over: His clerical garb was not up to the standard — authentic, as she remembered it. But it would be disrespectful to ask, should he be one of the clergy. Not knowing, however, she was reluctant to be too agreeable.

As she did with all strangers, she invited him to take supper with them. It was when he was conversing with Rolf at the table that she learned he was indeed of the faith! Fluster replaced reticence. One of the clergy here in these humble surroundings and sharing in the simple supper she had prepared, not knowing!

Rolf seemed not at all impressed with the status of their guest, conversing handily with him throughout the meal. She could contribute nothing to the conversation, for the minister was intent on acquainting himself with the area and her own knowledge of the region was limited.

Rolf showed no hesitancy in furnishing him with the information he wanted, but when he informed Rolf of his intention to establish a circuit and conduct services "in some settler's home" — pausing suggestively — Rolf merely grunted.

Now she found her voice: "We would be honored to hold services here, in our home, if you can overlook our humble circumstances. I'm sure you are accustomed to more refined surroundings."

"No matter. It is the spirit that counts," he assured her. He looked at her intently, seemed to take a measure of that spirit in her face. "I would like to ask a little favor of you. I would like a list of those who might be interested in attending the services."

To her embarrassment, she could think of none but the Engliens. But she said brightly, "I'll see to it before you leave."

After supper she realized that she must invite him to spend the night. But certainly they could not ask *him* to sleep on the floor on a pile of straw as had their other overnight guests. There was only one way: He and Rolf could sleep in the bed and she would sit up all night.

When the time came to retire, she turned the coverlet back on the bed and said to him, "Make yourself comfortable." Then she stepped outside to give the men an opportunity to undress.

After what she thought was a reasonable interval, she came back in. She saw that they were comfortably installed for the night — the minister next to the wall and Rolf on the room side. She blew out the candle, drew a shawl about her shoulders and sat down.

She had no sooner settled herself when she was startled to hear the minister's voice in the darkness, saying, "There is no need for you to sit up. In this place were shelter is at premium, one must not be too conscious of the proprieties. Take your deserved rest by the side of your husband. It is the usual arrangement under these circumstances."

Sleep in the same bed with a minister? She felt her face flush in the darkness. Moments slipped by. Then the utter silence became embarrassing in itself. Without undressing, she slipped in beside Rolf on the outside.

She awoke earlier than usual, slipped quietly out of bed. She felt she should prepare a special breakfast. *If only I had some coffee,* she regretted.

But I do have coffee! In her determination to exercise self-discipline, she had completely forgotten the small bag of coffee beans she had hidden in the straw tick months before. But how to retrieve it with the men still in bed? And what of Rolf? Her weak moment would be found out by him. Would he reprove her in front of the minister?

She hesitated but a moment, then shrugged her shoulders. It wasn't every day they had one of the clergy for breakfast.

She tiptoed over to the bed, carefully raised bedding along the edge until the straw was exposed and started exploring with her fingers. After some probing, she decided Rolf must be sleeping over the exact spot. Perhaps if she got *under* the bedstead and dug from beneath.... But how ridiculous she would look if one of them woke up and saw her crawling out!

Ominously, Rolf stopped snoring. She held her breath. But then, with a wide swing of his arm, he hove himself over on his side, facing the minister. Quickly and deftly, she dug in the warm straw where he had lain and retrieved the little brown bag.

Fresh water makes the best coffee, she reminded herself. She dumped out what was left in the bucket, made a trip to the spring to replace it with fresh. She took down her coffee grinder from the spot on the shelf where it had stood unused for months, took it outside and ground the beans. She sniffed; the beans had lost a great deal of their strength. But I'll use it *all* to make up for the staleness, she extravagantly resolved.

It must have been the smell of the coffee that awakened the men. Even before Rolf opened his eyes she noticed a twitching of his nostrils. Aware that he was awake and smelled the coffee, she avoided his eyes. She had the excuse of going outside while they dressed to forestall any glower from Rolf.

When she came back in to serve their breakfast, she nonchalantly poured the steaming black coffee in the minister's cup first and hadn't gotten to Rolf before the minister exclaimed, "You are indeed a fortunate woman! Not many of the remote homes I visit can afford to brew this heart-warming beverage so lavishly black. Your husband must be a provider of rare excellence!"

Was he rebuking her for extravagance? Thrown off-guard, she

now looked at Rolf's face. At least she need not worry about his disapproval! Rolf's face beamed, as he apparently was flattered by the minister's words.

Shortly after breakfast, the minister took his leave, informing her, "I shall be around again the second Sunday in October." His hand on the latch, he turned, "The list! If you will give me the list, I shall put it in my valise for the records and be on my way."

Her face flushed. "Oh—! I forgot all about the list! But I assure you, when you come again in October, we will have a packed house for the service."

She vowed to make it a truth.

❧

The minister's first visit was not to be the only milestone of that summer. There were to be new cabins: a simple one-room cabin for the Engliens and a more elaborate one for themselves.

Marit wasn't consulted in the matter, but she was pleased with the plan for their new one when she overheard Rolf outlining the layout to Odin: two rooms on the ground floor, one to be a large combination kitchen-sitting room, and the other a much smaller partitioned-off bedroom; a ceiling, making for a loft that would be accessible by means of a ladder built flat against the wall of the kitchen and, probably most pleasing of all, there was to be a wood floor, although of rough boards. Dirt floors were always "dirty" no matter how much one cleaned, she had found.

When Odin had returned from the drive in the spring, he and Rolf had gotten together and agreed to exchange work, the exchange involving the women as well. Sana would prepare the meals for both families and Marit would perform the tedious task of carrying water from the spring, mixing mud and chinking.

A bonus of all this building industry was to be that their old cabin would now become the barn. She had wondered where they would stable their growing accumulation of livestock the next winter, half worried that Rolf would partition off more corners of their one room as he had for the heifer!

The Engliens were not fortunate enough to need a barn for the next winter; they had not been able to afford to buy livestock. What was more unfortunate, the spring drive had taken up so much of the springtime that Odin had not gotten home to clear land before sowing time, so there would be no crop for them this year. It would be necessary for him to go to the pineries again next winter to earn the money for their livelihood.

Sana was glum at the prospect of being left alone again.

"With a proper roof over your head, it'll be different," Marit told her in an effort to cheer her.

Sana made a circling gesture with her arms, "Wilderness. Endless, endless wilderness...." Her voice trailed off.

"I'm here. And whenever you are lonely, all you need to do is come. You know that."

"But there's all that woods between. Those trees.... and shadows beneath them. I always have the feeling that something lurks in the shadows, some hidden thing waiting to pounce...."

"Nonsense!"

She knew immediately it had been the wrong thing to say. Sana rang down the curtain on her thoughts, her eyes becoming veiled as the same look of the springtime.

❧

The new cabin had taken shape and stood complete, save for the shingling of the roof. That would have to wait until a more immediate matter was attended to: The heifer had dropped her calf in the spring, and if she were to freshen again, she must be bred.

It had not been easy to locate a sire. Most bull calves were castrated and trained to the yoke since few could afford to keep a drone animal about. But by inquiry Rolf had learned that a homesteader about twenty-five miles away had a bull; it was a round trip they could not accomplish in one day. However, he had reconnoitered an abandoned cabin on their route. There they would camp overnight if necessary.

They had a week of rainy weather, but on the day that Rolf decided the time was right for the heifer, the morning dawned sunny.

Marit packed a basket of food in picnic abandon. She looked on the trip as an outing, a chance to see new terrain, meet new people; and perhaps contact someone who might be interested in the October service. Last thing before leaving the cabin she tied on her prettiest apron.

They had not gone beyond the boundaries of their own land before the excursion took on the aspect of an ordeal. With romance on her mind, the ordinarily docile heifer had become a cavorting Jezebel. Rolf led and she drove from behind, but the heifer was in no mind to be led nor driven, seemingly of the persuasion that she herself was the best judge of the direction they should take. By turns she would attempt to turn off into the woods on one side, then on the other. Thwarted, she would stop dead still, and at those times, all of Rolf's strength and weight at the end of the rope couldn't budge the animal.

Rolf soon became hoarse from yelling, by turns at the heifer, then Marit. Finally, he handed the rope to her saying sarcastically, "You're such good friends. You lead her!" But though she pulled and pleaded, she had no better luck. Finally, he broke a switch from a tree at the side of the trail, and whenever the heifer turned he ran up and rapped her on the side of the head. When she stopped, the rear end was the obvious pressure point.

Attempting to cover all the miles in this fashion would have been futile had it not been that the heifer — occasionally exercising the female prerogative of changing her mind — would suddenly decide that perhaps, after all, they were headed in the right direction. At such times she would run pell-mell down the trail, and they were forced to run with her, Marit hanging onto the rope. But these spurts of progress were made at the price of being spattered from head to foot with mud from the back-splash of the heifer's unfastidious steps, as the trail was muddy and puddled. And the mud soon streaked with perspiration in the humidity of the day, for the rain-drenched forest about them was steaming in the heat of the sun.

They kept up the sporadic advance until they reached a stream some time after noon; there they knelt and splashed water over their arms and faces. Somewhat refreshed, they ate in the cool of the shade. But tempting as it was to tarry, they lingered only long enough to eat.

The afternoon's pace, as the forenoon's, was geared to the whims of the heifer. But the tedium was broken by their sighting of several settlers' cabins. One was near the trail and a man and two children were outdoors. When these people saw them coming, they came to the side of the trail and stood waiting for them. But Rolf was in no mood for socializing. They passed them by with but a nod of acknowledgment from him. Even so, they were still far from their destination at dusk.

The sun had long set when Rolf came up, took the rope from her hand and led the heifer off the trail, Marit following. The sun had gone down behind a cloud-bank in the west. It could mean more rain, and he had decided to seek the shelter of the deserted cabin he had spotted previously.

Forbidding as the dark cabin looked in the gloom of the trees, she was glad to see it. She had thought they would have to camp outdoors, sleep on the damp ground. She approached it alone, for Rolf, after tying the heifer to a tree, had gone off to look for water. Where there was a cabin, there would of a surety be water nearby.

Suddenly she paused in her approach to the cabin. A moaning sound had come to her ears. But holding her breath and listening intently, she heard nothing more and decided it must have been the wind in the pines that hugged the cabin closely.

She pushed the door open and immediately backed away. The out-draft of stuffy air had carried to her nostrils the stench of sickness.

She took off her apron and tied it over her mouth and nose. Then, leaving the door wide open behind her and holding her breath as much as possible, she entered.

The far recesses of the room were dark, but labored breathing led her to a pile of blankets in a corner. She knelt, reached out, then drew her hand back quickly in recoil at contact with cold flesh.... a dead body. But concern overcame horror. Someone was alive! Overcoming her revulsion, she felt around. There were five: two, cold dead; three burning with fever.

She quickly lifted one child and carried it out into the fresh air, laying it on some pine needles she hastily scraped together with her foot. She re-entered, brought out the other live child. Then, half carrying, half dragging, she brought out a woman — evidently the mother. As she lay her down, the woman gasped, "Thank God.... thank God you have come."

Rolf had returned and stood unbelieving.

"Plague! A terrible plague of some sort! Go for help!"

In the desperation of the moment she commanded him, and

uncharacteristically he obeyed, thrown off-balance by this completely unexpected disarrangement of his well-laid plans.

No sooner had Rolf gone than she realized she must enter the cabin again. They could not lie on the ground with no covering, for even now the woman was complaining weakly, "Cold — I'm so cold...."

So again she tied the apron over her face, penetrated the evil-smelling closeness of the cabin. Feeling around in the darkness, by touch she identified some tools in the clutter. An ax, she could use that. She went to the corner where the two still lay and gathered up all the bedding she could carry, they no longer having need of it.

Outdoors again, she spread one quilt on the ground and lifted them up on it, then covered them with the rest. She chopped some dead branches, got matches from her basket and kindled a fire, more for illumination than heat, for it was a warm, muggy night. Only someone with a chill could be cold, she concluded.

Now the older of the two children was stirring and opened his eyes. "Water...." he begged.

Water! She had not thought to ask Rolf where it was! Maybe the woman could tell her. She questioned her; but the woman seemed now to have sunk, was unresponsive. And the child, in response to her questioning, only rolled his head from side to side, repeating, "Water...."

It was a pitch-dark night with no moon, the forest surrounding them a black palisade. But she must go look. She could not bear to listen to the boy beg for water until Rolf got back — which might not be for hours. She piled more wood on the fire, hoping the blaze would serve as a beacon.

Before leaving home, she had thought to tie a small bucket to the heifer's halter. She now went and got it, looped it over her arm. Then, she circled the small clearing, looking for a gap in the underbrush, a path. But the leaping light from the fire played tricks on her eyes, created shifting shadows that *seemed* to be openings. She plunged into several of these black "holes," the brambles tearing at her skirt. Finally, she decided to compass the clearing a little way into the woods, but no further in than she could keep the fire in sight.

Using her free hand to part the branches in front of her face, she stumbled through the tangle until she came to a place where openness suggested a passageway through the undergrowth. Probing with her feet, she found herself on a path.

Blackness such as she could not remember! She was as a blind person: sensing with her feet, shuffling for the reassuring feel of smoothness that told her she was still on the path....

A doubt arose. Suppose this were not the path to the water, just a deer-run.... She looked up, up, trying to see the beacon-glow of the fire above the trees. But, above as well, all was blackness. However, it was then, with that pause, that she heard it — though faintly: the sound of running water. She continued her cautious pace, the sound coming now to meet her.

She reached the bank of the brook, filled her bucket and started back at the same snail's pace. But the way back seemed longer and, after a while, too much longer. She became certain she had been led astray on an animal run. If so, it could lead further and further into the wilderness. She must retrace her steps, find where she had gone wrong. She turned and began to go back, but the path took a sudden turn and to her surprise she broke out of the brush, found herself on the trail.

She had no idea of direction; she was completely turned around in her head. But now the fire beacon paid off. She looked up, and with her scope unobstructed by interlocking branches, she saw the reflection of the fire in the fog that hung above the treetops. Following the trail to the left she found her way back to the cabin.

Finally he would have water. She eased an arm under his shoulders, and cupping her hand, dipped into the bucket and held water to his lips. He took several sips, then was seized by a violent chill. She lowered him, tucking the blankets tightly about him. Then, again utilizing her apron, she bathed their feverish faces with water poured over from the bucket.

Suddenly she remembered that the cow had not been milked that evening. She had brought the bucket along with the intention of milking her on the trail, utilizing as much of the milk as they could and disposing of the rest. Maybe if she could get some nourishment into them....

As if in protest against the outrages of the day, the heifer would not let down her milk. But stubborn tugging finally yielded enough to cover the bottom of the bucket.

She was now able to rouse the woman. She took some milk, as did the older child. But in the case of the younger of the two children, it had become apparent that nothing would avail.

It began to drizzle; keeping the fire alive became a vigil. It became to her as if the fire were the spark of life itself, the threat of its being quenched the threat of the powers of darkness and extinction. Only once during the night did she doze off, her back resting against the trunk of a tree. It was during those few moments that the younger one had slipped away.

A murky dawn groped its way through the mist; then, reluctant daylight. The two who were left seemed to be holding their own. She again milked the cow and fed them. Then she made another trip to the brook for water, in the light of day, a simple matter.

It was while she was bathing their faces with fresh water that she heard voices, knew that help had come. A buckboard came into view, Rolf and another man on it. They loaded the woman and the one remaining child in it and the man drove away with them.

No time had been lost; it was only yesterday morning that they had left home. But yesterday morning seemed like an age ago; that eternal night had come between. And now, propriety; "We must dig graves, bury them."

Rolf untied the cow, handed the end of the rope to her and released her with, "I'll catch up."

Some words should be said over the graves.... Yet she found herself so eager to be away from this place that she left all behind — bucket, basket and apron — and set off down the trail. And when Rolf caught up sooner than she had expected, she did not question. She saw smoke billowing above the trees when she walked back to driving position behind the cow.

They reached their destination midday and it was decided that they would stay the rest of the day and the night, leaving for home early in the morning.

At another time, the thriving homestead of their host family would have roused her enthusiasm, for here was all that she hoped theirs would someday become. But as the homesteader's wife proudly showed her around, on this day she found herself thinking: *This is good and well, but sometimes the wilderness exacts too big a price!*

She was glad when, before sun-up the next morning, they were on their way again. It was only then that she remembered that she had not thought to tell them about the October service.

The trip home went smoothly. The cow, now amenable, they moved right along. About noon they reached the homestead that they had passed by so rudely two days before. This time, Rolf stopped to talk, and they were invited to share the noon meal with the family.

"If we'd known you were headed for that cabin, we'd have warned you," the man of the house said when Rolf told him of their experience. "The family that homesteaded there came down with sickness this spring. The cabin must've still harbored it. Someone should've had sense enough to burn it down right off."

But it was to be several month's time before the whole story was pieced together to Marit's satisfaction. The woman survived and traced the identity of her benefactors. She wrote to Marit, thanking her and explaining the circumstances under which they were found: "My husband had been looking around for land to settle. He thought we were so fortunate to find this empty cabin to move into, and he hired a wagon to haul us there with our things...." She went on to say that they had become ill within two weeks of moving in and her husband, although ill himself, had left to get help. No trace of him had been found. "I think sometimes of going back to pay my respects at their graves, but I can't bring myself to it — at least, not yet. I'm so fortunate to still have Ingval, for he recovered too."

"It's better not to go back," Marit wrote in her return letter.

❧❦❧

For days after exposure, she watched for symptom of impending illness in herself. When for several mornings in a row she felt giddy upon arising, she feared. No fever developed, however, and after several weeks the spells of morning discomfort passed.

The bushes around the clearing were now festooned with wild berries. She was seeing to it that they would not have to spend another winter without fruit, and the aroma of the drying berries hung on the air of the cabin like a wine bouquet.

CHAPTER VIII

The promise of April had become the fullness of August; the clearing was an amber pool of waving grain set in green banks of forest.

Day after day Marit followed Rolf as he cut the wheat with the cradle scythe, her part being to bind the swaths into sheaves. Then, she shocked the sheaves to shed rain by standing two on their cut ends leaning in on each other and adding sheaves around the side tepee-fashion and thatching the whole with a sheaf lain on top.

It was back-breaking work, a convolution of stooping, twisting and stretching. And all under a relentless sun, for the height of summer was now upon them. The clearing, hemmed in by trees, was a stifling pocket of shimmering heat with not so much as a vagrant breeze finding its way through the trees to stir the air.

Their arms soon became raw from the rasping of the stems. Chaff worked its way under their clothing, stuck to the wet skin and goaded their flesh. To add to the torment, biting insects from the nearby woods swarmed about their sweaty faces and exposed arms. Their hands occupied, they could not swat them away.

Only night brought some relief, but reluctantly. For each evening, the sun sank an apoplectic red and the sky reflected the angry mood, taking up the hue and cry until the refuge of darkness was afforded.

Yet they pressed on, the clearing around the cabin shorn, the harvest accomplished. Now it remained for the shocks to be gathered into the wagon, arranged in cone-shaped stacks, again to shed rain until the threshing.

It was not until when the wheat was safely garnered into the stack that Rolf took off one day to furnish the table with fresh meat.

※

He thought later that it was luck that he only wounded the deer, that he tracked it out of sheer ire at the perversity of things. Had he not pursued the deer so far afield, he would not have come upon the patch of ginseng. He had received another letter from Nicolena, who was not to be put off: "Don't try to trick me, Rolf Monsrud!" In happening on the ginseng patch, he had found the solution to his dilemma.

That the Indians didn't find it first, haven't carried it off, that's an even chancier bit of luck, he congratulated himself. The plant grew wild, and white traders, their keen noses always sniffing for profit, recruited Indians to scour the forest for beds of the plant, paying them a pittance for digging and delivering the roots and then selling them at great margin. "Elixir of Life" the coveted root was labeled for its rumored powers. Rolf, thinking of this, smiled to himself at the knowledge of the child now growing in Marit's belly. *I don't need ginseng,* he crowed to himself.

"If you see any Indians hanging around, take the gun and run them off," he told Marit when he got home.

"But why? They don't intend us any harm."

"There'll be plenty of harm if they find that ginseng patch!"

Ginseng patch? But she knew better than to ask questions.

Early the next morning he picked up his shovel and some bags and informed Marit that she was to come with him, for he could not get though the tangled underbrush with the wagon and oxen and they would have to walk the several miles to the patch and tote the roots back to the homestead on their backs. From the size of the patch, he judged that even with her help it would take several trips.

When they reached the patch, he dug and she gathered and piled. When a pile was about as much as they could carry each time, they sacked and carried them home. It was a long round-way hike; the venture used up several days.

When they finally had it all home, he made a trip to Rice Lake, a trading post to the north. There he drove a hard bargain with the trader. "No Indian deals," he warned; and when a price that was to his satisfaction had been agreed upon, he delivered the roots.

He watched the weighing carefully. Even so, his eyes widened when he looked at the sum on the check he received. He had made a killing! The amount was more than sufficient for the fares of the Dahl family to America. He lost no time in dispatching the passage money to Nicolena.

All things considered, keeping his end of the bargain was the wisest way out, he had decided. With Nicolena *here,* he could find ways to intimidate her. For example, there was little danger that America would make a new man of Nils: Nicolena would toe the line or find herself destitute in a wilderness! It would take years before his own sons would be old enough to take over some of the work, and by this time, Nicolena would have a couple striplings who they could fill in in the meantime. But, above all, let it never be said that Rolf Monsrud had to resort to trickery to get a good woman! And she was a good one, the last requirement met now that she was with child.

᯾

The time had come for the threshing. Parking the wagon next to the grain stack, they used its box as a threshing floor. Then hour after hour, day after day, they flailed away at the sheaves to free the wheat from the husks. When a bundle had been beaten clean, the straw was thrown off to the opposite side of the wagon from the stack. Slowly the grain accumulated around their feet, and from time to time they stopped flailing to bag it, storing the bags in the barn out of the weather, the barn not needed by the animals now during the warm months.

The loose straw would pile up beside the wagon until it teetered over the side, and from time to time Marit jumped down to fork it back, make room for more, a welcome break from the monotony of flailing. Although the work was tedious, she enjoyed these days. The leaves had turned, and the woods encircling the clearing was a huge chrysanthemum-hued garland with the interspersed pine a green, ferny accent. Occasionally she paused in her work to drink in the beauty around her and to revel in the warmth of the late season sun on her skin, sensing that summer's flagon was almost empty. She imbibed deeply of the dregs, these hazy days, as if to bolster herself with an inner glow against the onslaught of the winter hovering near.

She was glad that they got done threshing in time for Rolf to finish applying the last shakes to the roof of the new cabin before the minister's return. They would have time to move in and she could tidy up the loft for him so the embarrassing sleeping arrangements of his first visit would not have to be repeated.

❦

He arrived on Saturday afternoon.

The evening was uneventful. He and Rolf spent hours before bedtime visiting; a conversation in which she took no part, having no knowledge of the topic under discussion: the relative merits of various species of trees for specific purposes. It seemed that the Reverend Holm favored maple and Rolf favored oak but that they agreed that nothing beat pine for all-around usefulness. In listening, she mused over the minister's knowledge of these things. In the homeland, ministers lived a life apart from the common folk, confining themselves to the sublime, a plane that commanded respect. She wagered that there were subjects that might be more edifying for Rolf than lumber!

In addition to preparing a bed for him in the loft with a tick filled with newly threshed straw, she had contrived a makeshift desk so he could study his sermon. When he was ready to retire, she took a candle, carried it up and placed it on the desk and lit it, returning to the kitchen to say, "If you wish, I'll press your suit for the service tomorrow. Just hang it over the edge of the trap door."

"That will be fine," he said, mounting the ladder.

She put the heavy attached-handled irons on to heat. Out of a corner of her eye she saw the suit descend part way for her reach.

She pressed it with care; it had seen its best days. She also mended several tears and sewed on a loose button. She then climbed a couple rungs of the ladder and placed it where he could reach it upon arising in the morning. She could not help but notice that the candle was blown out. He hadn't studied long, if at all. She felt a vague disappointment.

The next morning she arose early and started to prepare breakfast, sparing no clatter. It did awaken him, and he came down the ladder, saying "I suppose that even on the Sabbath, industry is commendable."

While she was serving him breakfast, he remarked, "I hope the service will be well-attended."

"Oh, we'll have a houseful," she assured him.

After straightening the house and finishing her chores, she changed her clothes and slipped away. She had but two hours to meet the deadline.

❦

The time had come to start the service. The minister paced nervously around the table that Marit had covered with a white cloth in deference to the function it was to serve today. Only the Engliens and Rolf were present, the three of them, with the children, seated on the two kitchen benches that had been pushed back against the wall. But aligned with the kitchen benches was make-shift seating Marit had contrived of rough planks held up at the ends by chunks of block wood.

What on earth had become of Mrs. Monsrud and of the goodly crowd she had promised? The minister took out his pocket watch for the third time, studied its numerals as if they were hieroglyphics. He cleared his throat. "Let us hope there was not some misunderstanding about the time."

Just then the door burst open. Marit stepped in and held the door open for her followers. The faces of those in the room registered gaping disbelief.

When the last of the Indians had filed in, she shut the door and indicated they were to sit. Most found room on the rough benches, but those who didn't sat down to cross-legged postures on the floor. She went to sit by Rolf. Looking around the room, she noted with satisfaction that the cabin was indeed filled.

The minister, his face flushed, passed out hymnals to the Monsruds and Engliens, then went to stand by the table. He designated the hymn, took his pitch-pipe from his pocket and sounded the key. Then, with startling volume, he began to sing. The Engliens and Marit followed his lead, vapid and always a little behind, like garbled echoes.

The minister had lain the pitch-pipe on the table. One of the Indian men who was seated on the floor reached over, picked it off the table and examined it out of curiosity; he put it to his lips experimentally. The ensuing sound caused a commotion; several others wanted to try it. The singing faltered, carried along only by the strength of the minister's sonority, which rose to the occasion, for a few bars. Then the singing halted entirely when he desisted to restore order by retrieving the pipe and installing it safely in his pocket.

That Rolf did not throw them out right then was not of courtesy to the Indians but rather of deference to the authority of the minister, seemingly determined to carry on in spite of the alien element. They took their cue from him, profoundly ignoring the naïvete of the natives, and the service was carried through to completion. That it had been an ordeal for all was evident from the relief that shown on their faces when benediction was pronounced.

The minister having been granted his due, Rolf now shot forward and began boldly shoving the Indians out the door. Odin went to his aid, herding them out from the rear.

When the last of them had gone, the room was a fastness of silence. A little too brightly, Marit broke it by saying, "Well, now you see how much they need the Gospel, Reverend Holm!"

The Reverend Holm's Adam's apple rapidly rose and fell twice. Then he slowly folded his hands and in a remarkably calm voice said, "I do not feel it is my calling to minister to the savages. From now on, we shall confine our services to the converts!"

Marit invited the Engliens to stay and take their noon meal with them, and the hours following were passed as a pleasant social occasion, with no mention made of the fiasco of the morning.

Early the next morning in an air of guarded forbearance, the minister took his leave.

꧁꧂

It was a crisp morning when Rolf hitched the oxen to the wagon to begin the long trek to market with the grain harvest. The trip that would take the better part of a week with the nearest flour mill at Chippewa Falls, some fifty miles distant.

The first yield from his land a bounty crop at that! In fact, he had not had bags enough to contain it and, consequently, the bottom of the wagon box was covered with the loose excess, the sacked grain riding on top. It made for a heavy load and before undertaking the trip he had waited for the first frosts to penetrate the ground and lessen the danger of miring. Also, he watched the sky signs. For several days now the weather had been typical of Indian summer with frosty nights and days of thin sunlight.

He made good progress the first day. He noted with satisfaction that the wheels rolled freely, though roughly, over the firm surface of the ground. At this rate, he'd be on his way back to the homestead — grain converted to cash — even sooner than he had expected.

Marit had prepared food for the trip. Driving until darkness set in, he camped along the trail the first night.

During the night he was awakened by a rising wind; with misgiving he noted that the stars had inked out. He did not go back to sleep but paced impatiently until daybreak and, in the first feeble light of a red dawn, he started moving again.

The red sky portended a change in the weather, but if luck were with him he would be in a settled area by mid-afternoon and some farmer's shed could provide protection for the wagon and its precious cargo.

Early forenoon was a perplexing mix of cold drafts with snow flurries and then sudden warm currents that would send the ragged troops of snow clouds scudding. Toward noon, however, warmth prevailed. But all of a sudden a bank of blue-black clouds streaked with lightning loomed in the southwest, making it apparent that a thunderstorm was in the offing. He turned off the trail into a pine grove and parked in the thick of it. The trees would act as an umbrella until the shower passed.

The choking-blue cloud lunged on the grove, coughing out pellets of a cold rain mixed with sleet. He ripped branches from nearby trees and thatched the wagon with them to further protect the grain. Then, to escape the bombardment himself, he crawled under the wagon for protection.

Time passed.... he became uneasy. This was no ordinary downpour and there was a river to be forded. If this kept up, it would be too swollen to cross and he would be stranded, the harvest jeopardized by seepage.

Across the river there was a homestead, he remembered. If he could reach there.... He made a sudden decision. Breaking off more branches, he thatched the top of the wagon even more thoroughly, then led the oxen out into the storm.

The hard rain had driven the frost into the ground and the wheels now cut in and became encumbered with mud, making for a heavy drag on the oxen, which he lashed mercilessly. Laboriously plodding, they finally gained a corduroy stretch and as the wheels rolled over the logs they sloughed off the accumulation of clay. He felt relief; this corduroy stretch was the approach to the river.

He tried to see ahead to the water, but the downpour was such that he could see but a few yards ahead of him. Dropping the lead rope he ran ahead of the oxen to gauge the level of the river. Already it was higher than normal, but he must risk it. He whipped the reluctant oxen into the stream. The wagon lurched precariously as it passed over the last of the logs, then leveled out as the wheels found the rock-strewn gravel bottom.

They were not halfway across before he realized that the river was more swollen than he had thought. The oxen were up to their flanks in the water. But now there was no turning back; he forced them on. At midstream their feet went out from under them for a few seconds and they threshed wildly, then found footing again and pulled forward. They heaved with their effort; he, with relief.

But it was a fleeting security. Even as the wagon jolted forward he spied the current borne log bearing down on the wagon where it lagged behind the oxen in midstream. He yelled at the oxen to spur them on and they jumped forward, but too late. The tree trunk hit the side of the wagon with splintering force, and through the breach wheat sifted out into the brown water like sugar dissolving in creamed coffee.

He jumped into the flood to dislodge the tree from the wagon. Little by little he maneuvered it around to the back end, where it floated away down the river. But the effort had been wasted; water, entering through the breach, whirlpooled in the wagon box, and when the oxen finally shored it on the bank he saw that a whole year's work had gone down the stream. The bags remaining in the box were sodden and, therefore, unmarketable.

In a rage he threw the sodden bags to the stream, swung the oxen around and plunged back into the torrent. The nearly spent oxen floundered, the wagon weighing them down, until the rushing water had flushed it of the residue of grain. Then the empty wooden box floated, drifting until the oxen, towing it like a barge, finally gained the far shore some way downstream.

The freak lightning-and-ice storm had disquieted Marit, and when she saw Rolf returning with the empty, splintered wagon, it was as confirmation to her: An act of God. *I knew no good could come of laboring on the Sabbath,* she rationalized. But seeing that Rolf was fuming inwardly, she decided that this would be the wrong time to point this out to him.

Marit could not know that most rankling to Rolf now was the thought of the money he had sent to Nicolena. If he had kept it for himself, as a backlog.... But now it was beyond his reach, on the way to Norway. And he would have to do what all of the settlers had to do when caught in a financial bind: seek work in the pineries for the winter.

It was not that they would starve if he didn't. Marit's industry took care of the essentials. But it was not his intention to plug along in this fashion year after year. He foresaw that as the land was cleared — to be replaced by waving fields of grain — that the first man in the area to own a threshing machine would be in an enviable position. *He* intended to be that man, the man other men must defer to, the one in command! He had a head start on the others. Now he had been set back — unless he made it up.

There was one drawback: Being gone would mean getting less land cleared this winter. He vowed he would make it home every weekend, working nights and Sundays as he had before.

In the meantime, it was a while before he must leave, and in a fever of ambition he hacked down trees, limbed and dragged them away. The limbs he piled near the cabin as a source of firewood for the winter. Marit would have to chop them herself.

The day he left he told her, "Don't let any man in the house while I'm gone. Anyone! Do you understand?"

The winter before, rumors had sifted through of a marauder who preyed on isolated women left unprotected, their men away at the pineries. She took this warning as a concern for her safety.

CHAPTER IX

N ow all the footprints in the snow around the cabin were hers and the tracks soon became hard-packed trails that circumscribed her daily rounds. With Rolf away at the pinery, all the responsibilities of the homestead fell on her shoulders alone.

First in the morning came the walk to the barn to milk the cow and feed the livestock, after which she cleaned their quarters, hauling the debris away in the unwieldy homemade wheelbarrow to the pile outdoors and then bedding the dirt floor with fresh straw carried from the stack by the forkful. Next came the several required trips to the spring to carry drinking water to them, an interlude drawn out by the waiting as each animal took long draughts from the bucket. Each evening the morning's chores must be repeated, save for the barn-cleaning. But to make up for it, evening brought the task of chopping and carrying in the daily supply of firewood. Finally, the day's rounds come full circle, she would knit by candlelight until bedtime.

There was that gap between morning's chores and evening's in the afternoon; this was when she made her daily check of Sana and the children. She always went with both hands full, milk in one bucket and water in the other. As the spring was on her way, she saved Sana a trip.

The Engliens were in much better circumstances than they had been in the spring when Odin went on the drive. Besides being properly housed in the new cabin, staples were assured; half the lumberjacks' pay was issued in script that had to be exchanged for supplies at the company store, and Odin, upon receiving each month's pay, trekked home with a big bag of groceries on his back.

Sana's outlook had not improved with their circumstances, however. On the contrary, she seemed to be drawing more and more into herself. Some days she seemed unaware of her children.

Marit often had the urge to shake her, as one would a sleepwalker. This can't go on, she decided; it's bad for her but even worse for the children. If she would only take an interest in something — anything — outside herself.

Marit was knitting when the idea occurred to her. She had started a pair of mittens for Little Odin the night before, and that afternoon she carried the half-finished mitten along to the Engliens, together with yarn and an extra pair of needles.

"See the mittens I've started. I'm knitting these for Odin. But Alma and Hilda need mittens, too!"

There was not a flicker of interest. She went on in a more specific way. "I would like for you to finish these so I can get on to the others."

Still there was no response; it was as if Sana were deaf. *I'll never get through to her talking.*

She walked over to Sana, put the needles in her hands. Then, as one would steer a child through her first lesson, she put her hands over Sana's, guided her passive fingers through the stitches. Gradually the fingers began moving of their own volition. Marit took her hands away and the fingers knitted on.

She made a pretense of not noticing and played with the children. But from time to time she stole a glance over to where Sana sat. Now that she had gotten started, she was knitting as if her life depended on it, her eyes following her own flying fingers as if they were something apart from herself. When Marit left, she was still knitting.

When Marit returned the next afternoon, she found the mitten almost finished. "It must have a mate," she suggested.

Sana went on knitting, but after a long pause she monotoned, "I haven't any yarn."

"I have plenty for both of us."

Now Sana stopped knitting. A look of futility came over her face. "What's the use of any of it? It's all so endless...."

"The use of it is for your children. That's what's the use of it!"

Marit immediately regretted her impatient tone. She had made the mistake before of not being understanding, driving Sana's eyes further into her shell. In a gentler tone — almost pleading — she qualified, "And it's not just for them. I need you, too. I'll need your help when the baby comes."

Sana's eyes widened. "I hadn't guessed."

She hadn't intended to blurt it out. *Women never told....* But her embarrassment soon was overcome in the observance that this confidence had penetrated Sana's indifference. Sana was looking at her as if she were seeing her for the first time.

"Are you afraid, Marit?"

"Well.... It's just that I don't know anything about it. I wouldn't know what to do — if I was alone, I mean."

"I know how it goes. I've had three — as you can see. I know what has to be done."

To Marit's relief, she did not elaborate. This business of being delivered of a baby — the *indecency* it entailed — was a mental picture that she modestly shrank from.

The knowledge of Marit's condition now seemed to become Sana's one link with reality. It seemed strange to Marit that, whereas her helpless children evoked no concern in Sana, *her* need did. Not that there weren't still days when Sana was withdrawn, but she seemed never to forget that Marit was counting on her for when her "time" came.

From time to time Marit tried to stimulate her with new projects, but she showed no interest, persisted in knitting, the rhythm of it seemingly soothing to her. She often rocked back and forth as her fingers flew.

It was best not to rush her, Marit decided. To do so might be to lose hold of the one raveled strand to Sana's cocoon she held in hand. But that in time she would unwind the cocoon completely — that Sana would find her wings — she had no doubt.

❧

Having homesteaded in the heart of what was now the boom logging area, the men were within hiking distance of home and usually made it back for Sundays. However, there came a weekend in December when they didn't come home. It started snowing on Thursday, continued on Friday, and by Saturday the storm had developed into a full-scale blizzard with dropping temperatures and a wind that whipped the snow about making visibility almost zero. Marit had all she could do to find her way to the barn to do the chores and make her way back to the cabin. She dared not venture to go so far as the Engliens on Saturday and Sunday, and she trusted Sana would know better than to leave the shelter of their cabin.

On Monday the wind went down, the sky cleared. The sub-zero temperatures had formed a crust on the snow that carried her weight and she found the hike to the Engliens an easy one in spite of the deep snow.

When she reached the cabin, she found that the family had come through the storm in good shape, save that they had run out of spring water. But Sana had melted snow for drinking and cooking — a good sign. She had used her head! Sana was nearly out of meat, however. But the men would be home next weekend to hunt and in the meantime Marit would divide with her what meat she had left.

Again a weekend storm blew up and the men did not risk walking the trackless waste in a blinding snowstorm to come home.

❦

They had been without meat for five days. Marit had never fired a gun, but now she took Rolf's musket down from where it hung on the wall, raised it and sighted through the window experimentally.

She had watched Rolf load it many times. Boldly she got down the ramrod, powder and balls and went through the process of packing it. She stepped outside, aimed at a knot on a tree at the edge of the clearing, and fired.

She thought for a moment that the whole firepiece had blown up in her face. But when the smoke cleared, she saw that both she and the gun were intact. She walked over to the tree and checked her accuracy. Several inches off.... It was margin enough for a *big* target, such as the broadside of a buck.

She had seen the big buck several times. Always wary, he came to drink below the spring where the brush grew down to the water's edge, affording a screen. He came early in the morning, usually before her, his tracks often told her.

Tomorrow, *she* would be there first. Putting down compunction, she asked herself: What's the difference whether it's one of the men or me? It's a matter of necessity.

Early the next morning, she went to the spring with the bucket in one hand — as to allay suspicion — but balancing the loaded gun on her shoulder with the other. She put the bucket down, went to a little rise that overlooked the spring and crouched down behind a windfall.

In the first minutes of waiting, she could hear her own heart pounding in her ears so loudly in the utter stillness that she was certain the buck would hear it — a drumbeat that would signal danger to him, keep him away. But as the minutes trooped by to become nearly an hour, she became calm, even a little bored.

Then from her vantage point she detected movement in the brush across the creek. She pivoted the gun on the fallen log, levelled it at the point of movement. The brush parted, but is was the doe with the twin fawns. She had encountered them so many times that they had almost lost their fear of her. She would starve before she would shoot one of these and betray their trust!

She had noticed, however, that when these three came to drink, the buck was often close behind, seemingly using them as probes, letting them go ahead, and if all went well, following. So when the doe and fawns had drunk and left, she waited on, now tensely alert.

She saw his antlers first; blending into the brush so as to seem a part of the landscape except for the forward movement. Kneeling in the snow behind the log, she attempted to get him lined up in the sights. She hadn't realized until now that she was trembling. The bead bounced wildly as she tried to keep it on him as he moved forward.

Now some brush came between. She waited and spotted his antlers again. But then they dropped from sight. He was drinking. She would wait until he was done, started to move away....

He raised his head, surveyed the woods across the creek. Suddenly he bounded across, much closer to her. He hadn't seen her and was taking his time. But soon he would be gone. Her finger, frozen on the trigger, refused to move.

At the very edge of the woods he paused, broadside to her, his head up, nose quivering. It had to be now or never. Aiming at his heart, she clawed at the trigger.

In her precarious crouching stance, the blast and recoil threw her off-balance. She fell over backward on to a bush behind her, facing the buck. She saw him take one great leap, then sink. There was one heave — as if to rise — but his legs bucked under him. Then he lay still.

She too lay still; the scene frozen, save for the slowly spreading dark stain in the snow.

She was roused by a chill. She got slowly to her feet, walked to where he lay. The eyes still stared, unbelieving. She reached over to an evergreen, broke off a branch and covered them. Then she drew the honed knife from her apron pocket, unsheathed it and began the task of skinning and quartering.

It took four trips to carry the quartered carcass to the cabin.

It had become her habit this winter to walk to Pine Fork every two or three weeks, exchanging what little produce she had in excess, after sharing with Sana, for the few things she required and to pick up what little mail they received.

Infrequently, there was a letter from her mother. But one day in January, she was handed a letter addressed to Rolf in Nicolena's handwriting. Since Rolf had made such a point of her not opening mail addressed to him, she left it sealed. It would have to wait until he came home on the weekend.

Nicolena's letters were *always* addressed to Rolf, never to her. She wondered why this was so, since she and Nicolena had been close in the homeland. But the fact that Rolf never shared with her what was in the letters she thought nothing of. It was his way with everything — the silent treatment.

But this time, after he had opened the letter, read it and burned it in the kitchen stove, as he always did with Nicolena's letter, she ventured to ask, "Is there anything new at home?"

I may as well tell her now, he decided. "Nicolena and Nils will be here sometime in February."

She stopped stirring the gravy, the spoon poised in her hand, its contents dropping on to the hot stove top, sizzling.

"Coming? Coming *here?*"

"People sail for America every day."

With that, he sat down to the table, looked expectantly toward the pots on the stove. As she served him, questions were tripping over each other in her mind. If only she could have read the letter! How could he be so matter-of-fact about it? Someone was coming from *home!* And of *all* people, Nicolena and Nils! How on earth could they have managed it?

"Aren't you surprised? How could they...? Get the money, I mean. It takes a lot of money."

She may as well have asked it of an empty chair. He was eating. That was that.

She could hardly wait to share the news with Sana. So many times she had tried to encourage her by telling her it was just a matter of time. That someday the country would be all settled, the woods cleared away so they could look across fields and see neighbors, that there would be roads, churches and schools like at home.

But even better than home because here there was plenty for everyone!

But when she told Sana, her cloudy reflection was, "Even if they all come — all the Norwegians in Norway come — they'll all be swallowed up in this wilderness."

⁂

February was ushered in by several days of thawing weather that shrank the snowdrifts to less of dirty white. But only those uninitiated to Wisconsin winters would be so naïve as to be misled by the season's benign mood. The temperature again dropped to below freezing and new snow fell as if to blot out an error.

It was toward the end of the month that there was one of those winter nights when a full moon shining on freshly fallen snow made the outdoors almost as light as day, bright enough to make the progress of the man on the trail appear apelike from a distance. Massive shoulders stooped as if weighted down by the large hands at the ends of his long arms, which he held out from his body and swung as he walked.

At the turn-in to the Monsrud cabin he paused, his labored breathing forming a vapor cloud in the crisp air above his head. He stood for long minutes staring at the place, as if to read some meaning from the appearance. He made the decision to move on.

On down the trail, he rounded the turn and the Englien cabin came into view, a window gleaming yellow with candlelight. He moved into the tree shadows at the side of the trail to make himself less visible.

When he reached the turn-in, again he paused, still in the shadows. He watched the illuminated square for movement, figures moving about within. Seeing none, he started toward the cabin, staying close to the brush by the side of the path.

He gained the small clearing surrounding the cabin and again paused, watching the window. Assured, he skirted the clearing to the windowless side of the cabin. Then, stepping carefully to minimize the squeak of his boots on the snow, he crossed the clearing to the side wall.

He sidled slowly around the corner of the cabin to a window-wall and, flattening himself against the frame to avoid candlelight, he looked in....

Sana and the baby Hilda lay sleeping in full view, Sana on the outside next to the door, the baby next to the wall.

Ducking under the window to cross to the other side, he surveyed the wall opposite from where Sana and Hilda slept. Emboldened, he straightened up, looked directly across the room to the door opposite, studying the bar and catch.... One *good run, using his shoulder as a ram....* He stole around the cabin to a position a few yards back from the door.

Sana did not have time to cry out. It was as if the splintering of the door-bar and the rough hand clamped over her mouth came at the same instant. Then the heavy, heaving body boring into hers.

⚜

Wakened by a sound outside the door, Marit raised herself up on one elbow to listen.... There is was again! And a fumbling at the latch.

Whoever was there — if his intentions were good — would knock, would not try to gain entrance stealthily. She threw back the covers, tip-toed to where the gun hung on the wall and took it down. It wasn't loaded, but the intruder wouldn't know that, she reasoned.

At the door, she lowered the gun, put her ear to the crack to listen. Perhaps he had given up, left. But then, right by her ear there was a whimpering sound.

"Who's there?"

Her question was answered by the wail of a child — Hilda's voice!

She set the gun down and hastily slid the bar, throwing open the door; Sana and the three children stood outlined in the moonlight. The whimpering sounds were coming from *Sana.*

"Sana! What on earth... what are you doing out with the children at this hour of night?"

They stumbled into the room.

Marit crossed the room to the table, lit a candle and turned to face the four of them in the light. "And they aren't even properly dressed! Have you taken leave of your senses — bringing them out like this?"

She hustled the children into the bedroom, helping them into the bed and covered them before returning to the kitchen.

Her first concern had been the children. Now she turned her attention to Sana. Something had happened. *Fire!* They must have burned out. That would account for the children being half dressed, Sana's devastated look....

Sana was saying something. "The door... broke down... broke down the door...."

"You broke down the door? Got out? Was there a fire?"

"A man... broke the door...." Suddenly she sagged. Marit rushed to her, helping her to a bench.

Had this really happened or had Sana only imagined it? A nightmare... the result of her fear that "something was always about to pounce on her from the shadows under the trees?" But she had seemed all right just this afternoon....

Marit knelt by Sana, putting her arms around her. "Tell me exactly what happened."

"He laughed...." With that, she slumped against Marit. She helped Sana to bed, tucking her in with the children.

She had to ascertain. The children had snuggled down; she did not want to disturb them to question them. Better, if it *had* happened — if they had seen something — that they find forgetfulness in sleep, thinking of it as a bad dream.

There was only one way to find out. She put on her coat, tying a shawl over her head. She hesitated.... What if it were *really* so and he were still about? She picked up the gun, this time, loading it.

She went to the bedroom, pulling Sana to her feet again and steering her to the door. "Bolt it after me!"

She had no way of knowing if Sana comprehended except to go out, shut the door behind her and wait. This she did, but there was no sound of the bolt sliding.

From the outside, she shouted: "Bolt it!" She heard a fumbling, the sound of the bolt sliding. She tried the door; it was secure.

"Go back to bed." She listened; thought she heard Sana move away from the door and did not hesitate further.

When she got to the Englien cabin, the door was standing ajar. But Sana could have left it open herself, she reasoned. The candle still burned on the table; she stepped in, looking about the illuminated room. Off to the side lay the splinters of the bar. Sana had not imagined it — the door had been broken open! Still looking about the room she recalled that Sana, in fear of the darkness, always burned a candle all night. And there were no curtains on the windows.

She went out and started to walk around to the side of the cabin to examine the snow under the window. At the corner, fresh tracks coming toward the door met hers. A man's tracks. She pointed the gun out in front of her, stole around the corner of the cabin.

No one was in sight. But the snow under the window was trampled. She had figured right: He had made certain there was no man in the house, that Sana was alone — unprotected — when he had done.... *what he had done....* Seeing his tracks, guessing what had happened to Sana, suddenly she was outraged. Such a man should be brought to justice!

In her anger she did not stop to wonder where or how far "justice" might be. Her only thought was to catch up with him. She followed the tracks back around again to the door, found the tracks leading out and followed them. They were soon joined by the tracks leading in. He had left in the same direction from which he had come, down the trail past their *own* cabin. Had she not cut through the woods, she would have seen his tracks and *believed* Sana.

She began to run, the moonlight so bright she had no trouble following the tracks even at this pace. On and on, she went, in the night; time meant nothing. Finally on the crest of a hill she was brought up short by the sight of a figure in the shadows of the trees on the trail ahead.

He did not seem to be in a hurry. This inflamed her even more: *I'll bet this isn't the first time — and he thinks he's gotten by with it again!* She quickly closed the gap between them to a couple of rods.

She had planned no strategy; now she wondered: Should she call "halt"? With gun in hand, she felt confident. And if the *sight* of the gun was not persuasion enough, she would point it at him and threaten him with it.

But her mind was made up for her. Warned by a sixth sense, he suddenly wheeled.

She felt no fear — only an overwhelming revulsion. "Surrender or I'll shoot!"

He eyed her for a moment, then threw back his head and laughed. Sana's words came back to her: *He laughed.*

Her voice was coarse with anger. "This is not Sana. This is Marit Maas!"

Again he laughed. Then he started coming toward her. She sighted the gun on him. He knew she was bluffing, kept coming.... THOU SHALT NOT KILL. In black capital letters, the words streaked through her mind. But now he was almost upon her. Deliberately, she lowered her aim, shut her eyes and fired.

She heard his yelp of pain and was afraid to open her eyes. She saw in her mind the buck, mortally wounded, *a convulsing heap....*

She forced her eyes open, only in time to see him disappear into the woods, hopping. She threw the gun down on the trail and started to pursue. She reached the spot where he had turned in, splatters of blood marking his trail.

She had heard him cry out — a part of that blind moment. But now, in a wash of cold realization, her anger ebbed. He might be badly hurt, or even be bleeding to death!

She stood and listened. The silence of the forest sang in her ears. She jumped when a dollop of snow slid off a branch with a soft plop. She cupped her hands to her mouth — then dropped them again. *How ridiculous! He wouldn't lead me to him by answering even if he did hear me call!* Then, in a manner of making a pact, she said aloud, "God will have to look after *him.* I'll go to Sana."

Daylight was streaking the east when she reached home. She lifted the latch; the door was still barred. She heard the children's voices and pounded in the door. There was a scraping on the floor, then the sliding of the bar. When the door was opened, she found it was Little Odin who had let her in by pulling a bench over to the door to reach the bar.

On entering she was greeted by a chilling sight: Sana sat in the middle of the floor, the two younger children clinging to her, trying to get her attention. And she was completely unaware of them.

"Mama won't get up," Alma lisped.

"Why is she sitting on the floor?" Little Odin asked.

"Your mama is sick. We must put her to bed."

❧❀❧

Rolf and Odin came home as usual that weekend. But only Rolf returned to the pinery. Odin resolutely packed their belongings, rented a wagon and rode away with his family out of their lives, leaving it to the Monsruds to tidy up their affairs.

CHAPTER X

Rolf considered the rout of the Engliens a stroke of luck; Nils and Nicolena could pick up where they left off. The cabin, though too small for Nicolena's family, was ready for immediate occupancy, the Engliens having left everything intact: table, benches, cupboard, stove and the two beds built into opposite corners. Come summer, another room with a loft could be added to accommodate the overflow.

Marit, on the other hand, considered the Englien debacle a defeat. The cabin, with bits and tatters of their belongings left behind in the haste of departure, was as a scene of a lost battle, and she had put off coming to clean it as long as she could. But calculating from what little Rolf had told her that the Dahls could arrive any day, she overcame reluctance.

Ever since early morning she had cleaned, the only break in her industry the time it took to return home to refuel the fire and grab a bite to eat, and the latter mostly for the sake of the baby.

Sana had taken little interest in her home. A layer of debris had accumulated on the dirt floor; and even after she had raked, swept and carried out litter until the virgin earth was exposed, the cabin still had a musty odor.

She had the door wide open for ventilation. Now she went to the window and attempted to open it also and get more fresh air into the place. But the window wouldn't budge. It never had been opened, she concluded, brushing at the cobwebs unmolested spiders had spun.

Caught in one web was a butterfly of last summer, its wings torn in an effort to extricate itself. She disentangled it gently. *But I'm much too late,* she thought ruefully. She sat down to catch her breath.

As she sat turning the butterfly over in her open palm, its brittle wings flaking away, some long-forgotten words of her mother came back to her, words her mother had said many years before, when she was a child: "A butterfly that blew in from over the mountain...."

Her mother had used the words in speaking of Lena Monsrud, Nicolena's mother — and Rolf's. She could recall having seen her only once. When she was a little girl, she and her mother had encountered her one day on the street of the village, flitting nervously about in a vivid but shabby silk dress, sylphlike. So different from the other mothers of village, she was purposeful and plain.

Marit had thought her the most beautiful lady she had ever seen, but of a certain brittleness that she had sensed even then with the discernment that small children instinctively have, but later lose to logic. Now of that logic, she pondered Lena Monsrud.... Had she been trapped in the village, futilely beating her wings, a butterfly who might better have been set free in the outside world? And Nicolena, so pretty once, was this same trapped feeling the root of her discontent? So much so that she had found the way to escape, come to America?

Leaving for the day, she paused in the doorway.... *We were neighbors in Lilledalen; now we will be neighbors again.* She tried to visualize Nicolena in the room, but somehow she didn't blend. In memory, only her person stood out — detached, unrelated to the surroundings. *Well, anyway, now it will be Nicolena who will be with me when my time comes,* she reflected. There was conciliation in that thought.

She returned the next day to accomplish the finishing touches. She had bought material and made curtains for the two windows and the wall cupboard; these she now strung up on twine. Wanting to make the cabin as inviting as possible, she also had bought oilcloth to cover the unsightly silvered surface of the table, a luxury she had not allowed herself. But by now her own tabletop was worn smooth by sand scourings. She spread the cloth and stood back. In its shiny newness and bright colors it decidedly added a cheery note to the room, justification for the outlay of hard-to-come-by cash.

But the musty odor still lingered. On sudden inspiration, she went out into the woods, found a pine and broke off a big armful of branches, carrying them back to the cabin. Then, walking around the room, she pulled the needles off tuft by tuft, scattering them on the floor until it was carpeted by aromatic green. When she was through, the cabin smelled as pristine as all outdoors.

She reminded herself that the needles would have to be swept up before a fire was kindled in the stove. Aside from that, she was now in readiness for Nicolena.

❧

It hadn't seemed real that they were coming until she had readied the cabin for them. Now, with all preparations completed, she found herself looking down the trail many times a day. And when she wasn't looking, listening....

Even as she went about her barn chores, her thoughts were preoccupied with their coming, questions crowding her mind. Would they come to Millwood, hire a rig to bring them the rest of the way? Or would they come as far as Pine Fork, expecting Rolf to meet them there with the wagon? Did they know Rolf was away at the pinery? Did they know he had the oxen with him there so there'd be no way to haul them? If so, could they find someone at Pine Fork to haul them?

These were questions that Rolf could perhaps have answered had she asked him when he was home on Sunday. But more and more, especially since having been alone so much this winter, she was becoming as incommunicative as he. And left with all the responsibilities as she had been, necessitating that she make decisions, she found it less necessary to communicate with him.

As it turned out, the arrival took none of the speculated forms.

She had gone to the barn to gather eggs. Upon returning to the cabin, she was startled to find a man sitting in the kitchen. Her eyes momentarily blinded by snow glare, she did not immediately recognize him.

"Who invited you in?" she bristled.

"Now what kind of a welcome is that?"

"Nils!"

She rushed to the table, setting the eggs down so haphazardly that one rolled out of the basket and onto the floor, splattering her skirt. "Is it really you, Nils?" she said, shaking her head.

"Well who were you expecting?"

"I... where is Nicolena — and the children?"

She was afraid he would tell her that he had left them back in Norway and had come alone. But he ignored the question.

"I had one devil of a time finding this place. You're really back in the woods! What with wrong turns, back-tracking, I've been all day."

Remembering his complaining nature, she interrupted him.

"— Nicolena and the children, aren't they with you?"

"They're at Pine Fork." Then, before she could question him further, "Would you have anything to eat in the house? A man can't be expected to do with out eating."

It was understandable that he would be hungry after the long walk. She prepared food, questioning him as she worked.

"How did you get to Pine Fork?"

"We just followed the directions Rolf gave in the letter. The arrangements he made."

"What arrangements are there for getting Nicolena and the children here to the homestead? Rolf won't be back until Saturday night. And he leaves the oxen at camp."

"I should think he would've thought of that, too!"

He hadn't changed a bit, always shirking responsibility!

"Well now that you're in America, you'll have to start doing some thinking for yourself. There are no parish paupers here!"

This reminder — that he had lived on charity in Norway — would have shamed most men. But not Nils. He nonchalantly swung a bench around and, straddling it, sat down to the table, discouraging further conversation by stuffing his mouth so full that he could not respond without dribbling or gulping. The room fell silent except for the animal sounds of his eating.

Then, arising from the table with a manifest belch, he ambled to the bed in the next room and lay down. Soon, she could tell, he was asleep.

So eager was she to see the others that she considered setting out for Pine Fork. But there were the evening chores; and it would be dark by the time she got there and no arrangements for transportation could be made at night. So, on second thought, she decided to wait until morning, cognizant that the hospitality of the wilderness was such that someone at Pine Fork would take them in and give them shelter for the night.

She did the evening chores and returned to the cabin to find Nils still sleeping soundly — an aspect that irritated her. She shook him awake. "It's time you start back."

"Back! I'm waiting right there until Rolf comes."

"I *told* you Rolf won't be back until Saturday night and it's just *Tuesday* today!"

He rolled over, turning his back to her.

"Who will see to them tonight?"

"They'll make out."

Although that surety was a comfort to her, she saw no reason that it should be a comfort to him. She set about making supper. The smell of food lured him from the bed, as she expected it would.

She tried to rouse some concern in him for his family's well-being by nagging him while he was eating. It wasn't just this night's apparent indifference to their welfare; what was to become of them if he didn't change? The wilderness was an even more demanding taskmaster than the sea — and far more treacherous.

Frustrated, she finally fixed a pallet for him in the loft and he ascended the ladder heavily, leaving it for her to work out some solution to the family's dilemma by herself.

Of one thing she was certain: That she had no intention of waiting until the weekend to see Nicolena and the children!

Early the next morning after chores she set out for Pine Fork, leaving it for Nils to find his own breakfast. He would have to shift for himself or go hungry!

The store was the most likely place to get information and she went there first. It was as she expected. The storekeeper told her they had been taken in by a family in the village. A woman had noticed the stranded family on her trip to the post office. The merchant directed Marit to the woman's house.

When she reached the house, there was no need to knock. One of the children spied her through the window and the door burst open with cries of "Tante Marit!" The older ones embraced her, the younger hung back, not remembering her. Nicolena stood in the doorway holding the last addition, an infant.

Encumbered by the children, Marit did not reach her for some moments, but when she did, held out her arms to embrace. Nicolena drew back, a flush coming over her face. Marit took her hesitation as recognition of her condition. Pregnancy to Nicolena was a re-pugnant state.

"I'm so glad you've come, Nicolena!"

Nicolena returned her earnest gaze for but seconds, then

dropped her eyes evasively.

"It's so good to see someone from home," Marit went on, but Nicolena was looking past her for Rolf. "I came alone. I couldn't wait to see you and the children," Marit explained.

"Wait! Where's Rolf? And what are we waiting for?"

"I'm sure something can be arranged."

"It's been no easy matter, I tell you, herding this bunch all this way! And where has Nils taken himself off to?"

"Just wait a little longer. I'll see to things," Marit soothed.

She returned to the store. She had seen no teams on the street; most of the men were away at camp, their teams with them. But if there were rigs for hire, the merchant would surely know of them.

"There's a homesteader a little way out who might be able to help you," he informed her. "He's not able to go to the pineries — a bad back. He has an ox and a sleigh."

"Is he Norwegian?"

The merchant replied in the affirmative, then directed, "Just follow the trail west of town. John Hagen's place is the second one to the right — set back a ways."

She had brought no money with which to hire transportation, but she felt certain this detail could be straightened out later, that her word would be surety enough between *Norwegians*. So she optimistically headed out west of town, finding the place without difficulty.

A woman came to the door in response to her knock. After Marit explained the situation to her, the woman invited her in, saying, "My husband is here. It's best you talk to him about it."

Marit stepped inside and the woman started to repeat Marit's story to him, but he interrupted. "I heard."

"Couldn't we help them?" the woman asked. "We have the sleigh." She turned to Marit. "If the load isn't too big. We have only the one ox, and he's not too husky yet."

"Oh, it won't be necessary to haul their things today — just them. Rolf can take care of the other later."

"Rolf, did you say? Would that be Rolf Monsrud?" the man asked.

"Why, yes. Do you know my husband?"

He did not reply. Marit turned to the woman again. "It's that some of the children are too small to walk that far."

There was a flicker of sympathy in the woman's eyes. But then she detached herself by saying, "It's up to my man."

Now they both looked to him for a decision. He returned Marit's pleading look with narrowed eyes.

He seemed to have taken a sudden dislike to her. The stony silence was broken by the wife's saying, "Well, I suppose we shouldn't hold it against *them.*"

He ignored his wife, addressing Marit. "Your husband drives a hard bargain."

He must know Rolf all right! She waited for him to go on.

"I'll haul you and your friends on one condition. I want the next calf your cow drops."

Nonplused, she asked, "How did you know we have a cow?"

"Don't play dumb with me. You know very well what I'm talking about!"

"No I don't. I honestly don't." But she could see that he did not believe her.

This much was clear to her. This man had some dealing with Rolf and he felt Rolf had gotten the advantage. And now he was trying to get back at Rolf through her. Well, she could take the same tack his wife had and make it none of her affair, but Rolf's. "This is something you must settle with Rolf. You know it's not a woman's place to make deals."

"Take it or leave it. That's my price."

She started for the door. But if he wouldn't haul them, who would? And Nicolena already in a state.... With her hand on the knob, she decided impulsively, "Well, all right then. But only on one condition. That you don't tell my husband of this bargain."

"How do I know you'll keep your word?"

"I'm a Christian woman."

"And Rolf? I suppose he's a Christian, too."

"Everyone has to answer for himself — and herself."

For a moment, their eyes locked. He looked away first. "I don't know why I should, but I believe you."

꧁꧂

Within an hour they were on their way. It was as a gay outing. Nicolena, holding the baby, rode up front on the seat with the driver. The next two youngest children sat on some straw in the box behind the seat. And Marit walked with the three older children, who frolicked along in the sleigh tracks behind.

They reached the homestead in early afternoon and, before starting back, Hagen went into the barn. He came back to say, "From the looks of it, I'll be able to come for my calf in about three months."

Standing in the open doorway with the babble from the overflowing room in her ears, Marit hardly heard what he said. She waved him gaily on his way and with this gesture erased from her mind the postponed payment as an assignment from a slate, filed away for worry when test-day loomed.

There was much to be told of the voyage, but the children's wide-eyed interjections and elaborations broke chains of conversation into disconnected links. She did ask at one point, "How did you raise the money to come?" She didn't catch Nicolena's vague answer but it wasn't important anyway. They were *here,* weren't they? That's all that mattered.

And none the worse for the trip, it appeared. When Marit commented on this, Nicolena accounted for it by saying that they took a Norwegian vessel as "sadder but wiser" emigrants were writing back home to advise, then added: "You don't get across as fast, but they don't treat people like animals, like those on big English ships and some others. Besides, we had favorable winds."

The rest of the week sped in a bustle of voices, slamming doors and eating — always eating. It had long been Nicolena's solution to the problem of cramped quarters to shoo the children outdoors and they popped in and out of the cabin all day at Nicolena's bidding like jacks-in-a-box. Their appetites whetted by the exercise, huge quantities of food disappeared and Marit came to appreciate Nicolena's impersonal way of referring to them as "mouths to feed."

The festivity came to an abrupt end with Rolf's arrival late Saturday night, a homecoming to a house and bed so layered with bodies of varying sizes that he took himself out to the barn with a quilt to spend what remained of the night.

Up at daybreak, he came back to the cabin to instruct Marit, "Get a fire going in the Englien cabin;" to inform Nicolena, "We'll be back with the baggage before noon. You'll be settled in your own home tonight;" and to order Nils, "You come with me."

The older children had already sought out the cabin that was to be their new home. But now, on this bright Sunday morning, Nicolena for the first time set foot in it.

She took it in at a glance. "I won't settle for this!"

"You won't have to — for long," Marit assured her. "This was built only to serve as temporary shelter for newcomers like yourselves, until you can afford something better. And you will be able to better yourself here. This is America, not Norway. Pretty soon our thinking will be different."

"And I suppose I'll be able to think away that I've got six young ones, too! How are we all going to squeeze into this little place? One room!"

"I've been thinking about that. We have the loft — some could stay with us for the time being. That is, if it's all right with Rolf."

"It better be all right with him."

When Rolf and Nils returned, Nicolena lost no time in passing along Marit's suggestion to Rolf. "There'll be plenty of room," he told her. "Nils won't be here most of the time. A man has to get out to make a living. That'll leave four for one bed and three for the other, or however you want to divide it up."

Nils frowned, but Nicolena brightened. "I think I'm going to like America."

Late that night, after hours of helping Nicolena unpack and get settled, Marit picked her way home through the darkness. When she left their cabin, the children had all been settled down for the night and were asleep while Nicolena was setting bread for the next day's baking.

꧁꧂

Now, with the weaving in and out of Nicolena and the children, the pattern of Marit's life took on more variation. Nicolena had no fear of the forest and she came every day, bringing the younger children with her, simply to escape her own cramped quarters, it seemed, for there was no need for her to set foot outside. The two oldest boys, Arne and Lief, kept her supplied with wood and water, looking on the forays of the woods as great adventure and making of them a game by stalking imaginary beasts and Indians. Within days, it was as if they had never lived anywhere but in the wilderness.

Quite often, Nicolena would bring knitting or mending with her. Then she would sit for hours, visiting as she plied the needles. It was during one of these sessions, in the easy give and take of small talk, that Nicolena mentioned Thorn.

"I think what I miss most about home is the sea," Marit had said.

"That you can have. I've had all I want of it! The only one in our family with sea legs is Thorn."

She should have gone on easily with the conservation, passed off his dropped name as of no interest; but Marit found herself waiting for Nicolena to say more, hoping she would, but his name hung in the silence.

Nicolena scrutinized her face. Marit had not in any way given indication that she was unhappy in her marriage to Rolf or had regrets. Nor, obviously, had Marit any knowledge of the part she, Nicolena, had played in Rolf's winning her. Nicolena was emboldened to go on: "Thorn is doing all right for himself. The master bought a new boat and put him in command. Says that when she's paid for herself, she'll be all his. Such a thing has never been heard of in Lilledalen before! Things just seem to fall into Thorn's lap! He'll be a master himself one of these days."

"If Thorn was offered such a deal, it's because he earned it!"

She shouldn't have sprung so quickly to his defense. Marit felt her face go red.

Nicolena didn't miss it. Marit still had a soft spot for Thorn! And the soft spot was her invitation for a barb. "It's too bad you didn't wait for *him*. Just think, you might have been a master's wife!"

"In America, there are no masters," Marit quickly parried. "Here, anyone who is willing to work can have his own domain, become a king in his own right."

"And I suppose that when Rolf becomes a king, that will make you a queen! That's one up on being a master's wife, I'll have to grant. But then, you always have held your head mighty high! All it needs is a crown."

The personal attack was so unexpected that it bewildered rather than anger her. As long as Marit had known her, Nicolena had been bitter, but now she was becoming vindictive as well! The insight braked her emergence from behind the impregnable wall she had built against Rolf's insensibility. It had the effect of shoring up her defenses, now against Nicolena as well as Rolf. And it had seemed so good to have someone to talk to at last!

In the days after the conversation, Marit found her thoughts turning to Thorn in spite of herself. She had buried him — alive to be sure — but buried. Now Nicolena had resurrected him. But Marit was confronted by a phenomenon: She could not recall his features distinctly. At first this intrigued her, then irritated her. He had *always* managed to elude her somehow!

Her time was drawing near and she welcomed the help Arne and Lief gave her, the chores becoming more of a burden every day as a result of Rolf's bartering.

The business of getting half his pay in script that had to be exchanged for goods at the company store never had been to Rolf's liking, so he devised a way to turn that portion of his pay into hard value. Many of the men who labored in the pineries had big families to feed and the pay was barely adequate, so he would exchange the script for such staples as he knew were most in demand, then barter them for whatever his hard-pressed fellow workers had to offer. In this way, he had not only acquired a wider assortment of tools, but more livestock as well.

In ones and twos a small flock of sheep had been accumulated that winter. Marit eyed their heavy fleece covetously. They would be sheared when warm weather arrived. Her spinning wheel, so long idle, would finally hum.

CHAPTER XI

For two days she had twinges in her back, but having no knowledge of the birth process and thinking them but a part of the discomfort of the last stages of pregnancy, she had gone about her work as usual.

And she had been unusually ambitious this day. The sun was bright and spring was in the air, and she carried all the bedding outdoors for airing. Afterward she scoured the oak plank floor on her hands and knees until the wood grain stood out like giant fingerprint whorls.

As she worked, she was obsessed by a craving for warm bread

crust slathered with butter. She could almost taste and smell its nut-like crunchiness. So although she usually set bread at night so as to have a head start the next day, she set a batch. It would not be out of the oven until late and in her mind all the roads of the day converged at one point, the moment when she would take the warm loaves from the oven.

It was when she was in the barn doing the evening chores that she felt the first pang, a cramp of fleeting duration. She halted her rhythmic forking of the hay, stood waiting expectantly. When nothing happened, she went on with the chores until she was finished. She was back in the cabin when the next pang came.

So this is how it starts.... Sana had asked her if she was afraid; she was surprised at her calmness. She got out the list that Nicolena had given her, methodically assembled the supplies — cloths, scissors, cord — and laid them out. She looked over to the water stand. Thanks to Lief and Arne, there was a good amount of water. She made up the bed with clean linens, sponge-bathed herself, combed her hair and bound it up tightly.

Her preparations were interrupted from time to time by the insistent spasms. But the bread was not ready to go in the oven yet; it must rise to the top of the pans. *It really isn't so bad yet — I have time for the bread....*

She waited until the bread had finished rising, put it in the oven before she started down the path to summon Nicolena, cutting through the woods. But just where the path left the clearing and entered the trees, she was gripped by a throe so paroxysmal that she doubled up and sank to her knees. Startled by the intensity of it, she pondered her situation....

It was not yet fully dark; twilight lingered a long time these days. *But I might not make it to Nicolena's, might be grounded between here and there... have the baby in the woods....in the darkness of night....* She decided not to risk it, returning to the cabin.

Maybe if I am still it will let up, pass....then I will go.... She lay down on the bed. The contractions, however, became more intense. *Maybe by chance Nicolena or one of them will venture up. If it hadn't been for that silly craving for bread....I waited too long.*

She tried to remember what she had heard of birth, but the experienced spoke of the ordeal only in dark hints. It was only by going through it that a woman knew.

Eden's curse.... Of this she had been informed. *But this is the way all human beings come into this world.* She considered that: All the people she knew or had ever known, all the people on earth and in it, thousands of people, millions of people.... She tried to hold onto the thought, forge a bond with all humanity in her situation. But in spite of the truism, she felt singular, a world to herself....

The hours dragged by and the smell of the burning bread seemed but a part of the searing gauntlet through which she was passing, until she began to cough on the smoke. She managed to get to the door and opened it. It was then, in the waft of cold air that cleared her head, that she remembered the bread. She made her way to the oven in the darkness, snatched at the loaves with her bare hands, letting them drop to the floor and got back to bed.

Later, she again rose, lit a candle. The loaves lay on the floor, in form perfect, but black char.... She crawled back to bed.

She had craved bread.... She had desired Thorn.... The bread had burned, its vitals seared out.... She was on fire.... She could feel the flames burning in her back... Twisting and convulsing on the bed, she screamed her protests to the night....

Nicolena stirred in her bed, awakened and listened. She thought she had heard one of the children cry out. But the sound came from the night outside the window. She lay back, turned over and went back to sleep. It was not unusual at night to hear a wolf's lament in the vastness of the wilderness.

It was Lief who found her in the morning; the baby had not yet been born. "Get Nicolena — get your ma," she gasped at him. He turned and ran knowingly. The eldest, he well knew the significance of a bulging stomach.

Nicolena is coming... finally coming.... She relaxed in the knowledge, giving in to the giant fist that grabbed her body and clenched until she groaned with the pressure. When Nicolena reached the door she heard the familiar wail, the vocal protest of the newborn against the ways of the universe.

It was as an affront to her. "Well! Aren't you the smart one! With most, the first isn't so easy."

But Marit's interest was all in the squirming red noisiness that Nicolena held in her hands. She raised her head.

"It's a girl. This isn't going to set good with Rolf. He was expecting you to give him a son."

Boy or girl — what did it matter! Nicolena put the baby beside Marit. She took one of the tiny hand in hers. "So perfect...and so small, so unbelievably small!"

"She is a small baby," Nicolena affirmed. "A Monsrud, I'd say."

Nicolena took the baby away to wash and bind it. Marit lay back, exhausted but sublimely fulfilled. She had never remonstrated against the quirk of fate that had placed her in this wilderness thousands of miles from home and married to a man she didn't know. But she had pleaded for this comfort of a baby to hold. She drifted into a contented sleep.

She was awakened by Nicolena's insistent prodding. "You have to be bound, too."

She submitted to the binding, lifting her body by her legs so the strips of cloth could be wound round and round her middle.

"I can hardly breathe."

"Good! That means I've done a good job. The tighter the better!"

"Why?"

Nicolena, playing to the hilt her role as High Priestess in the initiation to the secret order of Motherhood, gave no explanation other than, "Because it's a part of it, that's why."

When Nicolena had finished, she was winded and sat down to catch her breath. In a pre-biased tone of voice, she said, "I suppose you've already picked out a name."

"I was so sure it was going to be a boy...."

"I could've told you from the way you were carrying it that it was going to be a girl."

"But since it is a girl, I think I'll name her after my mother. She'll never see her, but when I write and tell her, it'll make her feel close to her."

"I think it would be more fitting to name her after my mother, in memory. In fact, she has a strong resemblance to my mother."

"It's a little early to tell, isn't it?"

"I've seen enough babies. I should know!"

❦

Nicolena spent the forenoon with her, then went home to attend to her own household duties, returning late in the afternoon to spend the night. She brought the children with her, bedding them down in the loft and came down herself to sleep with Marit. When she heard Rolf come home in the middle of the night, she got up and lit a candle.

He came into the kitchen and paused upon seeing Nicolena there.

"Well...?"

"It's a girl."

He did not approach the bedroom. He turned and went back out again, slamming the door behind him. Marit, hearing it, pulled the baby closer to her as if to make up for the slight.

"Pay no attention," Nicolena said. "He'll get used to the idea. There's not much else he can do."

He did not come back into the cabin that night. In the morning, Nicolena parted the curtain, looking out. "I think he slept in the barn. I see him fussing around out there. I'll fix breakfast and call him."

He ate sullenly. Nicolena waited until he was done, then chided him. "You haven't even looked at her! Take a good look. I think she's a Monsrud."

He stood up from the bench, walking over to the bedroom door, and looked over to the bed. Marit pulled the coverlet back from the little face, holding her up. He made no move to go closer.

"I was telling Marit, I think she's the image of Ma! That she should name her after her memory."

He stood stock-still, save for his fists, which he clenched until the knuckles turned white. Marit apprehensively pulled the blanket back over the baby's face.

"Well... what do you think?" Nicolena persisted.

"Call it anything you want. It's the same." He went out again.

The evident intensity of his reaction disturbed Marit. *Surely he can't hate her that much for being a girl, his own flesh and blood.* After minutes, she said, "We could name her after both of them...."

But Nicolena had lost interest in names. "I don't know what's gotten into that man!"

Nicolena decided to sleep at home that night. Before leaving, however, she put everything that Marit might need during the night within easy reach of the bed, warning her not to set foot on the cold floor.

Sometime in the night, Marit knew, Rolf left for camp again.

❧

Before Nicolena returned the next morning, Marit rolled to the side of the bed and sat up, putting her feet on the braided rug by the side. Her legs tingled, as if they had been "asleep." She swung them as one would to restore circulation to members that had been numbed by a cramped position. The prickling sensation passed. She tried to get to her feet, but in its tight casing, her body was unwieldy and would not bend. Using her arms as crutches, she managed to push herself to a standing position. Like pry-poles against a log, she thought impatiently.

On her feet, she had a moment of unsteadiness, but she ventured some steps. After a couple of turns around the room, she steadied. "I'm as good as new," she said to the world in general. "If it weren't for that *sausage* feeling!" She sat down on the edge of the bed and in several minutes of gymnastic unwinding, she managed to undo Nicolena's painstaking masterpiece. The bindings lay in a pile at her feet when Nicolena walked in.

Nicolena let out a horrified gasp. Marit, now unhampered, got to her feet and, exhilarated by the unaccustomed feeling of featherlightness and freedom, she did a couple of whirls.

"You sit down this minute and let me bind you again!"

"But I feel perfectly well! There's no reason why you should be waiting on me hand and foot like I was an invalid — really sick. You have plenty to do with your own."

"Do you want to ruin yourself?"

"Do you know that all squaws have their babies and get right up and go back to their work as if nothing unusual had happened at all?"

"They're animals!"

"They seem to be built the same as us."

"Well, if *you* want to put yourself in their class, go ahead. But leave *me* out of it."

Marit began to make the bed.

"And since you don't need help, I'll be going."

At the door she turned, warning, "You'll pay for your foolishness some day. Just wait and see!"

Later that day, Lief and Arne came as usual, carried wood and water, did the chores. She wondered if their miffed mother knew.

❧

Burgeoning spring sprouted a worry that had lain dormant: Soon the cow would drop her calf. Because of the bargain, what might have been cause for celebration now loomed as a crisis.

It would not be such a big worry if Rolf were still at the pinery. Then she could just let the homesteader know and he could come for the calf, leaving it for her to reckon with Rolf when he discovered the loss, which might not be for some time since tending the cow was her chore. But the thaw had put an end to logging, the winter's harvest was now being fed to the rivers, and Rolf had not gone on the drive.

She came to the barn one morning to find the cow licking her calf — a heifer. More the sorrow! Immediately she decided she would make a trip to Pink Fork and inform the homesteader that the calf had been born, that it would be delivered to his place. That way she would forestall his coming for it when Rolf was home, a confrontation that must be avoided. That Rolf would confront her when he discovered the calf was gone was a bridge she would cross when she came to it. She had given her word, and was determined to keep it. She would lead the calf to Pine Fork herself.

It could not be right away; the calf had to have mother's milk for some time first, a factor that the homesteader had taken into his reckoning. In the meantime, they would seed the grain and then, if Rolf ran true to last year's pattern, he would celebrate the accomplishment with an all-day outing. That would be her opportunity. That would be the day she would deliver the calf to Mr. Hagen.

❧

On that day, the weather was mild and although she had left the baby with Nicolena on previous occasions of trips to Pine Fork, she decided to carry her along on this trip. The outing would do her good and, besides, she wanted to show her off to Amelia. So, knotting a blanket to fashion as a sling so she could carry the baby on her back Indian style, and tying a rope around the calf's neck, Marit set off.

She saw right away she was going to have trouble. The calf did not want to leave its mother's side; she had to pull it forcibly out the barn door. And once she dragged it out, it found its legs, galloping a merry-go-round at the end of the rope, kicking up its heels in the joy of the frolic. She could only stand holding onto the rope — an axletree — until the novelty wore off. Then she moved out of the yard, the calf's stubborn hooves leaving a trail of dots and dashes in the dirt.

From time to time the calf found a second wind, gamboling intermittently. But in the contest of wills, superior strength was her ally. When need be, she simply dragged it along. When she stopped midway to nurse the baby, the calf flopped exhaustively down and napped. It took considerable prodding to rouse it, get it back on its feet and moving. But some time after noon, her mission was completed.

She had a sudden feeling of release, not just from being unencumbered by the calf; but with having finished with the matter — having done the right thing. She was in a lighthearted mood when she arrived at Amelia's.

The visit heightened her elation. Amelia gave the baby a gratifying amount of admiration and when she told her the name she had selected — Randilena — Amelia exclaimed in approval unlike Nicolena, who had wrinkled her nose in the distaste. Refreshed by the visit, she covered the miles home swiftly. But reaching there, she saw with misgiving that Rolf had beaten her home.

He was standing in the yard, studying the calf's tracks in the dirt.

She may as well tell him now, have it all over in one day — the matter concluded once and for all. "The calf is with its rightful owner."

He looked at her not comprehending. "John Hagen," she emphasized.

His face turned livid. "He came here and took it!"

"I led it to him."

For a moment he was unbelieving. Then, with doubled fist, he came toward her. She thought he was going to strike her, defenseless with Randilena in her arms.

But he drew up his fist within inches of her nose and shook it vigorously in her face, shouting, "Don't you ever interfere in my business again."

"I gave him my word."

"Your word means nothing! A woman's word means nothing. *No* woman's word!"

With that, he jumped back on the wagon, to which the oxen were still hitched, and left in the direction of Pine Fork. He did not return until late in the evening. When she went out to the barn in the morning, she found the calf back with its mother.

She had tried. But that thought was not enough to put her conscience at ease. Perhaps she had overstepped a wife's province by making a deal in the first place, she acknowledged. But she had given her word, and nothing she had ever read in the Bible gave her the solace that, on that *day,* the husband would answer for the wife.

The next time she went to Pine Fork, she again sought out the Hagen homestead. It was then she learned the whole story from beginning to end, with herself put on the carpet as an accomplice.

She would not live with this guilt for the rest of her life! She was appalled at Rolf's ruthlessness. Yet she was careful to not make it seem she was sliding against him when she came to an agreement.

She left the original deal out of it. That was Rolf's doing. The thing *she* had promised was a calf. She insisted Hagen set a price on it, took his word for its worth.

Thereafter, each time she went to Pine Fork to sell produce, she detoured past the Hagens on the way home, paying each time what she thought could be spared without notice, until the pittances had counted up to the full amount. By that day, the calf had become a cow.

༺✦༻

The summer sped by and it became apparent, if nothing unforeseen occurred, Rolf would not have to go to the pineries that winter. It was a good wheat year and the harvest went well. So as not to have a repeat of the previous year's folly, Rolf had invested in a large canvas. Now let the demons try to rob him of his harvest! He left for market in an amiable mood.

It was late in the season but the withdrawing sun benevolently tossed thin, golden coins of unlit days in the wake of the chariot, days that Marit revelled in, left to herself with Randilena and time that was not at Rolf's disposal, but her own. She spent hours outdoors with the baby, gathering the shiny mint days to revert as a hedge against the leaden ones of winter.

❧❀❧

It was on the day that she expected Rolf back that a man stopped at dusk and asked for a night's lodging. This was not an unusual occupancy. This summer had seen a noticeable increase of wayfarers, mostly on foot, and many had spent the night. If Rolf were in a mood for conversation, he would invite the man in and bed him down in the loft. At other times, he would send him to the barn with a blanket, particularly if he were not Nowegian.

This man was Norwegian and had a kindly face. She felt assured that she had nothing to fear from him and invited him in for supper.

Usually on these occasions, Rolf did all the talking and she remained in the background, gleaning what interesting tidbits she could from listening. But now, alone with their guest, she attempted to draw him out while she prepared food for him. But he was not a man given to glib conversation, seeming to have a load on his mind. However, with tactful prodding, she put together his story in the course of the meal.

His wife had died on the ship of passage, leaving him with an infant son. He had but three dollars in this pocket when he disembarked and knew no one in America. So when a family who had shared the voyage offered to take the baby, he had thought it best. All he knew of them was their name and that they were bound for Dakota Territory.

He had found work in New York splitting wood and had worked at this until he saved the money for the railroad fare to Chicago. Last winter, he had worked at a lumber camp in Michigan but the company held back his pay until spring. Then, the concern's owners being of shady character, they had not paid up in full. He had received ten dollars above his board for the winter's work.

Marit was bewildered by this. She had come to look on lumber in the same light as the manna by which the children of Israel were fed when *they* wandered in the wilderness. "I suppose there are a few bad apples in every barrel," she conceded.

All summer he had worked his way westward, hoping eventually to reach Dakota and locate his son.

When it came time to go to bed, she didn't have the heart to send him to the barn. "I'm expecting my husband home any time," she told him. "I'm sure it will be all right with him if you sleep in the loft. We often bed down travelers there."

She was awakened by Rolf's arrival. She had left the door unbarred and she heard him come in. She was aware that he lit a candle and then, as had always been his strange habit when he came home in the night, she heard him moving about as if searching for something. She heard him go partway up the ladder.

He came down again and burst into the bedroom. "I knew it, I knew it! You're all alike!" In the garish light of the candle he held before him, his face had a grotesque, twisted look. He set the candle down, turned and rushed from the room again.

She jumped from bed, just in time to see his feet disappear through the trap door above.

It all happened so fast. The man came half-falling down the ladder, catching himself and bounding for the outside door in his underwear with Rolf right behind him. His clothes were wadded up in his arms.

As when at night a bolt of lightning in a flash reveals the familiar in an altered light, she saw it had not been for her safety when he warned her never to let men in the house when he was gone!

"I hate you for this! Hate you... hate you!" she screamed at the door through which he had disappeared.

Startled from her sleep, Randilena wailed piercingly from her cradle. Marit went to her, picking her up and comforting her.

"It's all right. It's going to be all right."

With Trees on Either Hand

PART II

CHAPTER I

Two heads were bent over a book. Lamplight glow sparked copper in the hair of one and deepened the dark brown tresses of the other to black. The coppered one was deciphering aloud an *Eclectic Reader,* and the other stood beside her listening, helping when she stumbled over a word.

When the reading of the passage was completed, Marit turned to her bright-eyed tutor and asked, "How did I do this time?"

"Well... pretty good."

"You don't sound so sure."

Randilena sighed despairingly. "Mama, when are you ever going to stop rolling your *r's?*"

Marit laughed. "Is that all! From the look on your face I thought I had made some horrible mistake."

"Those *r's* of yours are a dead giveaway. *Anyone* could tell you came from the old country!"

"And what's wrong with that?"

But Randilena had lost interest, her mercurial mind already on to something else, she darted into the next room. Marit looked after her and smiled indulgently. Obviously, the lesson was over for this evening!

She set the book aside and reached for her mending basket, glancing over at Rolf who lay on the brown leather couch in the corner with his eyes closed, his head resting on the raised end. Was he only pretending to be asleep? Had he listened to her reciting of the lesson? She couldn't tell; his face was vague in the shadows of the corner.

She looked about the room, squinting to see. How dark it got at night! By contrast, in the daytime the kitchen was flooded with light from three windows. In that light, the kitchen range glowed velvet black and resplendent with mirroring nickel, the varnished oak table and chairs glowed golden and, in the glass-fronted cupboard, ranks of dishes glittered on perpetual dress parade. She turned from the room and bent her head over the mending in the pool of light at the table.

It was now nearly a year since they had moved into the new house, yet, she still sometimes — as now — looked about herself in disbelief. When the house was finished, it had seemed so grand in Rolf's eyes that nothing short of all new furnishings would do; he could not bear to see it sullied by as much as one shabby article. She had been staggered when he returned from a business trip with the heaped-up wagon of furniture, had stood back disapprovingly when he and Lief had carried it in piece by piece and arranged it to his liking. Hadn't he proved enough with the house itself, a house in the manner of a Boston sea captain, authentic even to the railed widow's walk on the peak, a house that stood out like a peacock in the flock of settlers' cabins that now dotted the area, a house that was really bait for newcomers?

For in recent years, the trickle of land seekers had swollen to a stream and Rolf, in seeming benevolence, made them welcome. Many found their first shelter under the ample roof of the Monsruds with Rolf relishing their surprise at such a fine home in the newly settled area. He led them to believe that they too could achieve what he had in a short time, talking up the opportunities of the area and encouraging them to settle nearby. With his cattle and machinery, he was in a position to capitalize on their needs. As strangers they could not know that the hand of friendship he held out could become an iron grip and, once he bonded to them, benevolence fled.

Yet, apparent as Rolf's motives were to Marit, it did not deter her from welcoming guests. She felt it her Christian duty to offer shelter, and should they stay to settle, she found ways to compensate. Well remembering her own first winter on the homestead when a fresh egg or pat of butter would have been a more welcome sight than a gold nugget, she went visiting carrying homely gifts of food. She took the occasion of these visits to inform them of the next scheduled visit of the minister, inviting them to her home for the occasion. For as it had from the beginning, their home served as the church, a church proper not to be built until the congregation could support a full-time minister, one who would reside in the community.

If the new house had a redeeming virtue, this, to Marit, was it: It served well the purpose of a *house of worship,* laid out as it was so the parlor could be thrown open by sliding the paneled-oak doors back into their slots in the framework, making of the two front rooms almost one, so any overflow could spill into the dining room and still participate.

And the monthly circuit meeting had come to play a much broader role in the life of the community than simply that of a religious exercise. The morning service was but a prelude to long hours of social interaction throughout the rest of the day.

After the service, the big pedestaled round oak table was grasped at each end and extended to facing half-moons, the gap filled in with leaves to form a generous oval, spread with a white cloth. Then the women carried in the pot-luck contributions they had deposited in the kitchen upon arrival and kept warm by the range during the formalities.

First the older children passed round and filled their plates, carried them to any convenient sitting place, usually the open staircase where they would seat themselves choir-arrayed. Next the men would seat themselves at the big table, and the women would serve them. After everyone else had been fed and the toddlers appeased meantime with some tidbit in hand, the women ate with the younger children in the kitchen what variety was left.

The meal over, the women did the dishes and the men retired to the parlor to visit and smoke their pipes. The boys were shunted outdoors to let off pent-up exuberance and the girls usually followed Randilena upstairs to share secrets and peek from behind curtains at the boys who frolicked in the yard below, their antics animated by the telltale curtain shifts that told them they were being watched. The young ladies made like matrons in the kitchen and the young men like peers in the parlor with their elders. But there was considerable flirting with eye and blush through the open doors and the monthly service had spawned at least one romance that had hatched a wedding.

The dishes from the noon meal would hardly be put to rest in

the cupboard before the huge gray granite-ware coffee pot was put
on the range to heat. The children snatched their afternoon lunch
from the kitchen table, but the men-folk were served their coffee
in the parlor where they sat, the circulating women causing no lag
in the conversation, snatches of which fell ambiguously on the ears
of the women-folk as they served.

"...nineteen-thousand acres skinned..."

"...four million acres — one-eighth of the state — where did it
all go?"

"...big forties..."

"...lumber sharks..."

"...the land commissioners in Madison..."

"...ten cents an acre..."

"...political henchmen..."

The women were content to let the *men* talk politics. But back
in the kitchen they might at the same time be deploring the long
miles the children had to walk in the bitter cold of winter to the
widely scattered schools, not realizing that they too were talking
politics: the corruption in Madison that had cheated the children
of millions of dollars in school funds, first in the timber pillage of
school endowment lands and then in the dissipation of twenty-five
percent of the accrued school funds in bad loans. It was only now
with the rising levies of school taxes and sifted rumors of scandal in
Madison reaching them that the men had become incensed — much
too late.

After several refills of coffee, the gathering up of the lunch dishes
was as a warning bell for departure, the interlude lasting only as long
as it took for the women to again do up the dishes. Then it was to
the rigs and dispersal and, for most, isolation for a month.

Nicolena, however, always lingered on some pretext such as, "It's
not right for them all to run off and leave you with a messy house."
She went about mincingly gathering up stray crumbs. But Marit
knew she was only trying to prolong the pleasurable day, one in four
or five weeks of unrelieved monotony.

Not that Nicolena was the only woman whose life was monotonous. For nearly all the women, life was a treadmill of work, the
pace slackened only from time to time by child-bearing, or the
rhythm altered by the equinoctial shifts of their men-folk from pinery in winter to homestead in summer. But, unlike Nicolena, most

were sustained by hope, a trust that their labor would assure a secure future for them and their children, a consolation Nils' shift-
lessness precluded for Nicolena. For when summers came, the time
that Nils should have spent developing the land was frittered away.
He found some excuse to walk to town every day, making his tot-
tering way home again in the wee hours; then slept late, getting up
in a surly mood and complaining about all the mouths he had to
feed while he wolfed down food with the children waiting on the
sidelines. Having fueled himself, he would thunder at them his orders for the day, then leave again. Winters were but little better,
but in the stipulation that half his pay had to be taken in trade at
the company store, there was surety of food on the table, though a
limited amount. "I'm actually glad when fall comes — when he
leaves," Nicolena once told Marit. "He's no help when he's home
and at least it's peaceful when he's gone!"

The children now numbered a dozen and with each birth,
Nicolena had become more bitter. Conversely, as Marit had held
each of Nicolena's new ones in her arms, she had coveted it, for
after Randilena there had not been another, an insufficiency that
made her feel a failure as a woman. "You're so lucky, Nicolena!"
she had once blurted out.

"That's easy for you to say — you, with your big house and
fancy furniture and no one to mess things up for you!"

Nicolena disregarded the fact that Marit had opened her home
to Nicolena's children. They would start coming early in the day,
sometimes in time for breakfast, and often spend all the daylight
hours, taking their noon meal there as well, while Nicolena took
no notice of their coming and goings. She simply prepared meals
and put them on the table. Then it was everyone for himself until
the set amount of food she prepared disappeared. If for a particular
meal there were less at the table, those who were there got greater
portions; when there were more at the table, the portions were just
stretched a little further. Once, upon dropping in at mealtime, Marit
had been shocked to find the children fighting over food like animals.

They still lived in the log cabin. The children had slept on the
floor of the loft in rows on straw ticks until just recently, the quilts
covering their bodies overlapping like shakes on a roof. Not really
too austere an arrangement, for with the heat sifting up through the

cracks in the floor and the chimney running through, the loft was the warmest place in the cabin. But Marit had become concerned about the lack of privacy for the maturing girls. "I think it's time the girls have a room of their own," she suggested to Nicolena.

Nicolena had taken it as a moral judgment of her children and had insinuated Marit had an evil mind. Undaunted, Marit herself had hauled some lumber and with the help of the older boys had erected a partition. And the cold water thrown by Nicolena had evaporated in the warm enthusiasm of the girls who, given the incentive of "our room," made that end of the loft a glaring contrast to the rest of the home: orderly, with touches of prettiness in curtains, braided rugs and coverlets on the pallets, items stitched up under Marit's guidance from materials salvaged from her scrap bag, finds too appropriate to be true.

The boys were not faring as well. Several seasons back, Rolf had given Nicolena a cow and some chickens, saying, "The boys can work it out." That had been in spring, and Leif and Arne had labored day after day from sunup to sundown until fall.

One late fall afternoon, Marit carried lunch to where they and Rolf were brushing. Lief stood a little aside from Rolf and Arne. She walked over to stand beside him, following his pensive gaze upward.

"I wonder how they know," he said.

"Know what?" she asked, but hardly listened to his answer, herself transfixed by the inexorable south-driving wedges in the sky.

"How they know when it's time to leave."

In the night she was awakened by one low-flying flock, their raucous calls ringing in her ears like distress signals.

Next morning, the boys were gone. "Blood will tell," was Rolf's summation of this turn of events — their running away.

She went to Pine Fork infrequently now. A combination post office and store designated as Sylvan Springs had been established nearby by at a crossroads, and it was there that she went these days to trade and pick up the few pieces of mail they still received from Norway.

Through the tenuous paper ties with home had come the news

of her mother's death. What will Pa do without her? She had worried, only to receive word several months later that, he, too, was gone. Now there were only the infrequent exchanges with her sister, and those usually only at Christmas time.

She felt that in America she had only Randilena of her *own*, and she sometimes envied others in this respect. In some instances she knew of, whole families had migrated to the New World, and family circles broken in the homeland had compassed again here, with only the setting different, as when a scene is changed in a play — same actors but against a different backdrop. But she saw no likelihood of such a reunion with her own family. Her brothers had gone to sea and she never heard from them. Her sister had married in Norway and, from her letters, it was evident that she was immune to "America fever." Excerpts from some of her letters had these things to say:

From all reports, it would seem that the climate of America is most unhealthy. The letters received here bring much news of death. It appears that ague, typhus, cholera, pneumonia, tuberculosis and influenza rage in the settlements of our countrymen there.

No doubt, this can in part be blamed on the inadequate crude huts they build to live in.

They could hardly be called houses! You yourself have been honest enough to admit that many live in one-room dwellings you call 'cabins,' homes such as only the poorest of cotters have here. Yet many write glowing letters designed to lure other unsuspecting people there.

I suspect that many of these letters are inspired by false pride, written to cover up the great error of leaving the homeland, the mistake of their lives. I put no stock in these letters, but rather pay heed to the minister, who cautions against such folly. I believe he can be trusted...

Most disturbing to me are the reports of deviation from the true faith, a great falling away.

Many, we hear, have rejected the faith entirely, even to the extent of working on the Sabbath, and that degenerates are common, those who spurn the chastisement of labor and spend their time in unbridled carousing. I shall be generous enough to excuse them for drunkenness in the light of the conditions under which they exist. Undoubtedly, many drink to forget their troubles.

But the rest I cannot excuse....

We hear that in some misguided notion of freedom, the pure teachings of the Church are rejected in the belief there are not applicable there. That traditional ritual and robes are cast aside, that many ministers are not properly ordained and that many so-called 'lay ministers' abound. And that many go as far as to think themselves equal to ministers in interpreting God's Word, scorning the edifying forms of their fathers and offering prayers of their own making. It is not surprising to hear that splits have developed, that the Church is falling apart in America as a result. When authority is undermined, childish quarreling among themselves is bound to be the result. It can only be in the assurance of a greater reward that clergymen will leave their secure posts here and go where they are expected to live in the same hovels as their parishioners and resort to common labor to survive, such as tending their own gardens and putting up their own wood for the cruel winters and ending up with hands calloused as a common workingman's! How vulgar this all seems to me...

You wrote in your last letter of the "public" schools of America. I think "heathen" schools would be a better description of them, since no religious instruction is allowed. How can reading for the minister compensate for a whole religion-centered education? Even counting Sunday school, how can it suffice? I think Mother would turn over in her grave if she knew that one of her grandchildren, your little Randilena, her namesake, was being reared in such a sacrilegious society, and I sometimes think it is a blessing that she did not live to hear of this...

Since I do not plan to ever come to America, we shall never meet again on this earth, but I hope to meet you with God. Because I trust, dear Marit, that you are holding steadfast to the faith. When we get our freedom from the Swedes, we feel certain that economic conditions will improve in Norway. I trust also that you speak out against the apostasy at every opportunity. Remembering you, I'm certain this is so.

Nicolena had only Thorn left in Norway and he seldom wrote. Yet, she frequently made the trip to the post office. "I'm going for mail," she would announce abruptly, grabbing her shawl. "Mind the baby and don't tear the house down while I'm gone." She would return a couple hours later, nearly always empty-handed but in the next thing to a cheerful mood, her cabin fever quelled. The older girls referred to these excursions as "Ma's mail spree," as a correlation to their father's aberration.

It was on a bright day in early summer that Marit looked out of a kitchen window to see Nicolena hurriedly coming up the path with a sheet of paper in her hand. Marit steeled herself: If it were a letter from home at *this* time of year....

But when Nicolena burst through the door it was evident that the news was not bad. Her usually dour face was flushed with excitement. "You'll never guess!" she said, clutching the letter to herself.

Marit waited for her to go on, but Nicolena stood eyeing her, wanting her to coax. She seemed to be taking a singular pleasure in the news she was withholding.

"Well, tell me," Marit said. "I'm too busy to be playing childish guessing games!"

"You'll never guess what Thorn has gone and did!"

Now she knew the game. She would not give Nicolena the satisfaction of appearing interested. It was evidently something she would relish in the telling anyway and would yield it without prodding.

When Nicolena saw that Marit was not going to wheedle, she went on. "Thorn has gone and got himself a woman! After all these years. I was beginning to think... Well, anyway, he's finally got married."

When Marit thought of Thorn now, it was as she recalled the tang of wild strawberries in winter, out of season, so not to be brooded over. And that torrid season of her life would never come again, she believed. So it was not hard to say, "That's good news, Nicolena."

"Aren't you going to ask who he married?"

"Does it matter? I'm glad he found someone. It's a natural thing for a man to marry."

Nicolena persisted. "He married Kari Eng."

Now Marit was gratifyingly surprised. "Kari Eng! Why... she's just a little girl!"

Nicolena laughed. "You forget. You've been gone for many years. Kari must be all of seventeen now. Children have grown up since you left."

It was true. She remembered people as they *had* been: perpetually arrested, frozen in memory as children, youths, middle-aged. She would always think of Thorn as eighteen! Her mind travelled back....

Kari Eng.... She tried to picture her as a young woman. But try as she might, she could not erase from her mind the picture of a little girl, her snow-white hair braided, the braids falling down on each side to her waist and bound on the ends with perky little bows to keep them from unraveling. But the face was too white, too thin! Kari had been a fragile child, and her parents had cherished her as one they would not have with them long. She recalled something else: It had been Thorn's delight to carve comic little figures to amuse the child who could not romp and play with the other children.

She had forgotten Nicolena was in the room. But now her penetrating stare punctuated the reverie, bringing her back to the present. "You're right. It's been a long time."

But Nicolena still nursed a smug look. "That's not all. Wait 'til you hear the rest of it!"

"What more could there be?"

"He's given up the sea — is coming to America!" This last, triumphantly.

"Is that all?" Marit turned away as if the dismiss her, to get back to work.

There was silence. Then, "I should think that you — you of *all* people — would be interested in this news."

"People sail for America every day." Where had she heard that before?

She heard the door slam. Nicolena was gone. Now she could think without guarding her face.

She had wanted to ask if they were coming here, to this *very* place. Would she see Thorn again, face to face? She shrank from the thought, putting her hands over her face to shut out the light. When she lowered them again, looking out the window, the grain field shimmered — a sea gilded with sunlight. And a whale's spout in that grain field would have been as easy to believe as Thorn here.

CHAPTER II

"How come you never told me I have an Uncle Thorn?" Randilena burst through the door shouting the question in a tone of accusation. "Signe says her Uncle Thorn is coming from Norway, and that he's my uncle too — Pa's brother!"

"Why.... I guess I just didn't think it was important."

She and Rolf's conversations were sparse at any rate, with only enough words exchanged to get the work done, but up until this moment she hadn't realized that she and Rolf never *had* made mention of Thorn in their home.

"You've told me about my other uncles in Norway — *your* brothers. Don't you like Thorn? Is he an old troll like Pa?"

"What an awful thing to say about your father!"

"Well, Pa is always crabby!"

"He has a lot on his mind."

It was a weak excuse and she knew it. Rolf had never warmed to Randilena; the very sight of her rankled him. It had been hardest when she was a toddler, when in her trust, she had dogged his footsteps, prattling constantly. For the most part he had ignored her, but irritated to the limit he would shout "Get" at her and she would come running, thumb in mouth. She would keep her distance until, in childish exuberance, she forgot and trespassed on his consciousness again. In time, she had learned to make herself unobtrusive, remaining silent in his presence, although it was her natural inclination to be talkative. It showed respect for him as her father, Marit thought, if not love for him. Respect was all that was required of a child, love not being commanded. Thus, it came as a shock to her to hear Randilena refer to him as "an old troll." She had come to feel assured that Randilena took his attitude in stride, hadn't guessed that she did not take his way with her for granted.

Randilena continued to labor the issue of Thorn's coming. "Did you ever know him?"

"Know who?"

"Uncle Thorn, of course! That's who we're talking about."

"I knew him when we were real young. When we were children."

"Tell me about him. Signe says he's a captain, that he goes to
sea in a big boat and that he's very rich."

"I don't know about that. So much has happened since I left.
But I remember that he was a sailor, all right."

"But what is Uncle Thorn like?" she insisted.

"If I know you, you won't waste any time finding out when he
gets here. Why don't you just wait and see?"

The words "wait and see" caught her fancy. During the next
weeks, Marit often heard her singing the words to a little tune she
made up. It was a gay enough little tune, but it tugged at her heart.
If she could not have her father's love, perhaps his brother's?

As for Marit, upon learning that she was indeed going to have
to face Thorn again, she had felt something of the accused awaiting indictment. She went over and over in her mind the circum-
stantial evidence against her, how it must have looked to him. But
one day she had taken a firm rein on her emotions: *I am a married
woman — many years married — with a daughter more than half the
age of Thorn's wife!* It had been a steadying thought. Her panic had
subsided, enabling her to concentrate on the practical matter of
readying for their visit.

Most certainly it would only be a visit. They would undoubtedly move on, perhaps to the Great Lakes where experienced seamen were in demand. She recalled all the boats she had observed
when they crossed the lakes on their way to the homestead. *I wonder if Thorn knows that things are different here — that boats are driven
by steam, not wind?* But no matter; what was certain was that Thorn
and his family would be sheltered under their roof while they were
here, for Nicolena had no room for them. And with that as a spur,
she set about giving the house a thorough cleaning from top to bottom.

If Rolf noticed the disruption in the house, he gave no outward
sign. But outward appearance aside, he was pleased: The house
would be shown in the best possible light! He, *Rolf* Monsrud, had
proven to be the better choice: He had made Marit the envy of every
woman she knew. Not that he any long had qualms about Marit
and Thorn; the fact that Thorn had taken a wife precluded any
dishonorable intent in his coming here. The past was a dead issue.

Yet, it was not as if he were really looking forward to seeing his brother again, the brother he only remembered as a toddler, a mama's boy. Well, he Rolf, would not cuddle him! He'd done fine as long as he'd stuck to the sea, a thing any Norwegian worth his salt could handle. But America was the test of a real man, especially if he decided to try his hand at farming! The thought of Thorn as a farmer curled his lips into a cynical down-cornered smile.

Nicolena's anticipation of Thorn's arrival was marred by frustration. With their cabin bursting at the seams, there was no way she could shelter him and Kari under their roof, but under *her* roof was where they belonged! Back home hadn't they always shared the same roof? And where had Rolf been all those years? Off looking out for himself! She and Thorn would stick together.

Since she had no man — Nils certainly couldn't be called a man — she could work out a partnership with Thorn. He could run the homestead. There was no reason he couldn't do just as well as Rolf. There would be a new house, a well would be dug for all the cattle they would have as well as for the household. And there would be new furniture. All could be won with Thorn in her camp. She would show Marit a thing or two! She would play Thorn against Rolf, and she would be the benefactress of the competition.

So real had all this become in her mind that Marit could not help but notice a change in her. These days, instead of the usual complaining, there was a smug reserve.

Curious as to what had brought about the change and not connecting it with Thorn, Marit explored one day, "Who left the lid off the cream crock?"

Not realizing she had been so transparent, Nicolena shot back defensively, "Some think the cream is just for them, that others should be satisfied with skim milk. Wouldn't *you* be surprised if you come some day and find me swimming in cream up to my neck!"

"Then I'd just dive in and pull you out so you wouldn't drown yourself in it."

"One doesn't drown if he holds his head high enough, as you very well know."

Marit hadn't intended to rile her; it was just that it was so apparent that something had changed. What was the thing that in

Nicolena's mind was the source of all her problems? Nils, of course!

"If you and Nils are working things out better these days, I'm glad for you."

"Nils!" Nicolena hissed.

So then it was something else. Marit couldn't imagine what, but didn't pursue it further. As it was, she had gotten Nicolena started again on the same old saw. Changing the subject, she asked, "Have you wondered what Thorn will do when he comes to America? Just think, your family circle will be complete again! It would be nice if they would settle down near enough so you could see them often."

Nicolena jumped up and started for the door. There, she turned. "Just you never mind what Thorn does! Or isn't one man enough for you? You have so much of everything, I suppose two men would be just the ticket!"

Marit usually shed Nicolena's gibes as she would shake snow-flakes from her shawl — the sooner the better so they wouldn't soak in. But this shaft went deep, hit quick and she felt her face go hot with anger. She had no opportunity to retort, however. Nicolena had gone, retreating rapidly behind the shield of the slammed door.

❧❀❧

Nicolena had received only the one letter from Thorn, the one telling of his marriage and his decision to leave the sea and his intent to come to Wisconsin and "look the area over." Thus, she ignored little Jens when he came running into the cabin, tugging at her skirt. "Come quick, Mama and see the fine rig that's coming up the trail."

Travelers were not uncommon now; she tried to brush him off. But he pulled her toward the window insistently. It was the fineness of the rig that had the boy excited. To satisfy him, she went to stand by the window and watch it pass by.

To her surprise, the rig turned in at their gate. Undoubtedly strangers stopping to ask directions, she surmised. So intent was she in scanning the rig and admiring the team of sorrels that drew it that she did not look observantly at the driver.

Anticipating a knock on the door, she turned from the window. But the knock was not forthcoming; she stepped outside. The children were clustered about the man and he was tossing them in the air, one by one.

In the late afternoon light she did not recognize Thorn immediately. But a familiar gesture — the way he always had of brushing his cap back from his forehead with his thumb when he was in a jocular mood — brought recognition. She rushed toward the group. "Thorn! It's you!"

He merely acknowledged her presence with a nod, continuing to give his attention to the children, who seemed to be everywhere at once. Some climbed over the rig, some stood patting the horses in admiration, and some stood about him, eyeing him in curiosity. He roughed the hair of the bigger ones and continued to toss the small ones in the air. The clamor made conversation impossible. But he finally disengaged himself and came to her.

"Did you rent the rig?"

"It's mine." So casually she hardly caught it.

He scrutinized her. "How are things?"

She was tempted to tell him right then and there how things were, but she bit it back. Following his lead of casualness, she answered, "Not too bad."

"Good!" He turned away, walking over to the rig. She had forgotten all about Kari! She was still seated in the rig, completely engrossed by the children, and seemingly bewildered by so many. Thorn helped her down and led her to where Nicolena stood.

"I'm sure you remember Kari," he said by way of introduction.

"Of course," Nicolena acknowledged, turning her attention to him again. "You must come into the house and have a cup of coffee." She led them into the cabin.

If they were at all taken back by the crudeness of the home, they gave no indication. Over coffee, news of home was exchanged and some comments made on the voyage. But all too soon they got around to the matter that had plagued her for weeks.

Looking about dubiously, Thorn asked, "Can you put us up?"

She had no alternative but to reply, "Rolf has a big house. I'm sure he'll put you up, for the night."

"It's best we be going then. Kari is worn out."

"It's the next place on the trail. You can't miss it. But I hope you'll be back tomorrow, spend the day with us. There's so much to be talked over...." Then, she qualified: "caught up with." She must not rush things.

Nicolena stood in the twilight and watched them drive away. Even in this light, the spanking rig glittered, testifying to Thorn's affluence. The sleek sorrels put Rolf's mismatched team to shame!

After they had passed out of sight, she was seized by an almost unbearable restlessness. She walked to the gate, peering up the trail. There was only obscurity. She considered following them, dropping in on the reunion, but restrained herself. She paced the yard until she was exhausted, then went to bed, leaving it for the children to scrounge supper for themselves.

❧

Rolf heard the jingle of the harnesses in the stillness of the evening. He went to the window and unable to make out the rig in the falling darkness, he started for the door, saying, "We'll probably have overnight visitors."

The thought pleased him; he was in an expansive mood tonight. Today, he had sold a cow to a settler for a good price.

The rig turned in and Rolf stood by the drive until it came to a stop. Expecting the usual request for lodging, he was startled when a vaguely familiar voice from the dusk asked, "Rolf?"

"It is Rolf."

Thorn got down from the rig and came toward him.... There was a going back in time. Way back in time.... The man who stood before Rolf in the semi-darkness could have been his father! It could only be his father's other son, his brother, Thorn.

"It's you then, Thorn."

"It is." The two stood eyeing each other in curiosity for a few moments. They did not shake hands.

"Well, take your woman and go in. I'll see to the team."

Thorn again helped Kari from the rig, but instead of going in with her, he told her, "You go in. I'll help Rolf put the horses away."

As Rolf led the horses to the stable, he could not help but admire them. But in the darkness he smiled to himself at the foolishness of squandering so much money for a fancy rig. He'll learn, he thought. But aloud: "As long as we're out here, I may as well light a lantern and show you my livestock."

Marit called "come" in response to the gentle tap on the door. What a beautiful child, was her first thought when she laid eyes on her diminutive visitor.

Kari stood expectantly. Then it occurred to her that Marit did not recognize her. "I'm Kari."

"Kari! Then... Thorn is here?"

"They're putting the horses away."

Marit had rehearsed the meeting dozens of times in her mind. Yet now, panic welled up in her throat like a potato dumpling.

"Come. Come sit in the parlor," she hastily invited, taking down a lamp from the shelf and lighting it with trembling fingers. She carried it before her, leading the way to the front parlor, usually set aside for special occasions. The kitchen, with its couch and abundance of chairs, was the routine place visitors were entertained.

She set the lamp down and turned to face Kari, who was looking around the ornate room in surprise. "I had no idea you had progressed so far! I had visions of makeshift furniture, rough uncarpeted floors... well, like Nicolena's house, implying no insult to Nicolena's home."

"Nicolena hasn't had things so good. Nils is a poor provider. I have a great deal to be thankful for." She surprised herself in her indirect praise of Rolf. She had never been able to gracefully accept compliments on her home from other visitors because of her guilt at Rolf's business tactics.

After they had seated themselves, the conversation turned to the homeland, as it always did with newcomers. Kari carried the burden of conversation and for the first time Marit focused her full attention on her.

Like the angels that float in luminous whiteness in the dark clouds of heavy religious paintings, Kari's presence seemed to light up the murky corner where she sat, an effect that stemmed in part from her extreme blondeness.

While it was not rare for Norwegian children to have snow-white hair — towheaded — at adolescence it usually deepened to wheat color or darker. But Kari retained the tresses and she wore them braided still, but with the braids coiled round and round on top of her head, giving a halo effect. The fairness of her skin contributed to the illusion, a blue-milk transparency that seemed a reflection of her cerulean eyes, except that there were two high red spots on her cheeks.

But there was a glow not of blondeness that emanated from her; a lightness of spirit that declared: *I'm alive and I'm here and I'm glad. Count me in!* Marit found herself so drawn by the positive charge of her personality that, for the moment, Thorn was shoved to the back of her mind.

The spell was broken by the sound of the men coming in, their voices sifting into the room. Marit no longer listened to Kari. She was listening for another voice....

Suddenly she realized that Kari had asked her a question. "I'm sorry. I wasn't listening. I had my mind on Randilena. She went to bed early tonight. A little stomach upset."

Kari did not repeat the question. Instead, she queried Marit about Randilena, and Marit, determined not to let her attention stray again, told her in detail about her daughter.

Their conversation was interrupted by Rolf calling her. She knew it was the signal to put coffee on. And there was no way out.

"Come with me to the kitchen," she said the Kari. "It's coffee time."

Thorn stood when they came into the room, a courtesy to their sex that was alien to Marit. He walked toward her with a decided limp, hand extended. But this bearded, broad-shouldered man couldn't be Thorn.

She shook the hand woodenly, looking into his eyes. The eyes did not waver. The *eyes* were Thorn's....

But if this was any more than a casual handshake between old friends, he gave no indication. "You're looking well," he said, then dropped her hand and turned to Kari.

"I think you need rest. You look tired."

"I was just going to put the coffee on," Marit said.

"We had coffee at Nicolena's. If you will just show us to our room." He continued to look at Kari as he spoke.

Marit went back to the parlor and retrieved the lamp, then led them up the broad open staircase where, on the topmost step, they found Randilena crouching.

"What have we here?" Thorn said, reaching down and picking

her up. He held her out from him so he could have a better look at her.

Randilena stared back at him. She reached out, as if to touch his magnificent black beard but then drew her hand back again.

"Is she always so shy?" Thorn asked.

༄༅༄

Although she had slept poorly, Marit was up when the furnishings of their bedroom swam into focus through the first milky light of dawn. They will sleep late, she thought, no need to start their breakfast until I hear them stirring she decided as she laid the pungent pine knots in the firebox of the range.

She thought back to her own first morning on the homestead. She had been aware of every travel-weary muscle in her body when she had pulled herself from bed that first morning. But that was a good kind of weariness, she reflected; it was just a matter of being winded over the finish line. It was different from the dull kind she often felt these days. Now there *was* no finish line to sprint for, to throw oneself across. Now it was a matter of going on and on.... She suddenly felt old this morning.

The fire blazed. She filled the coffee pot and grout pan with water and put them on the heat. Rolf would want breakfast at his usual time. Then she went to the window to draw back the curtain and let in the morning sun.

Like a Cinderella coach, the rig appeared before her eyes. Such a fancy one! And such a load! As she turned from the window, she admitted to her curiosity: *I just wonder what's in all those crates.*

While she was waiting for the pots to boil, her thoughts turned to Kari. She mentally compared her with the settlers' wives of the community: their styleless dresses of material selected with service in mind and made with few frills; their facial expressions of studied endurance, as if to show joy would be to tempt fate; their rough, work-worn hands. She had noticed that Kari's hands were like a child's. Evidently she had lived the life of a lady in the homeland with maids to do her work. That was highly likely, she pursued, since Kari was a master's wife and a whole year's pay for a maid was less than five dollars in American money! She pictured Kari ordering them about, stamping her feet when they did not jump at her commands. Then she was immediately surprised for assuming that Kari was such a person. As a rule, she did not think unkindly of people — at least not right off!

Rolf had seated himself at the table. She dished out his breakfast and was about to serve herself when she heard footsteps on the stair.

Thorn came into the kitchen. "Help yourself," she invited.

Had he, too, had trouble sleeping, she wondered, but thought better of asking when he accepted her invitation to breakfast without even looking at her. Why should she think he would lose sleep over *her?* She hadn't really lost sleep over *him* either. It was just the excitement — everything put together — that had brought on the restless night!

She served him her portion. This, he noticed. "What of you?"

"I was planning to eat with Kari," she covered neatly. "Will she be down soon?"

"I think she'll sleep late and I don't think she'll want breakfast," he said without explanation.

Turning to Rolf, he asked: "Is there any available land left in this area?"

"Plenty. Plenty of land! There's the timber company land, cut over, of course. And there's the railroad land with standing timber, and...."

Surely Thorn didn't plan to go into farming! She busied herself absentmindedly as she strained to catch his intent, her suspense prolonged by Rolf's launching into his well-rehearsed sales pitch of the area.

Finally, Rolf ran down. Thorn was talking again. "It's my hope that Kari can stay while I look the area over."

"She's most welcome," Marit assured him.

There was silence so she ventured, "If it's land you're looking for, I heard just last Sunday that the Larsons — they live just a little less than a mile up the trail — that they're thinking of selling out and taking up land in Minnesota."

Rolf frowned. He didn't like it when she butted in on business conversations and she usually didn't. "Just women's gossip, no doubt," he said.

"It might be worth looking into," Thorn countered.

So it *was* to be farming. But now Rolf grabbed the ball again, leaning across the table and speaking in a low, confidential tone. He advised, "He would want a fancy price for his holding, that you should know before you waste your time running up there. He has a fair set of buildings and quite a few broken acres."

"That can best be ascertained by asking," Thorn said, pushing his chair back as if to put distance between himself and Rolf. Then, "I'm not without resources."

Rolf's face flushed. "I suppose you sold your boat interests for a pretty fair sum," he fished.

It was as much as question as a statement, but Thorn ventured nothing more, so Rolf answered it to his own satisfaction. "It'll undoubtedly take a lot more money than you have stowed away. But even supposing you did have the money. Let me tell you it takes a lot more than money...." He launched into a long résumé of pitfalls, punctuated with thinly veiled hints that a good business head was required. And it was easy to infer that the thought he had one of the best — the reason he had succeeded while so many others were still plugging along.

When he had finished, Thorn made no comment. And to Marit, his silence was eloquent. His attitude of self-assurance — even of command — made Rolf's boasting childish by comparison. She wondered if Rolf also sensed this, for the conversation palled and Rolf became sullen.

The men were still at the table when Nicolena came. She entered without knocking, seating herself at the table without invitation. Marit got a cup and poured coffee for her.

The men said nothing when she sat down. She broke the silence, addressing Thorn, "I would like for you and Kari to spend the day with me. With me and the children, that is."

"That will have to wait," Thorn said. That, and nothing more. He has developed such a way of not explaining himself, Marit observed.

"What could be more important than spending a few hours with your sister after all these years?" Nicolena wheedled. Then, placing her hand on Thorn's arm, she added, "You know, you're almost like a son to me."

At this, Rolf glowered at her from across the table. It was as a slap; she drew her hand back.

Seeing this, Thorn assured her, "We'll have plenty of time for visiting later. I intend to be around for a long time."

Nicolena did not coax further, but Marit could see that she was disappointed, so she offered, "Kari will be staying here. Maybe we can walk down some afternoon."

Nicolena sniffed at this as if she had been thrown a dry crust. But she said nothing more until the men went out. Then, "You said Kari will be staying here. Does that mean they've made plans?"

"No definite plans that I know of. But Thorn asked if Kari could stay here while he looks over the area. It seems he's interested in buying land. He didn't really say so, but I gathered that he might talk to Larson about his place. You heard Bertina say that they were thinking of—"

"Who put him onto that!" Nicolena interrupted, bristling.

"I did. I thought it might be helpful, could save a lot of pointless running around. And since money seems to be no problem, a place that's already worked up—"

"I might have known you'd steer him around, fix things up to suit yourself! Did it ever occur to you that I, his *sister,* might want to have something to say about it? *Me,* who raised him from a sniveling whelp to the man he is now?"

"You're right about *one* thing. He is a man now! And from what I've seen, *no* one is going to steer him anyplace. He has a mind of his own. *That* you can bank on!"

Nicolena marched out. "I'm not giving up *this* easy! You haven't won yet!"

Now what did she mean by that? But Marit didn't have time to puzzle over it. She had heard stirring above, so she hurriedly cleared the table and reset it for three, then started a pan of fresh grout.

She heard footsteps on the stair. Kari came into the kitchen, her arm around Randilena. Kari looked surprised to find Marit alone. "I thought I heard Nicolena's voice."

"She just left. I hope we didn't wake you. I thought you'd be tired and sleep late."

"I took a long nap on the drive from Millwood yesterday, curled up with my head in Thorn's lap. The rig is very comfortable — springs in the seats and all. I really feel fully rested. And if I'd known Nicolena was leaving right away, I'd have come sooner. But I was getting acquainted with my niece. I can't get over having such a big girl for a niece! She has promised to teach me the language, the same as she taught you."

Randilena beamed.

"Thorn said you would not want breakfast," Marit said. "Is that the fashion now in Norway, for ladies not to eat breakfast?"

Kari's laughter, spontaneous and uninhibited, was an unordinary sound in the house. "No. It's not the fashion for most. Only for those who are expecting babies! A very old fashion, really."

Marit gasped at her frankness — and in the range of Randilena's innocent ears! The only announcement she had ever witnessed before was a telltale expanding waistline. She glanced over to where Randilena stood in front of the washstand, her back to them. Her reflected image in the glass told nothing. Randilena never had asked questions yet, and Marit felt there was still plenty of time for *that*. That babies grew in the mother's stomach, Randilena couldn't help but have guessed. But how they got there, well this was best left for a girl to find out when she married and it certainly could never be discussed. But such frankness as Kari's could start Randilena to wondering and even might make her so bold as to ask!

Randilena finished her morning toilet and Kari went to the washstand. Marit watched her, thinking: It must be that she's so young. That's it. It's all a big adventure to her — even having a baby. Like doll play. — But so soon! I waited so long for Randilena.... And it will be *Thorn's* baby....

She felt a pang of envy. *But could I love any child, even Thorn's, more than I love Randilena?* There was no contest. She slammed the shutter on that wishing star.

"Well, what else is new in Norway, besides what you told me last night?" Marit asked, steering the conversation to a safer course.

"War! And it's all because of that tyrant, King Oscar." She hissed his name. "And his attempts to dissolve our *Storting*," she continued, referring to the Norwegian legislature. "But Johan Sverdrup isn't afraid of him! He doesn't back down — it's King Oscar who's going to have to back down!"

Kari was so full of surprises! That she should bother her pretty head about *such* things. And express her opinion so strongly!

But Marit did not want to appear out of touch so she ratified without conviction, "Ya. When are the Swedes ever going to learn that they can't push Norwegians around."

CHAPTER III

To the villagers, the romance of Thorn and Kari had been as a reenactment of the "Sleeping Princess" fairy tale, save that the prince, as more befitting Viking tradition, swept in under sail rather than astride a steed. But quicken the sleeping princess he had and, after they were wed, she was ensconced in his "castle on the hill," the home Thorn built when he achieved master status, a high rank in the economic caste system.

That there had been another was remembered, as small villages have a way of remembering. But Marit had sailed away with Rolf and Thorn apparently had weathered it. It seemed of little consequence, that other romance, when Thorn began to take more than a brotherly interest in the house-bound Kari. And the pet of them all, no one could be so mean as to mar her happiness by dredging up something that had happened so long ago.

Back then Kari had been such a little girl and so ill that it had been the conviction of her parents and the villagers that she would not live to grow up, some commenting on how "exactly like an angel she looks already." Consequently, they had lavished love on her, and she had reciprocated by loving everyone in return, without reserve, a trait not common in Norwegians, who are inclined to bury their emotions deep and clamp and iron lid of stoicism on them. But despite the dark forebodings, Kari survived childhood and when she reached adolescence, the childhood fragility developed into a beauty exquisite in its delicacy.

Thorn had at first taken only a kindly interest in her. But it was noted that he spent more and more of his leisure hours with her when he was home from the sea. She was seen outside the house for the first time, walking hesitatingly at the start, but then with increased vigor down the lanes of the village, her hand trustingly in Thorn's. It was also noted that when Thorn was away at sea, and she was without him, that she wilted like a tender vine, the tendrils of which have been torn from their support.

To Thorn, it became a matter of priorities: His career or Kari's health and happiness. He could always find other work, he decided, but not another Kari.

He made the decision to go to America at the same time as the decision to leave the sea. Landed opportunities were scarce in Norway and he had heard that his brother was doing fine for himself in America as a farmer. Besides, swallowed up in the vastness of the American wilderness, the siren call of the sea would not reach his ears.

Now, he had found this new land all that he had expected it to be. Then why this feeling of disappointment, he asked himself. Was it that he had expected to find his brother and sister transformed, their natures altered in the new beginning? His childhood animosity toward Rolf had so mellowed with time that he was surprised to find himself still repelled by him. And Nicolena was *still* bitter. Granted she had reason to be bitter, for her financial circumstances were evidently even worse than they had been in the homeland and, understandably, her disposition had deteriorated accordingly.

Kari had commented: "Rolf has so much and Nicolena so little! It's really not much different from the homeland, after all."

"People are what they are no matter where they are," he had told her. "There's no boundary that people can cross where everyone becomes just like everyone else. Even the Americans haven't figured out a way to take ambition away from a man like Rolf, who has an over-supply, and give it to a man like Nils who is completely lacking in it."

"Then equality is just a phantom. It can never really be."

He had turned to her, pulling her to him. "The only thing in life that is not a phantom is what you and I have."

She loved him; needed him. And wanted nothing else — no one else.

❧

Thorn closed the deal with John Larson. But it would be at least a month before the place would be vacated and his offer of "I'd like to earn my keep while we're here" was snapped up by Rolf.

In the following weeks, working side by side with Thorn, Rolf gained a grudging admiration for him. It was not just the way he tackled a job — his initiative, foresight and self-assurance — but it

was that, although subconsciously, Thorn was in appearance, movement and voice a reincarnation of his father. This fellow has some
good stuff in him after all, Rolf acknowledged to himself.

During these same days, Marit was constantly in the company
of Kari, a prolonged contact that was as therapy, disarming her of
the protective shield she had raised against Rolf's single-minded
callousness and Nicolena's barbed bitterness. It was an armor that
had enabled her to plod on impervious to hurt, but also to joy. For
Kari's zest for life was a contagion that evoked response in kind.
Within days she found herself not only uninhibitedly laughing along
with Kari, but exchanging banter, a favorite device Kari used to
lighten the load. And this *very* lightness seemed her strength.

It had become evident that, in spite of the outward appearance
of vitality, Kari was not physically strong. She tired easily and there
were days when the translucence of skin revealed dark circles under
her eyes, stresses that she endured with no apparent loss of buoyancy, however. In fact, the very buoyancy seemed to have sprung
from physical limitation, from having risen above it in an achieve-
ment of spirit.

This spirit — her mettle — evidenced itself at times in ways
other than humor and lightness. She seemed to have well-formed
opinions of everything, and did not hesitate in expressing them, even
to the extent of intruding herself into purely "male" discussions.

There had been that morning when the men were appraising
Thorn's newly acquired property. "I think the price was fair," Thorn
had said. "The house isn't much, but there's a good barn, some fair
out-buildings...."

"Not to mention eighty acres of land with fifteen cleared," Kari
had interrupted. "Don't forget that! Compared to the farms in
Norway, that's an empire for one's family livelihood! I think we
made a good buy."

"What do women know about good buys!" Rolf had barked.

"I've found it's best to humor them," Thorn said, winking at
Kari. "It's easier to live with a good-natured woman."

❦

When the Larsons were loaded and on their way, Marit went
with Kari to look over the house at Kari's insistence. "I want your

ideas," she said.

But it soon became evident that Marit and Kari had different priorities. It was a two-room cabin with full loft overhead, and Kari decided that the smaller room downstairs should be a parlor, with the loft serving as their bedroom, completely contrary to local custom, that held the smaller room on the first floor *always* served as the master bedroom. Marit pointed this out to her, but Kari's mind was made up.

Marit went along with the plan against her own better judgment; especially in light of Kari's condition. When she cautioned Kari on the inadvisability of climbing stairs, Kari brushed it aside by informing her that she and Thorn already had discussed it, that he was going to build a railed staircase and enclose it on the bottom, "so we'll have a closet as a bonus. Thorn has a great deal of skill in carpentry. We won't buy much furniture. He'll make most of it himself this winter. We'll just buy the essentials in Millwood: a stove, maybe a couple of chairs to get by with, a sofa and, oh yes, wallpaper."

Wallpaper? No one in the neighborhood put paper on their walls, unless it was the tarpaper they sometimes put on the outside! Marit tried to imagine wallpaper, visualizing in the room the white of writing paper, the gray of newspapers, the brown of wrapping paper, all neutrals that presented in her mind an effect that was anything but pretty.

When Thorn left for Millwood, the dimensions of the room marked down in his notebook, Kari instructed him, "Since the room is so small that it won't take much, we can splurge a little. Get the prettiest you can find."

They spent the time Thorn was gone in remodeling drapes that Kari had brought with her from their home in Norway. "I decided to bring them along because I thought it unlikely I could get such fine material here," she explained. By the time Thorn returned the next evening, the drapes were ready to be hung.

When he came into the kitchen carrying the wallpaper rolls, Kari eagerly grabbed one and took it to the table, slitting it open and rolling it out.

A never-land of peace and abundance spread itself on the table: Verdant grape vines, heavy with fruit, twined round and round, the vines framing vistas of pastoral scenes where shepherds and shepherdesses, crooks in hand, stood steadfastly frozen in attendance of sheep suspended in the act of cavorting — all against a backdrop of hills topped with classic porticoed temples.

Marit was dumbstruck; but not Kari. "Oh, it's beautiful! Just beautiful!"

The rough log walls presented a problem. But by slathering paste generously over the flaws in the walls, as well as on the paper itself, they were able to make it stick. When all four walls were covered, they hung the festooned drapes and stood back to admire. The little room has been transformed into a cool grape arbor that opened into still another world of apertured illusion.

"It's so beautiful it's almost a sin!" Marit exclaimed.

Kari gave her a curious look. "That's a strange thing to say. Beauty is its *own* reason for being. If it but brings pleasure, it has served."

Marit never had looked at it that way. But she had little time to digest the philosophy, for Kari was pointing and saying, "and now it's just for Thorn to build the staircase and bookshelves along that wall and we can move in."

When Thorn had accomplished the carpentry, they spent a day moving all the boxes and crates that had been stored in a spare room at Marit's house. While they were still loading the wagon, Kari set one box aside and, when all else was loaded, she opened that one. "There's this one thing I couldn't wait to show you," she explained.

She drew a little chest from the box. It was of beautifully grained wood and intricately carved, a work of art. "This was my wedding gift from Thorn. He carved it himself and kept it a secret from me. It must have taken him months. He did most of it at sea, at night by lantern light." She stroked the little chest lovingly.

"I have only one such thing," Marit said. She went to a drawer, taking out the lace tablecloth, the family heirloom given her by her mother when she married Rolf. Kari fingered it gently. "Now *that* must have taken years of needlework," she marvelled.

The next morning, Kari invited, "Would you like to come along and help me unpack?"

Marit needed no coaxing. Now, at last, she would get to see what all the boxes and crates contained! And Randilena's curiosity matched her own. Through all this hubbub of readying the cabin, Randilena had been in a flurry of excitement and had once remarked to Kari, "It was never like this before. I wish you'd come to America sooner!"

At the cabin, Thorn clawed the crates open with a hammer. There were the posts and side-rails of a four-poster bed; a chest of drawers, small, but ornate. "Oriental," Kari said of a large gilded-frame mirror and some fine linens. These, he put in place.

But there remained many small unopened boxes and now Thorn went to work on these. When he had clawed them open, he left, saying to Kari, "I know you'll want to arrange these to suit yourself."

Books! Marit had never seen so many books together in one place in her life, unless it had been in the minister's study back home. What useless things to drag all the way across an ocean! What good would they be? "I thought you had brought, well, more things of a useful nature," she said with some disapproval.

Kari paused in her installing of the books on the shelf. She turned to Marit, her face earnest. "I couldn't bear to leave them behind. It would be like leaving a part of me." She sat down. "You see, Marit, I never lived — *really* lived — until Thorn made me believe I could. He gave me the confidence that I could live *fully.* Before that, I had only the books. They made available to me a world in which I could not participate, or so I thought then. And for that, I still love them, as one loves old, faithful friends."

"But where did you get so many? Only ministers have so many books in the homeland."

"And masters," Kari corrected. "The master had a big library and he was very generous." Her eyes went far away for a moment. "Sometimes I feel guilty about him. He counted so much on Thorn."

But then she jumped up again and went back to unpacking. "To get back to the books.... When Thorn became a master, he started his own library. But many go back to even before that. Since I liked books so much, Thorn bought me many through the years, and others gifted me with books. When the minister came to the house and I read for him in preparation for a confirmation, he said I had a quick mind. Since I would never be a wife or mother, he thought — *a woman's God-ordained destiny,* he put it — it wouldn't hurt to cultivate my mind. He felt that under ordinary circumstances, education is wasted on women, except for reading, writing

and ciphering, the rudiments being all that's necessary for a woman
to lead a dutiful life, since she is subject to her husband. But I have
come to disagree with him." She did not elaborate, turning to the
shelves. "See, here I have Kjelland, here Lie, here Gloerson — and
Munch, Ibsen, Bjornson...."

It took some moments for Marit to realize that she was referring to the authors, not naming the books themselves. *She talks like
she knows them, knows the writers in person,* Marit puzzled. She had
never contemplated authors as people, individuals. All the adult
books with which she had come into contact were of a religious vein,
and she put their authors in a sphere far above other mortals, thinking of their books as being conceived somewhat as Holy Writ, by
some miracle of God's guidance of the hand across the page, assuring Truth.

"What did you mean about not agreeing with the minister?"

"I have come to a conclusion: I believe that women have just
as good a brain as men. It's just that they don't use it, exercise it."

Marit turned a crate over and sat down on it. This was an irre-
ligious thought! It was clearly stated in the Scriptures that man was
set above woman, and since her own strength had disproved that it
was physical superiority, she assumed it was wisdom. She had never
challenged the admonition that man was the "head," that he must
be deferred to in matters of judgment, having the better head of
the two, except for that one indiscretion in the deal she made on
her own with John Hagen concerning the calf. Yet the thought,
sinful though it might be, was a fascinating one. Suppose it were
true....

"And there is talk that when we get our independence from
Sweden, women will be given the right to vote."

"How could they? Only men understand politics!"

Kari answered her question with another. "Have you ever read
Camilla Collet?"

"Why... no."

"Oh, you must read *her*, and Gloerson. They will open your
eyes. Gloerson goes especially far in elevating women. Here...." She
drew two books from the shelf, thrusting them on to Marit's lap.

Marit looked at the title of the top one, *The Commodore's
Daughters.* "Looks interesting," she said.

She carried the books home but when she neared the buildings, she tucked them inside her blouse, in case Rolf should be about. She was sure he would disapprove if he saw them. *Maybe I won't even read them,* she vacillated.

But in the next days, her mind kept turning to tantalizing possibilities. Might a woman come to the place where she understood business so well that she could become financially independent of men? Even have a bank account of *her own?* That Rolf had a bank account she knew, but in *his* name. And when Kari had said about women in the homeland getting the right to vote... Was it possible that women could fathom politics if they "exercised their brains," as Kari put it? Would there come a day in the homeland that when women gathered, they would talk politics, the way men did? She was sure it would never happen *here.* Women, what did they talk: home, children, church.... Well, that's because every moment of every day from dawn to bed of a woman's time is taken up with those things, she decided. Women don't have time to think of anything else, far less exercise their brains. Unless they steal the time....

The first few times she furtively opened the book, reading in the spare moments of the day, she felt guilty. But soon she became so engrossed in the contents that guilt dissipated.

꧁❋꧂

Throughout all their industry, Thorn had evidenced an amused interest in their accomplishments, coming into the cabin frequently to "survey the damage," as he put it. However, he focused all of his attention on Kari, sometimes becoming so engrossed in her that he seemed to forget Marit was there, physically displaying his affection for Kari in ways that were embarrassing. For it was the usual way of Norwegian men to feign disdain for women, at least in front of other people, so as not to appear vulnerable or unmanly. An open display of affection — touching — was a rarity, the carrying-on of Thorn with Kari, shameless!

There were times, however, when Marit suspected that he went out of his way to disregard her. She wondered if he had ever told Kari of the past to reassure her. Had he just passed it off to her as nothing? He seemed to have buried it completely, except for his elaborate way of ignoring her. *He must despise me,* she decided, *can't stand the sight of me for my faithlessness.*

This preyed on her. She considered telling him how it all had happened, if she ever got alone with him. But would it matter to him now? He had Kari. And nothing could be changed. Still, she brooded, I wish he wouldn't think so badly of me.

Her brooding, however, was benign; a virulent kind had Nicolena in its grip these days. Thorn had almost immediately taken a hand in managing her affairs. Under his guidance and with his help and encouragement, Henry, who had been poised to flee as had his two older brothers, had begun to assume responsibility and things had begun to go better.

But Nicolena felt left out. She couldn't forgive what she felt had been Marit's interference in her plans, which were so much more grand than the slow improvement that was coming about. And the close relationship that had sprung up between Marit and Kari aggravated her. Strange that *these* two should become so thick... I wonder if Kari knows, she speculated.

It was several months after their arrival that Nicolena decided to ascertain. She dropped in on Kari one day and, after a preliminary cover-up conversation, she got down to the real purpose of the visit. Looking around the cozy room, she said, "How lucky you are that Thorn has such a knack for making things!"

"Thorn has many admirable traits. This is just one of them," Kari said proudly.

"Well then, how all the more lucky you are to have been the one who snared him."

Kari chose to ignore the allegation that she had snared Thorn. "I realize that I am much luckier than most. There aren't many like Thorn. It seems to me sometimes that there never was a time when I didn't love him."

This *love* talk was nonsense to Nicolena. "But what of Thorn? He was mature of age when the two of you married. It seems strange that no one else set her trap for him since, as you say yourself, he was such a plum."

"If there ever was any other but me, Thorn has never told me," Kari admitted innocently. "Nor have I ever asked. What we have is *ours.*"

It was put as a shutout, which made it easier for Nicolena to abruptly take her leave, having gotten what she had come for anyway.

It's really Marit I want to get at, not Kari, she confessed to herself. And the usefulness of the information could only be determined by confronting Marit to gauge her reaction.

Seated in Marit's kitchen, Nicolena did not beat around the bush as she had with Kari. "I wonder what Kari would think of you if she knew about you and Thorn? Maybe she wouldn't like you hanging around if she knew you and Thorn had once been that way with each other."

Marit, as had Kari, ignored insinuation. "Maybe she does know. Maybe she and Thorn are so happy that it doesn't make any difference to her."

"She doesn't know. I made sure of that."

Marit was relieved. "I'm glad she doesn't. It's all in the past, anyway. Thorn and I were just children then." She said this matter-of-factly enough, even though as she said the words she acknowledged to herself that the pulsing had been anything but childlike!

"I think someone should warn Kari. It would only be right. So she could be on guard. I think it would really be the *right* thing to do." Nicolena said this as if she had already made up her mind and she noted with satisfaction that the prospect pierced Marit's composure.

"You wouldn't, Nicolena! That would be just plain mean! You wouldn't deliberately put suspicion in Kari's mind when she is so happy with Thorn!"

"How much do you bet that I wouldn't?"

"Why? Isn't there enough sadness in the world? Just because you and I aren't happy...."

"*You!* What do you have to complain about? You have everything a woman could want! What more do you expect?"

Marit did not answer the question. Instead, she impulsively averred, "I don't have anything in this house I wouldn't give up if it would make someone happy!"

Nicolena's face lit up. It had gone even better than she had expected. Anything that Marit had was now at her disposal, or Marit would be a liar!

"Nothing at all, Marit?"

"Nothing at all."

"Well.... I've always admired that lace tablecloth of yours. If I had that, I'd be a *little* happier."

Marit's face blanched. This was a thing that was of more than material value.... She had looked forward to the day when she would present it to Randilena, who was next in line of the long line of women who had cherished it.

"Well?" Nicolena said impatiently.

Marit went to the chest and gently lifted the cloth from the drawer. She had the impulse to clutch it to her. But she handed it over, hiding the hurt but imploring, "Please take good care of it. It's old, very, very old."

Nicolena grabbed it and went out the door.

❧

It was several weeks later that Kari dropped in on Nicolena to return her call. It was only when Nicolena made coffee and invited her to sit at the table that, up close, she recognized the cloth. Tugged to and fro across the rough surface by a half-dozen pair of grubby little hands, it had been reduced to a mass of filthy tatters. Kari lifted an edge, examining it minutely. "Isn't this... this can't be Marit's lace tablecloth!"

Nicolena's face flushed. "It was just... just a thing."

Kari got to her feet, backing away from the table as from a carnage. "I feel si— I don't feel well." She left at once without regard to the social amenities.

Outside, she put her hand to her throat. She did feel as if she were going to be ill. What had ever possessed Marit to give the cloth to Nicolena? It was a thing that should have been treasured. Marit's queer ideas about sin — pleasure being sin — was the only explanation!

She started to run, running until she was winded. But having gained her own door, she did not stop to rest in the kitchen but climbed the stairs to the loft. She opened drawers, taking objects from them and touching them, as if to assure herself that they were still there, that beauty still existed. There was the little Dresden figurine, a thing she had treasured since early childhood. She would take it downstairs, set it on a shelf where she could feast her eyes on it. Clutching it, she started for the stairs. She missed the first step, grabbed for the rail but missed again, plunging to the floor below.

Marit roused herself at once when the loud knock came on the door. She had been expecting it. Gena Moe was due. And having assumed the role of community midwife, a nocturnal summons was not an unusual occurrence.

Her proficiency in the skill of midwifery had come to be held in high regard, even to the extent that the superstitious held her powers to fall in the area of black magic. For she would come, go into the birthing room. Soon the shrieks of terror would subside, replaced by an interchange of voices, and ultimately, the triumph of the newborn wail. But her only potions were a long memory and knowledge gained from experience. She remembered her own terror — the feeling of being at the mercy of an unseen force — and it had become her conviction that no woman in her first labor should be left alone, even for a short time. For to fall prey to fear was to inhibit the naturally progressive intensity, an accommodation she believed every woman had in her power to endure, given counsel. She did grant the essential isolation of woman in birth-grip, but she gave no quarter to cowardice. "Take my hands and we'll ride the waves together," she said. Then, patiently, she would teach the art of labor. As the wave welled, she would instruct, "Good! Now, take a deep breath. There. Hold it so you don't go under. The trick is not to founder." As it ebbed, "The crest is passed. Now let your breath out slowly.... There. You made it through!" Thus, the woman no longer felt herself a hapless bit of flotsam tossed in a sea of pain, but the participant in a drama, with Marit the coach.

But when she thrust the door open this night, she was startled to see it was Thorn who stood there.

"It's Kari! Something has gone wrong!"

Marit grabbed her shawl, following him. Nothing more was said in the swift ride through the darkness, but fear was a tangible tie between them. It's too soon, much, much too soon, she despaired, and knew that Thorn also was cognizant of this.

Kari lay deep in the throes of labor. In the next hours she was valiant. But when it was over, when she knew she had lost the baby, she crumpled like a rag doll. "I did it. I did it myself! I killed Thorn's baby! I want to die...." She turned her face to the wall.

"Nonsense!" Marit said, then left her for a moment, going down to where Thorn waited in the kitchen, her face an agonized question mark.

"There will be no baby."

"But Kari. Will Kari be all right?"

"The worst is over."

"I couldn't stand to go through it again!"

It was not unusual for men to say things like this at such times, in unguarded moments, in guilt at the pain they had caused.

"Next time it will be different. There's no reason to think...."

He closed the two steps between them, grabbing her by the shoulders. "That's not what I mean, you idiot! I always lose the women I love." His fingers dug in, hurting her. "I won't let Kari go! *You* see to it that she comes through."

He dropped his hands, turning away. She stood frozen. *I loved you, too, Thorn, and I still do.* She put her hand to her mouth, biting hard on her lip. It was an admission she had not made to herself before. But this was not the time to explain to him, with Kari upstairs. Suddenly remembering Kari, she left him standing there, running back up the stairs.

Kari still lay with her face to the wall. Marit took one of her hands in hers; it was limp. She reached over, roughly pulling Kari around to face her. Kari's body was passive, her face resigned. A sudden anger welled up in Marit. She slapped the mask-like face hard. Kari's eyes opened wide.

"You're not going to die! You're going to live! Do you hear? You're going to live for Thorn."

❧

Toneta, one of Nicolena's daughters, took up residence at Thorn's to do the housework, sleeping on the sofa in the parlor. But almost every day, Marit walked the near-mile through snow, wind and zero temperatures to carry tempting foods to Kari, or perhaps to prepare something on Kari's own stove. Then she would sit down and, like a mother with a reluctant child, nag and scold until Kari had taken some nourishment; ignoring her evasions: "I had a big breakfast" or "Really, I'm not hungry right now. Just leave it on the stand and I'll eat it later."

One day, Kari said, "I'll be better when spring comes, just wait and see." But the weeks dragged into months and even when the days finally brightened and began to warm, Marit could see no change. Kari still had not left the child-bed.

Maple sugar time had arrived, a time with no outward show of the earth quickening, but with warm midday sun that stirred the life-juices of the trees, and frost-bitten nights that quickly turned chilly after the sun had gone down.

It was on one such evening that Marit paid a visit to Kari, not having found the time during the day. When she left home early in the evening, there still had been warmth in the air and she had not taken a wrap. But on the way home she felt the chill and, since it was dark and she was alone, she picked up her dark skirt by the hem and pulled it up over her shoulders and head as a shawl, the white petticoats she wore keeping her lower extremities warm enough.

She was near the little foot bridge that spanned the creek when she discerned a figure coming toward her on the path ahead. She quickly dropped her skirt and, in embarrassment, stepped into the bushes by the side to conceal herself and let whomever this might be pass.

Standing and waiting, she heard no approaching footsteps. Instead, the silence was broken by an oath and she recognized Nils' voice. Then, all of a sudden, in a headlong rush, he thundered by where she was hidden, all the while hurling curses to the night air.

She thought nothing of the incident until the next morning when, bright and early, a wide-eyed Gunnar appeared at the door with big news.

"Tante Marit, guess what! There are spooks in America, too! Pa saw one last night by the bridge that crosses the creek. He said it was monstrous, with black horns sticking out of its huge head and white at the bottom. And it slick and clean disappeared, just like that!"

It was easy to piece together: the black horns her arms, the quickly dropped skirt suddenly eclipsing her white petticoats a disappearing act, and Nils carrying a full load.

She hid her amusement from Gunnar, but assured him, "There are no spooks in America. If there had been, the Indians would have scalped them years ago! Your Pa must have been seeing things, like he sometimes does when he's drinking. It was probably just a cow."

He mulled this over. It sounded logical. The Indians used to be fierce. They weren't afraid of *anything!* His Pa saw something all right, but not a spook, he deduced with relief.

Seeing that his fears were allayed, she decided to keep her part in the incident to herself. Let Nils believe he had seen an apparition. Maybe a scare would do him good! But she could hardly wait to share her little secret with Kari.

When she reached Kari's house that day, Toneta, too, was goggle-eyed with the story, for Nils had been on his way to Thorn's when Marit met him on the patch.

Nils must have been really shaken up, Marit observed, for Toneta's skittishness had upset Kari. "If you want to go home for an hour or two, I'll sit with Kari," Marit told Toneta.

When Toneta had left, Marit launched into the story with gusto. "Picture this, Kari: Your bed is the bridge." Then, using the whole loft as a stage, she dramatized the incident from beginning to end. First she played herself: walking along with mincing steps as on a narrow path, developing a sudden chill, shaking as with ague. Then, the dawning of a bright idea, the pulling up of her skirt, the startled look when she saw someone coming and, finally, the modest dropping of the skirt, the covert stepping aside, the waiting in forward stance of strained listening. At this point, she crossed over to the other side of the loft, playing Nils: Staggering along, there was his blinking disbelief upon first seeing the spectre, next a dropping back, his indecision as to which way to run, then the headlong rush. She left out only the cursing, substituting "blanks."

Kari, caught up in it, clapped her hands in delight at each "act," and her tinkling laughter filled the loft. At the end of the performance, Marit, too, collapsed in laughter on the bed.

The abandon seemed to do Kari a world of good. For on that today, it seemed to Marit, her spirit returned. Soon she was able to be outdoors and take the sun. Color and strength returned.

CHAPTER IV

"Thorn is going to Millwood and insists that I go along, that it's time I get out and do some shopping, get something new. But I told him I'd go along on only one condition: that you come too! You need an outing even more than I do. How many time shave you been to Millwood since you came to the homestead?"

"Well... never," Marit admitted. "I've never had reason to go. Rolf takes care of the business and I can get everything I need at Pine Fork or the crossroads."

"No. Not everything! You don't find diversion at Pine Fork or the crossroads."

"Diversion?"

"A break from routine. Everyone needs it — even *women!*"

"But there are things that have to be done and only women can do them."

"In some cases that might be true, but not in your case. You are prosperous! Even the Bible gives license to enjoy the fruit of your labor."

Fruit of Rolf's ruthlessness, she thought, flushing.

Almost as if Kari had read Rolf's name when it crossed her mind, Kari continued, "I don't intend to pry, but I've often wondered why Rolf is so indifferent toward you, not at all the way Thorn is with me, and I think I've figured out why. He knows exactly what to expect from you, that you'll always do the practical thing! And he does take you for granted, Marit."

Quickly, Marit qualified, "I *have* thought many times that I'd like to see Anna Rolstad again. We've kept in touch all these years and many times in her letters she's invited me to come and visit her."

"Anna who?"

She realized now that she had never told Kari of the crossing. This she did, thankful for a detour around Kari's well-intentioned but misconceived advice.

After she had related all the hardships and tragedy of the voyage to an aghast Kari, who had crossed first-class, Marit added, "It would be fun to see the boy again. He must almost be a young man now."

"That settles it. I insist you go! It's time you had some fun. And it *will* be a gay trip, shopping, visiting and all."

Kari's enthusiasm was contagious. The contemplated trip was two weeks in the future and Marit found herself daydreaming often in the next days. In her mind's eye, she would go back down the long trail, up hills, down valleys, across streams. And then, at

the other end, Anna's surprised face.... All the things they would
have to tell each other....

It was not impossible, the trip, if she really set her mind to it.
Her pride would not let her ask Rolf to take over her chores while
she was gone, but there were all of Nicolena's boys. Surely one of
them could be spared for a few days. And Randilena could handle
the house. She already had her allotment of daily household chores
which she managed very well. Marit decided to put out some feel-
ers.

That same afternoon, Olaus stopped by to show her his bag of
squirrels from a foray in the nearby woods. "How would you like
to earn a little pocket money?" Marit asked him. "Your Tante Kari
wants me to go with her to Millwood for a few days. If you could
do the barn chores while I'm gone, I'll make it right with you later,
out of my egg money."

"Money? You bet!"

"Not so fast! It isn't for sure yet. And before I decide to go, I
want to make sure it's all right with your mother, that she doesn't
need you herself."

"*Her* need me — nah! But I'll ask if that's what you want."
Then, "I've never hired out before, not for *money!*" He ran out.

In spite of all that she had done for the Dahl family, Marit did
not consider taking advantage the way Rolf did. She got down her
sugar bowl, making sure she had the money to pay Olaus. But
recompensing him fairly would leave her with no spending money
for the trip. Well, she could help Kari with *her* shopping, sharing
in the novel dilemma of trying to make up one's mind among a
big selection of pretty materials. And Marit smiled to herself in
thinking of the store in Pine Fork where there were usually one or
two bolts of dress material, one of cotton print and the other of
heavy wool, the merchant not reordering until a bolt was nearly
gone, so you would see your own print coming and going on other
women. Even now she could envision Kari's face when confronted
with the grand profusion. In advance, Marit shared in her pleasure
and excitement.

Olaus was soon back. "She kicked up a big fuss, but I let her
have it right back. So here I am. When are you leaving?"

"Not for over a week yet."

"That long!"

Now that the problem of the outdoor chores was resolved, Marit informed Randilena of Kari's invitation. Randilena was as thrilled over the prospect as if it were she who had the chance to go. "Oh, do go, Mama. You'll have so much to tell when you come back!"

"Are you sure you can handle the house while I'm gone?"

"Oh, that! That's nothing. But I must remember...." Her eyes got a forlorn look. "Oh, it's nothing."

"What were you going to say? You must remember what?"

"Well.... not to get on Pa's nerves. But I'll be a little mouse while you're gone. A mouse in the house. See, I've made a rhyme, and rhymes help me remember, so don't worry."

Marit decided then not to go. It was not that Rolf would harm Randilena; he had never lain a hand on her. But Marit had always been there to compensate, making up for what she believed was his resentment of Randilena for not having been born a boy; and for the fact that she had not borne any more children, making the fault really *hers,* not Randilena's.

But when she told Randilena she had changed her mind about going, Randilena was even more upset. "I want you to go!" she kept insisting. Finally, Marit hit on the solution of having Nicolena's Ella keep Randilena company while she was gone. "So you won't bust from keeping still!" she told her daughter, making light of it.

So now it just left Rolf. Marit decided to broach it head-on. "Thorn and Kari are going to Millwood and have invited me to go along. Olaus will do the barn chores. Randilena will take care of the house with Ella's help. I will be gone four days."

He looked up at the terse statements, but said nothing. Maybe this will be all there is to it, she thought, yet somehow felt compelled to justify the trip for him. "Kari is going to pick out materials for some new clothes and wants me to help her. And if *I* go, I'm sure we will find lodging at the Rolstads. It will be nice to see them again, see how they've made out."

"No doubt Anna has borne a big brood of children."

This was the one thing in which she had failed; she felt chastised. Was the trip really so important after all?

In her moment of dejection, his next words took her by surprise. "The clothes a wife wears reflects a man's position, his success. You might take some lessons from Kari."

Was he saying he wanted her to go? Even to buy some clothes

for herself? He said no more to clarify things, but she decided that was his meaning and made her plans to go definite.

When the time of departure came, all doubt was removed. Just before they left the house, in the presence of Thorn and Kari, Rolf threw a wad of bills on the table, pronouncing, "The wife of Rolf Monsrud wants for nothing!"

She picked up the bills, dropping them into her satchel without counting them. It had been done mostly to impress Thorn, she knew, but already she was calculating what she would do with the unexpected bonus.

⁂

In the first miles of the ride, Kari was in a dither of anticipation. "These Rolstads you know.... Are they cultured people? Will they be interesting?"

"I gather from Anna's letters that they have done real well. Her man is in the timber business. He had good connections when he came to America. Some cousins had come on ahead. But I doubt if you'll find much culture in Millwood. It's a rough lumber town, you know."

"But they are well-off, you think?"

"Fairly well-off, I believe."

"Good! Then her clothes should be in fashion. We can get ideas and buy and sew accordingly."

Just having clothes to put on is all the fashion there is on the homestead was Marit's sober reflection. But she did not share it with Kari. She much preferred this enthusiastic Kari to the spiritless one of last winter!

Suddenly Kari tired and stopped talking. Thorn halted the rig and they all got down so Kari could move from where she sat in the middle of the front seat to the back seat where she could lie down, a pillow and coverlet having been placed there before leaving. As they went on their way again, Marit entertained her with a running description of all they passed. But when she eventually looked back, she saw that Kari had fallen asleep.

Now she seemingly rode alone with Thorn. There had been a while, after her admission to herself of her true feelings for him, when she had felt uncomfortable — guilty — in his company. But

I can't help how I feel, she rationalized. I have no control over that. The question is: Do I *covet* Thorn? I do not, she had vowed, so there's no reason to feel guilty. Besides, Thorn's own words, "I always lose the women I love," was to say that it was now Kari. She was just a sister-in-law to Thorn. He had no idea how *she* felt, so all she need do was play her role. Thus, the miles were spanned tranquilly, the passing panorama as reading a journal while the laps unfolded.

Mostly virgin forest had lined the trail the first time Marit had come this way. Now fields of grain rippled in the bright July sunlight. She mentally estimated the yield in bushels of each plot they passed. Sometimes only a turning-in indicated a homestead but often the buildings were in plain view of the road. To the uninitiated, they would have had a monotonous similarity, but not to her schooled eyes. She could approximate how long each place had been homesteaded by the metamorphic stages of the buildings. Fences, rock piles and ranked wood each lent clues to her of the sort the people were, their weaknesses and strengths; their chances for success. And when there were clothes on a line, she made a guessing game of the number of children and their ages.

They stopped at noon at a wayside inn to eat and give the horses their break. They leisurely dallied some time but got back on the road and covered the last stretch of the way by late afternoon.

Marit had not had time to write and inform Anna of their impending visit. Yet she was certain of a welcome, her musing on the long ride a telescopic exercise that had brought the past sharply into focus again from where it had receded into a dimness of years.

She had memorized their address and she had thought it would be a simple matter to find the street. But now, on the outskirts, nothing looked the same. The town had grown to a small city, a maze of streets from which she could pick no familiar landmarks. "Perhaps you'd better stop and inquire," she told Thorn.

He reined the horses to the boardwalk, handed the lines to her and hopped down, entering one of the numerous saloons that fronted this street — the main drag. On the walk itself, a veritable stag line of lumberjacks lolled in the varying degrees of sloven of men without the stability of home, wife or family. The summer was their slack season. They ogled Marit and Kari uninhibitedly.

One ambled over to the side of the rig. "Are you ladies strangers in town?" he asked by way of making conversation.

Marit stared straight ahead. But Kari, in her outgoing way, glibly replied, "Why, yes. How did you guess? We are in town to do some shopping."

"Then you've come to the right place! There are stores with just such finery as should grace ladies such as yourselves. How long are you staying?"

"Three days and four nights," Kari pertly informed him.

"Say now! I see that at least one of you ladies is unattached, that there is only one man. If either of you should need an escort while you're in town...."

"I'm the one with the man," Kari informed him.

He now edged closer to Marit, who still continued to stare straight ahead, and in a confidential tone said, "There are places.... Places with private dining rooms where ladies can go in the back door unobserved, have an evening of it...."

Now Marit turned, fixing her eyes coldly on him. "I'll have you know I'm a married woman! And I'm not in the least bit interested in back doors! I'd be caught dead first!" He backed away and left.

Marit turned on Kari. "It's your fault! You gave him the wrong impression, leading him on, being so friendly!"

Kari was convulsed with laughter. "If you could see your own face, Marit."

After some moments, curiosity triumphed over outrage. "Do you think it's really true? That there are places where ladies do sneak in, 'have an evening of it,' as he put it?"

"Undoubtedly."

"But they can't be *ladies!*"

"Well, I'd never set foot in one of them, but I've read that actresses in places like New York and London...."

But just then Thorn returned and they headed off down the street, running the gamut: graphically illustrated saloon fronts, open doors through which the raucous voices of carousers drifted down to the river and the foot of the hill. Now, for the first time, Marit got her bearings. This was the road that led to the ridge where the lumber barons aloofly resided apart from the shoddiness of the lower town; the incline a sluice that spewed wealth at the height and dross at the base.

When they reached the crest of the ridge, the street leveled into a broad boulevard and the homes seemed to increase in size and grandeur as they passed.

Lamps were being lit and they were treated to glimpses of the interiors before the shades were drawn. "I can hardly wait to get inside one of these places!" Kari exclaimed. "I hope the Rolstads live in one of them!"

Her hope was realized when they drew up in front of a massive house of hewn Dunville stone with a round tower set in an angle at the front. Partway up the tower, light streamed through a window set with jewel-like inserts of colored glass, giving the whole pile a cathedral aspect.

Taken aback by the imposing structure, Marit was suddenly struck with stage fright. "Maybe we shouldn't barge in like this. Maybe we should find lodging in an inn for the night and call on Anna tomorrow."

Thorn answered. "If there's such a thing that they can't put us up, I can go and look for lodging later. Right now, it's my main concern to get Kari in out of the night air."

Since he put it that way, Marit had no alternative but to climb down and walk up to the massive elaborately carved door. Its solid bulk mocked her timid tapping.

"Use the knocker," Thorn called from the carriage. Marit found the knocker, lifted and dropped it several times. The door was thrown open. But it was not Anna who stood there.

"Oh, I must have the wrong house! I thought this was the Rolstad home."

She was relieved at the reprieve and had turned away when the young woman said, "This is the right place, all right." The woman, who spoke in a thick accent, skeptically looked Marit over from head to foot. "Was it the lady of the house you were looking for?"

"Well yes. — I think so."

"Your name? I must announce you," she said importantly.

"Just say it's Marit Monsrud. We.... She knows me."

"Step in then."

The girl left Marit standing in the dimly lit paneled hallway, disappearing through a door at the far end, which she closed behind her.

When it opened again, it was Anna who appeared. She stood

for a moment as if not believing her eyes, then rushed forward. "Marit!" she cried, embracing her. Anna pulled her to beneath where the chandelier hung, studying her face. "When Mathilda told me it was Marit Monsrud, I couldn't believe my ears! Is Rolf here?"

"No. I came with friends. They're out in the rig."

Anna went to the door herself, calling out, "Tie the horses and come in."

She turned from the door. "After all these years.... I'd given up hope of ever seeing you again!"

Marit's face was flushed with the emotion of the reunion. "It wasn't my intention to surprise you, shock you. Things just worked out this way."

"I'm glad! It's the most pleasant surprise I've had for a long time."

Thorn and Kari came in and Marit made the introductions. Anna remarked, "You have the same name — you must be Rolf's brother. I didn't know Rolf had a brother in America. You never mentioned it in your letters, Marit."

The girl hovered in the background. Anna instructed her to take their satchels and wraps. They were then escorted to an adjoining room that appeared to be a parlor.

As they sat and listened, Marit faintly discerned the sound of children's voices coming from somewhere back in the house. "And the children, how are they all?"

Anna summoned the servant girl, instructing her, "Bring the children to meet my friends."

"They were not done eating."

"It's all right. For this one time, we'll make an exception."

The five came dutifully trooping in. And it was not hard for Marit to pick out the boy, Peder, who had already started the long-limbed stretch toward manhood.

When Anna presented him, she said, "Peder, this is the Marit I've told you so much about."

The boy looked at her with genuine interest. "She's every bit as big as you said and I'll bet she's strong, too! I'll bet she could lick a whole slew of sailors!"

Anna was embarrassed by the give-away appraisal but Marit indulged Peder by making a fake pass at his chin with doubled fist and the awkward moment dissolved in laughter.

After the children had been dismissed, Anna informed them that guests were expected, tactfully suggesting they would "undoubtedly want to freshen up before the guests arrived, then dinner." Thorn excused himself to attend to the rig and Anna led the way to the hallway again and up the broad balustraded open stairs, where the colored glass window was spotted at the first landing, to the second floor, a labyrinth of bedrooms. She showed Kari to one room and Marit to another, informing them, "We're having a late dinner. I'll have Mathilda bring you a little something to tide you over. I'll see you both later."

The girl soon appeared with warm water for the large china pitchers that stood on marble-topped washstands in each bedroom. A little later, she reappeared to announce, "If you are ready, clean up and you can follow me. Come in here." She led them to a little round sitting room in the tower, where she had laid a tea table with trays of open-faced sandwiches and a silver coffee service.

The condescending attitude of the servant had not escaped Kari. "She acts like it's her house, like we're intruders. You'd never find such impertinence among the servants in the homeland!"

"From the way she talks, I'd say she's not long *from* the homeland. You already speak English better."

"That's it, I'll wager! A newcomer. Probably some ignorant cotter's daughter with no proper upbringing. Putting on airs and trying to impress us!"

After they had eaten, they returned to their rooms. Marit lay down but she was too keyed up to relax. She wished she had something more dressy to wear for the evening. The thought of meeting guests was more than a little disconcerting in the light of the elegance she had so far observed.

She had assumed that the Rolstads had done well, but she never dreamed *this* well. The timber business must be a good one to be in, that is, if you were at the top of it, not at the bottom, she deducted. Downstairs, when Thorn had inquired as to the specific nature of Eyvin's work, Anna had answered, "He's a cruiser." It was an unfamiliar designation to Marit, whose lexicon of forest occupations was limited to the lower echelons: sawyer, teamster, leader, driver, cant-hook man and such. *I must ask Anna exactly what he does,* she mused, *so it'll make sense to Randilena when I describe this palace of a house to her.*

From time to time she heard rigs pass by on the boulevard with a rhythm-duo of jingling harnesses and thudding hooves. When ultimately she heard one turn in, she got up, peeking through the curtain. Immediately following, another turned in. In the light of the posted gas lantern by the drive, she watched the guests alight. Then the sound of voices faintly sifted up from below. She went to the mirror, patting her hair in place and, as she expected, there soon was a tap on the door. Mathilda came to announce that dinner was about to be served.

In the hallway, she was joined by Thorn and Kari and together they descended the stairs. At the foot, Anna and Eyvin waited with their guests. After the introductions, they proceeded to the dining room. A long table was spread with a snowy cloth and dishes. Crystal and silver scintillated in flickering candlelight from wall sconces and candelabra.

When they had been seated, Marit studied the other guests. Besides Eyvin's two cousins and their wives, there were three more people: Mr. and Mrs. Falk, who were a middle-aged couple, and Mr. Willard, a young man.

It was the younger of the two men — Mr. Willard — to whom Eyvin showed the greater deference, as did the cousins and Mr. Falk. The meal had not progressed far before it became apparent that Mr. Willard was to be the dominant figure of the evening. They hung on his every word and he had many, being a raconteur of some skill.

At first mention of his name, Marit took this man "Paul Bunyan" to be a mutual acquaintance of them all. For when Mr. Willard brought up his name, they all leaned forward in anticipation, as if anxious for news of him.

"You all know how Ole Olson was always spoiling for a fight," Mr. Willard began one story.

"No," they all chorused. "Tell us."

"Well it seems that Olson went looking for Paul Bunyan, aiming to challenge him. He heard Paul was at his farm, so he set off cross country through trees so thick he had to strip to his red flannels and smear himself with bear grease to squeeze through. When Olson came upon Paul, he was breaking a piece of ground with a plow and five yokes of oxen, the Blue Ox among them. Olson stood waiting for Paul to make his round and come back to that end. Paul came toward him slicing through twenty-foot stumps like they were butter. But Paul was too busy to stop, so busy that when he got to the end he didn't wait for his oxen to turn themselves around. He just picked up the plow and them — all ten of them — and set them down again headed in the other direction and went right on plowing. When Olson saw that, he high-tailed for the woods and hasn't been seen since!"

Marit, having caught on about halfway through the story, joined in the laughter and applause.

It was to be the first of many lumber-lore stories. After Mr. Willard's story, Eyvin took up on Paul Bunyan, adding "You all know how proud Paul is of his curly black hair and how his wife combs it every morning with a cross-cut saw after first parting it with a broadax. Well, he is just as proud of his beard!" Then, after a suitable pause: "Several times a day when he's out in the woods he pulls up young pine trees by the roots and brushes out the pesky frost-biters that like to build their nests in his big black bush."

" —And did you hear of the winter so cold that words froze solid and fell to the ground as soon as they were said?" Eyvin's cousin continued. "Well Paul had all the cuss-words sorted out and stored them 'til spring. Used the explosions as they thawed out for blasting powder."

And on and on, for jubilance seemed to be the mood of the evening. They were evidently all connected with the timber business and Marit inferred that the dinner was in celebration of some deal that Eyvin had effected that was of benefit to them all.

The meal progressed slowly and with a formality that fascinated Marit. It seemed to entail a great deal of unnecessary dirtying of dishes, a production that kept two maids scurrying with changes of dishes for the featuring of star foods. It finally culminated with the women adjourning to the parlor for the serving of demitasse cups of black coffee and the men retreating to what Anna referred to as the library.

Marit now realized that the room she had thought was the parlor when they first came was but an anteroom. For the room in which she now found herself was much larger, and shadow play from flickering fire on the hearth enhanced a busyness of patterned walls, drapes, rug upholstery and profusion of bric-a-brac. "I had Mathilda lay a small fire to take out the damp. These stone houses seem to attract it," Anna explained. After a time, the men rejoined them and the doldrums of woman talk was blown away in a gale of wide-ranging conversation.

Wine had been served with dinner but Marit had only made a pretense of sipping it. Now Mathilda came in with a decanter and fresh goblets on a silver tray. She passed among them, serving. The other women participated, so she did too, mimicking their swirling of the ruby liquid in the half-filled goblets. Experimentally, she took one sip. It really didn't have a bad taste at all!

Marit looked across the room at Kari. She had never been more beautiful. As always when she was excited. High rouge-like spots of color had come out on her cheeks and in the soft light of the room and her eyes flashed vibrant cobalt as they flicked from one face to another. When a clever remark caught her fancy, her laughter bubbled, having the effect of stimulating the men to competitive efforts of wit. And Kari, too, scored with the rejoinders.

Marit was glad she had picked a place to sit where she was out of the exchange, where she could merely listen and not be expected to contribute. She continued to sip on the wine and when Mathilda came round offering refills, she accepted it, then another.

She began to feel oddly detached from everyone in the room. From time to time, she was aware of Thorn's eyes on her but she did not return the glances. She knew he sensed she was ill-at-ease and was concerned. But she would not acknowledge to him by as much as a *look* that she did not measure up!

Her interest in the talk had flagged; it all seemed unreal anyway. The room spun in a carousel of absurdly gay faces. But suddenly she became aware that everyone's eyes were on *her*.

"... and only Marit Monsrud can reveal the *real* identity of the spook of the Willow Creek bridge!" Thorn was saying. He stood, bowed toward her with arm extended, as if to introduce her.

She felt her face going red. And now Kari crossed over, grabbing her hands and attempting to pull her to her feet, cajoling, "Show them Marit, just the way you did it for me. The whole thing from beginning to end!"

The *whole* thing? Her petticoats reached way down to her ankles — but underclothes were underclothes! They would think her a trollop!

They were all waiting expectantly, Kari applauding in advance. Now, she looked at Thorn. It was as if they were alone in the room...

the giddiness of the moment as the rocking of the sea.... *Now who's green,* Thorn's eyes were saying. *I'll show you, Thorn Monsrud,* her own eyes flashed back.

She went through the whole act, even improvising a sprawling fall in Nils' headlong rush down the trail. When she had finished and the uproar of laughter and applause had subsided, Mr. Willard commented, "Your rendition of the drunken gait was superb! Sarah Bernhardt could not best it!"

Throughout the rest of the evening she, too, was caught up in the whirl. It was as if she had been drawn into a square dance and, once in, must fill her place — keep up the pace — so they could all go on dancing. She complied to their demands for more accounts of her experiences in the wilderness. They found them all hilarious.

It was evident to her that these people put a high premium on being amused. Once, during a lull, she puzzled to herself: Strange, when these things were really happening, they didn't seem funny at all!

On the stairs again, the party over and the guests departed, Kari embraced her. "Your act was the highlight of the whole evening!" she exalted.

Marit was back in her room, undressed and in bed, when there came a tap on the door. It opened a crack. "It's me. Anna. Can I come in and talk, or are you too tired?"

"I'm wide awake."

Anna came into the room and lit a lamp. "I thought this would be our best opportunity to talk alone."

"I was wondering too when we'd get a chance to talk."

Yet when Anna sat down on the bed, neither said a word for several moments. Then, Marit confessed, "It wasn't like that, not really."

"I know. Now tell me what it was really like."

Marit filled her in on their long struggle. When she had talked herself out, she finished by saying, "I don't have to ask you how you've done. I can see for myself. The house, the servants. Did I hear you tell Thorn that Eyvin is a cruiser? What do cruisers do?"

"They seek out timber holdings, estimate, make deals. With a successful coup, Eyvin's commission runs into thousands of dollars."

"Coup?"

Anna looked down at her hands, examining a hangnail as if at that moment it were the most important thing in the world. When she looked up, it was to ask, "Have you ever broken a bad egg into the pan? Even if you shut your eyes, turn from it, the smell...." She did not explain further, going on to other things.

"Now, as for the servants, sometimes I feel I'm in the wife-importing business on that score! We've paid the way from the homeland for so *many* of these girls. They come ignorant, clumsy, but willing to learn. And they learn so fast. The language, the currency, the ways of the country and, in particular, that the social barriers are not as rigid here as back home. They can marry above their status and that with the shortage of women they can have their pick of an army of suitors. I've been Godmother to at least a half dozen of former maids' offspring! But I can't say that I blame them. Why should they be satisfied to be a servant forever in someone else's house when they can be mistress of their own?"

Changing the subject, Marit asked, "This young man... this Mr. Willard you had as a guest tonight. Who is he?"

"He's the Old Man's son, in town to check on the business for his father in St. Louis. The Old Man owns everything: the timber, the equipment, the mills, even the town. It's really *their* town. They own *everyone* in it."

Anna stood up and said world-wearily, "I suppose they are millionaires many times over."

She walked to the door, blowing out the lamp as she passed by it.

"Anna..."

"Yes, dear?"

"Who is this Sarah Bernhardt?"

CHAPTER V

It seemed to Marit that she had been gone much longer and so great was her eagerness for the sight of home that the horses seemed to her to be in a stall. She wanted to jump down and run on ahead of them. And when the place in all its familiarity *did* come into view, she burst out, "This is where I belong!"

So fervent was the avowal that Kari looked at her in surprise. "Why Marit! I do believe you've been homesick!"

"Maybe that is it. I don't know. I just know that I'm glad, so glad to be back! I never knew, never realized before, how much it has all come to mean to me."

Randilena had been waiting and when she saw the rig coming, she swiftly legged her way down the trail to meet them. She followed alongside, more up in the air than down, until the rig came to a standstill in the yard and, when Marit stepped down, Randilena threw herself on her mother.

In the house Marit quickly scanned the kitchen. Randilena had done her job well; everything was spic and span and in its place. "Good girl!" Marit complimented. "But I expected to find Ella here with you."

"Her Ma wanted her so she went home. She wanted me to go along and come back again together, but I was afraid you'd come while I was gone and that I'd miss you. I could hardly wait." She was busily eyeing and feeling the packages. "Hurry and open them," she begged.

"First things first. And first supper. Then the chores. After that we'll have the whole evening."

Rolf came in at the usual time for supper. It could have been any other evening. That she had been gone and returned he acknowledged in no way. However, in her own glow at being back, she told him, "It's good to be home." He did not respond but she went on anyway. "It's good to get away. It makes you appreciate what you have. I wouldn't trade this place for all of Millwood!"

This aroused enough interest for him to comment, "I take it that Eyvin hasn't done as well as I have."

That wasn't it at all! But would Rolf, in his single-mindedness, understand that it was the homestead itself. The fiber of it and it fiber of her, the tug of roots put down? And how firmly rooted she hadn't realized until she left it for these few days? That she felt a sense of belonging, that the homestead had become home as Lilledalen had once been home?

All she said was, "I gather from what Anna said that the timber business does have its drawbacks."

This pleased him, and was at least a half-truth. For although Anna hadn't said it in so many words, the opportunity for false dealing was a drawback to her way of thinking. But it would certainly not be a drawback to Rolf's way of thinking and it was better than telling him the whole truth and putting him in a bad mood by telling him that the success of the Rolstads made his trivial by comparison.

Supper behind, Randilena dogged her footsteps to the barn, pelting her with questions now that they were out of earshot of Rolf. And weary as Marit was from the day's long ride, she obliged by recalling those facets of the trip she knew would tickle Randilena's ears.

Olaus, not knowing she was home, had started chores, and though the faithful hireling up to now, he abdicated when she came in the barn door, not to go home but to listen, plying her with questions of his own. But Marit did not scold when in his preoccupation with vicarious adventure he shucked responsibility and followed her around as she did the work. She could have been Marco Polo returned for all these two had seen of their world outside the neighborhood.

"I have a few little things for you and the others," she told Olaus when the work was finished. "But come tomorrow morning. I haven't unpacked yet. And I'll give you your pay then too."

That way Rolf wouldn't watch her count out the money from the sugar bowl and it would give her the evening solely for Randilena. The opening of packages would be a showing, a production put on for her benefit.

For the extravaganza, she carried all the packages to the big table in the dining room. With a flourish she held a bag high above the table, shaking out the contents. Yards of silk ribbon of every hue spilled out, slithering over the tabletop like a collapsed rainbow.

"So much, Mama! How come so *much* ribbon?"

"I thought it would be nice if we gave each of your cousins enough for a bow of each color. Later, you can snip them, count them out and put them in the bag again for Olaus to take with him when he comes tomorrow. What's left, you can put away for bows of your own."

Marit opened another bag, just far enough to allow Randilena to peek in. She held the bag toward Randilena, saying, "These are for the boys." And, as she had expected, Randilena was not interested enough in things for boys to want to examine the contents.

There were many small bags, an assortment of notions. These Marit laid out in display on the table: buttons, lace, braiding, threads of various hue. Randilena fondled each card and spool, finally asked, as Marit hoped she would, "What do they go on?"

This was the cue for the main event. Marit began to undo the packages of materials. The scarlet velvet caught Randilena's eye immediately. She pulled its yardage to her, running her fingers sensually over the nap.

"I knew you'd like it," Marit said. "I picked it out just for you, for a dress."

"For me? Will I have a whole dress of it. Velvet!"

Randilena put the velvet to her face, rubbing her cheek on it. "I don't mean it as a slur to you, Mama, but I'm sure glad I took after the Monsrud side."

"I'm glad you're glad." And that you accept yourself as you are, she might have added, recalling how at Randilena's age she had found no compensation in feminine prerogatives.

As the thought crossed her mind, as it to confirm it, Randilena said, "How dull it must be to be a boy and never be able to wear pretty clothes!"

Randilena flipped disinterestedly through the pile of calico apron prints on the table. "What of you? You dress material? Didn't you get anything special for you?"

It was the last package, the most bulky one. When the material was exposed, Randilena's face fell. "Why didn't you buy something bright? I'll bet Tante Kari did!"

"I'm not the type for bright colors — like Kari."

"When I get to be a lady, I'm going to wear *pretty* clothes like her. — At least, until I get old."

Now she studied Marit. "Are you getting old? Is that why you wear such dull colors?"

The thought that she was getting old struck Marit as hilarious, until she remembered that she had always thought of her own mother as being old. *But in comparison to Kari, I must look like an old crone to Randilena,* she rationalized.

"This material suits me just fine!" she said firmly. "I've needed just such a dress for a long time. Something for special occasions... like weddings and funerals. And for all its *dullness,* it's very good material, very expensive. It will last for many years. Besides, I'm too big for bright colors, not dainty like you and Kari.

Randilena went up the stairs to bed clutching the velvet to her.

Halfway up, she turned, asking wistfully, "Do you think someday I might be able to go to visit the Rolstads at Millwood? See their fine house and all?"

"I'm sure you will. Someday."

Early the next morning, as Marit had expected, Olaus appeared to collect his pay. After she had doled out the coins, she handed two packages to him, saying, "This one is for the girls and this is for you boys."

He peeked in the latter. "Whistles! — And penknives! This is better than Christmas. At Christmas we only get clothes!"

He fished out a whistle, blowing on it. Marit clapped her hands to her ears. "Not in the house! You'll drive your Ma crazy! And the whistles are for the younger boys. The penknives are for you older boys, something that might come in handy."

As he darted out the door, she called after him, "I have something for your Ma, too. Tell her to come this afternoon so she can make her own choice of the apron prints."

Although she had learned the fate of the lace tablecloth through Randilena, at that time something far more precious — Kari's life — had been at stake and it had seemed to her then that both the cloth and Kari were too fragile for the harshness of this frontier place. When Kari survived, the cloth had seemed too frivolous to grieve over. And Kari, feeling she owed her very life to Marit, decided to never tell her of the part the tablecloth played in her fall. As close as she had come to telling her was one day, when she said, "If ever again in some moment of mistaken guilt at your own enviable circumstances you give Nicolena a beautiful thing to destroy, I shall never forgive you! I'd sooner you'd let me die." And in a flash of mind Marit had visualized Kari — beautiful Kari — dead, life sapped from her body. She was aware that there was a spiritual sustenance as vital to Kari as food and recalled the truisms, "Man does not live by bread alone," and more chilling, "Life is a vapor," a thing that could easily be wafted away, given Kari's delicacy.

But happily, these days a rejuvenated Kari was poring over *Godey's Lady's Book* that Anna had pressed on her. Introduced to it at Millwood, Kari had been so taken with the fashion magazine and the genteel life-style its pages of stylish clothing and houses conjured, that she had asked Anna for paper and pencil so she could make some sketches. Anna instead had insisted on giving her the magazine, saying, "I'll never miss it."

Already two creations had emerged, for Kari was gifted at dress-making to the extent of being able to duplicate a style simple by studying the pictures, patterning it to the contours of her own body. First came the cutting, then the fitting to her body by the jigsaw of pieces held together with pins; then the basting and a try-on for final adjustment before she would lift the lid of the Singer treading sewing machine that Thorn had purchased at Millwood and hauled on the return trip strapped on the top of the carriage. The seams firmly sewed by machine, she would finally add the frills by hand, then a final inspection in the mirror they had brought from Norway, its gilt frame making of her image, in chromatic hues and delicacy, a Renoir portrait. But the "dotting of the i's and crossing of the t's" did not come until she had modeled each for Marit and Randilena, pirouetting to their "oohs" and "ahs."

Kari generously offered to do Randilena's velvet dress, a miniature version of a style she had chosen for one of her own. When it was finished and Randilena modeled it, Kari gifted her with a fan that complimented the dress, one of several she had bought in Millwood, having been taken with the flirtatious device in watching Mrs. Falk and Anna wield theirs. She had practiced in front of the mirror until she had the manipulation down to an art, which she demonstrated for Randilena.

"Being a woman is like a game," Randilena commented.

"For you, only a peek-a-boo game," Marit said. "You've a long way to go before you're a woman."

"Not really," Kari countered. "It seems to me I was a little girl one day and a married woman the next. And, before you know it, it will be the same with Randilena."

❧

It was late fall before Marit got to her own dress. But it was just as well, she felt. With the harvest out of the way and with the termination of outdoor work, save the chores, she would have more time to devote to it and could do a *really* good job.

She finished the dress in early December and decided she would give its first showing at the Christmas Vesper service, which would be held a week after Christmas because it was not until then that the minister was due on his next circuit.

Kari burst in one day to upset this conservative projection. "I've decided to have a Christmas party," she announced breathlessly. "I'm going to invite all the neighbors! I want you to help me plan it."

It was easy for her to understand Kari's need for diversion. She had no children, no outdoor work, just her house, and reading. But what of the other women? With their sobering responsibilities, could they find it in themselves to have a party? Yet the season justified it. In the homeland, the Yuletide had been festive, with even the birds having their *Jule Neket,* a specially gleaned sheaf of grain put out for them at Christmas.

"Do you think," Marit asked, "anyone would come?"

"Why wouldn't they?"

"There's never been a party or a gathering only for the purpose of having a good time. They've always gathered for a reason before, a good reason, like threshing or christenings."

"There's only one way to find out. Give a party and see. Tell me you'll help!"

"I'm not against it. It's just so... so out of the ordinary. But I'll help. Tell me what you want me to do."

"Well, it's the usual way, you know, to go potluck whenever there's a gathering. But I'm giving a party so I'll want to furnish the refreshments. I'd like your suggestions as to what to serve and your help with the baking. And there must be decorations. Randilena and Nicolena's girls, I'm sure, will be glad to help with that part of it. And there's one other thing: We should have entertainment. I've often wondered if anyone in the neighborhood has talent, along musical lines, for instance."

Marit knew that a few had brought musical instruments with them from the old country, which they played solely for their own enjoyment since there was no public call for their talent. "I'll ask around and see what I can round up," she promised Kari.

The plans went forward. Many of the men were working at the pineries but the women were informed by the blanket word-of-mouth invitation: "Everyone welcome." Most evidenced that this novelty — a get-together just for socializing — was indeed welcome, especially so since at that time the men would be home for the holiday break and everyone would get to see everyone else. This was a circumstance that usually didn't occur until logging was over for the winter and the spring drive executed.

Since it was to be a Christmas party, they planned the decorations and refreshments to reflect the season. Even Nicolena got into the spirit of it and offered to help with the time-consuming task of baking the traditional Norwegian Christmas delicacies. The girls could hardly wait until the day of the party. It was their plan to gather evergreen boughs on the very day, so they would be fresh for the evening. In the meantime, they were fashioning adornments of anything bright they could find, material or paper; getting together to make chains, bows and braided baskets to be tied to the evergreen boughs for accent. Apple trees that Marit had planted in the first years were now bearing, the harvest packed in barrels in the basement. She donated a goodly amount of these as treats, the girls polishing them to a glow with beeswax. And Kari, on a shopping trip to Pine Fork, bought some oranges at a dear price. Here, as in the homeland, they were available only during the holiday season.

Expectation tingled the air more than the sudden sub-zero cold snap. None was more expectant than Kari, whose new wardrobe had hung unused — party dresses without a party! It was her hope that this party would only be the beginning, that the idea would snowball once she got it rolling. It was the idea that life need not be all drudgery and hard work. All that was needed was a different tack, one that took into account the need for respite from labor to renew the spirit.

꧁꧂

Christmas, usually the highlight of the year, was not of stellar importance this year, the twenty-fourth and twenty-fifth but prelude to the twenty-sixth and the party. On that evening, chores were completed early, by twilight rather than lantern light, so they would have plenty of time for the bathing and dressing up.

Marit donned her somber dress. It did not seem quite up to the occasion and she wished she had something bright to wear, just for this one time. Upstairs, Randilena burrowed her head and arms through the folds of velvet and after they emerged, the dress dropped into place on her body of its own weight. She had been determined to put her hair up for the first time this evening in spite of her mother's repeated, "You're too young for that yet." Randilena had practiced and practiced on her own but it never seemed to look right when she got done with it. Now, with dress in place, she picked up her comb and went downstairs. "Please...." Marit gave in and when it was done up and she stood back, her breath caught in her throat. The scarlet set off Randilena's dark hair and cast a glow on her fair skin, the effect a portent of beauty that was to come. Kari's words came back: "I was a little girl one day, and a woman the next...."

Rolf emerged from the bedroom in his Sunday suit, stood before the washstand mirror to part his hair in the middle and slick it down with water. Then, in still self-consciousness, they put on their outer wraps. Marit threw an apron over one arm as they picked up the party fare and went out into a night crystalled by full moon on frost.

Marit had planned to arrive early to attend to last-minute details. Yet, several families had preceded them and the air of the big kitchen when they stepped in from the cold was stuffy with heat from the kitchen range and pipe smoke.

Kari came bustling in from the little parlor. She took Marit's food contributions and installed them in a safe, up-out-of-the-way place in the cupboard, then directed Marit and Randilena to the upstairs, where they were to deposit their wraps. Marit took Rolf's coat and cap herself and followed.

Already, three infants slept blissfully, if haphazardly, on the counterpane. They put their coats at the foot of the bed, leaving room for more that were sure to join these three.

When Marit had taken off her coat, Kari quickly appraised her. "You need something to brighten that dress," she said authoritatively. She went to the dresser drawer, selected an ornate brooch, then came back and pinned it on Marit's bodice. "See!" she said, steering Marit to the mirror. "It makes a world of difference!"

They went down and joined the other ladies in the parlor, the women eyeing each other like strangers in the newness of this situation. More rigs arrived and soon the parlor was packed. And it was evident that most had put forth some extra effort for the party. Hair was braided, crimped or beribboned. At least three new dresses other than those of the Monsrud women were easy to spot. The cotton prints, as yet unintroduced to the ravage of strong lye soap were conspicuous in their brightness, making them look gala.

The party got off to a slow start, seeming at first to follow the pattern of Sunday gatherings with the men in one room talking of farming, logging and politics, the women in another room engaged in the small talk of their circumscribed world. Yet, there was a slight detectable difference in tenor, a strained chord of stiffness and voices hushed not present in the relaxed Sunday gatherings, after the formality of the service was behind.

Kari sensed this and jumped to her feet. "Let's join the men. Bring your own chairs." She initiated the move, grabbing her chair and moving to the kitchen. The rest followed.

The move, however, did not produce the hoped-for livening effect. If anything, sociality was quelled even more, at least for the women. When the men saw the women beginning to troop in with their chairs, they took their own seating with them and all moved to one side of the kitchen, vacating the other side for the women, who set their chairs neatly down in rows facing the men so that now conversation could only be carried on with those nearest, unless one leaned forward to draw someone down the line into conversation.

Kari called Thorn aside for consultation and he went outside. She stood by the door waiting for his return, opening it at a bump on the door and holding it open wide for him to roll in a keg. Having tapped it, Thorn filled glasses and Kari passed them, to the men first — with few refusing — then to the women. None was bold enough to accept, although it was common knowledge in the neighborhood that in the privacy of their own homes some relished the suds as much as their men-folk.

The glasses were refilled several times but still the party bogged in habit. Kari now went to the middle of the floor, clapping her hands for attention. "How about tuning up that fiddle, Harald?" A number clapped their approval of the suggestion.

Harald, after displaying the proper amount of modest reluctance, got to his feet, saying, "Well, if I'm going to make a fool of myself, I want company! Come you fellows. Karl, get your squeezebox. I know you brought it, and Olaf, didn't you bring your guitar?"

These two, again after the requisite coaxing, got to their feet and followed Harald out, returning shortly with the cased instruments. Then came the seemingly interminable tuning-up exercises, the procedure an enigma to most of the onlookers, who waited with patient expectancy.

Finally, an electric stance indicated that the tuning was mutually satisfactory and they were now going to get down to the real business of making music. Harald arched his torso over the violin, snuggled his chin on the rest, his hand holding the bow poised in the air. His foot began to tap. Then, with an agility that was unbelievable, his big, thick fingers began their ploy over the frets and the sawing bow gave voice to the pattern the fingers wove. Karl and Olaf followed his lead, they too lending their whole bodies to the rollicking polka and carrying the listeners along even as they sat. Feet began shuffling and tapping; entranced children unconsciously aped the body movements of the three musicians.

Nothing was said about dancing, but when Kari ran to Thorn, pulled him out to the middle of the floor and the whirling began, no one seemed surprised. Several got up, piled their chairs and benches against the wall to make more room, and as Thorn and Kari whirled by, they began to whirl in the couple's wake. The cavorting feet set the whole floor to undulating in time to the music. Soon hoofers were jostling each other for space and as each tune gamboled to completion, there was an immediate clamor for more.

When the dancing started, Marit busied herself in a corner of the kitchen making preliminary preparations for the coffee break. Dancing required a certain grace that she believed she did not possess. But Kari was determined that *everyone* should have a good time. As she spun past Marit, she called, "Forget about lunch! There's plenty of time for that!" And when that dance ended, Kari darted over to Rolf, pulling him to his feet.

Marit's eyes bugged as Rolf led Kari though the steps almost as gracefully as had Thorn! So engrossed was she at the sight of an unwound Rolf, she did not notice that Thorn had come to stand by her side until he spoke.

"How about it, Marit? Will you have a fling with me?"

"Oh no! I just couldn't. I'd never be able to keep up!"

But even as she protested, he was pulling her out on the floor. He put his arm firmly about her waist and took her hand. So masterful was his leading that she was surprised to find herself following his steps without difficulty.

She looked into his face, so startlingly close to her own. "It goes easier than I thought," she laughed.

He looked deeply into her eyes. "You're easily led."

The penetrating look seemed to go right through her, to something far away behind her and this moment. She didn't know why she said it, picking this time of all times to say, "Thorn, I'm sorry."

He looked away from her, but at the same time tightened his arm about her, drawing her even closer to him, the brooch causing a hurt in the press of his body against hers. The room and the blurred dancers became a phosphene pierced by bright flashes of lamp spots as they whirled. Then the music was drowned by a primitive drumbeat in her ears, the pounding of her heart, welling up in her throat and cresting until she thought she would burst with it. "Please... I've had enough," she begged.

But he did not release her until the music stopped. She fled to the washstand, grabbed the bucket and went out the door.

Immediately outside the door she paused. The frigid air stung her throat as she gasped it in. She went to the pump, taking her time about filling the bucket, pumping slowly, methodically, as if to invoke normalcy of the homely task.

Having pumped the bucket full, she stood still, looking up into the night sky. The moon had gone down and the stars were close, coldly twinkling diamond-blue in the black velvet-lined case of the heavens. The sound of the music drifted to her ears from the cabin as if seeking her out, unwilling to let her have a moment's peace even out here alone under the sky.

The devil is in the fiddle — I wouldn't have one in the house.... Her mother had said it many years ago and the recollection, conveyed in her mother's quiet voice, seemed so in character as to be audible. *Strange that she should speak to me now, at this particular time of all times, out of eternity.* Was it a warning? She picked up the bucket and went back to the cabin.

When she lifted the latch of the door and attempted to push it open, she found there was a press against it. When they gave way for her entrance, she saw that all had cleared the floor and moved back to the walls, the better to watch the two who were now dancing: Randilena led by the Tefft lad. Round and round they whirled with watchers clapping time to the music. They spun to a stop and everyone cheered them.

The fire in the range had burned down to coals and Marit replenished it with wood to bring the two big pots of water to a boil for coffee. Dodging the dancers on the outer fringes, she carried trays of food to the table, which had been pushed back against a wall to make more room for dancing. Even when all the food had been arranged on the table, she still had time to kill while waiting for the water to come to a boil. She wished herself someplace else, anywhere but here with the throbbing music in her ears and the memory of Thorn's arms crushing her close.

The water did finally boil and she made the coffee. The tempting aroma, together with the heat from the stoked fire, became too much for the dancers and the musicians, as well. The three men put down their instruments for a break. The musicians and most of the other men went outdoors, leaving the door open behind them to let out the heat. Those who stayed cooled themselves in the draft.

Kari occupied herself with her fan —no affectation at this point. Randilena retrieved her fan from where she had laid it up for safe-keeping and mimicked Kari.

The men came back in, passing round the table, followed by the youngsters. Finally, the women filled their plates and retired to find seating in the parlor to eat. And a far different mood now prevailed than when they had gathered there earlier in the evening. Restraint had fallen away and the room was a bustle of animation and laughter. Marit felt set apart by her own constraint.

After the dishes were done, a task in which many of the women pitched in to help, someone called for more music. Rolf came to Marit's side, saying brusquely, "This is enough. We're going home."

"That's fine with me."

She went to get her wraps and they prepared to take their leave. "Are you going so soon?" Kari objected. "The party's not over yet!"

Thorn was by her side, but Marit did not look at him. "Morning comes soon," she said by way of explanation.

On the way home, Marit began to chatter and Rolf hushed her curtly. Immersed as she was in her own confused emotions, she did not notice that he was in a black mood. It was not until Randilena had gone to bed and they were in their own room that she detected the change.

He had been good-natured enough in the early part of the evening. What had gone wrong for *him* at the party? Had he noticed her with Thorn or seen something pass between them?

It was some days later that Randilena came running down the stairs, saying, "Mama, did you take my velvet dress from the closet? I'm sure I hung it up but I can't find it."

Marit, too, searched the closet, then the whole room, drawer by drawer, but without success. "Now isn't that the strangest thing," she said. She searched the whole house, although it didn't make sense that the dress would be anywhere but in Randilena's room. It was not to be found anywhere.

Such a thing was impossible and she began casting about for explanations. Nicolena? She was spiteful enough to have taken the dress in a jealous mood. But she had not been to visit since the party. Of course, Marit was sometimes out of the house but Randilena would have been there.... The truth will out, she finally told herself, at the same time assuring Randilena, "It'll turn up, I'm sure."

It was two days later that she carried out the ash tray from the range to dump it. As the ashes slid from the tray, some bright objects caught her eye. She picked them up, at first examining them out of curiosity. Then curiosity turned to disbelief. But there could be no doubt what they were — the buttons from Randilena's velvet dress! The dress had been burned. *Someone* had burned the dress!

She couldn't bring herself to tell Randilena what she now was sure had been the fate of the dress. Randilena must never find out what happened to it, she decided. But if I ever find out who did such a mean thing....

"Never mind," she told Randilena. "Next time someone goes to Millwood, I'll order some more velvet and have Kari make another one just like it." She knew this was unlikely at any time soon, but it was not impossible at some time in the future.

"It has to be *some place,*" Randilena persisted. "It couldn't just walk off by itself." She didn't give up the search for weeks.

Even after Randilena had given up all hope of ever finding the dress, she still spoke of it wistfully. "Sometimes it seems the dress was just a dream, too beautiful to be real. Maybe if we'd left the party sooner — like in the Cinderella story, you know — maybe then it wouldn't have vanished."

CHAPTER VI

I n the buoyant wake of the party, the cold, dark days of winter that follow the holidays were less palling that year. The party was the talk for weeks after.

Kari was jubilant. "I think I'll make it an annual event. The Annual Willow Creek Christmas Ball. How does that sound to you? Or maybe The Holiday Homecoming Ball, because all the men are home from the pineries. It would be something to look forward to each year, to brighten these dull lives. People are short-changing themselves when they don't take the time to enjoy life while they are living it — taking their share of happiness before it's too late."

Take happiness? What would happen if everyone, including herself, took happiness, Marit speculated. What would happen to Kari, secure in Thorn's love as a sailor in oilskins, if she took her happiness with Thorn?

Marit had been so certain up until the night of the party that Thorn had found his happiness with Kari, that she was everything, even more, than she had been to him. But if that were so, why had he insisted on finishing the dance? Why hadn't he let her go?

His arm tightening about her.... Was he taunting her for the hurt she had given him, or was it something more? If it were something more... I mustn't even *think* such a thing....

It hadn't been hard for her to deal with her feelings for him as long as he had been indifferent toward her. But now, unbidden, those moments close to him crept into her thoughts, bringing a tide of emotion, a flush to her face, even though she told herself firmly: *This is wrong!*

Worst of all, she could not avoid him. Her close relationship with Kari threw her into contact with him constantly. She could think of no excuse that would be plausible enough to Kari to break off her friendship with her. But now when she was at Kari's house, she found herself listening for Thorn's footsteps, yet dreading when she heard them, for then she must pretend and make as if nothing had passed between them, that everything was as before.

But was it really different from before? Or was it only her?

Thorn gave no indication on their encounters. Now, as he always had been, he was maddening to her in his inaccessibility and the tension was such that she had the urge to confront him and force the issue, to have *whatever* this was out in the open. But in her more rational moments she shrank from the truth.

She had underestimated Kari's perceptiveness. One day, Kari confided: "I'm worried about Thorn. Sometimes I wonder if he misses the sea, if that's what he's brooding about these days. But he denies that there's *anything* on his mind."

This bit of conjecture on Kari's part served to disquiet Marit all the more. *Then, it isn't only me. It's him, too!* And she found no comfort in the thought.

The knowledge, in fact, preyed on her mind. She felt herself a sham, likening her lift to the false-fronted stores of the town, the even planes of the front hiding the irregularities of what lay behind.

For her relationship with Thorn was not the only irregularity of her life these days. There had been a change in Rolf in his attitude toward Randilena. And this, too, seemed to date back to the night of the Christmas party.

He had always seemed transparent to Marit, his boasting, greed and desire to be top man all part of his vanity. And his attitude toward Randilena, she had believed, also was of that vanity: the wound to his pride of the dearth of progeny. But since the party he had done an about-face, not ignoring Randilena but taking an interest in her, as if he were seeing her for the first time. Inexplicably despising what he saw, he seemed to have undergone an impervious turn-about that disturbed Marit and caused her to re-examine all the aspects of his behavior toward Randilena through the years.

Incidents to which she had attached no great significance at the time now took on singular importance, suggesting a pattern — but with a vital piece missing. Her intuition was that, were the vital piece to be found and put in place, the outline then presented would be grotesque and misshapen.

Bold action had always before been Marit's forte, but in her present twin dilemmas, the vulnerability of both Kari and Randilena, forbade rashness and for the first time in her life she had to learn to cope with the paralysis of undaring.

Sowing time came early that spring and everyone said it would be a good grain year, that the sooner the grain was planted the better. Some even maintained that a late snow on a sown field was a bonus and would assure a bumper crop.

Everything went well for Marit and Rolf in the fields and they were done earlier than most, early enough to catch the late snow that did come, quickly melting and seeping down into the humus sponge.

As had always been his self-dispensed reward for having accomplished the seeding, Rolf left one morning for an outing and, since the spring school term hadn't yet ended, Randilena also was gone. So on this day, Marit, contemplating uninterrupted hours, decided to prepare the garden plot and spade it over.

She had been spading for some time when she was startled to hear Thorn's voice behind her. "I've run out of seed. I thought Rolf might have some left over."

She turned to face him. "He has a great deal left over. All you want."

"A few pounds should do it."

He carried an empty bag over his arm. Because it had always been her way to help Rolf sack grain, she offered, "I'll hold the bag for you while you shovel."

They walked into the granary side by side, their conversation keeping with the concerns of the season.

"I see that Rolf is all done with his seeding."

"We were lucky. We got it in before the snow."

"I almost made it. It was just that one little jog around the woods I didn't make. It'll be a little later than the rest now, but there's no sense in letting it lay fallow all summer."

"No, there'd be no sense in that," she agreed.

She was keenly aware of the surge of spring in the air about them. How good it was to be alive on a day like this! In spring, nothing seemed unsolvable.

After the blinding brightness of the sunlight, entering the semi-darkness of the windowless granary was like going into a dark room. The grain bin was partitioned off, making an even darker recess, and she had a sudden awareness of Thorn's nearness and the fact that they were all alone.

She shouldn't have come! She was glad the gloom hid the trembling of her hand when she reached for the grain bag.

Thorn, too, was momentarily blinded. Groping for the shovel handle, his hand caught her arm. With a swiftness that gave her no time for protest, he pulled her to him.

There was nothing else in the world, nothing but her pent-up longing for him. She returned his kisses in an orgy of hunger. Her knees went weak and she felt herself sinking. *My God, no!* She unlocked her arms and flailed them, casting about for something — anything — to save her from herself. From the vortex of the whirlpool that sought its release, she discerned a face, swimming toward her, swimming into focus. The face suddenly clarified, aghast with illumination. "Kari!" she screamed.

Thorn recoiled as if stung by a bee, spinning round to face the door. Marit leaned against the boards of the bin, holding to one of the overhead bracing. He said nothing, even when he saw Kari was not really there.

Anger compounded by guilt and frustration welled up in Marit. "Then it's her — Kari — after all!" she spat out accusingly.

In the quiet, only the droning of the hornets from their nest in the peak of the roof could be heard. Then: "I do love her. I don't want to hurt her."

What was he saying? What was this thing between *them?* Did Thorn just think of her as something to be used, in the most despicable of ways, as Rolf had used her all these years? She felt sick — sick with shame and disgust at herself. So this was what he thought of her *now.* It had come down to *this!* But now he was talking again.

"I love Kari, just as you yourself love her. Who can *help* but love Kari?" He paused. "I've thought about this a great deal for months. Can you believe that it's possible for a man to love two women at the same time, but in different ways? I think it's like this: Do you remember the little brook that ran down from the mountains in Lilledalen? How often I've lain on its banks, spellbound by the clearness of it, every pebble in it I've memorized! And how often I've been lulled to sleep by its babbling." Now he paused again, taking a deep breath as if to throw a load off his chest. "But it's the sea that's in my blood. And you, Marit, you are the sea!"

In the silence that ensued after the confession, Kari's words rang in her ears: "Sometimes I wonder if he misses the sea, if that's what he broods about these days."

Thorn now turned to her again, but didn't reach out for her. His tone changed; there was no tenderness in his voice when he demanded: "Why! Why did you do it?" When she didn't respond immediately, he became more insistent: "Why did you run off with him?"

Could she make her understand? It seemed such a flimsy excuse, such a trifle now... that stupid figurehead gaping up at her from the ground!

"I thought you were lost at sea — dead."

"Why do you lie? I know better!"

Ordinarily it would have angered her to have her integrity questioned, but now it evoked only futility. It was no use. He would never forgive her for her lack of faith.

"I know you got my letter," he said. "I found the thongs along the path where you threw them."

"What are you talking about? What letter?"

"You know very well what I'm talking about! The leather scroll. Are you going to pretend you didn't get it?" He walked to the door. His face, turned halfway to her, was tormented in the light. "I know you don't give a damn for Rolf! If you did, that would explain it."

She had the sudden fear that he would leave and never again give her the opportunity to explain. But coupled with this fear was a need for time, time to think, to dredge up from the past something his words had snagged. She must stall him. "I don't know what you're talking about. I swear I don't. This scroll.... Tell me about it."

He turned from the door, as if to better read the veracity on her face. He must have believed her finally, for he explained in abrupt sentences, like hammering pieces into place. "I wrote on a leather scroll. Because I was among the Lapps. It was all they had. I sent it on with a hunting party. I found the thongs with which I had bound it on the path leading up the valley. I know they were the same because I carved them myself. They had to be the same."

At the end, his words were measured, as if he himself were puzzling as he related the facts to her.

"I never got it!"

They stood peering at each other, as if to read the answer on the other's face. But she was still groping for something out of the limbo of the past, trying to recall words vaguely remembered. They had been *written* words. *A letter.* The letter Nicolena had written to Rolf from Norway! The words came back. "I still have the leather scroll. I didn't burn it like you told me.... Our bargain...."

"Nicolena!"

"What about Nicolena?"

"It had to be Nicolena."

"But why?"

Suddenly truth was formidable. Nicolena had mentioned a bargain. Then Rolf was in on it too! So much — too much — was now clear. But Thorn was not aware of Rolf's part in it — not yet. If he found out the truth... Rolf's part... what these two had conspired.... She braked. "It wouldn't do any good, to try to get to the bottom of it. Not now. It's best to forget."

"I'll choke the truth out of her! With my bare hands I will! It was always you and me — right from the beginning. We belong together! It was meant to be...."

He raged on. She felt cold. The icy down-draft from the avalanche that threatened to sweep their lives away had blown away sensual wooziness and cleared her head. There was a way of forestalling it, perhaps even of escape....

"Nicolena is a bitter woman, you know that. You can't hold her responsible for some of the things she does. I think sometimes she has been driven a little out of her mind. Because she's so unhappy herself, she can't stand to see anyone else happy."

She did not speak from conviction. There was a mounting fury inside her even as she tried to quell his. But she must keep him from going to Nicolena, must save them all by vindicating her.

"We can't go on this way," Thorn was saying.

Kari had been her salvation but a few minutes before. "This would destroy Kari, if all this came out." She waited for that to penetrate, then went on in a logical tone: "If you talk to Nicolena and accuse her, she'll blackmail you and threaten to tell Kari." She related the incident of the lace tablecloth. "She would tell Kari out of spite, just to get even. Kari must not be hurt. This is none of her doing."

"But now that I know the truth of it, how can I go on with this masquerade? And you... when I think of you with Rolf...."

She knew what he meant and flushed as if guilty of adultery, but even *this* must be parried. "I can look out for myself, you should know that! And there's Randilena.... I have her out of all this."

"But what of you and me?" He reached for her again.

But cold reality was now her ally and she moved away from him.

"Please, Marit...."

"No, Thorn. No!"

"I can't accept that there will never be anything for us. There must be *something,* even if only stolen moments like now. We're alone. And right now, for me, that's all there is.... Us."

She did hesitate, but only seconds. She side-stepped him and walked to the door, stepping out into the sunlight. *Don't look back, don't look back,* she kept repeating to herself as she walked away, her head held high.

❧❧❧

All the hurts of the past — even the present circumstances of their lives — what did it matter? Their love had surmounted all! Now, it was just a matter of keeping it under control, the simple matter of never being alone together, never flirting with temptation. That could be managed easily enough; she would make it a point to remember that women were not made of the same weak fiber as men in this respect. Her own intensity of passion, she was certain, was an exception to the rule: As God had favored her with male-like strength, so had He given her the male cross to bear! And she had the fortification of *one* victory over self, giving her the assurance that she could successfully deal with any such situation that might arise in the future. Serenity displaced agonizing uncertainty. How could a love such as hers and Thorn's be a sin? It wasn't, unless they made it a sin.

But in all this mollifying, she discounted Thorn, thinking of herself as being in the driver's seat holding the reins. She failed to reckon with the male drive which, if thwarted in one direction, would turn and search for new worlds to conquer.

It was a tearful Kari who tapped at her door one day. "I can't face up to it," she sobbed.

He had told her! A flood of guilt rushed over Marit and she backed away from Kari as if from inundation.

"Thorn is going away."

It took awhile.... No accusation, this. Marit looked into Kari's brimming eyes and saw hurt in them, not hate. "Going away? What do you mean?"

"I've known for a long time that something was bothering him. He's been so restless. Now, he finally told me what it is. He is going to Dakota Territory, to look it over, he says. But if he likes what he sees, he will return for me. We'll move out there." There was another freshet of tears.

Now Kari came to her, clinging to Marit for comfort much as Randilena would. What could she say? Marit cradled the head of soft, tiered whiteness but all the while with a maddening frustration: *Like when he escaped me by going to sea....*

"It's the thought of leaving you. Next to Thorn, you mean more to me than anyone in the world, even my mother. She let me be weak, encouraged it. But not you. But he is so unhappy! And I can't stand to see him so."

At that moment, Marit did not share Kari's sorrow at *their* being parted. She could only think of Thorn's going. She wasn't so much trying to comfort Kari as to convince herself when she said, "Maybe he won't find the territory to his liking. Maybe when he comes back he'll decide to stay on here." But even as she said the words, she knew that Thorn had already made up his mind and that he was going ahead to smooth the way for Kari.

Why must he go away? Why couldn't they all just go on this way? And the answer that she got was: Because he's *Thorn,* that's why.

While he was gone, and in the certainty that he would return for Kari, Marit knew she should be helping Kari pack. But Kari clung to the forlorn hope that, when he returned, all would remain the same. Marit did not have the heart to snatch that shred from her by the finality of dismantling the house.

When he did return with the announcement that he had bought out the holdings of a settler in Dakota, he was in such a fever to get packed and on the way that the cutting edge of parting was dulled by the fast spin of events. While the women packed the household effects, he quickly disposed of all he had accumulated, save for the rig and land. The rig not lending itself to quick sale, being on the order of a luxury, he stored in Rolf's machine shed. The land he left for Rolf to dispense with as he saw fit, as it seemed not to matter a great deal to him. Rolf was flattered that Thorn gave him full authority, stipulating nothing — whether to sell, rent or lease — and stopping just short of signing the title over to him.

Thorn left without a farewell word to Nicolena. He chose instead of complicity as brambly as the landscape of Wisconsin itself, abnegation in a land that dwarfed man, making a mere speck of him in the expanse of prairie and sky of Dakota.

Nicolena, nonplused, came fishing to Marit for an answer. "Why? Why should he run off to Dakota? He had such a good start here. And so all of a sudden! And without even a good-bye to his sister!"

Seething, Marit did not trust herself to speak. She went on about her work, ignoring even Nicolena's presence in the room.

Nicolena got up to go, saying, "I suppose this means *I'll* be seeing more of you now."

Marit now acknowledged her presence with her eyes, which were twin glacial pools. "I hardly think so."

Nicolena was to learn that she meant it. Marit never sought her out and when she imposed herself on Marit, it was as if a drawbridge went up and she became a vastness across a moat of silence. Before, there had always been a vulnerability in Marit that gave her license to badger. But, like granite, Marit intimidated her and she ceased to prod, sensing that access would rain fire down on her head. And no longer having invective as an outlet, she was forced to withdraw into herself, take stock and search for ways out for herself. Tortuously, she arrived at a decision: She closed the door to the irregular coming of Nils. She didn't need him either!

⚘

It was so unexpected that it should be *Kari* that Marit missed the more! Thorn's absence was as a dismemberment of many years' standing. She had long learned to cope with it by compensating. But for weeks after Kari left, never a day went by without her thinking *I must ask Kari, I must tell Kari,* or *I must show Kari,* only to have the thought terminated by the poignant recall: *Kari is gone!*

In her opaque existence, Kari's transparency and sparkle had been as clear crystal, catching the light and reflecting it in rainbow colors to her. Now, without that rebounding presence, life seemed to stretch out into the future like a tunnel, and that summer the first streaks of gray began to dull the auburn of her hair. It was in a morphinic apathy that the realization came to her that she was pregnant!

Rolf had been completely oblivious to her resentment of him. As long as she adequately performed the duties as wife in and out of bed, his mind ran its burrow with no sensitivity to her moods, light or dark. The knowledge of the new life in her did in time dispel apathy. She found herself hoping it would be a boy this time. For its *own* sake.

But there were Kari's letters, poor substitutes for Kari herself. Yet the paper sheets were a bond that held with the stretch of hundreds of miles of physical separation.

The first communication from Dakota had made a bulky envelope. How could anyone possibly find time to write such a long letter, she thought as she opened it. But the use of various inks and leads made it glaringly apparent that the letter had not been written at one sitting; that it was a series of jottings made over a period of time. And jottings they were, with none of the stiff formality she had come to expect in correspondence. Her sister's letters had been a case in point, so unbending as to make her seem a total stranger. Marit had not read far before she further deducted that Kari wrote whenever she felt the need to talk to her. The chattiness was so characteristically Kari that Marit could hear her saying the words even as she read them. Portions of the letters were vignettes that vividly transposed Kari on her surroundings:

I didn't write en route because the trip was about all I could endure. You know my weakness of tiring easily. But now that we are here and I am caught up on rest, I shall try to make up for it.

We boarded the train in St. Paul and the ride was none too comfortable on the hard benches, although I cushioned them with pillows which we had to pay extra for. We could not lie because the cars were too crowded, so we had to sit up all the way. (It seems many besides Thorn have Dakota fever!) There was no way to amuse oneself to make the time pass faster. The constant jiggling made it impossible to read. I tried it and ended up with a headache from trying to hold my eyes to the lines. Watching out the windows was even more tedious to the eyes, or maybe I should say spirits, because soon after leaving St. Paul the land flattens out and there is mile after mile with nothing but grass and sky to focus on except the few homesteads one sometimes sees in the distance. They look so lonely! Even the towns along the tracks have a dreary sameness. All with a forlorn depot, and sometimes the glimpse of a main street and a square they call a park, which is just a patch of wasteland separated from the bigger wasteland only by the few build- ings that cluster around it. These towns have little population, making one think they must survive only on hope. Hope for a future....

I must say in fairness that they do make settlers feel welcome out here. The railroad and land companies provide reception houses where the women and children can stay while the men are out looking for land. I stayed in one of these the first night we got here and it was fine if you're not particular about privacy. The railroad company seems espe- cially eager to help with settlement. They will provide free transporta- tion for those who buy railroad land. And in some cases have even fur- nished free pure-bred sire calves and money for churches and school- houses....

One of the things that caught my eye when we first arrived were huge piles of what appeared to be driftwood stacked alongside many of the settlers' buildings. I took it for granted that it was driftwood be- cause the shapes and bleached whiteness from a distance looked so like the driftwood that washes up on the shores at home, and I thought, "This must be what they use for heat in winter" until I remembered that here we are hundreds of miles from the sea. I asked Thorn and he said they are buffalo bones! The settlers gather and pile them for they can be sold for as much as fifteen dollars a ton. It seems they make good fertilizer, so they are freighted east and ground up....

It is unbelievable how crudely most of the people live. It's even worse than the cabins in Wisconsin. Would you believe it if I told you that many of them live in shelters made of raw turf blocks? They are called sod houses but they are much like the earthen huts of the uncivilized Lapps of the homeland. They are horribly dismal on the inside and I wouldn't be surprised if the people who occupy them for any length of time go blind like moles! I visited in one of them to make the acquaintance of a neighbor and when I walked out again the light stabbed my eyes and I had trouble seeing for several minutes. But Thorn says they are very practical, that they are cool in summer and warm in winter and cheap to build because lumber is so scarce in this area. So different from Wisconsin! Though there is one thing here that reminds me of Wisconsin, something that helps people get a start called bonanza farms, where hundreds of men are hired to plow, sow and harvest thousands of acres held by absentee landlords. Mostly it is single men who work these places, but some of the married men also seek employment to get cash to make the improvements on their homesteads much as the men back there do with the money they earn in the pineries in the winter....

I'm luckier than most. We have a proper frame house above ground. It has three rooms on the first floor and an unfinished loft. It seems to have been built in two sections for there is a main wing of two rooms and then there is a side room that appears to have been tacked on later, making the whole thing shaped like an L. But it is a lonely place. The land stretches away in every direction endlessly and so empty. But Thorn seems to like it. I think it reminds him of the sea for he seems more content. It does, in fact, resemble the sea when the wind ripples the grass. One day I stood and watched until I became dizzy and felt a little fluttery of stomach just like sea sickness. I ran into the house and shut the door....

We haven't found time to cozy up the house yet and I will miss your help when we do. I'll miss someone to plan with. I'm going to try to make it look as much like our cabin in Wisconsin as I can, for I think of it often and miss it. Thorn will have more time here for carpentry because the land is much easier to work up. There are no trees, stumps or rocks to hinder the breaking and all that need be done is turn the sod over with a heavy plow....

In a later correspondence, Kari expressed a fear:

Almost every summer they say grasshoppers come in flocks so thick that they darken the sun as with clouds. That, I've learned, is why the man who homesteaded and built this place gave up. His crops were totally destroyed two years in a row and he sold the place to Thorn for a pittance. But I ask myself: What is to stop them from destroying our crops too? There is something uncanny about this scourge. They will destroy one farmer and spare another. Sometimes they pass over an entire neighborhood only to light farther beyond and devour the next neighborhood. Whole families turn out to do battle with them when they come, trying to drive them off. I detest crawling things! What will I do if they come?

When winter came, the letters went back to the fashion of the first one, each spanning periods of time in the writing. Marit gathered from the letters themselves that this was due to isolation, the difficulty of reaching town through the deep snows to post mail. The somber accounts were quite unlike Kari and did not reflect her blithe spirit.

There is nothing here to humble the wind and the snow does not lie still like it does back there where there are hills and woods. It whips about, lifts the snow up and flings it against the house, even forcing it through little cracks around the windows and doors. We often get up in the morning to find little drifts on the floor which do not melt in the draft. I have to sweep them up and carry them to the door and throw them out where they belong. At night in bed the wailing about the corners is unearthly, like lost souls trying to get in, and when you go outside there seems to be no leeward side to it. It hits you no matter which side of the house you stand on. Sometimes I envy those who live in the sod houses. The thick walls deaden the sound of it and they seem more snug than the frame houses. Some splash a white compound on the walls inside so they are not so dreary....

The snow has become so deep that it is way up on our windows and many of the sod houses are completely buried so the occupants must tunnel their way out. You would never know they were there under the drifts should you go looking for them, so fast do they fill in again. It is impossible to get to town for groceries regularly, and I plead for Thorn not to go for fear he won't find his way back should a storm come up, even though he studies the omens of the sky carefully before he sets out. But when he does go, he returns with so many tales of hardship that it haunts me. You wish you had not heard them. Rumors of people existing for weeks on only the grains they have stored for their cattle, grind-

ing them in their coffee mills to make grout and flat bread. And nothing besides unless it's milk, if they're lucky enough to have cows that still give milk with the irregular milking for not being able to find their way to the barn to tend them in the blizzards. We are lucky we are not out in the far reaches....

I don't know what I'd do without my books. I am so lonely, Marit! There is no joy here. I hate this country! But pray that I will be able to bear it for Thorn's sake. I hide it from him. He says this winter is unusual, that when spring comes again, things will look different....

Spring came, and did work its miracle of renewed hope — not only for Kari, as evidenced by her letters, but for Marit as well.

She had been so certain that the child she was carrying was a boy. She was much bigger than she had been with Randilena and the kicking had been so vigorous in the latter weeks of her term as to not allow her much sleep. But in April, she delivered another girl, this time a daughter created in her own image. Big-framed and long of limb, the baby weighed eleven-plus pounds. The granary scale did not lend itself to the reckoning of precise ounces.

In addition to the diversion of having a new baby in the house, a project of milestone proportion had Marit, and the whole community as well, in a whirl of preparation. Out of gratitude for a bountiful harvest, it had been decided the previous autumn that the men would during the winter months take out logs to saw lumber for the construction of a church. These would be donated as led by conscience, as each felt providently blessed. A goodly pile had accumulated and the logs had been sawed into lumber. It was planned to begin the foundation in the slack season between sowing and harvest, the dimensions already having been paced off and staked next to the scattered graves on the plot of ground that had been dedicated for a cemetery some years before.

The project would involve the women as well as the men for it would be the women's task to see that the builders were well-fortified with food carried to the building site. Not only must there be a hearty and warm noon meal, but the inevitable morning and afternoon coffee breaks must also be taken into account. All this necessitated a great deal of planning and organization, presaging many get-togethers. And sandwiched in between the preparation and carrying of food to the men must be the seasonal tasks of gardening and preserving for next winter, the usual treadmill of daily household and barn chores and, for Marit, a new baby to attend besides!

But Marit plunged into the busy rounds of the summer with inspired vigor. A house of worship, so long a dream, was now to become a reality. With a church, they might be able to secure a residential minister, perhaps by sharing him with one or more other congregations.

With Trees on Either Hand

PART III

CHAPTER I

P ine still reigned king, but hardwood had now come into its own, prime minister to the settlers in their increasing demand for such diversified lumber products as shingles, staves, headings, hubs and spokes. The need had given rise to small independent lumber companies. Bringing in their own crews and sawmills, they infiltrated the cut-over areas and the shrill feminine shrieks of steam whistles rent the crisp air of winter mornings.

A temperamental lady, the steam engine! It was necessary for the tender to rise hours before daybreak to coax her from her lethargy and get up a full head of steam. But once fully roused, she made her demands known in a shrewish voice that could not be denied. The crews swarmed from their warm bunkhouses in response to the summons and clambered about her in attendance.

No less demanding was she of her whining mate, the mill. Driven to gluttony, he devoured logs remorselessly, slavering trickles of sawdust all the while the straining men dragged heavy logs to him and held them to his maw in a vain effort to sate the mammoth appetite.

An area periodical reported that, on a bright winter morning, more than a hundred loads of logs in line were counted moving toward the mill at Barron, the county seat, and farther to the north, Rice Lake, laid claim to having within its limits the largest excelsior mill in the world.

However, there were still those who made the annual pilgrimage to the receding pineries. For some, it had become a way of life; for others, it was still a short-cut to security, a source of cash with which to purchase the hard goods required for homesteading. And for many a young man, the pineries filled the gap between childhood and married responsibilities.

It was still a wheat economy, but crying in the wilderness was a voice preaching a gospel of diversified farming and dairy-bred cattle. However, except for a few far-sighted farmers in the southern part of the state, the voice of William D. Hoard went largely unheeded. To reach a wider audience with his message, he founded a journal called *Hoard's Dairyman.*

❧

By chance, a copy fell into Marit's hands. And the seed planted by Kari — the challenge of the mind — having sprouted, such was her thirst for reading material that she coveted all printed matter that came her way. She read the journal from cover to cover.

It was an easy sell. Even she had noticed that virgin soil in its first years produced from thirty to forty bushels of hard wheat an acre but, after that, there was a gradual diminishing of fertility. At the end of a dozen years of steady wheat cropping, the yield got down to as little as five bushels an acre. Of course, there were always new acres to be cleared and broken. But when all the new land had been used up, what then, she wondered. She decided to show the paper to Rolf to have him read it and give an opinion. Rolf was a good farmer, if nothing else.

She placed the paper conspicuously within his reach when he stretched out on the kitchen couch at noon and he ignored it. Well, then, I'll just tell him, she decided.

He lay with his eyes closed while she gave her summary. Maybe he wasn't listening. She picked up the paper, opening it to a woodcut illustration showing a herdsman seated by one of the frail-looking new cows and held it up in front of him.

"See?"

He opened his eyes, glancing at the minutely detailed picture, then exploded. "Any man who would set himself down by the side of a cow and yank on her tits for a living is a poor excuse for a farmer!" With that, he slapped the paper away with such force that it went sailing to the middle of the floor.

"The paper tells of a new hay plant that has been discovered in the West," she persisted. "A plant that, once sown, comes up year after year, even in this cold climate. They call it lucerne." It later would become better known as alfalfa.

Rolf jumped up, retrieving the paper from the floor. He walked over to the range, lifted the lid and shoved it in. "That takes care of that!" he said with finality. Turning away from the stove, he punctuated, "Women shouldn't be allowed to learn to read. Their minds are like an unbraced corner fence post, easily toppled. They'll fall of nothing."

His opinion of women was not news to her and she scarcely heard what he said. But novel was the thought that crossed her mind: Maybe Rolf doesn't have such a good business head after all! Besides, in spite of his tirade on women's reading, he had no objection to her reading the *Decorah-posten.*

Rolf, in fact, took great pride in being a subscriber to the *Decorah-posten,* as did all Norwegians of the community. His disdain of the printed word did not extend to Norwegian-American newspapers, which were a hedge against assimilation and the erosion of old-county mores. But for Marit's part, although she went through the print as with a fine-tooth comb in her quest for the political ken that would enable to her to decipher Kari's letters, the paper did not fit the bill and left a lot unsaid. She could not know that the editorial policy of the *Decorah-posten* was to avoid anything controversial and that the editors took pride in the fact that theirs was a peaceable, tranquil paper that took no sides in politics. That the paper was a diversion, she granted, carrying as it did games and puzzles for the amusement of the children, and running classics in installments for the entertainment of adults. But uplifting as all this was, she felt a world apart from Kari, who had become caught up in the prairie fire of Populism that was sweeping the plains but had not penetrated the tree-sentried clearings of northern Wisconsin, where the lifelines were the abandoned tote roads of the lumber barons, not the monopolistic steel rails of the empire builders of the far West.

When Kari first started writing of an organization called The Farmers' Alliance, Marit had taken it to be of a social order, for Kari made many mentions of picnics and lodge meetings in such glowing terms as to make Marit's own church-oriented social life seem drab by comparison. But in time she inferred that the organization was not all for socializing and that it concerned itself with some very serious matters that were far over her head.

It seemed they got down to serious business at conventions. At those gatherings, speakers exhorted the members with grand words, samples of which found their way into Kari's letters in her recounting of the proceedings: hand-in-glove, monopolist, discriminatory, sugar-coated exploitation, cooperative enterprise. Marit's head fairly swam in her effort to comprehend Kari's outrage and she was sometimes driven to make desperate grabs for information in her attempts to appear well-informed in replies to Kari.

In one letter, Kari had written: "If you want to know the truth, read *Looking Backward* and *Thirty Years of Labor*. We can get these books in low-priced editions here. Can you? If not, let me know." But before Marit had solved the enigma of how one goes about locating low-priced editions, another letter came from Kari with the postscript: "The saying around here is, 'After the grasshoppers, we got Jim Hill.' What do you think of such as Jim Hill? I think something should be done about it."

Marit was hard-put to come up with a reply. Who in the world was Jim Hill? And what could he have done to make him as hated as the locusts in Dakota? Perhaps news of such magnitude had reached even Rolf's ears.... "From Kari's letters, it seems they're having a lot of trouble with Jim Hill in Dakota these days," she explored.

Rolf only grunted.

She casually introduced Jim Hill into other conversations, but the dropped name met only with blank looks. She finally formulated an opinion that she felt would not betray her ignorance. At the end of her next letter, she added a postscript: "As regards Jim Hill, don't worry about it. There's a remedy for everything."

The reply was more than satisfactory to Kari. "I'm glad Marit approves of the remedy," she told Thorn. "I wouldn't want our involvement with the movement to spoil our friendship."

❧❧❧

They were about to leave for church and, as usual, the girls came to their mother for last-minute inspection. The modest dress that Randilena wore did not disguise the fact that she was now a mature young woman, nor did the muted color tone down the bloom of the face above it. Conversely, no amount of frill could have made Thea look feminine at this stage. Already she was as tall as Randilena and the long skirt did not camouflage the awkwardness shown in the colt-like movements of her long legs.

Rolf, unbidden, now joined Marit to round out an inspection team. As usual, he did not approve of what he saw. "Is all that color natural?" he blustered, brushing his finger across Randilena's cheek and holding his finger up to the light of the window, as if her really expected to find rouge on it.

There being no rub-off, he said, "Well, if you don't call attention to yourself, maybe no one will notice."

It was as a taunt to him that in spite of his insistence that Randilena dress primly, she was a stand-out beauty and he watched for any show of male awareness. And if he noticed as much as a sideways glance, he accused her of deliberately drawing it. As a consequence, she had come to hang back, staying in the background as much as possible. The openness of childhood had been supplanted by an adult demeanor of pensive guardedness.

This metamorphosis Marit had observed with regret. But to challenge Rolf's autocracy was to aggravate it, bringing even more stricture to bear and, although she had long given up trying to find the missing piece — the key to Rolf's attitude toward his elder daughter — she philosophized that Randilena would find her release with time, as time had succored her own hurt. It was early yet.

❧

Marit and the girls took their usual pew in the church. Rolf went to seat himself with the men on the right-hand side of the aisle. Randilena immediately reached for a hymn book and began leafing through it, as if to pass the time until the service began. This had been her habit for some time now, a cover-up for the first moments of fear that he might not be there, then fear that he might and that her acute awareness of him might betray itself in her face.

He always sat two rows back, across and a little behind her.... *He was there!* Out of the corner of her innocently occupied eyes, she could tell he was looking at her this very minute. Her cheeks flushed brighter and she flipped several pages in quick succession.

She never in any way acknowledged his presence during the service. Though of fleeting and furtive quality, there was always that interval after the benediction when she joined the throng in the aisle.

His eyes would be only for her and she would lift her eyes to meet his, allowing herself those brief seconds of thirsty locked eye drinking him in. He waited for that moment, she knew. But she *lived* for it, from week to week. The service seemed interminable.

Thea sat on the other side of Marit. During the long service she, too, became impatient and began to scuff at the pew in front of them with the toe of her shoe. Marit shook her head at her and Thea shoved herself back up into proper sitting position, giving the pew in front a vindictive kick in the process. Finally, the benediction came and, like an animal released from halter, Thea broke with the staid gait of the throng moving toward the door, dodging out between them to gain the unhampered outdoors.

Randilena moved unobtrusively with the crowd, its unhurried pace a processional to the *moment.* He always paused, turning full-face to the aisle and waited for her to lift her eyes and acknowledge him before she brushed past. But today, although he paused, he did not look at her. She faltered a step and the lady behind her tripped on her heel. She turned to accept the lady's apology with a wooden smile. It was only when she turned back again that she realized he had slipped in beside her and was pressed to her side in the safety of numbers.

The sleight-of-hand movement happened so swiftly: the forcing open of her clenched fingers, the insertion of the tiny slip of paper and his hand closing her fingers on it tightly again in an unspoken pact of secrecy.

Immediately outside the door he strode away from her as if she didn't exist, as if it had never happened. Except that it had! She closed her fist tightly on the little scrap in her hand.

The usual pattern held outdoors. There was an interlude of exchanged greetings with some and short visits with others; during which the younger children amused themselves with a restrained game of tag among the impediments of the gravestones. The elders, not knowing this was part of the game, admonished them not to step on the graves, that to do so was a desecration. If in the dodging and weaving, one foot inadvertently trespassed, the children immediately a hushed foul-call of "You *descrated,* you *descrated"* and the transgressor automatically became "it." And since the diphtheria epidemic, there were many graves to dodge, mostly little ones. Four of them were Nicolena's She had come crying to Marit in panic: "He knows! He knows everything! He even knows I didn't want them in the first place and now He's taking them away from me! It's His wrath, His punishment!" Marit had gone to help and when the trying time had passed, Nicolena had conciliated, "In this Godforsaken wilderness, women need each other even more than they need men!" Marit had not debated the naked thesis.

Eventually, the little knots of people unraveled and strung out to their conveyances. It was not until they were home and Randilena was in the security of her own room, where she always went to change immediately after the service, that she relaxed her cramped fingers to unfold and read the damp, tightly wadded little note.

The scribbled words at first made no sense. Then they set her atremble when their full implication became clear: "Why is it always Thea who fetches the cows?"

The Valgard's land bordered on theirs and the pastures joined. But it had for some summers now been Thea's chore to round up the cows and bring them home. And it was much to Thea's liking, these twice-daily flights to the wild when she could be anything her mind fancied: a deer when her long legs traced the cow paths through the thickets and woods; a frog when she leaped from hummock to hummock in the swamp; a crane when she waded the creek stilt-legged with her skirts lifted high. And at all times she was an explorer, nothing escaping her in her bent for observation: the bouncing retreat of rabbits with stump tails waggling behind like the tassel on her winter stocking cap; the hollow trees where she periodically checked the gray squirrels' hoards of nuts, paying no heed to their furiously chattered objections; the birds that flushed from the deep marsh grass at her stealthy coming, giving away locations and yielding the secrets of their carefully concealed nests; the swift dark scribbling in the water that told her she had dislodged a hiding place for trout when she jarred a rock in the stream; and, far above and safe from her meddling, the aerial feats of flying squirrels. "Smart alecks, I'll show you!" she had once called up to them. Studying their aerodynamics meticulously, and believing she had it down pat, she had climbed a tree to a horizontal limb and carefully measured the distance to a branch on the next tree. Then, with arms curtsy-spreading her skirt for glide, she had leaped. But her reflexes had not been swift enough to drop the skirt and grasp the branch when she gained it. With the branch mercifully breaking her fall, her belly had come into abrupt collision with the ground, knocking the wind from her. She had lain quite still for some time.

Thus, when Randilena abruptly announced one afternoon that she was going for the cows, Thea objected vehemently. "Getting the cows is my job. Yours is to stay and help Mother with supper!"

"Couldn't we take turns?"

"Why should we? I've always done it before. Well, not always, but for a long time anyway."

Randilena did not make an issue of it. She had never quarrelled with Thea, the difference in their ages and interests heretofore precluding friction. And she feared that to bicker with Thea now over this seeming whim would be so out of character as to rouse Thea's suspicion and, given Thea's curiosity, that was the last thing she wanted. But there must be some way....

"Mother, don't you think it's time Thea took over some of the household chores? I mean, for training. It's not that I mind. She does tidy her own room, of course, but she had never tried her hand at cooking. I've been thinking.... Do you realize that I was about Thea's age when you went to Millwood and left me completely in charge of the house, including the cooking? Remember? I'll admit I'm not the outdoor type like Thea but I could get the cows, for instance, just as easily as she can. I used to do it before Thea took it over."

She *had* given Thea a great deal of freedom, Marit mulled. Perhaps she had even spoiled her, remembering too well her own childhood and the restrictions imposed just because she was a girl. In America it was different; they had a name for this kind of girl here. Tomboys they called them. And it seemed no disgrace to be a tomboy. Marit had even read a book about one such girl, Jo of *Little Women*, a book that Randilena had brought home from school and Marit had read with great interest, finding strong rapport with the indominitable Jo. But perhaps Randilena was right. There was such a thing as carrying something too far and not being realistic. Thea would someday have to act like a lady whether she liked it or not.

Almost as if she had read her mind, Randilena added, "There'll come a day, you know, when Thea will have to give up her boyish ways and her freedom and settle for being a woman."

"I think you're right. But I want to handle it my way. I was just like Thea when I was her age. There must be a better way...."

Randilena could see that her mother's mind had trailed off, as it was prone to do. Her eyes had the by-now-familiar "long ago and far away" look that seemed always to somehow exclude her. But knowing she had made her point, Randilena let the matter rest there.

It was about a week later that Marit informed Randilena in Thea's presence: "Thea is going to set the table and do a few little things for me. You'll have to get the cows this evening." To Thea, she had said, "I'm worried about your sister. She looks a little pale. I think she's shut in the house too much and needs more sunshine and fresh air." Thea had immediately suggested that she and Randilena take turns getting the cows, not remembering that the idea had initially been planted in her mind by Randilena, thus showing to Randilena the wisdom of her strategy in not forcing the issue with her willful sister.

The facile opportunity was so unexpected that Randilena almost protested in panic, a panic that did not subside until she had crossed the open pasture, gaining the woods so the buildings were hidden by trees. All the open way she had wanted to turn back to the familiar routine and the reassuring presence of her mother. But once in the woods, the dark recesses were as the warrens of her longings — secret, mysterious — and she walked as in an enchanted forest where at any step the evil spell might be broken and she could be her true self, not that other Randilena that wasn't her at all.

Tharal had only to *look* at her to make her feel real. *I want to feel real all the time.* She was near the Valgard fraction and the cows had started to head back. A little too loudly and prolonged, she called, "Co—boss, co—boss...."

No movement, no sign. Feeling suddenly wilted, she was about to turn and head back herself when the brush suddenly parted on the other side of the fence. For a long moment they stood and started at each other as if seeing the other there were the last thing that either of them had expected.

But Tharal gave the lie to this when he finally said, "I thought you'd *never* come!"

They walked as in disbelief toward each other and met at the line fence. Tharal reached across and lifted her over.

As the summer wore on, Marit came to the conclusion that the blinder she had used to harness her younger daughter with a minimum of balking had not been deceit after all and that Randilena had indeed needed more sunshine and fresh air. Her little walks seemed to have worked a transformation, gathering to Randilena an aura of radiance and serenity that bespoke of full-blown womanhood. Yet, happy as Marit was to see this change, it somehow made her wish that she could hold back time.

For this summer she had a sense of time getting out of hand, moving too fast. She acknowledged to herself for the first time that she was no longer young. Whereas before a good night's rest had renewed her strength, now, even when she arose in the morning, weariness clung to her like lingering night vapors.

She had always taken her great strength for granted. She had spread it thin and still had some to spare. But these days, she was finding it necessary to ration it. She had noticed certain irregularities but attributed them to her age, assuring herself, *when I'm done with this business they call "change of life," I'll get my strength back and be good as new.*

Winter moved in late that year. The first snow did not fly until mid-December; and even then it fell on grass unseared by frost so that the pasture land was as frothed green sea water until succeeding snows completely covered it. And it was not until then that the cattle were stabled for winter and denied access to the woodlands.

***

Tharal set his bundle down in a corner of the bunkhouse. For a time he remained aloof from the rest of the men, the corner becoming a vantage point from which to assay this: the fountainhead of the bunkhouse tales had enthralled ever since he was old enough to comprehend. However, romance evaporated as his eyes took in the unlikely assemblage of "heroes" in the chinked-log enclosure of crowded bunks with filthy straw ticks protruding from under even filthier bedding.

He had arrived at the logging camp at sundown, having hiked all the way, save for the last lap when he had hitched a ride on one of the camp sleighs in its evening retreat from the woods. Arriving in camp, he had promptly presented himself to the foreman and had been promptly hired. He had shared in the evening's fare of beans and venison, after which he had gravitated toward the bunkhouse with the rest of the men.

Feeling suddenly conspicuous in his detachment from the group, he left the corner and walked over to where the men were clustered about the spit-stained stove. They were in the process of peeling off their wet outer garments and there was a great deal of competition for drying space in the small circle of the stove's heat, but in good humor and accompanied by a rabble of voices — heckling, cussing, joshing, guffawing — and by a fluctuating odor of bodies long unbathed, tobacco, wet wool, dirty socks, scorching and, occasionally, a whiff of wood smoke.

When the men were down to their underwear, there was a wanton interlude of scratching. Then, as if at a signal, the men turned tail and headed for the bunks. Tharal was later to learn that the laggards must stoke the fire, blow out the last lanterns and find their way to their bunks in the darkness. In the jungle of bunks, the men climbed up like so many gorillas, with many a bare, heat-reddened behind exposed through the gap in the climb.

Tharal felt no part of this conglomerate, having not yet been caught up in its matrix. He was yet of that other world of which he had so lately taken leave, where stolen moments were as pyrotechnic star bursts that made all else seem bathed in pale light by contrast.

They had decided to run away together, to Dakota, they had determined. But they would need money, at least enough to get to Thorn Monsrud's house, where Randilena was sure they would find a welcome. The pinery was the only solution, they had agreed.

He would save every cent. Then, with the little hoard, they need not ask or tell anyone anything. They would become man and wife as soon as they were at a safe distance from home, before her father could trace them or catch up with them. Once she was legally his and with the distance between Randilena and her father, her fears would vanish, melting like the snows of springtime when he would return to claim her.

All these thoughts went through his mind as he lay on the uncomfortable tick, staring wide-eyed into the darkness with the

men in the bunks around him oblivious in exhausted heavy-breath-
ing slumber. Finally, his own tense muscles relaxed in an involuntary jerk, and mindfulness was overthrown.

❦

The work day started before sun-up. The fire had gone low
during the night and they dressed nimbly in air so chilled they could
see their breathing. A dash of cold water on their hands and faces
from the common wash basin filled with water dipped from the ice-
glazed bucket, a brisk drying with the rough towels and they were
off to the cook shanty for the invariable breakfast fare of pancakes,
maple syrup and fried salt pork floating in its own grease, ladled on
the pancakes in lieu of butter. They ate rapidly and, as each finished, he rose and headed purposefully for the door.

Tharal, having finished eating, imitated the knowing exodus
from the cook shanty. But having gained the outdoors, where the
crews were busily assembling their tools, he made offers of help that
were rebuffed and he stood awkwardly at loose ends.

He finally was spotted by the foreman, who confronted him
with, "What have you done before? Knitting?"

"I can do anything."

"One of *those,* ha?" He turned to a burly man who was engaged
in gingerly testing the whetting of a saw with a knowing finger.
"Hey, Lars! Take this greenhorn and break him in."

The burly one seemed to take malicious pleasure in the prospect. He came over to where Tharal stood, taking out a pouch of
chewing tobacco and packing his lower lip, all the while measuring
Tharal with watery blue eyes. The lips closed over the bulge, only
to pop and release an elongated missile that narrowly missed Tharal's
face, striking the wall of the shed behind him where it exploded in
a bird-shot spray of amber pellets.

"Follow me," the man said.

Angered by his contempt, Tharal resolved not to be shown up.
After all, he was not without experience as a sawyer. He had helped
his father saw down many a tree in the clearing of their homestead!

But, out in the woods, Lars' relentless pace taxed him even
before the first hour had ended. *He works like the demons themselves
are on his back,* Tharal observed. By the time the noon break came,

he felt as if he had already put in a long day's work.

To conserve time, the food was hauled out on a chuck-sleigh to where the men were working. Tharal got in line and filled his plate; then sought out a log on which to sit while eating as those ahead of him had done. Now, at last, he could rest for few minutes!

But he had just spied an empty spot and was about to sit down when he noticed Lars. He ate standing, wolfing down his food, and all the while surveying the uncut trees with the calculating eyes of a bowler counting spares. Tharal did not yield to temptation. Instead, he walked over to where Lars stood and ate on his feet also, feigning eagerness to get the business of eating out of the way so they could go at it again.

The seeming interminable day ended with the coming of twilight. They had worked all through the day silently. Now, in the dusk, Lars slapped Tharal's sagging shoulders with unabated strength, bouncing him on his rubbery legs. He knew the overture meant that he had passed the test, that this was Lars' way of acknowledging his grit. But weariness had blunted his pride and stolidity was his only ally as he mechanically mounted the sleigh that took them back to camp and supper.

When they entered the cook shanty door, the blast of heat that met him was as a physical blow, staggering him back. The venison and beans were downed in a glaze. Then came the bunkhouse and the ritual of readying for bunk that he had observed the night previous, but on this, his first night as a *bona fide* lumberjack, it held no novelty for him. And when his head found the dubious comfort of the sawdust pillow, Randilena only entered his mind as a chimera. Just before closing his eyes, her face floated before him in heat waves above the stove, undulating, her dark hair a smoke cloud that rose and fell over her face, covering it, save for the fire-red ember of mouth, bruised by his kisses. In the spring, he promised the phantom face, and immediately fell asleep.

The next day was even rougher, stiff as he was from the day before. But his resilient young body soon rose to the challenge as the weeks sped by. One day Lars was heard to comment: *"Dat boy is vun damn good vun!"*

There was a brisk rivalry among the sawyers and a team of Swedes known as the Mighty Moes — a title the two brothers had attached to themselves — held the unofficial championship. The rivalry did not escape the attention of the hard-driving foreman, for abetted, it resulted in a prodigious felling of trees for sake of manhood, family and country. For some time now the team of Lars and Tharal had given the Swedes reason for outdoing themselves, on more than one day they had bested the Moes. Some had put up money that the Norskes would show up the Swedes by Easter holiday and that there would be cause then for celebration of a Svenske humiliation. Tharal had not quite attained his ultimate gait, they figured.

❧

The days were growing longer. There had been a hint of spring in the air all day and the snow had turned slushy in the warmth of the afternoon sun. But in the perpetual twilight under the pines, deepening now with the setting of the sun, the snow still held.

On the edge of the clearing where they had been cutting all day, Tharal and Lars paused. Should they take one more for good measure? "We can finish in time to catch the sleigh if we really lay to," Lars decided.

He selected a tree and notched it with a few telling strokes of the ax. Tharal dutifully picked up his end of the saw and they moved around to the other side of the tree for the cut.

They rhythmic ritual began, the steel teeth noticeably biting deeper into the soft pine with each cross cut. It went fast, as the last tree of the day always did in the final spurt of mustered energy.

Lars raised his voice for the warning cry, not the storied "Timber!" but a primordial male bellow of victory.

The great tree shuddered, as if dreading the long fall to earth. For a moment it clung to its sisters with needle-fingered arms. Gradually, the fingers loosened their death grip and the arms became limp, and with a final resigned sigh of rushing wind though its branches, it came down. Caught in the web of trees, the sound of the fall reverberated through the forest.

As was their habit, they walked to where it lay to measure their slain giant. It was almost imperceptible, but, as they stood there, Lars heard that most dreaded sound in the forest: the sound of something breaking loose above. Instinctively, he gave Tharal a strong-armed shove that sent him sprawling face-first.

It was a huge limb, forty feet long and a full foot in diameter, devoid of foliage. It had been hanging there a long time, waiting.

Enigmatic *ifs* raced through Lars' mind: *If* we had not decided to take that last tree; *if* the limb had not chosen that precise moment to fall; *if* he had not given Tharal the shove that, instead of saving him, had placed him directly in the path of the falling "widow-maker."

Lars stood up from where he had knelt, raising his fist and shaking it at the innocuous slate gap above. *"Dat boy vus vun damn good vun, I tell you!"* he raged.

CHAPTER II

The door to the cavernous oven was open and Kari knelt before it in an attitude of postulant before a grotto, head bowed. It was a weekly ritual in the winter months, the thickness of her hair necessitating the drying of it in two stances, forward and backward to the spilled heat of the oven.

She lifted her arms to test the dryness by furrowing her hair's length with her fingertips. Satisfied, she flung the cascade back over her shoulders with a toss of her head, turning her back to the heat. She reached for her knitting, then thought better of it. She got up from the mat on the floor, went to the cupboard and took out paper and pencil, then again took up her position before the range, tablet in her lap. She dawdled with the pencil.

This was as far as she had gotten before with this letter to Marit, a letter that should be a missive of glad tidings but that she had put off writing in the indecision of whether or not she should mar it by disclosing... disclosing *what?*

How to verbalize the suffocating pall of fear that had descended and enveloped her when she had become aware that she was again with child? Even if she related to Marit the dark dreams she had at night, the premonitions that haunted even the daylight hours, how to convey the terror they invoked in her? How to *write* terror? And Marit hundreds of miles away....

She couldn't tell Thorn. He was so obviously delighted! In the awareness, he had become so attentive to her as to make her feel she had accomplished something novel when she really was only fulfilling woman's destiny, a function other men took for granted in their wives: the bearing of children. No. She couldn't spoil it for *him.*

For so long after the other time, she, too, had hoped for this, then had given up hope. Only now to have the hope — the promise — become an unreasoning dread that made her feel an island unto herself and gave rise to a need to be in touch with Marit in a way she had not needed for a long time, not since those first faltering years on the prairie when Marit's letters had been as a crutch, years when she had only to recognize the bold handwriting on the envelope to feel steadied by the large, firm lettering that conveyed strength and courage.

Once back then she had remarked to Thorn, "I wish I were more like Marit."

He had seemed startled at the prospect and had looked at her strangely before asking, "Why do you say that?"

"She never wavers."

"As much could be said of a stone wall."

Then it had been her turn to be startled. The comparison was an unkindness to Marit and unlike Thorn. "I thought you liked Marit! In fact, the thought has crossed my mind more than once that you and she would have made a great team. I'm surprised it wasn't the two of you who got together rather than Rolf and Marit."

"Well, we didn't."

"What do you know of their courtship? It always struck me that they aren't physically attracted to each other at all."

"You know that in the homeland marriage is more an economic consideration than a matter of physical attraction, secondary to a young man's prospects or his ability to support a family. It's the thing that's expected of young women: to find men to provide for them as their fathers provided for them before."

"I can't imagine Marit being so submissive."

"Maybe she just wanted to go to America."

"That would seem more likely. She does like challenge. But that's another reason why I wish I were more like her. I'm not really up to pioneer life, but Marit measures up. Now, if you had married her...."

He had cut her short. "Well, I didn't. I married you. And I'm not complaining."

He didn't like for her to be doubtful of herself. That accounted for his irritated tone, she had decided.

But at the present she must decide about the letter. She made several false starts, crumpling several sheets. She finally decided to leave out the dreams and premonitions. But in anticipation of reassurance from Marit, she wrote: "I wish I could have you with me again this time. Then I could be certain that everything would go all right. As it is, I'm a little worried."

❦

For the first time, a letter to Marit failed in rapport. Her return letter made that obvious in that her only reference to the fear Kari had confided was the glib advice: "Think only of the happiness that lies ahead for you and Thorn."

Kari felt marooned. But she would try, as Marit advised, to *think* happiness.

Her feigned bravado was no shield against Thorn's perceptiveness, however. "What makes you think you can't bring it off?" he asked one day.

"Why.... How did you know?"

"You forget. I practically taught you to walk. Now, when you hesitate, I sense it."

"To say you taught me to *live* would be more like it! You taught me to live and now I want to live. I want so much to live!"

The blurted words were not so much an eruption of fear as a plea, spoken as if she were a prisoner under threat of death sentence and he the magistrate who could grant clemency. But he saw the fear in her eyes and came to her, picking her up and carrying her to the rocking chair in front of the heater. Cradling her trembling body, he assured her, "You *are* going to live. You'll come through this just fine!"

"But my dreams...."

"What dreams? Why have you kept this from me?"

"Because it's so illogical, and you're logical. I've tried to be, but it doesn't seem to work. You see, it's not that I'm afraid of going through it again. It's what comes after."

"What do you mean 'what comes after?'"

"The *nisse*," she said, referring to a supernatural creature believed to steal infants from their cradles.

He stopped rocking. "The *nisse!* I'm surprised at you, Kari! You, an educated woman! You know the *nisse* is just a superstition of the homeland, only folklore."

"But I can't help what I *dream*...."

There was hysteria in her voice. He should not have chided her. This was a time for understanding. "Tell me about this dream."

She took a deep breath, making an apparent effort to compose herself. When she spoke again, her voice was calm and she articulated, as if the words would then make sense: "Well, the baby is born. But then.... Then this *nisse* comes. It walks over to the cradle. It reaches in." Now her voice was rising again. "I can't move.... I can't cry out...." Her voice broke and she hid her face in the front of his shirt.

This would not be easy to deal with. He could no more control her dreams than she. But there were the waking hours.... If she could be made to rationalize this during the waking hours, maybe it would carry over into the night and her dreams. And now that he knew, and she knew that he knew, the cork was off this brew of fear that she had bottled inside herself until the pressure became too great for her to hold it in.

"You should have told me about the dream the first time it happened. Now you'll really have to work to rid yourself of it — the grip it has on you!" Enough of scolding. He went on sympathetically, but firmly, "There is no *nisse*. No one is going to take our baby. And when it's over, you'll look back at this dream and laugh at its nonsense."

"If only I could have Marit with me! Marit wouldn't let anything happen."

What could Marit do for her that any other midwife couldn't, he thought. What could possibly happen? It was just her condition. Kari had never been superstitious before, but child-bearing was a primitive process. In child-bearing, women became primitive creatures again. All a man could do was indulge them for the duration.

She interrupted his thought. "You know, if it hadn't been for Marit that other time...."

He didn't want to think about that other time. He loosened the hair from the top of her head, unraveling the braids. He separated the strands and fanned them out so her hair enveloped them both.

"Is it really so important to you to have Marit with you?"

"Oh yes! But she has so much work she could never get away from the homestead for that long, I know that."

"But you could go to her."

She raised up, her face so close to his that her breath was his in the golden tent of her hair. "Go to her... I could go to her?"

"I don't see why not. If you don't wait until you're close up. The trains are quite comfortable now, not jarring. And I could come in time. After the harvest."

The words that were coming from his mouth were a surprise to him. He had never conceived of ever returning to Wisconsin, yet now he had practically promised her.

"Thank you. Thank you for understanding. You have no idea what this means to me!" She lay back down again.

"It was time you had a trip back to Wisconsin anyway. It's been a long while."

She was content, curled in his lap like a sleepy kitten limply relaxed. He stoked her hair, watching it spark under his fingers in reflection of the flame dancing behind the ising-glass of the heater door, making it almost look red.

Much later, he carried her to the bed and, as a fretful child rocked to sleep, he lay her down softly so as not to waken her, drawing the coverlet up from the foot of the bed to cover her. But though he tucked it gently, she sighed, reaching over to the pillow where his head usually lay. He picked up the limp hand, put it on his face and slipped in beside her fully clothed.

❧❧❧

It was decided she would leave in May. She would have as traveling companions, Hilma, a neighboring widow, and the youngest of her three sons, Adolph. When Hilma lost her husband, Thorn had taken over management of her farm and the supervision of her three sons. The two families operated as a single unit. The two oldest sons and Thorn would stay until the harvest was in. Then, it was planned, Thorn would join Kari in Wisconsin.

"Are you sure you'll make it? Have the harvest in by the time I need you?"

"Don't worry, I'll make it. Even if we have to harvest green!"

Summer — summer in Wisconsin! In her mind's eye, Kari again saw green hills as relief against the horizon, cool shadow pools beneath tall trees, earth napped with lush grasses cushioning footsteps. There was no better place to give birth. Or to be born. *Or to die?* No! She wouldn't think that way anymore. Everything was going to be all right now.

***

The words on the page blurred. Impatiently, Marit cleared her eyes with her knuckles. To dab at them with a handkerchief would be to admit to crying, a feminine luxury she had never allowed herself. She re-read the letter just to be sure. It was true; Kari was coming! And she had written that she wanted to spend the summer in their old cabin.

The cabin had stood empty now for several years, for when the last tenant had fallen behind on his rent, Rolf had evicted him and worked the land himself. He had made no attempt to sell the land since there was no advantage to him in such a transaction. Instead, at the end of harvest each year, he sent a lump sum to Thorn, and Thorn never questioned the amount. Evidently his small acreage in Wisconsin was of no great consequence in comparison to the vast acreage of the wheat farms in Dakota.

"For having been neglected, it's still in pretty good shape," Marit commented to Thea on a bright April morning as they walked about the deserted cabin, deciding what must be done to ready it for Kari's occupancy.

"I think it's horrid," Thea appraised, wrinkling her nose in distaste.

"When I say 'good shape,' I don't mean looks. I mean the important things, like being waterproof. Having a good roof over your head is something to be thankful for."

"Who hasn't a good roof over their heads?"

The younger generation.... They took so much for granted! But this was not the time to recount for Thea the hardships of the early years. There was work to be done and they were wasting time talking. "What it needs mostly is a good cleaning and that's a small matter. Between the two of us, we can lick that in no time."

So much was "between the two of us" these days, for there had not been a resurgence of her strength and, with Randilena away at Millwood, she had come to lean on Thea more and more. *What would I do without her,* Marit wondered as she watched the girl tackle the dirt and debris with a vengeance, and with a pace she could not match. In a few hours' time, Thea had the cabin in a purged bareness of walls and floors, save for the little sitting room where the wallpaper had let loose, making the room a shambles.

"What a pity," Marit said, standing in the door, looking in.

"What's a pity?"

"Would you believe it once was pretty?"

"That must have been an awful long time ago, before I was born. I've never seen Aunt Kari and Uncle Thorn."

Marit turned to look at her, measuring time by her size. "So, you haven't. It's unbelievable how time goes."

"I don't like it when you look at me like that, like you want me to stay little forever."

"Stay little!" Marit chortled. "My dear, you never *were* little."

"Like Randilena, you mean."

At the mention of Randilena, Marit turned away to hide from the ever-alert Thea the concern she was afraid her face would reveal. But she managed a matter-of-fact tone when she pointed out, "Randilena took after the Monsruds; you took after the Maas side."

"Lucky me!" Thea said, squeezing by her into the room. Then, she added, "Why you want to save this old wallpaper is beyond me. I could have it torn off the walls and out the window in minutes."

"No!"

"Give me a good reason."

"Because it once was beautiful, and brought joy."

❧❦❧

"See, Hilma? Didn't I tell you Wisconsin would be beautiful this time of year?"

They had hired a rig from the livery stable and were now on the last leg of their journey, the jaunt from Pine Fork to the old neighborhood.

"It is pretty," Hilma said. "But it doesn't look like grain country to me. Too hilly."

"It's the hills I love! And the trees. I'd almost forgotten what a real tree looks like! Wisconsin is a great deal like the homeland, don't you think?"

"No," Hilma differed flatly.

But her son, Adolph, was not of her prosaic turn of mind. "And I'll bet these trees are full of bears, too!" he embellished, and for the rest of the way amused himself by aiming an imaginary gun at dark recesses in the patches of woods, interrupting conversation with frequent ear-splitting "bangs."

"Adolph and Thea are almost of an age," Kari informed Hilma. "And from what Marit writes, Thea is something of a boy herself. The two of them should have a great time together."

At a fork in the road, Kari instructed the driver, "Go straight ahead." Turning to Hilma, she explained, "I want to see Marit first, not Nicolena." But when the big white house came into view, she suddenly fell silent, only tapping the teamster on the back and motioning for him to turn in when they reached the driveway.

They had pulled up to the back door when Marit stepped out. Shielding her eyes from the sun, she stood for moments on the step, peering into the rig, as to ascertain. She then came slowly forward and, reaching the wagon, put one hand on the sideboard to steady herself. Then, smiling up at Kari, she held out the other hand to help her down.

Kari took the hand but, having gained the ground, didn't release it. Shock on her face, Kari's first words were, "Are you *well?*"

"I'm just a little under the weather. Nothing to worry about." Seemingly unconvinced, Kari continued clinging to Marit's hand. "We don't stay young forever," Marit added.

"But you're so much thinner than I remember."

"I'm fine!"

It was stated with finality. Kari dropped Marit's hand and embraced her. Then, still in embrace, they looked closely into each other's faces. Both winced with the synchronization of time and memory.

She's as young and beautiful as ever, had been Marit's first conclusion upon spying Kari in the interior of the covered rig. It was the way she always liked to think of Kari. But now, up close and in the bright spring sunlight, Marit observed with a pang that the delicate texture of Kari's skin was traced with fine lines, like crazed china.

Hilma had paid the teamster and he had driven away. She now stood aside. Kari apologized, making the introductions. Leaving the baggage in the yard for later, they followed Marit into the kitchen.

Kari looked around expectantly. "Where are the girls?"

"Thea is still in school. The spring term hasn't ended yet. And Randilena... Well, you remember Anna Rolstad at Millwood? You remember what a hard time she had keeping maids? When she wrote asking for Randilena, her offer of pay was so generous that even Rolf felt she could not afford to turn it down, especially since a part of the agreement was that most of her salary be sent home each month. Anna promised Rolf she would guard her as her own daughter."

"Guard her?"

"Well.... Supervise her, you know. Rolf feels that young women need a great deal of supervision."

Recalling Rolf's attitude toward Randilena in the early years and his indifference toward her, she started to say, "From what I remember...." But warned by something in Marit's face, she stopped. Perhaps it was Hilma's presence. Instead, Kari turned her concern again to Marit: "I should think you'd need Randilena at home to help *you*. It's time for you to slow down and take things a little easier."

"I manage very well with Thea. She's a lot of help already, big for her age and strong like I once was. I mean, like I was when I was her age."

"I can't wait to see her. *Where* have the years gone!"

❧

The cabin stood in readiness for Kari's homecoming, having been rudimentarily furnished with spare furniture from Marit's house, including her laundry stove for cooking purposes.

When Kari walked in, she was overcome. Tears of happiness welled, making all the effort well worth it, especially the frustrating business of salvaging the scenic wallpaper, patching it back together again and getting it to stick despite its brittleness. Battle-scarred though it was, Kari ran her fingers over it affectionately.

Within days, something of the old pattern of the former years was resumed; and the short-cut path between the two houses over fence stiles years lost in tall grass soon became clearly defined again.

Kari hit upon a way to mine more time for her and Marit to spend together. Hilma, to whom idleness was anathema, found time heavy on her hands and Kari suggested that she relieve Marit of some of her household chores, allowing Marit to serve her as companion during the daylight hours. And Hilma found the arrangement to her liking, so much so that she often came in the morning and spent the whole day taking over, a proprietary attitude Marit might have resented had she not been so grateful for the assist with a work load that was becoming increasingly taxing to the strength she had available.

There was only one fly in the ointment of these balsamic weeks: Thea. For rather than take Adolph in league, as Kari had expected she would, Thea took his presence, in company with his mother, as trespass on her territory. She challenged him everywhere he turned. "If that girl was mine, I'd soon teach her the proper place," Hilma complained to Kari. Not wishing to be caught in the middle, Kari suggested it would be best for Adolph to amuse himself at Nicolena's, where there were two boys his age, rather than accompany his mother each day to Marit's. Hilma somewhat dourly went along with the compromise.

Tranquility restored, the high months of summer passed all too swiftly. The sunny days were a rosary of quickly strung golden beads, with Kari's confinement looming as the terminal cross; its shadow, as a patina, only making time more precious and Marit and Kari's hours of camaraderie more dear in the knowledge that they were measured. And each respected in the other a reluctance to project beyond, allowing a degree of lightness in their hours together.

The idyll came to an end with Thorn's arrival. After his coming, Marit rationed her time with Kari, even though he scarcely looked at her. It was as if the incident in the granary had never occurred, his concern seemingly all for Kari as it had been that first time when he had brought her from Norway as his bride and had showered her with his attentiveness.

⁂

The letter had come from Anna that morning. Marit had torn it open with trembling fingers. It was over, Anna's cloaked words told her, and all had gone well. A great longing to see Randilena had welled up in her. But it couldn't be.

Torn as she was, the day had been wearing in the conflict of emotions. She was even more tired than usual by nightfall. But it was that evening that Kari's baby decided it was time. Thorn came for her, bringing Hilma along to take her place at home.

It was well he did bring Hilma to spell her because Kari's pains were sporadic throughout the night and ceased entirely for some hours in the morning. Marit didn't like this; it could make stress for the baby. But by mid-afternoon, Kari was in deep labor. By sundown, it was over.

Marit knew it was hopeless even before she tried to blow life into the blue baby by expanding its lungs with her own breath. It had been born dead.

No wail roused Kari from her exhaustion and she *sensed* something was wrong. She raised up and saw Marit bent over the little scrap of humanity, then *knew*. Her eyes opened widely. She started to say something and Marit turned. It sounded like "Don't let...." But the last words were lost when Kari collapsed on the pillow.

Marit left the baby and rushed to her side. She was about to reach for Kari's hand when one of the hated spells of weakness overtook her. She did find the hand but sank to her knees by the side of the bed, pulling Kari's hand down with her.

"Don't Kari, don't give up," she pleaded. But her plea was vapid, clinging as she was to Kari's hand in her own weakness that seemed to transmit as she felt Kari's hand go limp in hers. Tears welled up and she had not the strength to dam them. They oozed out silently as from a morass, leaving her wrung out.

She must have slept. The room was dark when she opened her eyes. She did not light the lamp. Yet, as one who has been wandering in a subterranean chamber for what seemed like an eternity, following one dark tunnel after another to a dead end, to have given up, sitting down to await the inevitable and only to see the opening right in front of her. She saw light. She had only to muster strength and take the few necessary steps.

She got to her feet. Thorn was waiting.

He read her face. He only asked, "Both of them?"

"Both of them."

Rolf has two of our horses stabled here and Thorn has tinkered up the rig.... "There's something you must do for me. You must go to Millwood, get Randilena. I will take care of things here, do the things that are necessary. If you leave right away, you should be back tomorrow night. I'll write a note to Randilena. I'll do that while you hitch the horses."

He obeyed as in a trance. When he returned, she had the note sealed in an envelope. "Don't stop and tell anyone. It's best to save this for morning. There's nothing anyone can do tonight anyway. They might as well get their rest."

She stood by the window, waiting to hear the rig pull away.... *It will work out. Prolonged labors are not uncommon. I'll somehow cover up until he gets back with Randilena.* She stood with her hands resting on the little chest that had been Thorn's wedding gift to Kari. As she backed away from the window, her eyes fell on it. It was a thing Kari had loved; it would be fitting.

꧁☙⚹☙꧂

Thorn whipped the horses homeward through the darkness. Randilena was a shadow beside him. Shock compounded by shock! He had been numb, had done Marit's bidding mechanically when she told him to go get Randilena. He had even been vaguely relieved when she told him not to stop and tell anyone what had happened, for not to have to say the words made it seem somehow less true. But if the first shock had stunned him, the second had revived him. It had been as ice water flung in his face, clearing his head. And not a small part of the chill was the remembrance of Kari's voice, saying, "It's what happens afterwards."

It was in a frenzy of apprehension that he turned in at the gate. He jumped down with no thought of Randilena, rushing into the cabin.

Marit sat in a rocking chair by the stove. He sped past her into the bedroom. In an instant, he was back to confront her, his eyes dark in his blanched face.

"What have you done with Kari's... with my baby?"

Her voice was harsh with weariness. "He had a proper burial. I christened him myself."

This couldn't be happening! In the unreality of the moment, the words came as from the mouth of a stranger: a gaunt old woman sitting in a rocking chair, her hands folded in her lap; the face pinched — grayed around the mouth, hair of ash save for a spark here and there that told of the former fire.

He turned and walked to the dark window, stood looking out, his eyes the vacant focus of a sailor contemplating the sea, seeing nothing, yet mesmerized by the vastness of the nothingness.

"I know the words from memory," she added, as if to further reassure him.

Randilena had slipped in quietly and stood leaning with her back against the door, clutching the baby to her. Marit got up slowly, walking to where she stood. She embraced Randilena fleetingly, her eyes on the bundle. She reached out her arms to take it. "Mama...?"

"Trust me," Marit whispered.

Randilena relinquished the baby. Marit turned down the blanket, smiling at the comical little-old-man's face. She lifted him to her shoulder, laying her cheek on the downy little head. And in that posture she walked over to where Thorn still stood, his back to the room.

"Your son, Thorn. Look at him!" she said.

EPILOGUE

It was never questioned. I was raised as Thorn Monsrud's son. It was as it on that fateful night a knot were tied in the skein with me at its center, a cocoon of protective threads drawn about the chrysalis that was my existence — and just the one loose end to be tied: Randilena's hiding until her "return" from Millwood and Thorn's hiring her to care for his "motherless" child.

Knowledge came with maturity, but the knowledge was imparted with the firm admonition that the word "mother" must never cross my lips and I'll confess that for some time in youth this was a torment to me. Origin is the warp on which the tapestry of life is woven and to deny your own is to deny the very fabric of one's self! — But no longer. Viewed down the dappled vista of many years, it now seems of no great consequence.

Thorn was all my real father could have been to me. And if he found a son in me he found two daughters, as well, in Randilena and Thea; for he moved back to Wisconsin and Thea, too, came to live under his roof when, after Marit's death, Rolf proposed marriage to Hilma and she accepted.

It was Thorn's observation that Thea had a keen mind and he saw to it that she availed herself of all the education that was to be had locally — and even more. When James H. Stout, scion of the founder of the lumber company of the same name, fittingly established Stout Institute at Menomonie — an educational facility that opened the door of opportunity to the generations that followed in the wake of the forests — Thea was in one of the first classes of graduating teachers. She married well and it was in her home that Thorn spent his later years.

There is in the nature of the Norwegian people an inherent brooding melancholy; I have seen it many times in the eyes of people

I have known. But when I was a child, I often saw in Thorn's eyes a deeper, more immediate sadness. As time went by, however, I saw this look infrequently and, finally, not at all. For he found great joy in his adopted family and lived to be very old. There was just this one thing: In the last months of his life, he took to calling Thea by the name "Marit."